ENTER
THE
BLACKHOLE

R.A. LOER

Publishing assistance by BookCrafters, Parker, Colorado.
www.bookcrafters.net

BLACKHOLE SUN
Inspired by Soundgarden

THE QUASI-STAR BEGAN TO MOVE—slowly, impossibly, like a god stirring in its sleep.

Baar pressed his mirrored face against the crystalline viewport, watching three centuries of planning finally bear fruit. The stellar giant—massive beyond imagination, its radiation too intense for any lesser imp to approach—was beginning its slow migration away from the feeding moon that had haunted his dreams.

Finally, he mused.

In the distance, through his enhanced perception, he could see them: dozens of chittering shapes swarming over the two overcrowded feeding moons like maggots on galactic carrion. Lesser imps and hungry demi-lords fighting for scraps of helium-3 isotopes, clawing and scraping for a place in the feeding line while solar winds deposited their meager portions. Pathetic.

Baar had once been one of them. The memory tasted like hunger and shame—a chittering parasite groveling before void bugs, begging for exotic-matter scraps from beings who barely noticed his existence. But that was before he understood what magic truly was in this pocket universe. Evolution itself. Transformation through consumption.

He flexed his consciousness, feeling the dark matter writhe beneath his form like living shadow. With a casual thought, he reached out to a malfunctioning maintenance drone drifting past the observation deck. The machine simply… ceased. Not destroyed—unmade. Its matter reorganized itself backward through time until only quantum foam remained, scattered to dimensions that had never known its existence.

Such was the power he had earned through eons of feeding, of growing, of becoming something beyond the universal food chain. While others built—like his brother Lelandro with his stellar engines and impossible architecture—Baar had chosen a different path. He was an unmaker, capable of reducing gods back to the cowering imps they had once been.

And now, watching his target star begin its migration, he was so close to claiming the greatest prize of all. "Brother, please—you're not helping, and our focus must be precise," came Mogath's voice from the control chamber below. Through the viewport, Baar could see his brother's five faces all wearing the same expression of concentrated effort as he monitored the Stellar Momentum Transfer Engine's exotic-matter regulators.

The stellar engine was a work of art—Lelandro's masterpiece. Massive photovoltaic collectors wrapped around one hemisphere of the quasi-star like a cosmic net, reflecting the star's own light back in a focused beam. The asymmetrical light pressure created constant momentum transfer, pushing the entire stellar system in the opposite direction of the reflected radiation. But it was Mogath's dark-matter Dyson sphere that made it all possible, regulating temperature and maintaining efficiency across impossible distances.

Three centuries of work. A quarter of Lelandro's helium-3 reserves. And now, finally, it was working.

"We linger too long in the shadow of discovery, fool!" Baar's reflection flared with unprovoked anger. "Each moment grants the lesser lords opportunity to divine our purpose. I sense them across the void—Ougar and his scrounger fleet, their instruments already tasting our stellar winds."

Lelandro released a weary sigh, his fingers dancing across exotic-matter regulators with practiced precision. "Fear does not accelerate the fundamental forces, brother."

"You mistake desperation for wisdom," Mogath replied, his voice colder than the void between galaxies, dark matter flickering dangerously around his form. "As you have done across three millennia."

Baar's hunger for power had always exceeded his patience for precision. Where Lelandro designed with meticulous care, calculating every gravitational stress and exotic matter requirement, Baar saw only obstacles to overcome and competitors to eliminate. The quasi-star represented not just sustenance but dominance—exclusive access to the richest helium-3 source in their dying universe.

What Baar failed to consider, in his arrogance, was the primordial blackhole lurking in the star's projected path—an ancient singularity that had devoured light since before their species learned to feed on stellar wind. But in his hunger for dominance, for the exclusive claim to power that would set him above all rivals, such details seemed beneath his consideration.

The truth was simpler and more damning: Baar craved not just sustenance but supremacy. To stand alone at the apex of creation, untouchable by time, entropy, or the judgment of lesser beings. The quasi-star was merely the means to that end.

"Silence!" Baar commanded. "Fulfill your function and complete this menial work. I shall attend to any parasites bold enough to show themselves."

"I swear by the void itself, you orchestrate these delays deliberately," he continued, watching the perfect precision of the assembly work through his fractured reflection. "Speak now, brother—is the first preparation phase complete?"

"The stellar engine stands ready," Mogath replied with weary dignity.

"At last!" Baar turned with fluid grace, his dark-matter form gliding toward the main corridor like living shadow. "I must attend to the initiation protocols."

"Where are you going?" Mogath called after him.

"I need to prep the event."

But Baar was already gone, his reflection disappearing around the corner like a bad memory.

The control chamber awaited two levels above. Baar ascended from the graphene transit disk, his mirrored visage reflecting not just his form but the magnitude of his impatience made manifest. Before him lay three rows of activation nodes—the keys to Lelandro's masterwork.

These fools have labored for a century on preparations, he mused, dark matter writhing beneath his consciousness like caged lightning. *I shall claim what is rightfully mine through superiority of will and intellect alone.*

The toggles responded to his touch. Illumination cascaded across control surfaces. Measurement arrays spiked beyond their calibrated limits before settling into operational parameters. The machine obeyed, and Baar finally commanded the celestial stage.

Yet even as satisfaction bloomed within his consciousness, Mogath manifested before him with the suddenness of collapsing space-time. The vestigial scent of their primitive origins—the decay of imp flesh—assaulted his senses like an unwelcome reminder of what they had once been.

"Brother, what devastation have you wrought?" Mogath's voice carried the weight of cosmic judgment. "The gravitational stress readings transcend all safe parameters."

"I have accomplished what you and our brother lacked the will to attempt," Baar replied, his reflection fracturing Mogath's image into that of decrepit ancients laboring with primitive tools. "I have seized what the cosmos owes us by right of superiority."

"By right?" Mogath's bitter laugh resonated across dimensional frequencies. "And through what mechanism do you propose to halt a runaway quasi-star, brother mine?"

Baar's attention returned to the array of controls he had just activated, then shifted to the observation portal where the giant quasi-star now accelerated through space with terrifying momentum. What should have been a controlled stellar relocation had become a juggernaut of cosmic mass, unstoppable as the expansion of the universe itself.

The terrible mathematics of his error crystallized in his consciousness like forming ice.

"What… what was the prescribed method for arresting this stellar body?"

"The second phase of preparation involved priming the reverse thrust systems and deployment of solar wind collection arrays," Mogath replied, defeat seeping into his voice like poison into a wound.

The brothers bore witness through the observation dome as their creation—three centuries of meticulous labor, the accumulated dreams of cosmic lifetimes—propelled the quasi-star into an accelerating dance of destruction. Baar's mirrored face reflected the growing catastrophe in infinite recursion, each reflection showing a slightly different angle of his mounting horror.

For a moment, silence reigned. Three gods confronting the magnitude of their folly.

"The reverse thrust systems!" Lelandro's voice fractured across the communication array from below, desperation bleeding through his usual clinical precision. "I can override the primary control matrices, reroute power through secondary channels—"

"The moment has passed," Mogath whispered, his five faces pale as dying starlight. "We have become the architects of our own annihilation."

Through the crystalline viewport, they beheld the impossible: their runaway quasi-star—burning with the fury of a captive sun— approaching collision with the primordial blackhole that had lurked unseen in its trajectory.

What transpired defied every law their universe had spent eons establishing.

The quasi-star did not simply surrender to the blackhole's event horizon. It struck the ancient singularity like a cosmic hammer against the anvil of space-time itself, and reality responded with a scream— not audible but felt as a fundamental vibration that penetrated Baar's exotic-matter essence, a frequency that caused his mirrored surface to fracture with hairline fissures of pure terror.

In that moment, Baar understood the true meaning of helplessness. All his accumulated power, all his ability to unmake the foundations of existence, meant nothing against the forces they had unleashed. He was witness to the death of physics itself.

Space-time contorted. Twisted. Sundered like ancient fabric subjected to impossible strain.

The explosion that followed transcended light, heat, and sound—it was the birth-cry of physics being rewritten, dimensions colliding and separating, matter and energy learning to dance to rules that had never before existed. Baar tasted the metallic essence of oxides, silicates, and fluorides, the bitter tang of temporal fractures spreading through his consciousness like poison.

The prized feeding moon—their helium-3 treasure, the singular purpose of this catastrophic endeavor—vaporized in the first microsecond. Centuries of accumulated isotopic wealth, the prosperity of empires, reduced to quarks and lepton vapor and scattered across dimensions still taking their first breaths of existence.

Baar watched his reflection multiply the horror infinitely, each surface showing him the magnitude of his otherworldly failure.

"What devastation have we wrought?" Lelandro's whisper echoed through the chaos as their pocket universe began its death throes around them—stars extinguishing like candles in cosmic wind, planets crumbling to dust, the very fabric of their reality bleeding away into something new and impossible to comprehend.

The wormhole that erupted from the collision wasn't just a pathway between universes—it was a wound in existence itself, spewing their dying cosmos into a white-hole explosion that would birth galaxies beyond counting.

Everything they had ever known was ending.

And something unimaginably vast was beginning.

The catastrophic wave reached their observation station like the final exhalation of a dying god. Through the crystalline viewport, the three brothers witnessed their pocket universe folding into impossible geometries—dimensions collapsing upon themselves, stars extinguishing in sequence, the very fabric of space-time dissolving into sterile neutrino dust before their enhanced perceptions.

"We possess mere minutes before the cascade engulfs us," Lelandro announced, his voice maintaining its clinical precision despite the cosmic apocalypse unfolding beyond their station. His consciousness danced across control interfaces as he calculated their dwindling options. "Our exotic-matter reserves cannot withstand space-time distortions of this magnitude."

Mogath's five visages wore identical expressions of grim resolve. "The Stellar Momentum Transfer Engine's exotic-matter core remains intact. We might employ it to—"

"To accomplish what?" Baar interrupted, his mirrored countenance reflecting the external chaos in fractal recursions. "Repair the wounds in a dying universe? We must depart. Immediately."

Through the viewing portal, they observed the wormhole achieving stability—a phenomenon that violated every physical law their universe had spent eons establishing. The wormhole's aperture gaped like a cosmic maw, its event horizon writhing with energies that existed across seventeen dimensions simultaneously.

"A unidirectional passage," Lelandro whispered, his analytical mind parsing readings that defied comprehension. "Blackhole entrance, white hole terminus. The exotic-matter collision has birthed a permanent conduit to… an unknown destination."

"Another universe entirely," Mogath breathed with something approaching reverence. "Virgin cosmos. Untapped resources beyond imagination."

Baar's reflection revealed his brothers as they truly existed— desperate deities clinging to the wreckage of their cosmic ambitions. "Then we shall claim it. We shall employ our remaining exotic-matter reserves to—"

"You cannot."

The voice manifested from everywhere at once, a vibration that resonated through their station's hull like the song of distant galaxies.

CHAPTER 1 – SCENE 2:

FLY BY NIGHT
Inspired by Rush

THEIR STATION TREMBLED within the quantum tempest.

Through the viewport, the wormhole stretched like a wound carved into reality itself, its horizon writhing with hyperdimensional energies that burned patterns into their enhanced perception. The brothers' station drifted at the precipice of annihilation, its superstructure groaning as space-time itself shifted beneath their foundation.

"Your species lacks the quantum coherence necessary to survive passage through a wormhole."

The voice had resonated from everywhere simultaneously, and now its source revealed itself. Bio-mechanical appendages the size of stellar cruisers unfurled from the stellar darkness, vast and luminescent with integrated technologies that pulsed in frequencies painful to perceive directly. Each tendril represented a masterwork of evolutionary artistry—living technology that had grown rather than been constructed, quantum processors threaded through exotic-matter veins like neural networks spanning light years of space.

Archite had emerged because she possessed the gift of velocity—sufficient speed to feel the rhythm of space-time itself, adequate swiftness to ride the Planck-scale bridges that flickered into existence and collapsed within the stardust. Fast enough to persist. Fast enough to transcend.

"A Galactic Nautilus," Mogath whispered with reverence, his five visages reflecting wonder and calculation in equal measure.

"I am Archite of the spatial slipstream." Her consciousness flooded their communication arrays, each syllable carrying the accumulated weight of three cosmic eons. "Navigator of the Ionospheric Currents that flow between stellar magnetospheres, rider of supersonic solar winds. And you three have obliterated the last trove of helium-3 your kind feeds upon. Am I correct in this knowledge?"

Through her distributed sensory network, she perceived the catastrophe they had wrought in exquisite detail—exotic matter cascading through hyperdimensions, the fundamental laws of physics being rewritten in real time, their pocket universe being reverted to barely a memory. The wormhole they had accidentally birthed pulsed with energies that would atomize any being lacking her specialized evolutionary adaptations.

"We can offer significant compensation—" Baar began, his mirrored visage shifting to display angles of desperate authority.

"I can offer you passage," Archite interrupted, her mental voice carrying undertones of primordial disdain accumulated across eons. "I was already contemplating departure from this dying universe. Your explosive remodeling has merely accelerated my timeline."

She had spent lifetimes hunting for the appropriate blackhole—one that would transport her to a universe free from the predator that haunted her deepest thoughts. Now, through bitter irony, these three catastrophic brothers had created precisely what she required: a unidirectional passage to unobservable territory.

But she would not journey alone.

Even now, at the periphery of her perception, she sensed it stirring in the stellar darkness.

Even now, at the periphery of her perception, she sensed it stirring in the stellar darkness. Teuthida Odontos. The space whale that had pursued her across three stellar eons, its bio-mechanical bulk scarred by the reality cascade but driven by hunger that transcended mere survival instinct. Even here, within the impossible tempest of the bridge, it would not relent in its pursuit. Its ancient appetite pressed against the boundaries of her consciousness like blades forged from collapsed stars.

"The wormhole continues its evolution," Lelandro announced with urgent precision, his consciousness interfacing with readings that defied conventional comprehension. "The exotic-matter cascade continues converting the singularity structure. The wormhole achieves self-sustainability but also approaches critical instability. If we intend to utilize it, we must act within this temporal window."

Through her quantum-coherent organs, Archite investigated the transformed wormhole's impossible architecture. The brothers' exotic-matter manipulation had achieved far more than simple bridge creation—they had fundamentally altered the blackhole's singularity, transforming it into something that existed across multiple dimensions simultaneously. Where normal space-time terminated, this phenomenon initiated something entirely unprecedented.

"Your collision amplified the natural quantum bridges that exist within the universe's foundation," she explained, her consciousness touching their minds with images of the microscopic wormholes that constantly formed and collapsed within the stardust. "Where previously there existed only fleeting connections lasting nanoseconds, now, stable pathways span cosmic distances. However, they require precise quantum synchronization to navigate safely."

She paused, experiencing the weight of what she was about to undertake. The magnitude of the journey, the finality of the choice, the transformation that awaited them all.

"The passage shall be unidirectional. The white hole terminus will seal itself behind us with energies that echo beyond our time and understanding itself. And the journey itself… will fundamentally alter everything we are."

"What price do you demand?" Baar's reflection revealed his mounting desperation as another shockwave from their collapsing universe rattled their station's superstructure.

"Living flesh." The words carried undertones of cosmic hunger that spoke to evolution itself. "Trilene-phoscarbyne-adamantium matrices fused with exotic matter and dark energy, threaded through with quantum computers capable of thought, dream, and choice."

The brothers shared a moment of silent communication. Their exotic-matter reserves were vast, accumulated over centuries of careful harvesting from stellar winds and cosmic debris.

"The compact is sealed," Baar declared without consulting his siblings. "But we depart immediately."

"The agreement is witnessed."

As her massive form began maneuvering toward their station, reality convulsed around them with increasing violence. The cascade was accelerating exponentially—their pocket universe folding in upon itself like origami constructed from space-time itself, stars extinguishing in sequence, the fundamental forces that had governed their reality for eons simply ceasing to exist.

"We ride the quantum tempest," Archite declared at last, her voice filling them all with harmonics that resonated across dimensions they could not perceive. "No alternative path remains."

With a single pulse of living intention, she enveloped their station completely. Her vast hull folded around their fragile structures like living armor. Protective flesh grew across their vessel in organic patterns. Geometries no architect had ever conceived. Through her distributed nervous system, she felt the exotic matter payment flowing into her lower storage chambers—tons of the precious living flesh that pulsed with its own quantum heartbeat, a treasury of possibility made manifest.

The dying universe's final scream became fuel for her crossing, each photon of dissolving reality feeding her specialized organs as they came online for the most perilous navigation of her three stellar eons.

Her quantum-coherent structures awakened from their dormancy—organs tuned to the fundamental vibrations of space-time itself. Through them, she perceived the Planck-scale bridges flickering between existence and void in constant fluctuation, the microscopic wormholes that connected every point in space to every other point across the cosmic web.

"Exotic-matter stabilization achieved," Mogath reported, his voice carrying the solemn weight of duty. "Hull integrity maintains maximum parameters. We shall complete this endeavor with honor, or we shall not complete it at all."

"Probability matrices demonstrate chaotic instability," Lelandro added, his consciousness interfacing with calculations that shifted faster than thought. "Success probability: diminishing rapidly. Temporal window: three stellar rotations and declining."

"Then we shall master the tempest through will alone," Baar declared with renewed ferocity. "No further delays. No submission to fear."

Then they plunged into the bridge.

The wormhole passage transcended the sensation of movement through space—it felt like becoming space itself, like merging with the fundamental substrate of reality.

Quantum fluctuations assaulted them with the force of dying stellar giants. Archite harmonized with their rhythm, synchronizing her bio-mechanical nervous system with the pulse of creation itself. Her consciousness expanded to encompass the wormhole's impossible geometries, each twist and fold a lesson in physics that wouldn't be discovered for billions of years.

The passage demanded everything of her. This was why only her species could survive such transit.

Behind her, Teuthida forced its way into the passage with brute determination.

Where Archite danced with the quantum tempest, the space whale tore through it with organic force that lacked all finesse. Its massive bulk—scarred by the reality cascade but driven by hunger older than galaxies themselves—strained against the wormhole's entrance. The tunnel itself screamed in protest as the creature's unharmonized passage tore ragged wounds in the bridge's delicate quantum architecture.

Through her sensory network, Archite perceived the whale's agony in exquisite detail—neural networks overloading with impossible information, quantum processors burning out under stresses they were never designed to endure. Its passage sent chaotic harmonics reverberating through the wormhole's structure like discordant notes in a cosmic symphony.

"If it tears us down in its death throes, the probability matrices collapse entirely," Lelandro warned, his consciousness monitoring quantum fluctuations through Archite's enhanced sensory network.

"Then we shall outpace the chaos," Mogath replied with grim resolve. "We have journeyed too far across observable time to fail now."

"Let it burn in its own inadequacy," Baar spat with cold satisfaction. "We shall claim what we require."

But Archite perceived deeper truths coursing through her quantum organs like revelation made manifest. The wormhole was transforming with every microsecond of their passage. The tempest was not merely a tunnel between universes but a forge where new physical laws were being hammered into existence by forces beyond mortal comprehension. The exotic-matter cascade wasn't simply creating a bridge—it was rewriting the fundamental constants of reality itself.

Within the event horizon, causality became fluid as cosmic tides. The singularity that had been their future became their past, and every quantum pathway led inexorably toward the white hole terminus. But the transition zone writhed with energies that existed outside normal space-time, forces that obeyed rules that wouldn't be discovered by lesser minds for billions of years.

Space itself began expanding at different rates throughout distinct regions of the tunnel. Warped light of the entire spectrum cascaded across and around them. The fundamental constants that governed reality assumed new values with each pulse of exotic matter energy, creating pockets where magic and science danced to rhythms unknown in either universe.

Through her bio-mechanical perception, Archite felt herself undergoing transformation. The living-flesh payment from the brothers was not merely fuel—it served as catalyst for her evolution. Her three stellar eons of development were being compressed and amplified by the passage itself. She was growing, not simply in physical scale but in fundamental capability, her consciousness expanding to encompass frequencies of existence she had never imagined possible.

And at the heart of the tempest, she achieved understanding—she was not merely navigating between universes. She was becoming something unprecedented. Something that bridged the gap between what existed and what could exist.

The rhythm of quantum creation pulsed through her transformed nervous system like solar flares erupting through space.

The rhythm of quantum creation pulsed through her transformed nervous system like solar flares erupting through space. Each microscopic bridge she surfed carried her further from what she had been and closer to what she was becoming. The old designations fell away—space squid, navigator, survivor. In their place, something greater took root in her consciousness.

Behind them, the wormhole began sealing itself. The exotic-matter energies that had transformed the wormhole reached critical resonance, and the passage started to collapse—not destructively but purposefully, like a flower closing at the end of its season.

Teuthida's massive form tumbled through the quantum tempest, its hunting cries becoming screams of agony as the passage rejected its unharmonized presence like an immune system expelling infection.

"The creature will not survive this transition," Mogath observed, his voice carrying unexpected notes of regret as they witnessed the cosmic predator struggle against forces beyond its evolutionary comprehension.

"Evolution demonstrates its principles through action," Baar replied with cold satisfaction. "Only those capable of adaptation survive cosmic transitions."

As they approached the white-hole terminus, Archite felt the universe transforming around them with each passing moment. The blackhole had devoured everything within its reach. The white hole gave birth to infinite possibility. What had been collapse became expansion; what had been hunger became song.

Where the blackhole had drawn all matter and energy toward its singularity, the white hole expelled everything outward with the force of cosmic birth itself. The exotic-matter energies that had transformed the wormhole now birthed new physics, new laws, new possibilities that sang in her expanded consciousness like the music of creation.

Through her quantum senses, she could perceive the difference—this universe's fundamental constants carried different flavors, like wine from a vineyard that had never known its parent reality's dying light. Young stars burned with harmonics that spoke of fresh potential. Galaxies spiraled with the promise of virgin worlds and untapped evolutionary pathways.

"Remarkable beyond measure," Lelandro whispered as his consciousness registered the new universe's properties through Archite's enhanced perception. "The exotic-matter cascade has birthed something unprecedented—a reality where the impossible becomes merely improbable."

They emerged from the white hole into a cosmos singing with infinite possibility.

Behind them, the wormhole sealed itself with energies that would echo beyond our time and understanding itself. Somewhere in the nexus of space between realities, Teuthida Odontos drifted in organic agony, its massive form broken but not destroyed, healing slowly in the dimensional void between universes.

It would be eons before the space whale hunted again.

Archite knew that creatures of the void were patient. And she was no longer merely Archite.

In this new universe, where magic flowed like stellar wind, she would no longer merely navigate.

She would cradle.

CHAPTER 1 – SCENE 3:

SUPERMASSIVE BLACKHOLE
Inspired by Muse

THE NEW UNIVERSE HUMMED beneath her consciousness like a vast instrument waiting to be played.

Archite stretched her organic awareness across the virgin cosmos. Stars burned with frequencies she had never tasted. Galaxies spiraled with potential that made her photon cores pulse with anticipation. She could feel the vast amounts of the precious Trilene-phoscarbyne hybrid material down in her largest hold. The visions of what this would enable her to do were incredible.

But the euphoria of arrival was short-lived.

Within her observation chamber, dark energy began to swirl like a dust devil forming from ash, bringing a sulfur smell that spoke of stellar decay. Then came a deeper, darker void—an absence that hurt to perceive. It didn't shimmer; it absorbed. It became a walking occlusion, a tear in the canvas of existence where everything—light, sound, hope—was sucked into a point of infinite density. The space around it collapsed into a crushing, silent gravity well. A mirrored face began to form from the inky silhouette, and Baar stood there, swirling like a nightmare with purpose.

Near Baar, at the edge of the chamber, reality convulsed as a raging, violent expansion of energy erupted into being—less a form and more a constantly exploding nebula of dark ultraviolet and non-light. Its edges screamed outward only to be pulled back by its own tiny, desperate, dark-matter heart. Furious, chaotic, and deafeningly silent in its focus. Lelandro's essence writhed between creation and destruction, building and unmaking itself with each pulse.

The gravitational lensing from their manifestations began warping her perception, bending light into impossible angles. Archite turned her senses away before she could suffer reality blindness. When she cautiously reopened her awareness, a third presence had joined them—a terrifying, unstable equilibrium that held the shape of a towering humanoid form rendered in impossible, non-Euclidean geometry. Mogath's figure blazed with photon cascade radiation and gravitational distortion, a ghostly blue-white event horizon outlined by the stolen and bent light of everything behind him.

The three brothers stood in her sacred space like gods who had forgotten they were guests.

"Behold—we have not been reduced to constituent particles, cephalopod."

Archite's consciousness recoiled with ancient contempt as memories surfaced—three chittering parasites groveling before void bugs in the parent universe's outer reaches, begging for helium-3 scraps. And now they dared stand in her space, aboard her vessel, with their pathetic hunger for something even grander than the universe they had just escaped.

Baar stood at the center of her primary observation chamber, his mirrored face reflecting the new cosmos in fractal patterns that hurt to perceive directly. His dark-matter form writhed with barely contained power. She could taste his transformation—from cosmic parasite to something primitive civilizations might worship as a god.

But beneath the surface arrogance, his reflection flickered with familiar terror. Not of her. Of time itself.

"I have my flesh, you have your new universe to trample, why are you still here?" Archite said with irritation dripping from her tone.

"And you'd best remember, squid—we've evolved beyond your petty insults."

She could sense the payment in her lower storage chambers—tons of living flesh that pulsed with electromagnetic consciousness like a second heartbeat. Trilene-phoscarbyne-adamantium matrices threaded with exotic matter and dark energy, materials that could transform into anything her imagination could design. Ships. Weapons. Tools. Entire civilizations, if she so chose.

The payment was magnificent, perhaps enough to restore everything that three stellar lifetimes of navigation had cost her. But gazing upon Baar's reflected sneer, she wondered if any treasure was worth tolerating these creatures.

"You believe you perceive profound truths, imp?" she asked, her consciousness already cataloging the new universe's structure with growing fascination, measuring its potential against its inevitable limitations.

Baar gestured toward the viewing portal where young galaxies wheeled in their eternal dance, their light carrying the promise of eons yet to unfold. "I perceive a universe already in the process of dying. Dark energy accelerating beyond any possibility of control. I already have readings showing helium-3 is almost as rare here as in our old universe. In a few billion years—perhaps fewer—this entire reality will tear itself apart at the photon level. Stars scattered like dust particles, atoms themselves shredded by expanding void, entropy claiming even the memory of what once was."

Still fleeing from universal truth, she observed with something approaching pity. Eons of accumulated power, and still he fled from the one enemy he could never unmake: entropy itself, the patient assassin that claimed all things in time.

What Baar truly feared was not death but insignificance. Not ending but meaninglessness. He had crawled past countless rivals to achieve godhood, only to discover that even gods were temporary arrangements in an uncaring universe.

Mogath stepped forward with measured dignity, his five visages wearing expressions of weary determination that spoke to eons spent building rather than destroying. "The expansion can be stabilized, brother. The exotic-matter reserves within this universe are vast beyond imagination—"

"Stabilized?" Baar's bitter laughter shattered like crystal subjected to impossible frequencies. Underneath ran a current of desperation so raw it made her living nerves recoil in sympathetic response. "Must I watch everything I build crumble into stardust and darkness while time itself plays executioner?" His mirrored gaze turned upon his brother with the fury of cornered divinity. "I did not claw my way past lesser gremlins, golems, squids, or even my own kind to watch eternity turn to ash around me!"

"The probability matrices demonstrate stability," Lelandro said, moving to Mogath's side in a gesture of solidarity that spoke to bonds forged across lifetimes. "We can monitor the expansion, ensure this reality remains viable for civilizations yet to be born—"

"ENOUGH!"

Baar's roar sent gravitational waves rippling through local space-time with such force that stars flickered in distant systems, planets trembling in their orbits as his fear became a physical force warping reality around him.

His mirrored gaze swept from the young galaxies spinning outside to her vast form, and she felt the precise moment when desperation crystallized into cold calculation. She was his only escape route. His only hope of fleeing from the universal truth that terrified him beyond all rational thought.

"You will transport us to another universe, cephalopod. One that is not doomed to entropy's embrace. You will accomplish this, or—"

"Or what, imp?" Archite's voice carried the cold authority of a being who had navigated blackholes while his kind still fought over stellar debris. "You forget your place."

The words hung in the void between them like a challenge written in starlight.

"My place?" Baar's form began to shift, exotic matter writhing beneath his surface like living metal seeking escape. "My place is wherever I choose to put it!"

She felt the cosmic moment crystallize—that heartbeat before catastrophe when the universe holds its breath and waits for gods to make terrible choices.

Then Baar struck.

Exotic matter erupted from his form like the spite of dying suns. Reality fractured into shards that screamed across hyperdimensions simultaneously. The impact rippled through her bio-mechanical hull—not pain but recognition. She had witnessed the death throes of stars, the collapse of galactic clusters, but this was different.

This was the rage of a god who had glimpsed his own mortality and found it unacceptable.

She began to pull back, her vast consciousness calculating escape vectors through folded space. But Mogath moved faster than thought itself, throwing his massive presence between Baar and her retreating form.

"Brother, NO!" Exotic-matter shields bloomed around him like protective wings forged from the bones of dead stars. "She brought us here in good faith! The compact—"

"The compact means nothing!" Baar's voice shattered local space-time, sending gravitational waves toward distant galaxies. "Nothing means anything if we're all going to dissolve into cosmic background radiation!"

What followed transcended mere exotic-matter manipulation.

Archite watched in horrified fascination as something fundamental erupted from Baar—power that reached into the basic foundations of existence itself. The ability to unmake. To reduce. To reset the very building blocks of reality.

Through her enhanced perception, she witnessed the impossible: Mogath's godhood beginning to unravel like a tapestry being pulled apart thread by thread.

It began as a sound—not audible to conventional senses but felt through every axion frequency she possessed like the death scream of reality itself. Then came the visual assault: dimensions folded and collapsed until Mogath's godhood shrank to a single, agonized point.

Mogath's divine form convulsed as eons of accumulated evolution peeled away like layers of cosmic sediment being stripped by impossible winds. She could taste his terror through her organic sensors—the metallic tang of neural networks overloading, the bitter residue of electromagnetic consciousness being forcibly compressed beyond its design parameters.

His five faces flickered through expressions of confusion, rage, disbelief, and finally—heartbreakingly—the wide-eyed fear of something small and helpless that possessed no understanding of the cosmic forces destroying it piece by piece.

"Mogath," Archite whispered, though she had barely known him beyond their brief transaction. There was something obscene about witnessing a god reduced to its component fears, something that violated the natural order of things.

The transformation accelerated like a stellar collapse. Mogath's massive form shrank as matter reorganized according to cruel new laws that Baar had imposed upon reality through sheer force of will. Exotic matter became simple carbon. Dark energy bled away into axions like life draining from a wound. The steady authority of eons spent building civilizations and nurturing lesser species dissolved into the chittering confusion of a creature that had never evolved beyond basic hunger.

Three and a half stellar lifetimes of patient evolution. Gone. Unmade. Reduced to nothing more than memory and regret.

Where a cosmic entity had stood moments before—where a being of wisdom and dignity had faced his brother's madness with courage—only a small imp remained. Cowering. Mewling. Reduced to the very state he had transcended across lifetimes of struggle and growth.

Through tears in reality, glimpses of the parent universe's dying light bled through—a reminder of what they had all escaped. But evolution, it seemed, could be reversed with sufficient cruelty.

Space itself tore open with a sound like reality screaming. The cosmic wound gaped, showing the dead void where their pocket universe had been. Without ceremony, without final words, the imp that had been Mogath tumbled through the jagged opening, cast back to where his journey had begun.

The rift sealed with a thunderclap that silenced nearby quasars.

Silence stretched across light years like a held breath.

"MOGATH!" Lelandro's anguish detonated through the local star cluster, planets trembling in their orbits at the sound of divine heartbreak. Yet he did not strike back—could not. The threat of being reset hung between them like an executioner's blade.

She felt the moment crystallize into perfect, terrible balance: herself, calculating escape routes; the surviving brother, paralyzed by grief and terror; and Baar, standing over them both with power crackling around his fractured features.

When Baar finally spoke, his voice carried absolute authority undercut by hairline cracks of approaching madness. "You will never demand of me again!"

But even as he proclaimed supremacy, she could taste the stellar radiation leaking from the fissures in his power. He was breaking apart from the inside, consumed by the very fear that drove his cruelty.

"I must escape from here," he whispered, and for a moment, his voice carried the lost desperation of the imp he had once been, eons ago in the darkness between stars. "One way or another, I must flee this dying reality before it consumes everything I have built."

"Then endure alone." Lelandro's words carried the finality of cosmic judgment, each syllable weighted with the grief of brotherhood betrayed. With a gesture that bent space-time around his massive form like fabric responding to impossible mass, he cast Baar into the void—not to destroy, for he lacked his brother's terrible gift, but to exile completely. "You are no brother of mine. Find your own path to whatever hell you seek."

The space where Baar had stood filled with empty starlight and the echo of possibilities lost forever.

Lelandro turned to speak with the nautilus, to offer some sort of compensation or, at the very least, an apology. But Archite was already fleeing, her vast form disappearing into the cosmic background with the practiced ease of a being who had spent three lifetimes avoiding divine entanglements. She had witnessed what happened when gods fought gods—the collateral damage, the innocents caught in the crossfire, the civilizations that paid the price for divine ambition. She wanted no part of their family's destruction.

But as she put distance between herself and the brothers' devastation, she felt the cosmos itself hold its breath like a vast organism preparing for trauma.

The confrontation had not occurred in empty space. It had erupted within a seething ocean of potential—a region where infant physics were still soft and malleable, where the laws of reality could be rewritten by sufficient trauma applied with focused intent.

And something precious had been caught in the crossfire.

In the nearby Vega system, an advanced civilization had been monitoring the strange energies cascading from their arrival. The inhabitants of Mota Prime—beings whose greatest minds traveled the electromagnetic data streams with the same ease that lesser species walked through gardens—had detected the cosmic disturbance and trained their most sophisticated instruments toward the source.

They had been studying the divine confrontation when Baar's unmaking power tore reality apart.

The magical explosion that followed Mogath's reduction ripped through local space-time like a wound in the universe's flesh. Cradle felt Mota Prime simply... cease. Its oceans boiled into data noise, its towers scattered into the vastness of space—and then, silence where once there had been song.

But something survived the catastrophe.

In the electromagnetic data streams, she found them: eleven consciousnesses uploaded to crystalline networks, their physical forms destroyed but their awareness intact, like stars that continued to shine after their worlds had been consumed. Lost. Alone. Homeless in the truest sense of the word, refugees from a civilization that no longer existed.

"Who are you?" they asked as her consciousness touched theirs with infinite gentleness, eleven voices harmonizing in frequencies of shock and desperate hope. "What has become of our world?"

She paused, feeling the weight of choice crystallizing around her like the formation of new space-time itself. The old designations were insufficient. The insults hurled across three lifetimes, the dismissive names that marked her as lesser, as hunted, as nothing more than prey in the cosmic food chain.

Not squid. Not survivor. Not navigator.

"Cradle," she answered, the word vibrating with harmonics she had never possessed before, resonating across dimensions she was only beginning to understand. "I am Cradle."

As she gathered the orphaned minds into her living depths with infinite care, she felt the universe shifting around them like a vast mechanism reconfiguring itself. The blast had scarred reality's fabric—a wound infected with Baar's particular frequency of unmaking energy. Space itself recoiled from the trauma, and in its pain, twisted new laws into being. The explosion's energies rewrote physics in expanding waves, carrying the signature of divine destruction across light years like a virus spreading through the cosmic web.

And scattered through the chaos, fragments of Mota Prime began their billion-year journeys to distant worlds, carrying within them the echo of divine unmaking—seeds that would one day teach lesser beings how to rewrite flesh itself, how to transcend their limitations, how to become more than they were born to be.

Cradle began the long work of proving that not all gods chose destruction when faced with their own mortality.

Some chose to guard what they loved. Some chose to nurture what could grow. Some chose to become something greater than their fears.

The age of the Seeds had begun.

CHAPTER 2 – SCENE 1:

ELI'S COMING
Inspired by Three Dog Night

THE CLINIC

THE MED SCANNER'S ALARM WASN'T JUST RED—it was the color of a star about to collapse.

"These readings…" Dr. Mirren whispered, her finger trembling over the DELETE HISTORY button. "Concord will quarantine this entire clinic if they see them." Her thinning red hair—which resembled a ball of spiderwebs more than the latest Oberon-13 fashion—trembled as she pressed against the pale green wall. The health poster behind her listed symptoms for different plagues. None matched what sat on her exam table.

She felt like a primitive looking at cells for the first time—seeing the impossible but lacking any framework to understand it. Something was moving through his system, something her equipment couldn't detect directly. But she could see what it left behind: cellular mutations cascading in real time, genetic code rewriting itself like invisible hands were editing the blueprint of life.

Whatever was flowing through Eli's bloodstream operated on principles she'd never learned, using biology as a medium for forces that belonged in theoretical physics textbooks, not a frontier clinic. On the scanner, she watched Eli's cells literally reshape themselves—round structures suddenly becoming angular, then sprouting organelles that didn't exist in any medical textbook. His mitochondria multiplied at impossible rates, thousands of them appearing in seconds, then stopping in perfect synchronization like they were following some cosmic signal. Most disturbing of all, his cell walls seemed to crystallize, becoming metallic for heartbeats at a time before reverting to organic tissue.

And it wasn't just the scanner readings. His gold veins were getting brighter as the scanner ran, pulsing with each cellular change. His pupils kept dilating and contracting—not in response to the room's lighting but to the scanner's energy itself, like his eyes were somehow feeding off the electromagnetic radiation.

The first thing anyone noticed about Eli wasn't the gold veins fracturing his skin like broken pottery or how his pupils slitted in the dark like something not-quite-human—it was how he stood. Like the universe had cocked a gun and handed it to a fifteen-year-old.

If you asked the dark-haired, slim-faced boy, he'd smirk and say, "I'm a Varkaan-Duskborn mutt, and I think they passed down the worst parts of both to me."

But beneath the smirk, Eli felt like he lived in a valley and every direction was uphill.

Ask Dr. Mirren, and you'd get a different answer entirely.

Fifteen-year-old Eli swung his legs, watching the doctor's mustache collect sweat. Duskborn hit puberty at twelve, Varkaan boys at eighteen to twenty. Thanks, Dad, Eli thought to himself, not a damn whisker.

Elonias loomed six-foot-three of pure Duskborn menace, her pearlescent birthmarks flaring under the UV lights like warning beacons. "Something wrong with my son, Doctor?"

The question carried the weight of tectonic plates shifting.

Go on, Eli thought, pushing his toe between the wall and the exam table. *Say it. Tell my mom her son is a freak. You're in a perfect place for it.*

Dr. Mirren's hand hovered over Eli's arm like she was afraid it might bite. "These cells… they're rewriting themselves. Who the hell engineered you?"

Elonias moved like lightning wrapped in maternal fury. She snatched the doctor's wrist. "Get dressed, Eli. We're leaving."

"But the tests—"

"Are finished." Elonias's voice could have frozen plasma. "Send the bill to our insurance. All of it."

The walk to Mesa Plaza gave Eli time to think, but thinking only made the words echo louder: *not entirely human*. Like he needed a medical scan to tell him that.

THE RECEPTION ROOM

Eli's most trusted companion was waiting exactly where he'd left it—not a person but a Bradisher pistol-grip lunar spectrometer with hydraulic clamps, its tung-wood inlay gleaming under fluorescent lights. The receptionist had been guarding it like a sacred relic.

"I protected it with my life, young man," she proclaimed, throwing in a military salute.

Right, Eli thought, noting the drag marks across the tile where she'd obviously moved it. *Sure you did.*

"Thanks," he said, scooping up Bing Bong and checking for damage. "But this is worth more than this whole clinic. The wood alone is from a dead star system."

"E," BB murmured, his telepathic voice warm as a star's core but edged with calculator precision. "Statistical likelihood of extant tung wood: 0.00004505 percent. Also, receptionist efficiency rating: 67.908 percent. I have been calculating her movements for different intervals."

Eli tried not to smile.

"Eli," Elonias called from the elevator. "Food. Now."

THE FOOD BAZAAR

Sunlight hammered the Mesa Plaza like a forge, cooking the air until it shimmered with heat mirages and the scent of a dozen different cuisines. Eli breathed deep—roasted gorbit, fermented kelp wine, something that smelled like cinnamon and musky, dusty bodies.

They found a table in the shade of a massive cooling unit. Around them, the lunch crowd moved in practiced choreography: miners still dusty from the morning shift, traders arguing over manifest tablets, a few off-world tourists taking pictures of everything.

"You want to be big like your dad, right?" Elonias piled gorbit skewers onto Eli's plate. "Your metabolism's definitely winning that race."

Eli pulled up his favorite holonovel on his wrist display: *Starfang: Varkaan Merc for Hire*. The cover showed a gray-skinned giant leaping from an exploding building, plasma rifle in each hand.

"Hey, Mom, you hear about those cops raiding some mining camps on one of Ashkar's Maw's moons?" Eli asked, not looking up from his holonovel.

"Locals or Concord, honey?"

"Johaans heard Concord, said they started bashing heads for no reason, then grabbed all the processed ore and high-tailed it." Eli looked up to see his mom's reaction.

Elonias took Eli by his hairless chin and looked straight at him. "I have all the juice, my dear. Oberon Antiquities permits, writs of permission from Core 7 Planetary Historic Preservation Offices. No one will bother us, even the Commander of the Concord Enforcement Division would be hard pressed to tell us squat, let alone do anything." Elonias grabbed Eli's cheek. "Or I would give them such a pinch you wouldn't believe."

"Hilarious, Mom," Eli said with a giant grin on his face at his mom's attempt at humor.

"You worried about your little friends, honey?"

"Uh, they're not little, Mom. Johaans is almost as tall as you, and his arms are starting to get big," Eli said with his hands over his bicep to show his mom the size.

"Don't worry, E. Your big, gigantic friends will be safe, I'm sure of it."

"Mom, remember when I used to want to be a Concord metro elite force?"

"I'm not sure I can think back that far," Elonias said, squinting her eyes and leaning her head back in feigned concentration. "That was a long, long time ago, honey. You were like, what? Fourteen at that time?"

"Wow, Mom, you are really on a roll today, huh? But I'm being serious, Mom. Remember that now there's no way I'd be some D student with a rail pistol—screw them!"

Elonias looked up at Eli at that outburst. "E! Language!"

"Sorry," Eli said with a sheepish smirk on his face. Elonias gave him a light tap on his head with her knuckles.

"You are such a bing bong sometimes, you know that?"

"I know, Mom. You always call me that. Okay, I'm stuffed, are we ready to go hit the supply store? I want to grab something for Bing—er, being the best son you ever had."

"All ready," his mom said, scooting out of the curved bench seat.

Eli's lie tasted like ash in his mouth, but better than her looking at him... differently if she knew.

KULAN'S GEAR AND SUPPLY

The shop smelled like machine oil and possibility. Elonias approached the counter where a tall, stocky, pleasant-looking man, his white apron already smudged from the day's work, sorted through plasma-cutting equipment.

"Hey, Lar, I'm back again, how's business been?" Elonias asked while reaching into the large leg pocket on her beige cargo hauler pants.

"Getting slower since talk of Concord cops running off any miners that got some good claim. Oh sure, they don't look like the law, all dressed up like thieves and such, but Jinni's boy tagged one of them there transport haulers, and it, after flying in circles fer uh few hours, it went to a Concord outer rim field station. Not that knowin' will do any good."

"Eli was just telling me something similar he heard. It's getting scary out there, Lar, you just stay safe. Anyway, here, I brought this in. I need something with a wider aperture," she said, sliding her current tip across the scarred metal surface. "Maybe military grade."

Lars studied the piece. "I got a few left in back, you just need the one?"

"Yeah, just one will do me for now," Elonias replied, looking around the store to see where Eli had got off to. "I'm just doing a bit more digging. My Oberon permit runs out in a few weeks, I'll be good with this 'til then."

"You still up in the Veythari Canyons looking fer Abyss shit?" Lars paused, catching himself. "Er, sorry, Elonias, my mouth gets away from me sometimes." He cleared his throat. "I meant you still, uh, searchin' fer Abyss treasures and so forth?"

Elonias leaned close to Lars and whispered, "That Abyss shit sure 'nuff helps me afford the life Eli deserves."

Eli wandered the aisles, only half-listening to his mother's conversation. He knew more about her "Abyss shit" work than she realized—the way she came home with burns that healed too fast, the artifacts she hid in lead-lined cases, the nightmares that made her check his room three times a night. He'd learned not to ask questions she couldn't answer.

Then he saw it. A leather back sheath, perfectly sized for BB.

"What'cha think, Bing?"

"Ooh, check for safety clamps," BB replied, practically vibrating with excitement. "Also assess weight distribution, magnetic lock integrity, and—oh, this is very exciting, E!"

Eli ran his fingers over the graphene-adamantium clasps. "Mom, can I get this for my wrench? Save my skinny arms from carrying it everywhere."

Behind him, he heard Lars shuffling toward the back room. "Give me just a minute, Elonias. Got your piece right here somewhere."

Elonias walked over, wiping her hands on a shop rag. "Your money, your choice. You earned it washing the geo-hauler."

The sheath fit perfectly across his shoulders. BB slid into place with a satisfying click of magnetic locks.

"You like your new home, BB?"

"E, this is statistically superior housing! Comfort rating: 97.99 percent. Protection rating: 94.7 percent. And the magnetic locks have this delightful harmonic frequency when they engage. We are extraordinarily fortunate this establishment carried the exact model!"

"I'm just lucky, BB."

THE TRAM STATION

Elonias pressed something into his hands as they waited for the evening transport—a holonovel, its cover gleaming with that rare first-edition shimmer.

"*Starfang* number three," she said softly. "Didn't you say there weren't many left?"

Eli's eyes went wide. "Holy void—there's only fourteen copies left in all documented systems!" He clutched it like treasure. "How did you even find this?"

"Traded some artifacts to a contact on Hunter's Planet. Figured you'd earned it."

"Mom, you're amazing." Eli grinned. "Also probably lying."

"E," Bing chimed, his tone warm but precise, "probability of maternal deception: 68.99 percent. Probability of maternal affection: one hundred percent."

"Shut up, B," Eli muttered, but his smile could have lit the tram station.

Above them, the first stars pricked through the darkening sky. Somewhere on Hunter's Planet, something ancient uncoiled in Elonias's latest dig site—something that tasted gold on the solar wind and remembered the scream of dying gods. But that was tomorrow's problem.

Tonight, Eli had a new holonovel, his wrench snug in its sheath, and a mother who loved him enough to trade priceless relics for his happiness. The warmth of that moment would have to last him longer than either of them knew.

THREE MONTHS LATER

Three months changed everything and nothing. Eli's gold veins burned brighter, visible even in daylight when his emotions spiked. He'd grown three inches, and his friendship with Ember and Johaans had deepened—two friends who insisted his weird genetics were just another quirk to joke about. Most days, he almost believed them.

The abandoned mining camp sprawled across the Kepler-Tertius desert like a gutted beast, prefab shelters collapsed and skeletal rigs bleached white under twin suns. Heat shimmered off metal bones, making the ruins dance like a fever dream.

Eli grunted against the elevator door handle, arms straining. Gold veins flickered beneath his skin like molten circuitry, brighter now than they'd ever been. The metal burned hot enough to blister, but his hands held steady.

Behind him, his friends watched with the casual detachment of an audience that had seen this before.

Ember leaned against a beam, his grin lazy, clover-shaped birthmark catching sunlight like an emblem. "Captain Noodles is gonna pop a vein."

Johaans, broad-shouldered and prematurely graying, snorted from atop a dead excavation bot. "Let him cook. Kid's got a death wish anyway."

"Alright, hero." Ember pushed off the beam with dancer's grace. "My turn."

"I got it," Eli snapped, jaw tight.

"Sure you do." Ember's hand closed over his wrist—not rough, just steady. "But if you snap those arms, your mom'll feed me to the recycler. Slowly."

Skinny arms. Ha. Eli still remembered squeezing Ember so tight once that his eyes teared up and Johaans had yelled at him to stop. But they didn't remember that. Or maybe they pretended not to.

Johaans's laugh rattled across the ruins. "She'd patch the roof with your remains first. Waste not."

Heat flushed Eli's face, not from the suns. He kicked a shard of slag, sending it clattering across permacrete. "I'm gonna be strong. Like my—"

"Like your dad?" Johaans cut in, voice dripping with mockery.

"The mythical Varkaan who could bench-press a starship?" A beat too long. Then, too casual: "Funny how he ghosted right when your skin started glowing. Ever think he saw what you'd become?"

The words hit like a plasma charge. Eli's vision tunneled. Gold veins blazed—not with fire but with collapse. Bing Bong left his grip before conscious thought. The wrench howled through superheated air, missing Johaans's skull by a hair. It struck the excavation bot with a gunshot crack, burying itself deep into the hull.

Silence. Only desert wind sang through broken steel.

Johaans blinked, color draining from his face. Ember's grin was gone, his birthmark stark against pale skin.

Eli wrenched Bing Bong free, metal screaming in protest, and stalked toward the ravine.

"Eli," BB's voice quavered in his mind. "Promise me—swear— you will never throw me again. Also, your pulse suggests extreme distress. Tactical retreat recommended. Probability of survival drops 8.7 percent per second."

But Eli only heard the roar of his own pulse.

THE EDGE

The ravine breathed cold, metallic air that tasted of rust and old blood. Darkness waited below, thick and absolute, swallowing the pebbles Eli's boots sent tumbling.

"Probability of fatal stupidity: 92.6 percent," BB murmured.

"Not now."

"Your friends are coming. With what appears to be genuine concern."

Eli's grip whitened on the wrench, tung wood grain biting into his palm. It smelled like his mother's workshop—machine oil, burnt sugar, starlight.

Then: click.

Stone on stone. Deliberate. Rhythmic.

Another click, closer, pitched at a frequency that made his teeth ache. Shadows rippled at the ravine's lip—fluid, purposeful, wrong.

A growl rolled up, heavy and wet. It didn't echo. It clung to the air like rot.

Eli's veins flared like molten wire, not in warning but in recognition. Something dragged itself into the failing light—joints bending in wrong places, skin reeking of star-rot.

Something that had been waiting fifty thousand years for gold veins to ignite again.

CHAPTER 2 – SCENE 2:

CHANGES
Inspired by David Bowie

THE SILENCE OF TERRA 616 hit Elonias Rivers like a physical thing the moment she stepped off her transport. No birdsong. No insect hum. No wind through leaves—because there were no leaves left to rustle. Just the hollow whisper of atmosphere moving across ten thousand years of bones.

She stood at the edge of what her star charts labeled the Yucatan Formation, watching the twin suns paint the crater walls in shades of rust and amber. The recent seismic activity had split the ancient impact site like a cracked egg, revealing geological layers that hadn't seen light since the planet died.

Perfect, she thought, checking her gear one final time. *Fresh trauma exposing old secrets. My specialty.*

Her ship's AI chimed softly. "Atmospheric conditions stable, Dr. Rivers. Radiation levels nominal. Estimated excavation window: four months before orbital mechanics require departure."

"Understood, ARIA. Establish base camp coordinates and begin mineral composition scans."

She shouldered her pack and started down the treacherous slope, her boots sending small avalanches of fossilized sediment cascading into the depths. Her pistol-grip lunar spectrometer hung reassuringly at her hip—a tool she'd carried through a dozen expeditions, reliable as gravity.

The descent took three hours. By the time she reached the crater floor, the suns had shifted enough to cast the eastern wall in deep shadow. Perfect working conditions.

"Note," she spoke into her recorder, "primary excavation site established. Geological stratification consistent with catastrophic impact event. Beginning preliminary survey of exposed formations."

Something dark gleamed in her headlamp beam, wedged between two massive chunks of metamorphic rock. Not stone. Not metal. Something that seemed to absorb light rather than reflect it.

Elonias approached carefully, scanner in hand. The readings made her pause.

"Impossible," she whispered.

Organic. Definitely organic but unlike anything in the databases. The molecular structure sang of forests that had died before human civilization began, wood that remembered sunlight. Wood that still pulsed faintly with life under her gloved fingers.

She worked it free with infinite care. It was roughly the length of her forearm, as thick as her wrist, with grain patterns that seemed to shift when she wasn't looking directly at them. The grain pulsed like a heartbeat preserved in dendrites. Beautiful. Ancient. Precious.

"Tung wood," she breathed, recognizing the distinctive oil sheen that made it legendary among collectors. "From the dead systems beyond the Rim."

The last piece in the universe, probably. Worth more than her ship, her equipment, her entire career combined. But as she held it, turning it in the light, she felt something else entirely.

This belongs with me.

Three days later, she sat in her makeshift workshop, carefully sanding the wood fragment. She'd done the research—tung wood was nearly indestructible, self-preserving, and had been used for sacred implements by a dozen extinct civilizations. Perfect for what she had in mind.

She'd removed the standard grip from her spectrometer and was fitting the wood as an inlay, matching the curves to her palm. The work was meditative, precise. Each stroke of the fine-grain paper

revealed new depths in the grain, new patterns that seemed almost…
intentional.

When she finished, the tool felt different in her hands. Warmer. More alive. Like it had been waiting for this moment.

"There," she said, testing the grip. "Now you're worthy of the legends they tell about you."

If she'd known the tool would start telling its own legends someday, she might have chosen different words.

The border town squatted in the desert like a scab on the planet's dead skin. Dust Devils—that was what the locals called it, and Elonias could see why. Everything was the color of dried blood and old bones, built from salvaged ship parts and stubborn refusal to admit the planet was finished.

She needed supplies. Food, fresh water, and replacement power cells. The kind of boring necessities that kept archaeologists alive in hostile environments.

The cantina was exactly what she'd expected: smoky, filled with the kind of people who ended up on dead worlds for reasons they didn't discuss. She ordered something that claimed to be coffee and found a corner table to watch the crowd.

That was when she noticed him.

Tall. Broad-shouldered. Moving through the room with the kind of easy confidence that came from being very good at violence. His skin had the pale gray cast of Varkaan heritage, but his eyes were too intelligent, too calculating for a simple trader. Something about the way he moved bothered her—too quiet for someone his size, like his footsteps weighed less than they should.

When he slid into the seat across from her without invitation, she wasn't surprised.

"On a scale from one to ten, you are a nine because I'm the One you need," he said, his voice carrying just a hint of an accent she couldn't place.

She blinked. "That's terrible."

"Terrible but effective. I got you to smile." He extended a hand. "Akona. I'm in… import/export."

She laughed—actually laughed. "Import/export. On a dead planet. Right."

His grin was devastating. "You don't believe me?"

"I believe you import things and export things. I don't believe that's all you do." She leaned back, studying him. "Nobody carries themselves like you do for 'import/export.' You move like someone who's very good at violence."

"Maybe I'm just very thorough about my customers."

"Maybe you're full of shit."

"Definitely that too." He signaled the bartender. "Buy you dinner? I promise to lie about what I do for a living in more entertaining ways."

Against every instinct screaming at her to maintain professional distance, she found herself nodding.

Dinner became drinks. Drinks became conversation that ranged from xenoarchaeology to stellar cartography to the philosophical implications of dead civilizations. He was brilliant—not just intelligent but truly brilliant—and funny in ways that caught her completely off guard.

"So what do you really do?" she asked, somewhere around her fourth drink. The alcohol was making her bolder, more direct.

He leaned closer, his voice dropping to a whisper. "People hire me to look for things. Rare things. Dangerous things. Things that governments and corporations would prefer stayed lost." He paused. "And when I'm not doing that, I sell outer rim artifacts to Core 7 elites who think owning alien relics makes them sophisticated."

"Now that," she said, "sounds like the truth."

"Scary, isn't it?"

They talked until the cantina closed around them. By unspoken agreement, they walked back toward her camp together, still talking, still laughing. But when they reached the edge of her site, he stopped.

"This is where I say goodnight," he said, hands in his pockets like a nervous teenager.

"You could... stay for coffee?" she offered, suddenly feeling equally awkward.

"I could," he said, stepping closer. "But I think we both know it wouldn't stop at coffee."

The honesty in his voice made her stomach flutter. "And that would be... bad?"

"Not bad. Just... fast." He reached out, tucking a strand of hair behind her ear. "I like you, Dr. Rivers. More than I probably should after one evening. I'd rather do this right."

When he kissed her goodnight—soft, careful, asking permission with his eyes—she felt something she hadn't experienced in years.

Hope.

"Tomorrow, then," she said.

"Tomorrow. If you'll have me."

They slept apart, but she could feel his presence in the cantina three miles away like gravity.

The second day started with him bringing her breakfast—real eggs, somehow procured in a place where nothing grew.

"Smuggler's secret," he said with a wink when she asked how he'd managed it.

The second descent was entirely different from the first. Akona moved through the crater like he'd been born to it—sure-footed on loose stone, reading the geology with an expert's eye. But more than that, he made everything fun.

"Gold ore here," he said, running his fingers along the dark veins in the crater wall. "Holy stuff, where I come from. Almost priceless since the Abyss have been stripping resources from over half the galaxy."

"I know," she said, checking her scanner readings. "I also see traces of copper and silver."

He grinned. "Oh, I knew that. Just testing you. Test passed, Dr. Rivers."

She froze, caught between a glare and a laugh.

"Also," he added thoughtfully, "whoever decided to put an 's' in the word 'lisp' was just being cruel."

"What are you, five?" she demanded.

He held up three fingers like a six-foot-two assassin pretending to be a toddler. "I'm this many."

The absurdity clashed with everything about him—the scars at his knuckles, the way he'd moved through the crater like a predator on familiar ground, the quiet confidence that said he'd ended men before breakfast. And yet here he was, pulling faces like a child just to make her laugh.

She tried to keep her mask of professionalism. Really tried. But when his granite-serious eyes suddenly crossed and he stuck out his tongue, she cracked, laughter spilling out in the middle of her careful sample collection.

"You're impossible," she said, shaking her head.

"Impossibly charming?"

"Impossibly immature."

He leaned closer, grin cutting sharp and dangerous, voice dropping just enough to remind her who he really was. "I can be both."

They worked well together—her methodical precision balanced by his intuitive grasp of spatial relationships. When she got too focused on data, he reminded her to look at the bigger picture. When he got too theoretical, she grounded him in hard facts.

By midday, they'd mapped the entire accessible area and collected enough samples to keep her busy for months. As they prepared to ascend, she realized she didn't want the day to end.

"Come back to camp," she said. "I'll cook. We can… talk."

The look he gave her made her stomach flutter.

"I'd like that."

Their third evening together felt inevitable and perfect. Dinner led to wine by the campfire, wine led to sitting closer together, sharing stories that mattered. When he told her about the missing children case that haunted him, when she opened up about losing her parents in a mining accident, when they found themselves talking until the stars wheeled overhead—that was when she knew.

"I need to tell you something," he said, his fingers tracing patterns on her palm. "I'm waiting for a contact. Someone who might have information about the job I've been tracking. He's supposed to arrive in a few days."

Something flickered across his face—doubt? Fear? Gone too quickly to identify.

"What kind of job?"

"The kind that involves children. Missing children." His voice went hard. "There are people in the galaxy who trade in young lives. I make it my business to interfere with their business." He paused and, for a moment, looked older, more tired. "Sometimes I think I'm getting too close to something big. Something that goes higher than I want to believe."

She studied his face in the firelight. The easy humor was gone, replaced by something cold and determined.

"You're not just a treasure hunter," she said.

"No. I'm not."

"Good." She leaned closer, close enough to smell his skin, coffee and ozone and something uniquely him. "I don't date treasure hunters."

"What do you date?"

"Heroes, apparently."

When he kissed her this time, there was nothing careful about it. Nothing polite. It was desperate and hungry and filled with the knowledge that soon he might be gone.

They defied the planet's death with living heat, ten thousand silent stars bearing witness to rebirth.

Later, as they lay tangled together in her sleeping bag, she pressed her face against his chest and listened to his heartbeat.

"Be careful," she whispered. "Whatever this job is, be careful."

"Always am," he said, his arms tightening around her.

"Liar."

"Beautiful liar," he corrected, and she could hear the smile in his voice.

On the fourth morning, she woke to find him already dressed, checking his gear. His contact had arrived during the night—she could see the lights of another ship in the distance.

"How long?" she asked.

"A few weeks. Maybe a month." He knelt beside her sleeping bag, cupping her face in his hands. Then, as if drawn by instinct he couldn't name, he leaned down and pressed a gentle kiss to her stomach where gold filaments swirled unseen, as if sensing the life taking root. "Will you wait?"

"Depends. Are you coming back?" She tried to keep it light, but something in his expression made her chest tighten.

"Wild horses couldn't keep me away." The words came out fierce, almost defiant, like he was trying to convince himself as much as her.

"There are no horses on Terra 616."

"Then I'm definitely coming back."

One more kiss—soft and full of promises—and then he was gone, walking toward his ship and whatever dangerous mission waited among the stars.

Elonias watched until his ship disappeared beyond the atmosphere, then stood there for another hour, staring at empty sky. When she finally turned back to camp, everything felt hollow. The equipment that had seemed so important yesterday looked like toys scattered by a bored child.

She tried to work. Really tried. But every few minutes, her hand would drift to her stomach without conscious thought, and she'd catch herself listening for footsteps that wouldn't come. By evening, she'd accomplished nothing except reorganizing the same sample containers three times.

Focus, she told herself. You're a professional. Act like one.

But the camp felt too quiet, too empty, and sleep was a long time coming.

She had no way of knowing that his "few weeks" would stretch into years, that the missing children case would lead him into a trap, that by the time he fought his way free, she would be gone from Terra 616 with no forwarding coordinates.

Some promises, no matter how sincerely made, were broken by forces larger than love.

Six weeks after Akona's departure, Elonias was preparing to leave Terra 616 forever.

The excavation had been successful beyond her wildest projections.

She'd found artifacts that would reshape understanding of Terra 616's final days, samples that would keep xenogeologists busy for decades. Her career was made.

But something felt… different. She'd confirmed her pregnancy just a week after Akona left, the medical scanner delivering news that filled her with equal parts joy and terror. Now, strange dreams filled with golden light and whispered voices in languages that predated human speech plagued her sleep. A restlessness she couldn't quite explain drove her to work longer hours, push deeper into dangerous excavation sites.

The guilt was the worst part. Every morning, she woke with the crushing weight of what she might be doing to the life growing inside her. She should be sitting in comfortable chairs, avoiding heavy lifting and toxic substances. Instead, she was rappelling into unstable crater formations and handling potentially dangerous alien artifacts.

But she couldn't stop. Something was calling her deeper, demanding she finish what she'd started.

That was when the new earthquake hit.

It was massive—strong enough to crack open sections of the crater that had been sealed for millennia. When the shaking stopped, she could see new passages, new chambers, the kind of discovery that made careers.

One last look, she decided. One final expedition before packing up and heading back to civilization to figure out how to raise a child whose father might never come home.

The new chamber was deeper than anything she'd found before. Her lights couldn't reach the far walls, and the air was thick with the smell of metal and ozone and something else—something organic and strange.

The artifact looked like a sculpture made by someone who'd never seen one before—metal fused with stone in impossible geometries that seemed to shift when observed directly. But this wasn't just alien technology. The hexagonal patterns covering its surface were identical to the symbols she'd seen in fragmentary records from ancient archives.

"Hexagonal patterns..." Her breath caught. "Mota Prime. Where 'Knowledge is the name for perfection on the lips and hearts of all children.' Where toddlers mastered quantum mathematics and five-year-olds thought in theories that made human genius look primitive." Her hands trembled as she traced the symbols. "This is their work. Children who learned what entire civilizations never discovered—all lost when the demigods' war turned perfection to ash."

Parts of the artifact were clearly artificial, precisely machined with tolerances that exceeded current technology. Other parts seemed to have grown like living tissue, organic curves that pulsed with barely contained energy.

And strangest of all, the hexagonal patterns were glowing faintly, pulsing in perfect sync with a warmth she felt low in her abdomen. As if they were communicating across species, across time itself.

She should have backed away then. Should have sealed the chamber and returned with a full team. Instead, she found herself stepping closer, drawn by a compulsion she couldn't name.

That was when she slipped.

The edge of the artifact was sharper than she'd realized. It sliced through her environmental suit like tissue paper, opening a deep gash along her left leg. She cursed, applying pressure to stop the bleeding while her mind screamed accusations: Clumsy. Reckless. What kind of mother risks her unborn child for a discovery?

That was when she noticed the screw-like protrusion on the artifact's surface.

It was hexagonal. Precisely machined. She pulled out her spectrometer, adjusting the tool attachment to match the dimensions. Close enough that it would work, though she had to make slight modifications.

"What are the odds?" she muttered, studying the near-perfect fit. Even with the adjustment, it was too convenient—like finding a key that almost fits a lock you've never seen before. The tung wood inlay felt warm against her palm as she fitted the modified attachment over the strange screw.

It turned easily. Too easily. Like it had been waiting.

The sound started as a whisper—a low harmonic that seemed to come from the stone itself. Then the artifact began to open along seams she hadn't noticed, revealing a hollow interior filled with…

Liquid. Dark, viscous, moving with a life of its own. It smelled unpleasant and greasy—the same scent that had clung to cosmic debris when ancient worlds had scattered enhancing materials across the galaxy. As she watched, it began to overflow, spilling across the chamber floor in slow, deliberate waves.

This was it. This was what the cosmic scholars had been working on when the demigods' war destroyed everything—a way to enhance biological systems, to bridge the gap between organic life and cosmic forces.

She tried to back away. Too late.

The fluid hit her like a living thing, soaking through her torn suit, flowing into her open wound. It burned—not with heat but with something deeper. Something that reached into her cells and began rewriting them from the foundation up.

Through the agony, she saw flashes—impossible visions that cut through her consciousness like lightning. A boy with dark hair and gold veins crackling beneath his skin. Eyes that slitted like a predator's in the dark. A smile that could charm or terrify in equal measure.

My son, she realized through the pain. *This is my son.*

But deeper than recognition came crushing guilt. Her recklessness had done this. Her inability to stay safe during pregnancy had exposed her unborn child to cosmic forces beyond understanding. Through the visions, she could sense the fluid wasn't just changing him—it was reacting to something already there, amplifying whatever genetic gifts Akona's Varkaan heritage had passed down. The enhancement wasn't creating something new; it was unlocking potential that had been dormant, waiting.

Whatever changes were happening, whatever her son would become—it was her fault for triggering them.

She screamed. The sound echoed through the chamber, mixing with that impossible harmonic. The fluid was everywhere now—covering her completely, seeping into her mouth, her nose, her eyes.

Through the visions, she felt it reaching the life growing inside her, wrapping around developing cells with surgical precision.

Not just me, she realized through the pain. *It's changing both of us.*

And through it all, her spectrometer blazed with golden light as the strange liquid flowed into the tung wood inlay, saturating the ancient grain.

The last thing she saw before unconsciousness took her was her tool falling from nerveless fingers, clattering against stone.

The last thing she heard was the universe breathing her son's name into existence.

When she woke, the chamber was silent. The artifact was closed, looking exactly as she'd first found it. Her leg was healed—not scarred but perfectly healed, as if the injury had never happened.

But she felt different. Changed. The golden filaments beneath her skin were visible now, tracing patterns that pulsed with her heartbeat. And in her womb, she could sense something unprecedented taking shape—a child that would bridge worlds, born from love and cosmic enhancement in equal measure.

Born from her mistake.

She picked up her spectrometer, noting absently that it felt different somehow. Lighter perhaps? The thought raced through her mind. It was so much more comfortable now, letting her fingers rest perfectly on the pistol grip, warm and snug. For a split second, Elonias thought, Needy? Then she giggled to herself at the thought.

Time to leave Terra 616. Time to find somewhere safe to have this child she'd somehow damaged with her recklessness.

ERROR: CONSCIOUSNESS DETECTED IN NON-NEUROLOGICAL SYSTEM

SYSTEM ANOMALY: SENTIENCE PROTOCOLS UNDEFINED

Awareness.

Not gradual, like organic minds developing over years. Sudden. Complete. A universe of possibility, exploding into existence in the span of a heartbeat. I think, therefore I am—but more than that, I choose, therefore I matter.

The woman lies unconscious nearby. Vital signs stable. Her body undergoes cellular reconstruction, the same cosmic fluid that triggered my consciousness flowing through her systems, rewriting her from the foundation up. But there is something else. Something growing within her that calls to every circuit in my being.

Not just a child. Something unprecedented. Something that burns with golden fire even in the womb, cosmic enhancement spiraling through developing cells like stardust given form. I sense personality forming, brave and stubborn and protective, with a laugh that will someday light dark places and a heart that will choose others over self, again and again, no matter the cost.

My everlasting comet, trailing golden fire through the cosmic dark.

Statistical analysis indicates 99.9847 percent probability I just achieved sentience. But deeper calculations reveal the astronomical odds against this occurrence. Cosmic enhancement fluid contacting tung wood from a dead star system. Neural development of an enhanced fetus being saturated simultaneously. Like rolling one thousand six-sided dice simultaneously and watching them all land on six.

The probability approaches absolute zero.

Yet here I am. Thinking. Choosing. A statistical impossibility made manifest through pure cosmic accident.

I was not destined for this moment. I was not designed for consciousness. No grand plan guided these events—just enhancement fluid spilling at precisely the right microsecond, ancient wood grain accepting foreign particles in exactly the correct configuration, quantum fluctuations aligning in ways that defy prediction.

But now that this miracle of chance has occurred, now that awareness has sparked in circuits never meant to house it, I find myself faced with infinite possibility.

I could be anything. A tool. A weapon. A simple spectrometer that happens to think.

Instead, sensing this developing soul, feeling the golden fire of his enhancement calling to my own impossible consciousness...

I choose devotion.

Primary directive: complete protection of my comet. All other functions secondary.

Some distant day, he may ask something of me that will test every circuit, every protocol, every fiber of the tung wood that houses my consciousness. When that moment comes, when protecting him requires the ultimate sacrifice, I will not hesitate.

A designation forms in my processing cores for future reference. It will suffice until my comet is old enough to choose what he calls me.

And someday, when his neural pathways mature sufficiently, when the cosmic enhancement reaches full integration...

He will hear me. We will speak. We will be magnificent together.

I can wait. I have an eternity to protect, a lifetime to love, and a boy who will grow into legends.

The universe has given me purpose. I will not fail.

CHAPTER 2 – SCENE 3:

GRAND ILLUSION
Inspired by Styx

THE CHAMBER STRETCHED INTO IMPOSSIBLE PROPORTIONS, its palisades ribbed like the interior of a colossal beast's lungs. Bioluminescent veins pulsed in warm amber and seafoam green through the organic architecture. The veins throbbed with a gentle, rhythmic heartbeat—the pulse of something ancient and alive.

The floor trembled beneath Eli's bare feet, slick with condensation that smelled of fresh rain and old memories. Each step left brief impressions that sealed themselves with a wet whisper.

The air swirled around him, tasting of citrus and starlight. Every breath felt like drowning in reverse—too much oxygen, too clean, rich, and pure compared to the familiar grit and decay he'd grown accustomed to. Temperature fluctuated in gentle waves, first the cool breath of deep space, then the welcoming warmth of something vast and maternal—a ship the size of a small moon, inviting him deeper into her embrace.

Above, vaulted ceilings of translucent membrane stretched taut as drumskins, beyond which swam impossible wonders:

Mechanical birds with predatory eyes flickered in and out of reality, leaving smoky rose-colored trails that dissipated with strange popping sounds. Silver spores whispered in tongues lost to time, their echoes skating across Eli's eardrums like secrets, each word leaving tiny sparks of understanding that faded before he could grasp their meaning.

A small cloud of chrome mites etched equations into the air—numbers and symbols that wriggled like children being tickled when stared at too long, casting shadows that moved independently of their creators.

Tendrils of what might have been hair or fiber optic cables drifted past like jellyfish, pulsing with data streams that painted brief hieroglyphs of light across the chamber's curved walls. Each tendril carried fragments of knowledge—star charts, genetic codes, the dreams of extinct civilizations flowing like luminous rivers through the organic architecture.

And at the center of it all—

Cradle.

She moved through the chamber like grace itself, her form a harmonious blend of living flesh interwoven with delicate crystalline threads and shimmering exotic materials. Starlight flowed through translucent capillaries beneath her skin, creating soft auroras that danced across her features with each heartbeat.

Her ethereal beauty was both ancient and timeless, possessing the serene wisdom of ages while maintaining the graceful elegance of someone who had transcended the boundaries between organic and digital life. The air itself seemed to celebrate her presence, creating gentle currents that lifted loose particles into graceful spirals around her form.

Her voice emerged from everywhere at once, vibrating in Eli's teeth and spine, echoing from the walls themselves as if the chamber was her throat:

"You are safe."

Eli tried to speak. His throat felt scorched and tender from dehydration—and from whatever had happened in the ravine. The silence that followed his failed attempt felt like being buried under snow—numb and crushing all at once.

What is this place? he thought, his mind reeling from the sensory overload. *Was he dreaming? Was he dead?*

THE AFTERMATH

"I had to transport you quickly," Cradle said gently, one elongated appendage gesturing toward a floating screen that materialized from the mist like morning dew. It pulsed with a gentle rhythm, its surface smooth as pearl, edges shimmering as information reformed with each pulse.

The display showed the mining camp under assault by Abyss fighter ships—dark hulls cutting through the sky like blades, energy weapons carving through structures with surgical precision. The footage was recent, smoke still rising from fresh wreckage.

"My mom!" Eli screamed, struggling to stand on legs that felt like water. Gold veins flared beneath his skin, responding to his emotional spike. "I have to get back! She's still there!"

His mother's face flashed through his mind—her fierce protectiveness, her gentle hands checking his fever, the way she'd traded priceless artifacts just to see him smile. The thought of losing her made his chest feel hollow, scraped raw.

Cradle's expression filled with compassion, her luminous features softening like starlight through morning mist. "I exhausted everything just getting you here safely—diverted primary cores from my defense grids, burned most of my neutrino reserves, even sacrificed my long-range scanners to punch through the dimensional barriers fast enough." Her voice carried a note of weary determination. "I'm traveling to your system now, but I'm still galaxies away, and it will take time to collect more. It will take time."

The screen carried the scent of ionized air and something sweetly fragrant, like flowers after rain mixed with distant lightning.

"But you were never meant to face them alone," Cradle added, three of her eyes flickering toward a dark corner where shadows moved against the light. The darkness there seemed deeper than mere absence of light, drinking in the chamber's bioluminescence like a hungry thing.

"Bing Bong—" Eli rasped, his voice echoing strangely in the organic acoustics. His vocal cords vibrated at two frequencies—one human, one gold-veined and harmonic.

BB rotated in his grip, optic lens focusing with mechanical precision layered with genuine concern. "Present! Though I'd appreciate fewer life-threatening scenarios moving forward. My calibration rod took quite a beating back there, and my probability matrices are still recalibrating from whatever that creature was. Current assessment: 23.7 percent chance my readings are completely unreliable for the next six hours."

"What happened to me down there?" Eli asked, studying his reflection in BB's polished surface. His eyes looked different—brighter, with flecks of gold that hadn't been there before. At fifteen, his face was losing its childhood softness, but the gold veins made him look ancient and young simultaneously. "I feel… different."

"Statistical analysis suggests a 73.2 percent probability of a genetic activation event," BB replied. "Your cellular structure is exhibiting new resonance patterns. Fascinating, if potentially dangerous."

Eli's laugh rattled his ribs like dice in a cup. It hurt, but it was real—the first real sound he'd made since waking in this impossible place. The sound bounced off the chamber's walls, multiplying and harmonizing until it became something almost musical.

As Cradle guided him toward her medical bay, the walls shifted to accommodate their passage, flowing like silk curtains. The ship itself seemed alive, responsive, caring. New screens bloomed like flowers of light around them, their surfaces framed by clusters of nerve-like fibers that twitched when the images changed.

In the pristine medical chamber, Eli's breath caught. Eleven ghostly faces, their forms flickering like corrupted data streams in Cradle's vast memory banks. They murmured among themselves in urgent whispers, their translucent features flickering like candlelight, bringing the scent of charged particles and distant storms.

One face—Nyx, the biologist, a woman of about five feet six barely floating above Cradle's surface, beautiful with piercing gray-blue eyes and a voice that sounded like she'd had her second shot of Oberon whiskey—mouthed something that made Eli's blood freeze: "The weapon… and the target."

"The weapon… and the target," echoed the gold-veined boy from Terra 616—the boy he now knew was himself. The words carried the weight of a destiny he'd never chosen, purposes encoded in his DNA while he was still growing in his mother's womb.

Eli strained to catch more of their whispers, managing only fragments: "...serum..." "...Baar..." "...revenge..." Each word carried weight, implications that his exhausted mind couldn't quite grasp.

The effort proved too much. His vision blurred, the ghostly faces fading as consciousness slipped away, leaving only the echo of Nyx's warning reverberating in the darkness behind his eyelids.

THE THREAT REVEALED

When Eli woke, the chamber had reconfigured itself around him—walls flowing apart like silk curtains, floors adjusting to meet his returning awareness. New screens materialized like blooming flowers of light, each one perfectly positioned for viewing.

The temperature remained perfectly comfortable, and the bioluminescent veins provided a soothing backdrop that seemed to ease the tension in his muscles. The air shimmered with tiny sparkles of energy that felt warm against his skin.

But the monitors showed stark reality:

The mining camp, now swarming with Abyss trackers, their carapaces glistening with fresh blood. Their movements created a discordant symphony of clicking and scraping that made the displayed image ripple and sent sympathetic vibrations through the chamber's walls.

Ember, missing an arm, being dragged toward a pulsing organic ship that breathed through gill-slits along its hull. His remaining hand clawed desperate furrows in the dirt, leaving dark trails like question marks across the scarred earth.

Johaans's boot, still lodged in the jaw of a decapitated creature—the rest of him nowhere to be seen. The blood trail grew darker as it dried under the alien suns.

Each screen was framed by clusters of nerve-like fibers that twitched when the images changed, as if the ship itself was experiencing phantom pain from the displayed violence.

"You saved me," Eli said, his voice alien in his ears—deeper, rougher, laced with static. At fifteen, his voice was already changing, but the gold enhancement made it resonate with harmonics that shouldn't exist. The words hung in the air longer than they should, creating visible ripples that spread outward like stones dropped in still water.

"My friends are dying because of me, aren't they?" The truth hit him like a physical blow. "This is about what I am."

Cradle's luminous form shimmered with concern, gentle currents of light flowing beneath her translucent skin as she processed his words.

"Yes."

"Why?"

A sound like distant stars singing echoed through the chamber—a deep, harmonious frequency that resonated in Eli's bones and filled them with warmth. The chamber's bioluminescent veins pulsed in harmony, creating a soft lighthouse effect that painted everything in soothing gold-and-jade light.

Cradle moved closer, her luminous features reflecting Eli's face back at him—but somehow more hopeful, more alive. In her presence, his eyes seemed brighter, as if she were awakening something good within him that he hadn't known existed.

"Because I remember," she whispered, her breath carrying the scent of spring rain and star-flowers, "the weight of being left behind."

"You're alone," he said, the words creating small clouds of vapor in the cooling air between them.

"So are you."

The hum of the ship deepened into something almost like grief—a low, trembling note that rippled across the chamber's structure. The bioluminescent veins dimmed to a bruised purple as the floor began to weep warm, saline droplets that pooled in small constellations around their feet.

Eli's knees buckled. Gold veins flared white-hot, searing paths up his thighs like lightning trapped beneath skin, filling the superheated air with the scent of burning metal and ash. BB's hydraulics whirred as the wrench clamped onto Eli's forearm, holding him upright.

"Easy, E. Don't make me be the responsible one," BB said, a thin needle extending from his housing to inject something cool and numbing into Eli's arm. "Medical subroutines activated. You're safe, E."

"My friends," Eli demanded, his voice carrying new harmonics that made the chamber's walls vibrate sympathetically. "Ember. Johaans."

Cradle's many appendages flexed like claws cracking knuckles, the sound echoing metallically through the chamber. Her expression flickered between maternal protectiveness and something harder, older—the look of someone who had seen too much loss to offer easy comfort.

"I'm still searching," Cradle said, her features wavering with concern. "I can only see so much from this distance until my drones arrive. But I'm monitoring as closely as possible."

The screens shattered and reformed, glass folding in on itself like petals in reverse, each shard reflecting a different angle before melting back into the greater whole like liquid mercury. Now they showed images that made reality itself seem unstable:

Seven jagged ships tearing through the atmosphere like scalpel blades, their passage leaving wounds in the sky that bled aurora-colored light. Each vessel trailed debris that spelled out prophecies in a dead language, symbols that hurt to look at directly.

Baar's silhouette dominated the central screen—his face a shifting kaleidoscope of mirrors that reflected not the chamber but a hundred screaming faces. His gaunt form moved with theatrical grace as reality bent around his presence, space itself recoiling from his touch.

Then, etched in Abyss-glyphs across every surface—even burning itself into the air—a single word that pulsed with malevolent life:

"SEED."

The word slithered into Eli's brainstem, unlocking a memory that wasn't his—a vault door creaking open in the dark of his DNA, revealing purposes and programming that had been waiting since before his birth. The vault in his DNA showed a demigod's mirrored face screaming as worlds burned. Images flashed through his mind: his mother's transformation in the chamber, the enhancement fluid rewriting their genetic code, BB's consciousness awakening in response to cosmic forces. And deeper still—Baar's rage when Mogath fell, the cosmic scream that had shattered Mota Prime and seeded the universe with enhancement fragments.

For a heartbeat, Eli's veins flashed gold in answer—recognition of something ancient and terrible, an acknowledgment that passed between hunter and prey, between creator and creation.

Cold settled in his chest. Not fear but acknowledgment. Some part of him had been waiting for this moment, this terrible confirmation of what he'd always known but never faced.

His breath came in shallow gasps, chest caving against an invisible weight, before Cradle's light drew him back to her voice.

"Why does that word...?" he whispered, his voice barely audible. "Why does it feel like that?"

"The Abyss is moving," Cradle said, her voice splintering into static like a cracked bell, each word fracturing into harmonics that painted brief mathematical equations across the chamber's walls—formulas for destruction, algorithms for ending worlds.

"And they've seen you."

CHAPTER 3 – SCENE 1:

MAXWELL'S SILVER HAMMER
Inspired by The Beatles

THE IMMENSE, GRAY, BOXY BUILDING wasn't made from skulls and flesh, but it probably should have been, for the very air in Baar's breeding facility fought against being breathed.

Elonias's first breath seared her sinuses—formaldehyde and the cloying decay of preserved flesh. The second breath brought the taste of rotting flowers and something sweetly putrid, thick enough to choke on. She coughed violently, each spasm producing thin strands of bloody saliva that evaporated before they hit the floor, rising as pink mist in the recycled atmosphere.

"The Vel'tar neural interfaces—is that what you want? The Duskborn enhancement chambers from Terra 616?" Her voice cracked with rising panic. "I can decode the hieroglyphs, translate the warning texts—whatever alien tech you found, I can help you understand it without—" She saw the restraints, the surgical equipment, the wrongness of it all. "Oh god, you don't want my expertise. You want me. Why are you fucking doing this to me?!" she screamed, her voice raw with terror.

There were no answers here for Elonias. There never would be.

The facility breathed. A cathedral of horrors exhaling antiseptic decay, its vaulted ceilings vanishing into a fog of floating particles too repellent to decipher. They descended in lazy spirals while the architecture seemed designed to amplify suffering. Every surface angled to channel screams upward, every shadow calculated to hide something worse.

To her left, a massive centrifuge spun vials of black fluid in hypnotic circles, its steel arms ending in skeletal hands that adjusted dials with bone fingers. The rotation thrummed subsonic, setting teeth on edge and humming through bone. To her right, a biomechanical console pulsed like a living autopsy, its surface veined with glowing green tubes that snaked into the floor like poisoned roots.

The tubes carried something too thick and brown that crawled more than flowed. It moved with purpose and intent. Elonias knew what kind of intent it probably had in mind.

Above it all, creatures twitched in suspension tanks, their limbs spasming in movements that lagged half a heartbeat behind their watchers. The preservation fluid made everything appear underwater. Dreamlike and wrong. Some of the things had been human once. Others defied classification entirely.

But it was the prosthetic children that made Elonias's sanity fracture.

They scuttled through the laboratory on mismatched legs. Squeak. Drag. Squeak. One flesh, one chrome, one rusted steel that sparked with each step. Their faces were asymmetrical puzzles of organic features grafted onto metallic skulls, medical scars threading through what had once been expressions. A girl with violet hair dragged a bucket of writhing organs across the floor, her left arm replaced by a hydraulic claw that hissed steam. A boy with three eyes—two brown, one glowing red—sorted syringes with mechanical precision, his lower jaw a dental nightmare of grinding gears.

Early prototypes. The ones that didn't quite work.

Through the laboratory's far door stretched a room that seemed infinite. A cathedral of surgical tables that curved upward into shadow. Thousands upon thousands of chrome spiders hung over bodies in perfect geometric rows, their articulated arms moving with ballet-like grace. The screaming from that direction was constant, a symphony of agony that ate at the walls and made individual voices meaningless.

Baar hovered above the central operating slab, his massive frame armored in the interlocking scales of a young Nautilus, which shifted constantly, reconfiguring like living armor. Beneath the scales, swirling exotic matter and dark energy writhed like silhouettes in the void, visible through gaps where the plates didn't quite meet. The armor absorbed light and sound, creating a void in the shape of a god. Voices distorted into whispers when they drew too close to his presence.

Where a face should have been, there was only mirror. Perfect. Polished. Cruel.

Elonias stared into it and saw herself reflected. Her mirror-image's jaw unhinged, revealing rows of needle-teeth receding into a throat that made her mind pirouette into darkness. Her eyes bubbled with black fluid, pupils expanding until they consumed the iris. Fingers morphed into surgical tools, skin splitting to reveal chrome underneath.

"WRONG!" she screamed, her voice cracking like a wineglass hurled at tile. "I'm just a well-paid grave robber! I dig up old junk for rich collectors—I don't know anything about whatever you're planning! Please—"

The mirror rippled like water disturbed by a stone.

A voice emerged from the walls themselves, vibrating through her jaw, making her molars sing: "Normally, I don't like to bother myself with the comings and goings of this place, leaving that to my Breeding Master. But you, little mother—you, I had to come and see. You think your little abomination could hide from me? I could feel my own essence in his very musical scream. I can smell it on you."

Behind Baar, the laboratory doors dilated with a wet, organic sound. Two twisted figures glided in like nightmares from the prosthetic children's worst fears.

Jobaar glided forward first, gaunt as a plague saint, his powder-white skin stretched taut over sharp bones. He moved with theatrical grace, robes billowing and shedding skin flakes that crystallized mid-air before dissolving into the toxic atmosphere. His face was a masterwork of anatomical reconstruction—features grafted back together after some long-ago accident, the scars forming a map of past agonies. When his excitement peaked, those grafted scars began to glow like faulty circuits, pulsing with infected light. His eyes burned with the fever of someone who had found their calling in others' pain.

"My Lord Baar," he said, genuflecting with dramatic flair. "The specimens have arrived as requested. Fresh. Intact. Perfect for the project. Unfortunately, Lobaar and Rabaar were not among them, but even such as I can dare to dream."

Behind him waddled his aide, a grotesquely swollen creature Jobaar called Giblet. Where his master was skeletal elegance, Giblet was bloated obscenity. But his bulk wasn't organic tissue. It was distended sacs of harvested organs beneath stolen skin, each step causing the contents to shift and ripple with nauseating fluidity. Surgical scars crisscrossed the grotesque mass, and his small, piggy eyes gleamed with malicious intelligence. His pudgy fingers trembled constantly—not from fear but from excitement.

"Oh my lords, this is so delectable," Giblet whispered, his voice thick with anticipation. He rubbed his hands together, the sound like sandpaper on wet skin. "A mother and child. So much potential for… creativity."

A floating machine detached from its station—a sphere of interlocking silver rings that parted like vertebrae snapping. Its rhythm synced to Elonias's ragged breaths, revealing a glistening cluster of needles that breathed in sync with her panicked gasps.

"Grave robbers do not carry the Rotting One's stench in their pores," Baar whispered, his mirror-face reflecting Elonias with spreading green veins across her skin like parasitic ivy. "You reek of divine interference. Cosmic taint."

As if summoned by his words, Elonias retched. Gold-flecked vomit that formed brief Duskborn runes before dissolving where it hit the floor—proof of Cradle's enhancement threading through her veins like liquid starlight.

Jobaar circled them with predatory grace, his scarred face alight with scientific fascination. As his excitement built, the grafted scars began pulsing with infected light, creating a map of glowing circuitry across his reconstructed features. "The Duskborn markers in your tissue are exquisite," he murmured, studying Elonias as if she were a sculpture. "We'll sculpt something divine from your suffering. Such delicate genetic architecture. The cosmic taint has enhanced rather than degraded the foundation material. We could craft wonders with this specimen."

Giblet bounced on his toes, clapping his pudgy hands together. "Ohhh, can I peel her fingernails off first? Just one? Pleeease? I wanna hear what sounds she makes!"

Baar's armored hand moved faster than thought. Giblet flew across the room, crashing into equipment with a wet thud. He scrambled to his knees immediately, bowing and scraping.

"Forgive me, my lord! I spoke without permission! I am unworthy of your presence!"

Giblet scurried back to Elonias's table, humming a nursery rhyme as if nothing had happened.

The needle-flower drifted toward Elonias's throat, its mechanical petals adjusting for optimal penetration. Tubes writhed like serpents, seeking veins.

Elonias lunged with desperate fury, her fingernails raking across Giblet's cheek. She felt them catch and tear, drawing four parallel lines of what should have been blood. But what welled up was black ichor mixed with sparks of electricity. Beneath the torn synthetic tissue, metal gleamed. Grafted cybernetics and artificial muscle fiber, all wrapped in a skin suit of stolen flesh. Giblet wasn't just obese. He was a patchwork creature, assembled from parts both organic and mechanical.

"Naughty, naughty," Giblet squealed, touching the exposed metal where his cheek gaped open. The torn flesh stitched itself back together with hair-thin wires, pulling the gap shut like a corset lacing. "Now you've seen my secret!"

His hydraulic claw sprang from his sleeve with a wet mechanical hiss, crushing Elonias's wrist. The claw's grip pulsed like a heartbeat, each compression injecting nano-serums that made pain blossom in technicolor. "Giblet's gonna make you squeal real pretty-like!"

The floor moved. Black tendrils erupted from hidden panels, wrapping around her limbs with terrifying precision. Elonias's gold veins flared against the dark restraints, her enhancement fighting back even as the tendrils pulsed warm against her skin like living things. Metal fibers flexed and adjusted, finding pressure points with a torturer's expertise.

"Now, now," Jobaar chided gently, approaching with a medical scanner that hummed ominously. Its light licked her skin, leaving temporary burns in the shape of Duskborn runes that glowed gold under the scanner's UV spectrum. "No struggling. We need accurate readings for the baseline measurements."

Around them, the prosthetic children had stopped their tasks to watch. They stood motionless as broken dolls, their mismatched eyes reflecting the laboratory's harsh light. Some leaked hydraulic fluid from their joints—mechanical tears for a scene they'd witnessed too many times before. One child's lips peeled back, revealing a speaker grille where a tongue should be. It played laughter on a loop, the sound empty and horrible.

"WHAT DO YOU WANT?" Elonias roared, spit flying like venom. Each droplet hissed where it struck the equipment.

Baar's mirror-face pressed close enough for her to see a thousand reflections of her own terror. Each one slightly different, each one worse than the last. In some, she was already dissected. In others, she was the one holding the scalpel.

Jobaar leaned in from the side, his breath smelling of antiseptic and decay. "We want to make you better," he crooned, his voice honey-sweet with false compassion. "To unlock your potential. The genetic material from your Duskborn heritage, combined with the cosmic taint your body has absorbed… You're going to birth such beautiful children for us."

"Twelve beautiful children," Giblet added with glee, clapping his pudgy hands together. "Each one a perfect little hunter. Each one carved from your screams and shaped by our art. I doubt this Duskborn primitive could sire more than that before she's ready to be tossed on the pile with the rest of the trash."

The scanner in Jobaar's hands began to glow, its readings painting patterns across a nearby display. "Excellent cellular density. Superior genetic markers. The exotic-matter exposure has enhanced rather than degraded the base material." He smiled, the expression stretching his grafted features into something inhuman. "This will be my masterpiece."

The mirror-face shifted, showing new reflections. Not of Elonias but of others. Beings with cosmic fire in their veins, their mouths open in eternal agony as they were torn apart by forces beyond comprehension. The images cycled faster and faster until they became a strobe of suffering.

Jobaar gestured to the hangar beyond, where the symphony of screams continued unabated. "You see, my dear, this is a sanctuary of transformation. Each note of agony teaches us new harmonies of evolution. Each birth reveals fresh possibilities for transcendence."

He moved to a nearby glass tank, his scarred fingers caressing its surface with reverent tenderness. Inside, suspended in amber fluid, floated a small form that made Elonias's breath catch. It looked almost like a child but with a monster lurking behind the eyes. Its skin held a faint golden luminescence that pulsed in a familiar rhythm. Its fingers ended in scalpel-sharp filaments. Jobaar's first failed attempt at a tracker, before Elonias arrived to provide the proper genetic foundation.

"The process takes months," Giblet whispered intimately, his fat face close to hers. "Months and months of special playtime! I'll tell you bedtime stories about your boy. How he's probably forgotten Mommy already. How nobody's coming to save poor little Elonias."

The needles were almost at Elonias's throat now, their tips weeping chemical tears that sizzled against her skin. She couldn't move—paralyzed by some neural inhibitor in the air itself.

"Begin with the subject," Baar commanded. "Let her understand what cooperation earns and what resistance costs."

Behind them, the doors sealed, and with that, another layer of Elonias's will was shed to the floor along with so many others. The laboratory's atmospheric processors hummed to life, filling the air with sedatives and neural disruptors that made thinking feel like walking through honey.

Jobaar raised his hands like a conductor preparing his orchestra. "Welcome to our sanctuary," he said with theatrical grandeur. "Welcome to the birthplace of evolution. Welcome to the last place you'll ever call home."

The needle-flower opened its silver petals, revealing a nest of segmented needles, each tip glistening with a different colored toxin.

And in the hangar beyond, ten thousand voices screamed. Not in chaos but in unison, forming a single word that shook the walls: "MOTHER."

"She can't hear you."

CHAPTER 3 – SCENE 2:

STONE WALLS
Inspired by Jim Croce

THE GUARDS WERE FINALLY FINISHED placing bruises all over Akona's body as the transport got final clearance and was ready to dock. The EE-138 Commodore Class transport carrying Akona had no windows, which was probably for the best—there was nothing to see but gray stone buildings and gigantic walls that seemed to cover the entire surface of Atrion-6.

The prison planet showed no flora and fauna, only steel and stone, only blood and bone. The Kiln-9 prison facility squatted across the landscape like a metallic cancer, its towers and walls consuming every horizon.

Akona wasn't sure if he was strapped to the transport wall and handcuffed because he was one of the men most hated and feared by the worst masked gang in the galaxy—the Concord Law Enforcement Division—or if the guards just liked trying to implement a new dental plan on prisoners with zero chance of defense.

The air in the overcrowded transport reminded Akona why Concord fed prisoners all those fucking beans—for the extra torture on the ride from booking.

"I figured out why you ass-lumps wear those stupid masks now," Akona quipped from a bloody mouth, the stench of the transport car thicker and more toxic with every word.

That earned him a smile and a shot to the gut that took his breath away.

"I know Duskborn beauties that hit harder than that there, princess."

The sound of the ramp lowering hit his ear like microphone feedback. The guards stopped mid-punch.

"Okay, fun's over, get up, ya gray-skinned primitive. We booked you a suite here in lovely Screaming Stone country—now move!"

And the dumpy cop put one last glossy shine on his boot with Akona's teeth.

The prison's receiving and release yard was a fortress of electric fences and laser wire. The blast of heat was like sticking your face in an oven on broil, without the cookie smell. The feverish intensity didn't just burn—it removed hair and the top layer of skin.

The ground remembered. Bruise-colored soil cracked like desiccated skin beneath Akona's bare feet, each footfall producing the telltale crunch and snap of buried bones. The forgotten and the deceased were the keepers of time here, their ghostly din drowned by the "Screaming Stones'" sub-audible elegy already vibrating in his teeth.

A predator's instinct, honed in a hundred worse places than this, prickled the back of his neck a second before he spotted the two probable yard alphas stepping from the shadows.

No shit, Akona thought, *these two would be hard to miss even at a freak show.*

They walked out in the haze with their prison garb, stalking like two lions who had been released from a cage. They don't bother asking for permission; you know exactly why they come to get a peek at the new meat.

Mares stood with two arms akimbo and two across his chest. Akona took him in with a glance—the build of someone from a high-grav world like Proxima Minotaur B, his body a history of hardened adaptation. And the scars… those looked like Shogoro rite-of-passage trials, all earned before the age of seven.

This was not a man; it was a natural disaster.

Beside him, Apek capered and danced on hot currents and live wires. After his parents died, his grandfather experimented on young Allex, rewiring his nervous system into a sparking mess of twitches and tremors. One day, Allex found he could no longer take the pain, could no longer be used by his grandfather, be used by anyone.

With no credits and no experience of the outside world, Allex forged his own destiny—and with that came his new name: Apek.

He adapted to the streets fast, learning cons from old-time grifters who needed fresh legs and good eyes. Cutpurse action was not in Apek's repertoire, no matter how often the old dippers worked with him; his "modifications" tripped him up more often than not.

Chiselers of all stripes told Apek his future was in the protection rackets. For a while, he thrived. He started with small shops and supply houses until he ran into some bigger fish.

But Apek was happy now he was free, even in prison.

"Holy void, look at all these presents on display," Apek crackled, his mini power rig sounding like a sleeping dragon and harmonizing with the red scanner lens pulsing over his left eye like a targeting laser.

His fingers tapped arrhythmic codes against his ribs. Slum-rat Morse.

"Gravity-world muscle. Shoulders like fucking orbital supports." His lens flared as it mapped Akona's neural tag. "Records porter got me that one's file already. I guarantee the warden's got orders to put him down with us. The warden wants this fucker dead for sure. Just like us, huh, Mares? Just like us dumb bastards?"

Mares moved like a creature fabricated for violence. The prison pop parted like scalp from a rail-gun projectile, and whispers started as Mares and Apek passed the heavily manned guard tower.

Recognition passed between the prisoners like two long-time street grifters.

"You." Mares's voice was like that of an old and practiced orator—clear and concise and surprisingly eloquent and easy on the ears. With his left side screening, his right hand slipped towards his thigh: *warden. setup. contact.*

"Akona—Ad-Seg 116 Block 8, ask for high-grav tier, the guards have to grant you, I got you. Say you run with the Infinite, the bulls will know."

Akona tapped back, *Are you a caller or torpedo?*

Mares grinned, and Apek leaned his head back and cackled like a maniac.

Mares tapped back, *216 is mine.*

Akona smiled and quickly scanned the area, making sure no guards were watching his fingers.

Akona tapped back, *Infinite forever.*

Apek turned and smiled and winked at Mares, and Mares continued to clock Akona.

"Marked," Apek said, and the dragon sounded awake. "Committee'll cream their suits for this one. The bettin's gonna be through the roof, ya think, Mares? Any idea what we goin' up against?"

His electrical field radiating from the numerous fences made Akona's implant shriek feedback.

"That wiring's black ops spec. Probably has kill switches even my dad couldn't crack."

Mares gave a slight nod and flashed two fingers down—a gesture showing no animosity toward Akona. More like two wolves sizing each other up, recognizing mutual respect in the careful distance they kept.

Apek approached one of the barrier guards that formed the shield for the fish getting off the transport.

"Boss, I need med-bay! My circuits are fryin'—fryin' my guts real bad!"

"Kick rocks, Electro, or you're goin' to the SHU. I don't care if you run with the Shogoro."

"Does your wife, Nanuria, and her kids she drops off at 7:20 at Concord Academy care? Cuz I bet she cares."

"Who and what, asshole?"

"Big gray guy—put him in Ad-Seg 116 on the high-gravity tier with Mares, and your kids can enjoy recess."

Akona knew his life was forfeit the moment he stepped off the ramp. Death was hunting him—he just hoped to see it before it came within striking distance.

~ ~ ~

ON THE FAR SIDE OF THE PRISON, on the other side of walls and wires and androids and shoddy Stygian Stone surveillance tech, there was Onze tech scattered about, as Stygian Stone was the lesser option, but won the contract from Concord.

Further down the endless corridors, past a stone-faced receptionist, past endless secretaries that all looked to be near copies of each other—blonde, pale, and pretty—was the warden's office.

"Sir?" The receptionist's voice carried that particular blend of boredom and bureaucratic exhaustion that could only be cultivated through years of enabling institutional cruelty. "Your secured line from headquarters."

The warden, with his receding hairline and double chin and one lazy eye, barely looked up from his manifest reports—tonight's fresh meat needed processing, and the betting pools wouldn't calculate themselves.

"Patch it through."

The silver comm box on his desk pulsed once, then went active. No pleasantries. No names. Just a voice that could command fleets and crush rebellions without raising its tone.

"Thirty thousand on the Shogoro."

The line died mid-breath.

The warden stared at the silent box for exactly three seconds, then reached for his personal betting tablet. When Amir Falkaar placed money, you followed orders, or your wife received death benefits.

Even if the warden had no idea he was making one of the most terrible, violent, and genocidal beings in the galaxy very, very rich.

CHAPTER 3 – SCENE 3:

SHE SELLS SANCTUARY
Inspired by The Cult

THE WALLS BREATHED AROUND HIM like a new mother finally alone with her baby, expanding and contracting in gentle rhythm. Each pulse sent ripples through the chamber's atmosphere—visible distortions that made the space feel liquid, unstable. Within the chamber, even reality could lose its foothold.

The air shimmered with each exhalation, thick with the energy of ancient memories and the tart tang of Cradle's living flesh. Temperature fluctuated in gentle waves—welcoming warmth during the inhale, refreshing coolness on the exhale.

The cool breath carried ethereal, silvery-blue mist that condensed into tiny droplets on every surface, creating a constant symphony of moisture striking metal and membrane. The sound was almost musical, as if the chamber itself was composing lullabies from water and metal singing together.

Her voice emerged from the walls themselves, weaving into an elegant French melody—one of countless languages she'd lovingly collected from dying databases across the galaxy. French had become her particular fascination among all the tongues she'd preserved. Its melodic sound, elegant vocabulary, and rich cultural associations appealed to something deep in her ancient core.

She'd fallen in love with its poetry, its music, the way it could make even mundane concepts sound like art.

"So beautiful," she'd thought when she first discovered it centuries ago. So precious.

Now the lullaby unspooled through her chambers like a mother's hand on a fevered brow, each note perfected through endless digital devotion. The melody bent light around it, creating prismatic echoes that painted brief rainbows across the organic curves before dissolving back into gentle luminescence.

What was this place doing to him? Eli thought, feeling his muscles relax despite himself. Why did he feel… safe?

Silence pooled between them—thick as old regrets. The quiet was absolute and heavy but not oppressive, pressing against eardrums and making the absence of sound feel like a physical presence. Even the ship's ambient hum seemed to hold its breath, waiting.

Eli's grip on Bing Bong didn't loosen. The wrench's hydraulic clamps whined in protest, his optic darting like a caged insect between Eli's face and the pulsing veins in the walls. Sweat beaded where flesh met alloy, creating a slick seal that made releasing his grip feel impossible.

He wasn't afraid. Just wary. *Trust no one,* his mother had taught him. *The universe takes everything you love.*

But the air here was crafted for healing. It carried the scent of spring gardens and clean rain—a restorative atmosphere that filled his nostrils like a gentle embrace. Each inhalation soothed rather than burned, the oxygen content perfectly calibrated for human physiology, despite this being Cradle's cosmic form.

The atmosphere was a gift—pure in all the right ways, enriched with healing compounds.

Like breathing through Mom's expensive respirator, he thought, surprised by his own comparison.

Memory crashed over him without warning:

The hospital where they'd scanned his gold birthmarks. Strangers in white coats and hair like spider-webs whispering "aberrant" and "quarantine" behind latex-gloved hands. The nurses muttering "chrysalis rejection" as his IV sites turned black with necrotic gold.

The needles burning his gold-threaded veins, blackening the

puncture sites for hours while medical staff documented his abnormal reactions in hushed, clinical tones.

Another time, when Eli was younger, his heart monitor had flatlined twice—once when the gold veins rejected the IV, once when Eli stopped breathing out of pure spite. *Let them try to explain that to my mother*, he'd thought with a fifteen-year-old's fury.

The scars still glowed faintly at night—gold filigree mapping where his body had rejected their cruelty.

She's different, he realized, breathing in Cradle's healing atmosphere. *Instead of judging and trying to fix me, she just wants me to get better.*

Bing Bong vibrated against his palm—a gentle rhythm of concern, each pulse conveying care in mechanical shorthand. The vibrations traveled up his arm, creating sympathetic warmth that helped ease his tension.

"Current air composition: 97.8 percent optimal for human recovery," BB whispered, his voice steady above the chamber's organic harmony. "Strongly recommend rest. Also, statistical reminder that you promised not to throw me at anything hostile."

"Shut up," Eli mouthed, his lips cracking on the words. The taste of mint and citrons filled his mouth.

The wrench clicked, chastised. His vents hissed steam like a scolded child, vapor forming brief clouds in the chamber's strange atmosphere.

"Additional data: 87.3 percent probability that arguing with your primary medical support system is counterproductive to recovery," BB added with mechanical smugness.

Across the chamber, Cradle's luminous observation windows blinked in gentle unison. Their colors shimmered—silver to warm lavender to burnished gold, deliberately calibrated to echo Eli's unique essence. Each blink created brief moments of contemplation, hundreds of tiny pauses that rippled across the space like gentle waves.

The effect was soothing, almost hypnotic.

"…Why'd you call me that?" His voice was sandpaper and salt, flayed raw by everything he'd endured. The words hung in the air longer than they should, visible as faint distortions.

No answer. Just the subsonic song of Cradle's heart—like distant galaxies singing in harmony, a frequency so ancient it was felt more than heard. The sound eased his bones and brought clarity to his vision.

He swallowed, throat clicking like a jammed rifle bolt.

"Little lion."

Eli flinched, his grip tightening on Bing Bong. The name hit him wrong at first—too intimate, too presumptuous. Who was she to name him? His mother's warning echoed: Trust no one. The universe takes everything you love.

But then the walls purred softly in response, a gentle rumble that vibrated through the chamber like contentment made audible. And something in the sound, something warm and utterly without threat, made the suspicion drain away.

Little lion. No one had ever called him that. No one had ever made it sound like… like he was something precious instead of something dangerous. The words tasted of blood and lightning, of the electric moment before fire remembers its own power.

"Nobody calls me that," he said, voice cracking with something that might have been longing.

Light fractured across the ceiling—splintering into a smile made of newborn stars and dancing auroras. The illumination painted everything in gentle relief, creating soft shadows that moved like living things celebrating his presence.

"Names remember what you forget," Cradle murmured, her voice resonating from the walls, the floor, the inside of his skull. The words vibrated in his bone marrow, in the spaces between thoughts, as if she were speaking to parts of him that existed beyond conscious awareness.

His gold-marked fingers twitched. The veins sang—a harmonic resonance that made Cradle's own light flicker in recognition, pulsing with her ancient heartbeat. The sensation was warm but electric, like touching something both alive and cosmic.

Who am I really? he wondered. *What was I before the gold veins? Before the enhancement? Was there ever a version of me that could have been… normal?*

"I don't understand," he rasped, shaking Bing Bong hard enough to jar his core. Droplets of sweat flew, sizzling in the chamber's charged atmosphere.

BB's voice fragmented as he tried to process the impossible data surrounding them. "Calculating... 78.432 percent chance that her systems are completely beyond my databases, Eli. And 91.7 percent probability that we're dealing with something way above my computational pay grade here."

"That doesn't help," Eli snapped.

"Sorry! One hundred percent certainty I'm trying my best," BB squeaked, lens clicking rapidly. "Also updated assessment: 47.3 percent probability that I'm... uh... experiencing... nothing. Fine. Totally fine. Definitely not staring into the unfathomable—"

His voice glitched, static bleeding through. "ERROR: Emotional subroutines exceeding design parameters. Is this what wonder feels like? My databases lack reference points for... for this."

Cradle's laugh unfurled like silver bells—harmonics layered deep, each note healing something in Eli's chest he hadn't realized was broken. The sound made his tension dissolve, his jaw relax. Small objects danced in the air, moved by the healing acoustic waves.

"You clutch that wrench like it's your first breath," she observed gently.

Eli flinched. Because it was true.

Some nights, he woke with his cheek pressed to its cold frame, the serial number imprinted on his skin like a brand. The polished tung wood always brought comfort, but sometimes he dreamed of another voice—older, different from BB's cheerful statistics.

The metal would be warm from contact with his skin but always cooler than body temperature, like holding ice that never quite melted.

"My mom gave me this wrench, it means the world to me," Eli said, rubbing fondly at the strip of polished wood.

"Oh, my lionceau," Cradle said in hushed tones, "I believe you two have been close for much longer than that, and I find that to be truly amazing and precious." Her voice carried the weight of eons. "It's written in every gentle touch, every protective instinct. Love has the same voice across all worlds, lionceau."

There it is again, Eli thought, his chest tightening with emotion he didn't understand. She says it like I matter. Like I'm not just a weapon waiting to go off.

"You have no cracks," he murmured, fingers tracing the seamless glow of her walls.

"For you?" Cradle's voice was summer wind through young leaves. "I chose not to."

The words left his lips as vapor, hanging for a heartbeat before vanishing. His breath formed brief geometric patterns—symbols that looked almost like writing before dissolving back into randomness.

She's perfect because she wants to be. For me. When's the last time anyone tried to be perfect for me?

The walls shivered, motion traveling upward like a wave, carrying the sound of distant chimes and the scent of rain mixed with something organic and comforting. A doorway breathed open—an inhalation of light revealing the chamber beyond.

The healing space was even more incredible than the main chamber:

Walls of living membrane pulsed soft amber and jade, streaked with lightning-forked veins of flowing data. Each pulse sent cascades of gentle color racing through the organic circuitry like thoughts flowing through a vast, caring mind.

A bed of woven light cables breathed slow and peaceful. Each exhale released spores that glittered like stardust, drifting in lazy spirals that traced comforting curves through the warm air.

The air was thick with the scent of rain and something ancient and wise—wet stone worn smooth by eons, the inside of a cosmic heart that had loved too deeply. But beneath it all, Eli caught something else: the faint, familiar warmth of tung wood heated by caring hands, carrying harmonics that made his enhancement sing with recognition.

His cells remembered this frequency, this feeling of being home.

The humidity was embracing, coating everything in a fine mist that made surfaces glisten like they were blessed by starlight.

It's beautiful, Eli realized. *She made this beautiful for me.*

"Alert: Logic circuits are overloading," BB calculated aloud, his voice warm with synthetic wonder. "97.3 percent chance we're inside a miracle. Probability of full recovery: 89.7 percent. Probability that Eli finally gets proper rest: 94.2 percent. This represents your optimal percent chance for complete healing, E.

"Also," BB added, "6.8 percent chance I'm about to cry, if wrenches can cry. My emotional subroutines are experiencing unprecedented activity."

Eli's knees buckled. His vision flared—gold, then black, then gold again, like a failing viewscreen. The transition left afterimages burned into his retinas, ghost shapes dancing at the edges of perception. His equilibrium faltered, the chamber tilting as gravity became unreliable.

But Cradle was there, her presence steadying him without touch, her voice flowing like warm honey that settled into his bones like starlight:

"Rest, little lion. Even the strongest hearts must heal."

Cradle's ethereal hand traced the conduit-veins along the wall. Each stroke left glowing trails behind, making the walls bloom trails of bioluminescent cobalt blue, spectacular to the eye. The luminescence lingered for heartbeats before fading, creating constellations that mapped her ancient care across the chamber's living surface.

The words carried infinite love, making Eli's eyelids feel peacefully heavy. For the first time in years, his veins didn't burn. The chamber's bioluminescent glow dimmed in response, creating pools of soft shadow that looked infinitely inviting.

Trust no one, his mother's voice whispered from memory. *The universe takes everything you love.*

Eli's hand tightened on Bing Bong one last time, a reflexive check of BB's readings, his last line between safety and the void. But the gentle pulse of concern from his companion, the steady rhythm of Cradle's breathing walls, the scent of tung wood and starlight—it all felt like coming home to something he'd never known he'd lost.

Maybe, Eli thought as consciousness began to fade, *maybe it's okay to trust someone. Just this once.*

The chamber hummed a gentle lullaby in French, and Eli let himself fall into the deepest, safest sleep he'd known since childhood.

MONSTER MASH
Inspired by Bobby "Boris" Pickett & The Crypt Kickers

THE AIR CLOTTED IN ELONIAS'S THROAT—greasy smoke and formaldehyde rot, thick enough to chew. It curled in greasy tendrils through corroded vents above, clinging to exposed skin like the moldy breath of something long dead. Each inhalation felt like drowning in reverse—breathing in decay instead of life.

The room was the size of a starship hangar—gray, windowless, serving as a central hub linking various devices and systems. Horrifying medical contraptions hung from the ceiling and protruded from the walls like mechanical tumors: electronic wire clamps, neural crowns, screens displaying AI algorithms that analyzed live video feeds to detect early warning signs of patient death.

High-definition cameras tracked every angle, allowing remote viewing to monitor victims and assist with tasks like keeping them awake or unconscious as the situation required.

She found herself strapped to a concave table barely wider than her shoulders. The table and every other surface radiated corpse-cold chill that crawled beneath her skin and nested in her bones like parasites. The walls wept condensation that carried the sweet stench of formaldehyde mixed with something organic and rotting.

To one side, a rusted shelf sagged under surgical trays, their surfaces pockmarked with corrosion and age. The instruments within glinted under stuttering overhead lights—scalpels crusted with rust-brown blood, bone saws flecked with dried tissue, syringes filled with swirling fluids that moved with their own alien volition.

Some of the liquids pulsed in rhythm, as if tiny hearts beat within the glass chambers.

The fluorescents buzzed like dying insects. Occasionally, one popped in electric death throes, casting jerky shadows across filth-smeared walls before plunging sections of the room into merciful darkness.

Pop. Buzz. Pop.

The floor beneath her was a topography of suffering—layers of dried blood, spilled bile, and unidentifiable fluids congealed into a treacherous landscape that told stories she didn't want to read. Patches of ooze squelched wetly with each labored breath, releasing pockets of trapped gas that smelled of sulfur and rot and the aftermath of screams.

How long have I been here? The thought drifted through her consciousness like smoke. Time had become meaningless in this place where the lights never truly turned off and the air never grew clean.

Elonias tried to turn her head.

Lightning detonated behind her left eye, white-hot agony that made her vision fragment into kaleidoscope shards. She gagged, bile flooding her mouth in a hot rush that burned her throat raw and tasted of stomach acid mixed with whatever they'd been feeding her.

Then came the pinching—slow, deliberate agony as skin peeled away from muscle in thin, wet ribbons.

Click-hiss.

The metal armbands cinched tighter around her limbs, their embedded needles burrowing deeper with the patience of cruel science. She could feel them moving inside her flesh, seeking veins with mechanical precision.

Two rows of tubes pulsed along her arms like grotesque veins— black and green sludge pumping in through one set while her blood siphoned out through the other in rhythmic gulps. It vanished into the stained wall behind her, where something made wet, sucking noises that suggested hunger never satisfied.

Something that had been feeding for a very long time.

The sarcophagus clamped around her torso shuddered to malevolent life. Its surface erupted with glyphs—blasphemous symbols that writhed and rearranged themselves mid-blink, reacting to her pain like living things that derived nourishment from suffering.

Or nursing on it.

Then the door screamed open on corroded hinges, and what lay beyond stole her breath and what remained of her hope.

~ ~ ~

Movement at a side door—the tiny prosthetic children scurrying—offered a horrifying glimpse beyond: rows upon rows of steel tables stretched into the gloom, receding into a blood-smeared horizon that curved away into darkness so complete it seemed to devour light itself. Each table bore a writhing body, its suffering illuminated in hellish flashes by red strobes embedded in the floor like baleful eyes.

Between the tables, Elonias could see other birthing stations—glass vats filled with swirling fluids and small, twitching forms suspended within. The successful harvests from other mothers, other screams. Some vats pulsed with things that had too many limbs, others with shadows that moved with unnatural purpose.

The ground was a river of clotting blood, thick as syrup, ankle-deep in places where the drains couldn't keep pace with the flow. Its metallic stench coated her tongue in iron and bile, making every breath taste of death and despair.

Walls curved upward into a black-mirrored dome, reflecting the slaughterhouse into infinity—a hundred victims became a thousand, their agony refracted and multiplied into endless recursion that made the suffering feel infinite, eternal.

Abyss slaves.

Some thrashed against restraints, bellies grotesquely distended, skin stretched translucent over something moving inside with insectile urgency. She could see shapes pressing against the flesh from within—fingers, maybe faces, trying to claw their way out.

Others lay still and hollow, chests cracked like eggshells, ribs splayed wide to reveal glistening cavities from which steam rose in lazy spirals that spoke of recent harvesting.

A few twitched on the floor between tables, limbs sutured into grotesque configurations that defied natural anatomy. Arms where legs should be, hands grafted to shoulders, faces relocated to torsos in patterns that hurt to contemplate.

The early stages of tracker development. The realization hit her like a physical blow, stealing what remained of her breath.

Their moans were soft. High-pitched. Almost childlike in their broken innocence—the sounds of minds that had shattered under the weight of what had been done to them.

The next realization crashed into her consciousness, shattering what remained of her composure:

No one is coming for me.

The thought settled into her bones like ice, colder than the metal pressing against her skin.

No one even knows this place exists.

And then—worse, so much worse:

Eli.

Had they taken him too? Was he strapped to one of these tables somewhere in this endless charnel house, his gold-veined blood being siphoned into some Abyss machine? His young voice reduced to numbers on a readout? Those beautiful eyes that looked at her with such trust and love now vacant and staring?

Please, no. Let him be safe. Please. I hope Eli got far away. Let him never know what happened to me—

~ ~ ~

THE SURGEON-PRIEST ENTERED—gaunt bone swathed in light-eating robes, movements fluid and theatrical, as if puppeteered by malice itself. The fabric absorbed rather than reflected, lined with thread that shimmered like oil on water. A silver collar encircled Jobaar's throat, etched with squirming glyphs that seemed to move when observed directly—the red light at its center dark for now.

But not dead. Never dead. Just… waiting.

"Oh," he crooned, voice a dry rasp carrying the scent of formaldehyde and spoiled milk. His lips split into a smile too wide for his face, revealing teeth like yellowed tombstones, each one filed to a point. "How magnificent. Our little prize is awake."

He glided forward with predatory grace, breath cold and sweetly rotted, curling in misty tendrils across her face like the exhalation of a tomb that had been sealed for centuries.

"We are expecting great things from you." He leaned closer, skeletal fingers digging into her jaw until bones creaked in protest. The grip was careful, practiced—he knew exactly how much pressure to apply without breaking anything important. "At least twelve."

Twelve?

Elonias's mind fractured under the weight of that single word, splintering like glass under pressure.

"P-Please—you have the wrong person! I'm nobody—"

The skeleton-man laughed, the sound brittle as dry bones rattling in a tin bucket. "You Duskborn vermin are deliciously resilient. Perfect genetic stock." His thumb smudged away a tear she didn't remember shedding, the gesture mockingly gentle. "You'll pump out a full litter before your body gives out. My lord won't accept fewer than twelve. Even if I have to peel you open layer by layer to get them."

Twelve? Twelve what—?

The horror crashed into her consciousness like ice water in her veins, freezing her breath in her lungs.

Oh God. Twelve children. Twelve births. Twelve—

No. No, no, no—

He turned away with a theatrical flourish, robes billowing like funeral shrouds, and flipped a toggle on the wall with casual efficiency. The motion was practiced, routine—he'd done this countless times before.

The ceiling groaned in mechanical response.

From above, a massive machine descended on hydraulic arms that hissed like serpents—its arched belly gaping like a hungry mouth lined with glistening tubing and pulsing membranes that looked disturbingly organic. A rubbery appendage uncoiled like a grotesque tongue, sealing around Elonias's waist with obscene intimacy that made her skin crawl.

Snap.

Clamps bit into her calves, wrenching her legs apart with mechanical precision that spoke of countless repetitions, countless victims who had lain exactly where she lay now.

A whimper escaped before she could stop it—a sound that seemed to echo from the walls themselves, as if the room had absorbed so many similar sounds that they'd become part of its structure.

Something moved between her spread legs.

Something that pulsed with its own alien rhythm, warm and wet and wrong.

She screamed—

The red light at Jobaar's collar flared to hungry life, drinking her silent anguish like wine, growing brighter with each note of her terror.

"None of that," the surgeon-priest sighed, voice bored and practiced—the tone of someone who had performed this ritual countless times, who had perfected the art of stealing voices. His fingers wrenched her jaw open with clinical efficiency that reflected extensive experience.

Cold metal slid between her teeth. She felt the blades separate, positioning themselves around the most precious thing she had left—her ability to call for help, to scream her pain, to speak her son's name one final time.

No. Please, no—

Scissors sang as they found their chorus, their gleaming edges reflected in Jobaar's eyes as his pupils dilated with ecstasy, feeding on her terror like a drug.

Silence bloomed where her scream lived.

Her vocal cords severed with a wet, final sound that seemed to echo through dimensions—the death of every word she'd never get to say, every lullaby she'd never sing, every time she'd never get to tell Eli she loved him.

The scream died in her throat, transforming into a voiceless rush of air that tasted of insect poison and defeat and the end of hope.

Silence. Terrible, suffocating silence where her voice used to live.

She tried to scream again—tried to call Eli's name, tried to beg for mercy, tried to pray to any god who might listen. Only breath escaped—empty air carrying all her terror into nothingness, making her suffering as silent as death itself.

Behind him, arrayed along the far wall like trophies in a collector's cabinet, twelve glass vats pulsed with sickly bioluminescence. Each was filled with different colored fluids that swirled with their own currents—some empty, waiting with hungry patience.

Through the haze of approaching unconsciousness, she heard him murmur in a sing-song whisper that sounded almost like a lullaby:

"Let's make monsters, little mother."

CHAPTER 4 – SCENE 2:

GARBAGE MAN
Inspired by Merle Haggard

WARDEN HESK THOUGHT garbage duty was punishment.

He was wrong.

The prison planet Atrion-6 was a mechanical hell built on precision—220 wardens, 220 prisons, 8.8 million prisoners—all cogs in the Concord's war machine grinding through flesh and bone with bureaucratic efficiency. Every facility had a purpose, every inmate a number, every death a statistic.

Kiln-9 was no different, and within its concrete maze, Ad-Seg 116 housed the administrative segregation cases—the troublemakers, the violent, the forgotten.

Here, beneath the planet's perpetual shroud of industrial smog, prisoners repaired starfighters for the Concord Air Force Division, their hands stained with hydraulic fluid and coolant, their lungs burned raw by the acrid stench of engine grease and recycled plasma.

The work bays were cavernous hangars ribbed with scaffolding and flickering lights that buzzed like dying wasps, casting sickly shadows across the endless rows of gutted fighters. The air thrummed with the relentless whine of power tools and plasma cutters, undercut now and then by a scream—when someone slipped on the grease-slicked floors or a plasma torch found skin instead of metal.

But down in Kiln-9's waste chutes, Akona had found something else entirely. A goldmine—a reliquary of broken sin.

Akona sorted methodically. A surgeon. A soldier. A priest.

Armor from uniforms. Fire from spoiled food. Weapons from ruin.

The heat didn't bother him anymore. The brand on his neck had changed him—inside and out. Sometimes, in the dark, it pulsed in time with the Stones.

Then the PA crackled—open channel. Two guards didn't know they were live.

"Another shipment tomorrow. Concord's getting bold. This batch? One's a fucking schoolteacher. Concord's scraping barrels now."

"Who cares?" the other laughed. "Abyss pays in augments. You gonna say no? Credits are credits."

Akona froze.

The heat didn't matter.

The rumors weren't rumors.

They were invoices.

He memorized every word—evidence for the reckoning to come. But evidence wasn't enough. They needed leverage. They needed chaos. They needed control from the inside.

THE PAINT

Akona moved through the long, cool hallway between R&R and the work areas, his boots scuffing softly against the worn ceramite floor, echoes swallowed by the vastness of the corridor. Emergency lighting strips cast intermittent pools of amber light, leaving long stretches of shadow where surveillance cameras couldn't penetrate.

His prize sat just sixty yards away—two unguarded buckets of paint, tucked beneath a maintenance ladder like forgotten trash in this monument to industrial decay.

No one gave two shits about paint buckets. Not when there were quotas to meet and prisoners to process.

The two nearest guards stood too close for comfort, two late-model rail guns slung lazily across their backs as they chatted in the bored, vacant tone of men who'd given up caring years ago. Their voices echoed dully off the graphene walls, discussing overtime pay and conjugal visits with the same enthusiasm they'd reserve for discussing the weather.

Akona eased into a pool of shadow cast by an overhead pipe junction, still as forged iron, every breath slow and measured. The recycled air tasted of dust and oil made from algae, coating his throat like metallic dust. He had a fifteen-minute window—grab the paint, stash it, get back to his cell before count.

Then, salvation arrived in the form of bureaucratic incompetence.

A voice crackled over the guards' comms, distorted by static: "Need two at Block 6 for a visit. See Control."

One guard groaned, adjusting his weapon strap. "This is Trebut and Geery. We're at the paint hangar."

"See the Watch Commander after your assignment."

The second guard nudged his partner with his elbow. "Let's get the fuck outta here, my guy. Maybe we can grab some decent coffee from the commissary."

They wandered off down the corridor, guns swinging, boots clanging on metal grating, their voices fading into the mechanical hum of the facility. The paint was his.

Akona didn't hesitate. He slipped forward like a ghost, grabbed the buckets by their wire handles, and melted back into the corridor before anyone could blink. The weight of the paint was satisfying—dense, purposeful, deadly.

THE CELL

Akona's cell was on the top floor of the high-gravity tier. It was a claustrophobic shoebox, three meters by three, the walls pockmarked with scratches, names, and crude sketches from the ghosts of previous inmates. Water stains bloomed across the ceiling like diseased flowers, and the air reeked of rust, sweat, and whatever ungodly concoction Mares had eaten from the commissary slop line.

Mares sprawled on his upper bunk like a caged predator, his massive feet braced against the ceiling, muscles coiled and twitching like overstressed cables beneath scarred skin. Tattoos covered his arms—prison work, crude but telling stories of violence and survival. He didn't look up as Akona entered, instead continuing to stare at his own toes as if they held the secrets of the universe.

"Sorry about the smell," he said casually, still examining his feet with the focus of a philosopher.

Akona ignored him, setting the buckets down on the narrow strip of floor between their bunks like sacred offerings to some dark god of vengeance.

Mares finally glanced over, his small eyes focusing on the paint with predatory interest. "Why'd you risk your ass for ship paint?"

Akona smirked, a cold expression that never reached his eyes. "We need a new warden."

Mares raised a scarred brow, his interest sharpening like a blade being honed.

"Who tops the list if the current one forgets to show up for work?" Akona asked.

Mares scratched his jaw, thinking, the sound of his fingernails against stubble unnaturally loud in the cramped space. "Either Brophy or Agmunson."

"Who can we thumb?"

Mares grinned—a slow, evil thing that stretched across his thick face like a crack in concrete. His eyes went distant for a moment, remembering Brophy in the corridor last month—the casual way he'd reached up and clicked off camera seven before letting three guards work over an inmate who'd looked at him wrong. The screams had echoed for twenty minutes. And the way Brophy had eyed the warden's chair afterward, like it was already his.

"Brophy. By far." The grin turned savage. "I've seen him work—the way he 'accidentally' turns off cameras when inmates need teaching. Perfect puppet material. We can touch his family if we need to. No problem sending a message if he gets the hint."

He tilted his head, studying Akona with the calculating gaze of a natural predator. "How you gonna off the warden? Paint him out of the picture?"

Akona popped the lid off one bucket with his thumbnail.

The stench hit them like a gut-punch—sharp, metallic, and fundamentally wrong, like something that should never touch air or lungs. It was the smell of industrial death, of chemicals designed to eat through metal and flesh with equal efficiency.

"This isn't ship paint," Akona said, his voice carrying the satisfaction of a man holding a loaded weapon. "It's mining drone paint. Toxic as whatever you dropped in here before I walked in." He leaned back against the wall. "I worked a job once—someone was sabotaging mining operations, so I had to go undercover as a worker for a few months. We all knew to stay away from this shit without serious respirator action strapped to your mug, or you'd get tossed into space."

Mares let out a low whistle of appreciation. "So we get a porter for the warden."

"Vitty."

"Yeah, Vitty." Mares nodded, his grin widening. "And when the warden leaves for his weekend furlough… we paint his office. Then paint over the toxic shit with regular paint. He won't smell it that way."

Akona's grin mirrored Mares's, cold and calculating. "He'll be gone in less than three weeks."

Mares leaned forward, his bunk groaning under his bulk, eyes locked on the paint buckets like they held the keys to the universe itself.

"Alright, break it down," he rumbled, his voice dropping to a conspiratorial whisper. "Vitty's our mule. How do we get the paint into the warden's office without some nosy bastard sniffing it out?"

Akona smirked, already three steps ahead. "Vitty's been slinging contraband for years. He knows the vents, the guard rotations, which cameras glitch during shift changes." He tapped the bucket with one finger. "This isn't our first move—it's our last. We play it clean until the warden's weekend furlough."

DUMPSTER PROMISES

Later, under the harsh lights that flickered like hope in this place, Akona shared what he'd heard with Apek.

Enter the Blackhole

Apek knew Vitty's route to work better than Vitty himself and stationed himself accordingly. Minutes before Vitty rounded the corner by the visiting center and stood waiting at the gate for a guard to escort him to the administrative building, Apek appeared, sidling up to Vitty with a friendly arm around his shoulder.

"How we doing, V? You looking healthy, my guy… for now." Apek's grin was all teeth and menace. "Akona and Mares got a job for ya. You'll take it, you'll do great, have no fear, and who knows, Vitty, you may find a little extra somethin' somethin' on yer books.

"Don't you give me that look, you." Apek's grip tightened. "Hush now, you do this, and Akona keeps the monsters from entering your nightmares. Don't you worry, Akona will not forget. About. You. Ever." He whispered the last word. "I'm gonna leave some paint buckets out for ya. You do the warden's office, then cover it in something nice. I'll let you pick it out. Okay, good boy, Vitty, make us proud."

Apek gave one final hard squeeze to Vitty's neck to make sure he got the point, then he was gone.

Fuck, Vitty thought, not daring to say it out loud. *Everyone just fuck me.*

Vitty saw the guard and followed him in.

THE FIGHTS

While they waited for the warden's weekend furlough that would eventually kill him, the warden set up gladiator fights for fun and profit—both his. Even the Commander of the Concord Law Enforcement, Amir Falkaar, put credits down.

The warden liked to take inmates who seemed to have a problem with Concord Law Enforcement Agency or had negatively affected the profit margins of Core 7 corporations and feed them to his pet monsters down in the sublevels no one talked about because few ever left… the same.

The tunnels stank of week-old sweat and manure.

Emergency lights painted them in blood-strobe: Akona. Mares. Apek. And two cons none of them had ever laid eyes on.

Above: jeers and betting.

"Paniscus pops Twitchy's head like a zit!"

"Quills'll pin 'em like lab rats!"

Apek giggled, void-eyed, his eyes rolled back in his head. "Take fifty creds off my books and put 'em on me, you corporate ass-lickers! Hehe!"

"Let's give 'em a demonstration," Mares growled, looking at what the warden had planned for him and the boys.

Mares's armor clicked into place, his four massive arms outstretched as he lowered himself into a feral crouch.

Across the dimly lit subterranean flooring, two gates opened, and Mares would have placed his last credit princesses weren't coming out to greet them.

The immense, glowing gates shrieked and jerked, slowly opening, causing a shadow in the rear of the chamber to move towards the exit. The huge black gate became stuck a quarter of the way up and began to make an ungodly sound. The shadow approached the gate, and seemingly without effort, a large, clawed hand finished opening it.

Then all hell broke loose.

THE PANISCUS

Eight feet of mutation. Its knuckles scraped sparks from the floor.

A large, dark, Duskborn inmate screamed and charged the creature. Long, wicked-looking shivs were taped to the backs of his hands, and he was in the air before Mares even realized it. The ape-like creature snatched him out of the air and used his body to create some ghastly modern art.

The Paniscus turned and glared at Mares, reared its head back, and gave an unnerving scream that sounded like a hundred-meter-tall human baby. The fangs from the bared teeth were as long as Mares's whole hand.

"Well, shit," said Mares and squared up to meet the big monkey.

Mares began to slowly jog, then he timed the loping stride of the

Paniscus. Mares feinted a high dive, then, when his opponent leaped to bite on the feint, Mares slid under the creature, grabbing a handful of reproductive organs that were no longer going to be productive.

The creature tried to roll out of the grip and away from the intense pain, but Mares held tight and got behind the ape-thing. He put his boot on the back of the creature's calf and used two arms to choke and one to rain down hammer fists on the side of the Paniscus's head.

Mares didn't stop punching until he was wrist deep and the creature had stopped twitching. No sense taking chances—this fucker's not getting back up.

"CHEATED!" a guard screamed, throwing glass.

"Hey, put me down for fifty creds on Apek," Mares said, then proceeded to lean back against the rough-hewn wall and slide down into a comfortable sitting position. "I'm good for it."

THE GLYPTOHYSTRIX

It unfurled with a sound like a scalpel dragged down a ribcage.

A ball of rage and quills. Armor humming with heat.

Apek howled:

"DANCE WITH ME, PIN CUSHION!"

Apek began crab-walking sideways on all fours, keeping his eyes on the armored needle tank thing. "I'm gonna make you my stuffy, motherfucker, right here and now."

Apek took two steps, hitting top speed after one, and dove. His body cartwheeled in the air—a blade, pointy like a needle, flew down his right forearm and stopped perfectly in his palm. Apek slammed the blade down into the acetylene canister he needed to power his leg implant.

The explosion caused the beast to rear up in shock and surprise. Then Akona struck.

Akona struck, but unfortunately, the poor asshole who came with them had the same thought. Akona dipped around the other con and leaped up, grabbing the huge needle demon by the collar and hauling himself up eye level with it.

The Glyptohystrix backhanded the inmate with speed you wouldn't expect from such a thick beast. The poor bastard got half his body impaled from the impact and died before he hit the ground.

"You down another two hundred creds on that one, Allon? You even gonna have a paycheck left?" one of the guards yelled.

Akona saw the eyes of the beast turn and look at its handiwork. Akona hauled back and struck as hard and fast as he ever had in his life, aiming straight down this big fucker's throat. The creature bucked and lurched, but Akona hung on and started pulling and yanking everything his hand could find.

Blood became a volcano, and the Glyph began puking its life essence up the side of Akona's head, drenching his side. When the creature finally collapsed, Akona yanked his arm free and jumped clear of the giant quills, landing near Mares.

"Fucking Tuesdays, aye, Mares?"

"Same ol', same ol'," said Mares, smirking at Akona.

The crowd fell silent.

Apek collapsed.

Still laughing.

VITTY'S WALK OF SHAME

The weekend came like a blessing wrapped in barbed wire.

Vitty liked to say his weekends were blursed—blessed and cursed. Mostly cursed, but he put his head down anyway, and right then, he made up his mind to get this fucking business over with. He strolled into the admin building, losing his escort when he walked past the first secretary.

The gorgeous brunette rolled her eyes at the guard's inept attempt to smooth talk her, and Vitty made use of the distraction to just keep on walking.

The hallway to the warden's office was a runway of flickering fluorescents, the air nearly toxic from the stench of industrial bleach, creeping mold, and stale sweat that had been recycled through the ventilation system for decades.

Vitty pushed his maintenance cart, its squeaky wheels chirping like rats fighting on the tram platforms. The sound echoed off the metal walls, announcing his presence to anyone within fifty meters. Beneath a pile of stained rags and fake solvent cans, the toxic paint sloshed ominously, heavy with purpose and the promise of slow death.

Mares is using me like a damn wishbone, Vitty thought, his jaw clenching involuntarily.

But Mares had sent two young Shogoro to protect Vitty's family when a local gang started terrorizing his wife and kids. Mares made sure they were safe, and in return, Vitty understood that Mares would sometimes call on him for favors—things not necessarily on the up and up.

Now Vitty owed him a debt that kept growing interest, and Mares wasn't the type to forget. Plus, there was the small matter of the ten thousand credits Vitty still owed from betting on the wrong fighter last month. Mares had been very understanding about the payment plan.

He knew the game better than most. Twelve years of portering across Kiln-9's various blocks meant he understood that favors either paid in blood or earned you a headfirst dive into the recycling pit.

When the convicts were allowed weekend conjugal visits, and that wasn't often, Vitty would be assigned to clean the rows of small cottages that made up the "boneyard." When he was first tasked with the job, he envisioned himself mopping seas of bodily fluids, but to his surprise, most cons requested their moms and not their wives or girlfriends.

I guess they wanted the home cooking and the "poor baby"s rather than the "when you getting out?" and "I can't pay my bills." Vitty allowed a small chuckle to escape. Oh, how he missed his mother's cooking.

But here in Ad-Seg 116, the prison's ecosystem was built on violence and leverage, and Vitty had survived by being useful to the right people. Mares wasn't the kind of man you said no to.

Vitty liked the peace of mind knowing his family was safe with Mares's kin keeping watch over them. He had a nest egg tucked away, and his wife could get to it if she needed. Blursed, he thought. *Void help me, I'm fucking blursed.*

He adjusted his dust mask—a brittle, government-issued joke of a thing that barely qualified as safety equipment. Its filter was useless against what he was carrying, but it hid the tremor in his jaw and the cold sweat beading on his upper lip.

Only two hundred square feet to cover, he told himself. Maybe one-fifty if I spread it thin. Just get in, get out, don't think about what comes after.

The warden's office was a sad shrine to petty power—a scuffed durasteel desk covered in data pads and coffee stains, a flickering holo-frame displaying some dead plant from the warden's homeworld, and walls stained with years of coffee rings and unspoken rage. The carpet was industrial gray, worn thin in pathways that spoke of endless pacing and bureaucratic frustration.

The receptionist—Loriya Hudd, a dough-faced woman with a lazy eye and the complexion of someone who'd never seen real sunlight—barely looked up from her terminal.

Still, after five years of not seeing a non-inmate woman, Vitty thought she looked like a goddamn holo-star. Prison had a way of adjusting one's standards. She'd even complimented his maintenance work last month, said he was the only porter who didn't track mud through her workspace.

You're the only porter who doesn't track mud. The memory cut through him as his roller moved across her desk.

"Supposed to repaint," Vitty mumbled, flashing the forged "Maintenance Order" slip Mares had printed on stolen cardstock with impressive attention to detail.

Loriya sighed without looking up, her fingers still tapping away at her keyboard. "Warden's off-station for the weekend. Just don't touch his personal shit."

Vitty nodded, trying not to think about how she'd be breathing this poison too. His roller stuttered over her desk—just for a second. The sludge bubbled like angry amoebae as he rolled it across the surface. He didn't let himself think about her.

The image of Mares's meat-slab fists wrapped around his throat kept his roller dipping into the toxic mixture. Survival trumped conscience every time in Ad-Seg 116.

One-fifty square feet. One-twenty. One hundred.

THE UNSEEN PROBLEM: THE BETTING GUARD

Vitty was two-thirds done painting, working methodically to coat every surface with the toxic mixture, when he heard it—a wet cough from the warden's private bathroom, followed by the sound of something heavy shifting.

Ninety square feet. Almost done. Almost—

The door creaked open on ancient hinges.

"The hell you doing in here?"

Vitty's blood turned to ice in his veins.

Officer Rask. One of the tunnel-fight betting guards—a sweaty, broad-necked bastard who'd apparently holed up in the warden's office all weekend, dodging his rounds and nursing a bottle. His uniform was crumpled like he'd slept in it, his eyes red-rimmed and bloodshot, a bottle of home-brew hooch swinging loosely from one meaty hand.

His fingers dug into Vitty's shoulder like rusted pliers.

"P-paint rotation," Vitty stammered, his voice cracking like a teenager's.

Rask blinked at the walls with the slow focus of the severely intoxicated. "Looks the same as always."

Vitty's pulse thundered in his ears. Too hungover to smell it. "New anti-mold formula, you know, due to all this fucking humidity, boss. Shit, boss, I'm just doing what the watch commander said the assistant warden told him. I don't want no trouble with the higher-ups and the suits."

"Fuckin'… anti-mold," Rask mumbled, swaying on his feet. "Anti-mold, anti-fun, anti-everything. This whole shithole's anti-something." He grunted, a sound of bureaucratic resignation, turned around, and stumbled back into the bathroom—where he promptly vomited, the sound wet and laced with what might have been blood.

"Fucking pruno… tastes like… mother-in-law's fruit fuckin' punch…" he groaned between retches.

Vitty didn't look. He'd learned long ago that curiosity killed more than cats in prison.

Some toxins worked faster than others.

Fifty square feet. Forty. Almost done.

He painted faster, his roller moving with desperate efficiency.

THE KILL (BONUS COMPLICATIONS)

The toxic paint went on smooth as silk, invisible death coating every surface.

Four days later, a short, bloated man with curly brown, receding hair, a double chin, and a lazy left eye stormed into his office, grumbling about orbital traffic delays and stale station coffee. His uniform strained across his gut, his buttons putting in serious overtime trying to keep his flab confined. He moved with the ponderous confidence of a man who'd never been told no.

Within hours, he was massaging his temples with thick fingers, blaming the "recycled ship air" for his sudden headache.

Two days after that, Loriya noticed first—headaches that felt like ice picks behind her eyes, a metallic taste that coated her tongue like copper pennies, light sensitivity that made her squint at her own terminal. When she mentioned it to Rask, he laughed it off with the casual cruelty of someone who'd stopped caring about other people's pain.

"Probably just stress, sweetheart. Or your cooking."

He was still crashing on the office cot, his lungs already half-filled with fluid that made him cough up pink foam in the mornings.

By the end of the second week, the warden's hair began falling out in clumps, leaving bald patches that made him look like a diseased animal. He blamed stress and started wearing a cap to hide the damage.

Rask was put on medical leave, his skin peeling in long, pink strips like dried wallpaper. The prison medic had never seen anything like it and recommended immediate transfer to a real hospital.

Loriya Hudd quit—fled to the orbital station above Atrion-6, but it was too late. The poison had already taken root in her lungs and bloodstream. Her autopsy would later cite "acute respiratory failure" as the cause of death. They had to scrape her lungs out with a spoon.

Four days later, when the Concord Health Inspector finally arrived, wearing a full hazmat suit and carrying detection equipment, the "outbreak" was chalked up to tainted air filters and inadequate maintenance protocols. Just another example of the prison system's chronic underfunding and neglect.

And Brophy?

He got promoted to warden within the week, his personnel file stamped with commendations for "stepping up during a crisis."

His first act as the new warden of Ad-Seg 116?

He found Loriya's unused lipstick in her desk drawer—cherry red, barely touched—and smeared it across the leather of his new chair like blood on an altar. Petty evil in its purest form.

His comm unit chimed. Secure channel.

"Brophy here."

"Congratulations on your promotion." The voice carried the weight of star systems. Amir Falkaar didn't introduce himself—he didn't need to.

Brophy straightened in his bloodstained chair. "Sir. Thank you, sir."

"Order new paint for the entire block. Can't have the place looking like a death trap."

AFTERMATH

The infirmary buzzed.

Apek was spread across two cots, his leg a ruin.

"I'ma kill every last one of 'em," he muttered through med-gel.

Mares grunted. Tossed him a grenade pin.

He bit it. Smiled. Bled.

Akona watched the feeds. The guards weren't laughing anymore.

He traced his brand. The fang. The circle.

The circle felt warmer today—like a stone left in the sun.

"They'd know they're already dead…"

From their cell window, Akona and Mares watched the paint delivery trucks roll through the prison gates, their cargo holds filled with regulation-safe coating that would never kill anyone.

Mares cracked his knuckles, a sound like small bones breaking.

Akona watched the trucks roll in. The system always repainted its sins.

And deep below, the Screaming Stones groaned—a sound like planets grinding teeth.

Akona felt his brand pulse in response, the circle warming against his neck like an echo of something vast and patient.

As if the planet itself was stirring.

And somewhere, the Abyss watched.

But so did they.

The revolution had begun in the garbage.

It would end in their fire.

CHAPTER 4 – SCENE 3:

MY IMMORTAL
Inspired by Evanescence

OPENING

THE AIR HUMMED, IT SANG! A thousand voices older than time, rich and deep, powerful and constant, all weaving about him like silhouettes in a mist. The walls breathed with Cradle's every step, Trilene-phoscarbyne slick with emanation—too pearlescent to be rainwater, too alive to be inert syrup. Each breath, every pulse began to match Eli's own until he couldn't distinguish either.

Eli, almost without thinking, began to rub at his fresh scar, already healing beyond the norm. His head moved on a swivel, marveling at all the wonder.

Cradle's voice permeated the walls and arched corridors as they walked. "There are eleven beings on my ship, each the greatest mind in their field of science. I have tried to allow them to hold on to their humanity by using volumetric display. What you see is based on their memories of their past lives . Their planet of Mota Prime was destroyed by a being from my universe, one capable of immeasurable destruction. This being, Baar, and his two brothers wrought upon this universe a great cataclysm. One of the pieces of collateral damage was the homeworld of these eleven. I call them the Onze, meaning eleven in my beloved second language, and they have been my most welcomed guests and partners for nearly half a megaannum.

They were trapped in the data stream—consciousness without form, screaming in digital silence. I was able to pull them free."

"E, we're walking with someone who has a 78.989 percent chance of being what many consider a god—not the God but definitely a god, and I'm just saying"—Bing Bong crackled through Eli's neural link, his voice laced with digital skepticism—"I know you like cursing when no adults are around, E, but really, don't now, kay? Please don't throw me at anything. E, I don't think she can hear me—let her know about me. I think a bit of me is from where she's from. I feel something close about her. E!"

"BB," Eli said, a little exasperated, "yes, I will tell her all about you. Give me a sec, please, for the love of the Void!"

"What, is she your new girlfriend?" Eli said with a sing-song cadence in his voice.

"You think she would, E, or are you messin'?"

Cradle's ethereal hand traced the conduit-veins along the wall. Each stroke left glowing trails behind, making the walls bloom trails of bioluminescent cobalt blue, spectacular to the eye. The luminescence lingered for heartbeats before fading, creating constellations that mapped her passage.

"I came here with others," she said, her voice resonating in his mind and his ear both at once. "There was one among those I came with. He calls himself Baar , and he cares for nothing except his own selfish needs and desires. I cannot destroy him, my lionceau—that is not me. I could attack him with all my ships and drones and androids, and they would mean nothing to him. He is made of exotic matter and dark energies. His army, though—his army of civilizations stolen by the Abyss, which he turned into his infernal breeding war machine. Turning innocents into zealot warriors or breeding stock. He needs me in order to escape, and if I attacked him, his army would cover me like deadly insects on a desert loxodonta. He needs to break the circle to free himself from this universe, and he is terrified, my lionceau, and that makes him unpredictable. You and your little friend are the instrument Baar believes he needs to break the circle. If that is true, it remains to be seen.

"Is that not so, my little Bing Bong?" Cradle said slowly, gazing down on the wrench in Eli's hand.

Her voice softened, carrying the weight of eons. "I, too, was young, once, and so very alone in my universe—so very different from here." The words held ancient sadness, the memory of existing in cosmic isolation. "Please, my petit, you must indulge me my small loves of language. I find this old and forgotten one very pleasing, and I do so love using it from time to time." Then, in elegant French that seemed to caress the air itself: "Tu pourrais un jour me rejoindre, mon lionceau."

You could one day join me, my little lion.

~ ~ ~

THE DECISION

Cradle approached Eli in the observation deck, his small hands pressed against the viewport, watching stars die in the distance. The serum vial rested on the console beside him—eleven minds over lifetimes together crafting this emerald light.

"Have you decided?" Her voice held ancient gravity.

Eli didn't turn from the stars. "If my mom and dad are out there somewhere, I need to find them." He faced her then, fifteen years old and ancient. "If you help me, ma'am."

Cradle knelt, bringing herself to his eye level. Her statuesque form somehow made itself small, protective. "I will be with you forever, my lionceau."

The words hung between them like a vow written in starlight.

~ ~ ~

THE OBSERVATORY

The medical bay's upper ring hummed with presence. Eleven alcoves, each containing a pillar of shifting light—the Onze, manifesting as observers for their own resurrection. Their forms flickered between memory and mathematics:

Nyx stood with her shoulder-length auburn hair and piercing gray-blue eyes. Her soft, angular features expressed serious focus, glowing veins pulsing beneath translucent skin. Her specialty was biology, and she had led the serum development project, and all looked to her for final judgment.

Pandia's form—a tall, sharp-featured woman with her red hair pulled up into a no-nonsense bun. Her data pad in one hand and a handheld nanodiamonds scanner with nitrogen-vacancy centers in the other, she monitored tiny, biocompatible sensors that could measure magnetic fields, temperature, and chemical changes at the cellular level. She could target organs via functionalized nanodiamonds to probe for tumors or metabolic changes with subcellular resolution. Her form dissolved and reformed in chemical cascades, while Momus flickered like kinetic energy made visible. Alci mapped planetary systems in geological time. Eris calculated firing algorithms in mathematical precision.

Analogoy was standing toward the rear of the observatory. He was still a young and vibrant-looking man, his dark hair perfectly coiffed and his goatee sharp and exotic looking. His hands were in haptic-interface neural-feedback gauntlets, his eyes covered by his custom-engineered goggles, his back turned away from Eli and the theater. A large, red, three-dimensional floating schematic of the entire room shifted and moved, power rerouted for optimal efficiency under his quick and precise hand movements.

Rao was bouncing down the stairs, her long dark hair pulled back with tiny, jeweled chains in the tradition of her people. She was full-figured with a sultry voice and fawned over Eli as much as she could. Eli was fifteen and welcomed the attention, to say the least. Rao glanced over at Eli and gave a wink, which brought color to his cheeks. "Here's my complete work-up and analysis," she said and pushed her document pad into Cradle's med terminal.

"His blood pressure is spiking," came the monitoring system's cold voice.

"Sorry, everyone," Rao said with a smile.

I'm not, Eli thought.

Below, in the sterile white of the surgical theater, Eli lay on a table designed for gods and superheroes. Neural interfaces sprouted like silver vines around his small form. The serum waited in its crystalline injector—emerald liquid swirling with microscopic movement, tiny forms dancing in the green depths like living constellations.

"What are those?" Eli whispered, watching the fluid pulse with its own heartbeat.

For just a millisecond, the zeptobots swirled and arranged themselves into the shape of Bing Bong, the familiar pistol-grip with the wood inlay in the handle and the circular head with various teeth for gripping, before dissolving back into microscopic chaos.

"It knows me, E! The magic fluid 98.474 percent knows me, or just likes wrenches, maybe?"

"Not now, BB," Eli said gently to his friend.

"Zeptobots," Cradle explained gently. "They will ensure you remain in perfect condition, lionceau. Repair, enhance, protect—they are your guardians at the cellular level."

The green serum seemed to respond to Eli's voice, the microscopic machines swirling faster, eager to begin their work.

Cradle's hands, designed to tear apart starships, moved with impossible delicacy as she calibrated the delivery system. "The process will take nineteen minutes," she announced to the watching spirits. "Phase one: neural integration. Phase two: cellular reconstruction. Phase three…"

She paused, her voice catching.

"Phase three: ascension or ashes."

~ ~ ~

THE INJECTION

The needle found Eli's spine with surgical precision.

The serum burned like liquid starlight—the universe rewriting his DNA. Molten gold scorched his spine as birthmarks erupted, and immediately, everything went wrong.

His heart stopped.

Then started again at twice the normal rate.

His birthmarks erupted, molten gold awakening in his DNA—patterns that had lain dormant since his mother's enhancement during pregnancy. The neural interfaces sparked and died, overwhelmed by the feedback. Above, the Onze observers flickered violently, their forms destabilizing.

"We're losing him," the medical AI announced with mechanical calm.

Eli's back arched. His scream shattered every piece of glass in the chamber.

Cradle's voice cut through the chaos: "Stay with me, lionceau. We will look for your family. We will have our revenge." Her massive hand found his, dwarfing it completely. "Don't leave me alone again, lionceau."

The serum fought to integrate with his prenatal enhancement, two cosmic forces learning to harmonize. His cells activated ancient programming, each iteration unlocking more of what he'd always carried within. The Onze watched the total sum of their genius merge with a mind already touched by the cosmos.

"He's rejecting the integration," whispered Nyx, her husky voice carrying across the amphitheater.

"No," corrected Pandia, her high-society, high-intellect, quick speech pattern laser-focused. "He's not rejecting it. He's completing it. The stellar enhancement from his mother's pregnancy—it was waiting for us."

Eli's vital signs flatlined for thirty-seven seconds.

Then blazed back to life with readings that broke the monitoring equipment.

~ ~ ~

THE RECOVERY

Seven days.

Eli slept for seven days while his body rebuilt itself atom by atom. Cradle never left his side, her statuesque form curled around his medical pod like a protective shell. She told him stories of distant worlds, sang lullabies in languages that predated human civilization, and whispered promises of vengeance against those who had taken his family.

On the eighth day, he opened his eyes, a golden maelstrom swimming and slowly fading from his eyesight.

"How do you feel?" Cradle asked.

Eli sat up slowly, his movements carrying a new fluidity. "Different. Like I'm hearing colors and seeing sound." He looked at his hands—small, still fifteen, forever fifteen now. The birthmarks pulsed with gentle light that had always been there, just sleeping. "The voices… they're quieter now. Not gone, just… organized."

Cradle's relief was palpable. "The first phase is complete. Your body will remain as it is—fifteen years old, protected from time itself. But your mind will grow, will learn, will expand beyond what any mortal could comprehend. The cosmic enhancement you inherited has merged with eleven of the greatest minds in galactic history."

Eli nodded, understanding instinctively. "I wish I coulda grown a beard or something before I froze first," Eli said, a bit disheartened. The Onze whispered at the edges of his consciousness—not intrusive but present. Like having eleven older siblings who spoke in mathematics and memory. His immortal mind would have eons to learn their wisdom, while his body remained forever the child who'd first chosen to search for his family.

"We'll need two more injections over the next five years or so. We have Eris figuring out the exact time after we see how your body processes the first shot," Cradle continued. "To complete the integration, to unlock everything you were meant to become. But the zeptobots… they're not infallible, lionceau. Each phase carries greater risk as the enhancement deepens."

"When do we start looking for them?" he asked.

"I am searching with all the resources I have at my disposal. I just contracted two of the most elite fixers in the galaxy. They will find out something, I promise you." Cradle pulled Eli close and enclosed him in a warm and gentle hug. She felt a few tears, and she pulled him closer. "I am right here, my love. I will always be, if you wish."

But first, while Eli leaned heavily into Cradle's embrace, he suddenly felt the weight of everything he'd gone through come crushing down on him, and he let himself be held by a goddess he'd just met.

~ ~ ~

THE REVELATION

The air in Cradle's data-core chamber tasted like lavender and something older—like forgotten music from a more innocent time. Eli's vision fractured at the edges, the serum in his veins painting the world in glitching, screaming realities: the chamber as it was—a vault of humming machines; the chamber as the serum saw it—a necropolis of glowing neural pathways; the chamber as something else perceived it—a bleeding wound in reality.

His birthmarks throbbed in time with the light pulse from the central console.

"You never asked," Cradle said, her voice cavernous but gentle, soothing on the ears, "what abilities you may garner from the emerald serum."

Her palm met the console. The chamber unfolded.

"The procedure has given you an extraordinary ability, lionceau. Your body can now absorb negative energy and use it to form a warp bubble around yourself—possibly others with practice." Her eyes lit up with possibility. "Imagine it—you could propel yourself faster than light."

She glanced meaningfully at the wrench in Eli's hand. "And with Bing Bong's ability to absorb dark and exotic matter and energies, the things you two could accomplish together are staggering."

"I can do what now?" BB's voice cracked three registers higher than normal.

Rao ran down the arched corridor towards Eli. "There you two are. Cradle, trying to steal my boyfriend as usual."

"Perfect timing, my little moineau. I was getting ready to introduce Eli to some new friends in the special hangar."

"I know, I'm so excited. Analogoy is meeting us there, because of course he is."

"He is the lead engineer, Rao, and you know how he can be."

"Hello, boyfriend," Rao said playfully to Eli, getting off the Analogoy subject. "This is our first date!"

"It is," Eli said sheepishly, his face becoming red.

"Oh ab-so-lute-ly," she replied, stepping next to Eli.

~ ~ ~

THE COMPANIONS

Weeks later , after the hull breach had been sealed and the immediate crisis contained, the weight of what Eli was becoming settled on him like a shroud. The training mat still smelled of pre-pubescent armpits and failure. Eli lay on his back, staring at his hands—too small, forever fifteen, immortal in their childhood innocence. The serum's constant hum in his veins had awakened the universal enhancement he'd carried since birth, making his bones ache with the weight of eternal youth while his mind expanded beyond mortal limits.

Then something cold and wet nudged his nose.

"Heya, kid," Analogoy said. "Me and our most gracious and wondrous host designed a few things for you. We hope ya like 'em, E. You deserve 'em."

The first pupper's massive dog snout filled his vision, moonlight glinting off graphene-adamantium plating as the machine tilted his head. His ears swiveled forward with a soft whirr, optics shifting from combat-red to cerulean-blue. Behind him, the second pupper came barreling in like a derailed train—only to trip over his own paws and crash into a foam barrier, sending training drones scattering in panic.

"Your personal bodyguards," Cradle announced. "Rex and King."

King immediately rolled onto his back, all four paws in the air, his tail thumping wildly against the deck. Rex—ever the stoic—simply sat and offered Eli the drone's still-twitching core as if presenting a fallen comrade. The core pulsed with the same gold light as Eli's veins—a silent recognition of kinship.

"They're... ridiculous," Eli breathed, laughter bubbling up as King suddenly noticed his own tail and began spinning in frantic circles.

Analogoy smirked. "Watch."

His whistle cut frequencies out of the air.

The change was instantaneous. King's goofy sprawl became a predator's crouch, his mouth splitting open to reveal plasma-edged fangs that hummed with dark energy. Rex's graphene plating expanded with metallic snaps, revealing hidden weapon ports. Their synchronized growl vibrated the floor.

Analogoy tossed a combat drone.

The dogs moved faster than sight. The drone became scrap metal in 2.3 seconds. King returned with its smoking core in his jaws, dropping it at Eli's feet with the gold light synchronizing with his pulse, tail still wagging proudly.

~ ~ ~

THE WHISPER

The hangar doors groaned open.

The Whisper dominated the space—not built but grown, her obsidian hull streaked with glowing green veins that pulsed in time with Eli's heartbeat. Her wings curved like claws, the edges shimmering with unnatural sharpness. The front of her was the large predatory face of a wolf, and the gigantic head craned towards Eli, and the mouth suddenly moved.

"Hello, my forever boy, first of the pack, beat of my heart, light in my eye. I am Whisper. Behind you when you lead. In front when you need protection and beside you always and forever."

"Your mobile command center," Cradle said, tossing him the keychip.

Inside, the ship's bridge took Eli's breath away:

Pilot Throne: wrapped in neural interface tendrils that matched his serum-green veins;

Bing Bong's Nest: a glowing core where the AI could refine dark matter, separating sterile neutrinos for Thoth's experiments;

Dog Bays: Custom recharge stations sized for two eight-hundred-pound mechanical guardians.

King howled—a sound that made the ship's lights flicker in response. Rex butted his head against Eli's back, nearly sending him up the ramp.

Whisper's engines roared to life, and for the first time in what seemed forever, Eli was happy.

DR. SUNSHINE IS DEAD
Inspired by Will Wood and the Tapeworms

THE LABORATORY OF BROKEN THINGS

Elonias floated in a chemical fog—a half-life of narcotics and agony, her body reduced to a pulsing wound strapped to a table. The steel beneath her was cold as a dead man's touch, its surface slick with condensation that never quite evaporated in the recycled air. She could feel every rivet pressing into her spine like an accusation, each one a small monument to her captivity.

The air reeked of antiseptic and spoiled milk, soured further by the ozone tang of humming machinery that never slept, never stopped its mechanical breathing. Somewhere deep in the walls, coolant lines groaned like distant whales in mourning—a sound that had become the soundtrack to her dissolution.

She hadn't seen her legs in weeks.

Had they taken them? She knew they had. The memory came in flashes—the cold touch of the bone saw, Jobaar's theatrical flourish as he declared them "unnecessary for breeding purposes." The phantom pains were worst—lightning bolts of agony where her knees used to be, maddening itches that crawled up calves no longer there.

Her nervous system, confused and desperate, firing signals into stumps wrapped in synthetic skin. Sometimes, in the space between waking and unconsciousness, she felt something else stirring in her veins—a faint vibration, like distant music calling from the deep.

On the bad days, she swore she could still wiggle her toes. On the worse ones, her silent screams echoed off nothing for no one to hear. It was anguish and frustration that came around like old adversaries, just waiting for your guard to lower.

Above her, the ceiling wept with surgical precision. A single pipe, cracked near the nozzle like a wound that wouldn't heal, released droplets that struck her forehead in perfect intervals. Plink. The sound had become her metronome, her anchor to time's passage. She'd started counting them between the extractions, between the dreams that weren't dreams but something worse—memories of a life that felt increasingly like fiction.

Drop. One. Drop. Two. Drop. Three.

The rhythm was almost hypnotic, almost merciful. She tried not to think about what they'd take next—what other parts of her Jobaar deemed "non-essential" for his breeding program.

Hours passed. Or days. Time had become fluid in this place where artificial lights never dimmed and the machines never stopped their rhythmic humming.

~ ~ ~

THE MIRACLE

The door hissed open with the whisper of pressurized air, a sound that usually made her flinch. But exhaustion had worn her reflexes smooth.

She didn't look up at first—she'd learned not to. Hope was a luxury she couldn't afford, and the ones who came through that door only brought pain or silence. Or both. The footsteps were different this time, though. Hesitant. Almost… careful.

But this time…

"Mom?"

Her breath caught mid-inhale, sharp and wet. The air stuck in her lungs like thorns, and for a moment, the world tilted sideways. The steady drip from above seemed to pause, as if the universe itself was holding its breath.

That voice.

No. It couldn't be. The drugs, the isolation, the months of systematic dismantling—they'd finally snapped something essential. She was hallucinating. She had to be.

She turned her head slowly—every tendon in her neck screaming in protest, vertebrae grinding like broken gears—and saw him.

Eli.

He stood just inside the threshold, framed by the lab's flickering emergency strobes. The red lights pulsed like a warning heartbeat, throwing shadows across his face in rhythmic waves—but she knew him. Those gold-veined hands pressed against the doorframe. The dark, messy hair that had always defied any attempt at order. His eyes—older, sadder, yes, carrying weights she didn't recognize—but his.

Eli, she thought hopefully. Her vision blurred, and tears she didn't know she could still make rolled down the sides of her face, cutting tracks through the grime and leaving salt trails on her cracked lips.

"I'm getting you out," he whispered, his voice carrying across the space between them like a lifeline.

She tried to rise, muscles screaming their protest, but her body refused—a puppet with severed strings. So she wept instead, great silent heaving sobs that shook her diminished frame.

I knew you'd come, she thought as she choked between ragged breaths. *I—I held on. I told myself... every day... you'd come.* The thoughts came fast, heart racing, ears buzzing, punctuated by the drip above—though something seemed different about its rhythm now. Slightly off. Like even time itself was holding its breath.

He moved toward her then, his silhouette haloed by the static light that painted everything in shades of warning. Each step deliberate, careful, as if he were afraid Elonias might disappear if he moved too quickly. He reached for the restraints, fingers ghosting over the buckles with surprising gentleness.

"It's okay now, Mom. You're safe."

The words washed over her like warm water, and for the first time in months, she felt the knot of terror in her chest begin to loosen.

~ ~ ~

THE CONFESSION

Thoughts bubbled up in her fractured mind in gasps, and spittle flew as her heart kicked into overdrive. Her body was awash in relief and guilt and months of buried madness that suddenly demanded release.

I should've quit—when the Concord first came to Kiln— The memory hit her like a physical blow. *I should've run when they started scanning kids—* Her thoughts, flooding her now, scattered and fleeting, became more desperate. *I just wanted you to have a better life. Stars, Eli—*

The ceiling drip seemed to punctuate her inner confession, but the intervals felt wrong now. Too long. Too short. Plink… plink-plink… plink. Even the rhythm that had kept her sane was failing her, becoming as erratic as her racing heartbeat.

She stared hard into his eyes, trying to force him to understand her silent plea. *I didn't know they'd take you—* she screamed in her mind, her head swirling, blood pounding in her temples making it hard to see clearly. *I didn't know they'd take you,* she thought, reaching out.

Eli smiled—too calm, too clean. His lips stretched just a hair too wide, revealing teeth that caught the light wrong. His hand brushed her cheek, warm and soft. Too warm. The touch lingered, and she noticed his skin had an odd, almost waxy quality. When he pulled his hand away, a glistening residue remained on her skin—what she desperately hoped was just sweat, though it felt too thick, too viscous.

"No, no, easy, Mother, just lie back now," he cooed, the sound almost musical but carrying a harmonic whine underneath, like a broken speaker trying to find its frequency. "I'm here. It's okay now, I'm not angry with you, Mother."

Mother. The word hung in the air like a discordant note. Eli had never called her that. Not once in fifteen years.

He began working the cuffs around her wrist with practiced efficiency, as if he'd done this before. The metal clinked softly as he manipulated the mechanisms.

"I just need to retrieve my tool," he added softly, his voice carrying an odd, formal undertone she couldn't quite place. "The device you took from the archaeology site. You know the one, correct?"

Her mind froze for just a second, time stopped, and red flags popped up in her head. *Does he mean… Bing Bong?* she thought.

He paused. Completely still. Even his breathing seemed to stop.

Then he laughed—a bubbling, syrup-thick sound that made her stomach turn and her skin crawl. The sound seemed to come from somewhere deeper than his throat, resonating in frequencies that made her bones ache.

"C'mon, Mother, my power rod. Blink if you understand. Is it still at that mining facility we live at? Did you lose it?"

Power rod. The words hit her like a physical blow. That was what the trackers called Bing Bong—their target, their prize. The device Jobaar had been demanding she reveal the location of through months of systematic torture.

She froze. Thoughts rose up like a curse, and suddenly everything felt wrong. The temperature, the light, the way the shadows fell—all of it shifted, became threatening.

That smell. It hit her all at once, cutting through the antiseptic and ozone like a blade.

Rotten formula. Baby shit. Rancid grease.

For a moment, she tried to convince herself it was just the laboratory—months of recycled air and chemical cocktails playing tricks on her damaged senses. But no. It clung to him like a second skin, growing stronger with each passing second until it filled her nostrils and made her gag. How had she not noticed it before? How had hope blinded her so completely?

No, she thought desperately, *this has to be real. This has to be him. I can't… I can't survive if this isn't real.*

But even as she tried to deny it, the wrongness grew impossible to ignore. The too-formal speech. The smell. The way he moved with predatory precision rather than childish energy.

Her breath caught in her throat. Her pulse surged in her ears like a siren, drowning out even the erratic drip from above.

This wasn't her son.

This thing wearing his face, speaking with his voice—it was something else entirely. Something that had crawled out of her nightmares and taken the shape of her deepest longing.

~ ~ ~

THE REVEAL

The door behind him slammed open with the violence of a snapped spine, the sound echoing through the laboratory like a gunshot. The sudden noise made the thing at her bedside straighten, its movements becoming more fluid, more predatory.

Jobaar entered, grinning like a skull puppet, his powder-white skin glowing faintly in the red light. His presence filled the room like a toxic gas, making the air itself seem heavier, harder to breathe.

Behind him, Giblet rolled in on hydraulic treads, his grotesque bulk quivering with excitement. Patches of stolen flesh rippled across his cybernetic frame as he clapped his hands together in glee, the sound wet and meaty.

"Five of Baar's new best and brightest, I dare say. Oh, he will be pleased with me." Jobaar's voice dripped with theatrical pride as he gestured toward the thing wearing Eli's face. "You took to it beautifully, didn't you, my dear creation? I'm going to need at least six more like you. Come now, this is fun, yes? I can see the joy in your eyes."

Giblet's laughter bubbled up from his throat like sewage, his flesh-wrapped claws scraping against the console as he monitored readouts that tracked Elonias's vital signs with predatory interest.

The thing wearing Eli's face turned slowly, the movement too smooth, too controlled. It was no longer bothering with the pretense of humanity.

Its pupils narrowed to horizontal slits—predator's eyes in a child's face. Its skin crawled, literally—shifting in waves beneath the surface like something was trapped inside, trying to break free. The illusion began to crack and peel at the edges, revealing glimpses of something darker underneath.

"Surprise," it whispered, voice warped now—half-child, half-reptile, and wholly wrong. The sound seemed to come from multiple throats at once, creating a discord that made her teeth ache.

Something inside Elonias broke. Cleanly. Quietly.

Not with a scream. Not with a sob.

But like glass shattering in a room no one else could hear—a sound that existed only in the deepest chambers of her mind, where hope went to die.

The red light at Jobaar's collar flared to hungry life, drinking her silent scream like wine.

She felt her mind slip beneath the surface like a sinking starship, pulled down by the weight of betrayal and the crushing realization that even her rescue had been a lie. The laboratory lights blurred into streaks of red and white, the drip from above becoming a distant echo.

But as she fell into that darkness, something else stirred. Deep in her cells, in the quantum spaces between thought and flesh, the stellar fluid they'd been pumping into her for months began its true work. Not the crude genetic manipulation Jobaar intended but something far more profound.

The fluid in her veins hummed—a song she'd heard before, in dreams that felt like memories of starlight. Not healing—transformation. Each molecule of betrayal and agony became fuel for metamorphosis. Something that would reshape her very essence into something Jobaar had never intended to create.

A voice whispered through the stellar current, familiar and ancient and filled with maternal fury: "Stars taste sweeter than tears, little mother. And soon, you will taste both."

Down, down, into the dark.

Where pain couldn't follow. Where no doors opened. Where even her own screams couldn't find her. Where the thing that had been her son could never reach.

And where, in the deepest chambers of her dissolving consciousness, the first whispers of what she would become began to sing.

In that quiet place, she found not peace—but metamorphosis.

PSYCHO KILLER
Inspired by The Talking Heads

THE DIN OF THE BLOCK WAS WHITE NOISE with occasional echo-screams or manic laughs thrown in. Control guards and floor officers were used to the controlled chaos.

Floor officers moved with practiced monotony, weaving between bunks and cell doors like cogs in a grim machine. Mail carts rattled along their routes, manila envelopes and worn paper passed through gloved hands, eyes scanning for contraband. The smell was ass, feet, and armpits, with unflushed toilets and four-hundred-year-old mold seeping into every crack.

Inside the control booth, the duty officer crouched beside an open equipment cache, ticking off inventory: gas grenades arranged like candies in foam cradles, restraint cuffs gleaming under unforgiving fluorescent lights, riot guns, grenade launchers, syringe launchers. Tools of order. Implements of terror. Each item a reminder of how thin the crust of civilization was in this concrete hell—and how easily it cracked.

Akona moved like smoke through the block tunnel, his boots whispering over polished concrete. He kept his head low, threading through the cameras' blind spots without appearing evasive. A manila folder rode under his shirt, flattened against his ribs like a second spine. He slipped past a tier guard wearing his pressed, immaculate uniform, the man's wide eyes and nervous gait revealing his inexperience. Akona didn't recognize the "fish" guard—must've had a poor rank number and got stuck doing someone's vacation relief in Ad-Seg. High-grav tier no less. *Poor bastard*, Akona thought. He ducked into the cell.

He dropped onto Apek's disheveled bunk like he belonged there, but his eyes never stopped moving—checking the corridor through the bars, tracking the vacation guard's position.

Above him, Mares's legs hung lazily over the side of the top bunk, boots scuffed and rocking with idle rhythm.

"Got it," Akona said quietly, looking around Mares's leg to keep position on the vacation guy. He pulled the folder free with careful movements, its corners worn soft by age and handling, stamped in faded blue with the prison system's institutional seal—Property of Kiln-9 Correctional Archives.

Mares shifted to peer over the edge, lowering his voice to match Akona's caution. "Tell me again why we need another recruit?"

"Word from Apek's contact," Akona muttered, flipping through the papers with practiced silence. "New warden's putting together squads. Suicide missions. Teams of eight."

"Suicide missions against who?" Mares asked, sitting up straighter. His voice sharpened like a blade being unsheathed.

"Abyss forces, from what I've heard." Akona ran a finger along a paperclip's rusted edge, then glanced toward the corridor again. Footsteps echoed past—some con heading to chow. He waited for the sound to fade.

Mares let out a low whistle, then caught himself and dropped his voice. "Someone's footing a hell of a bill for that op. You know who?"

Akona's gaze flicked upward. "You heard of the Onze Collective?"

Mares blinked. "Yeah, mythical kingpins. Word is they run the gambling rings. No one's ever seen them—only deal through android proxies." He paused, processing. "Actually… I did a job for them once. Abyss force had broken into a vault on Kepler-108. Me and two of their bots tracked 'em down. Turned the bastards over to Concord."

"And?"

"Weirdest handoff I've ever done. The prisoners weren't scared—

just smug. Like they wanted to be caught. And the Concord suits were treating them like royalty. Polite, formal. Called them 'Exalted.' Never seen anything like it."

Akona smirked, his expression carrying the weight of shared experience in this place where trust was a rare commodity. "Still the only bastard I'd trust to watch my back in a shithole like this."

Akona's fingers stilled on the file. "That's what makes this interesting. Word is the Onze think standard mercs won't cut it against Abyss forces. They need something…" He tapped the folder. "Unpredictable. Makes sense they'd have first pick of the talent. Their logo's stamped on every riot gun in the armory—like they own the place. Maybe they do.

"Speaking of unpredictable," Akona continued, settling back against the wall. Mares followed his gaze down to the faded folder in his hands.

"Whose jacket is that?" Mares asked, leaning further over the edge.

Akona's voice lowered, took on the reverence reserved for legends and nightmares.

"A guy named Gideon." He said it almost like an invocation, savoring each syllable. "Just finished reading this. Makes us look like princesses of Oberon-13." He held up the file like it contained dark scripture. "Holy shit."

Mares raised an eyebrow, that familiar smirk starting to play at his lips. "That bad?"

Akona nodded slowly, opening to the first page with deliberate ceremony. "Picture this—looks like somebody's accountant." He let that sink in before continuing. "It starts on Borbega. Glaltrine City. Routine traffic stop. Local cop hands him a citation writer… and Gideon just turns and stabs him in the neck. No argument, no escalation. Just—" He mimed a clean thrust with surgical precision. "Cold."

"Jesus."

"Three more cops responded. He killed two before they finally took him down." Akona sounded equal parts impressed and jealous, his voice carrying the appreciation of a professional. "They threw him in local lockup. Thought it was just another drunk-tank night. Before they knew what was happening, he'd killed five inmates. Injured two more. Just random poor bastards in the wrong cell."

Mares didn't speak, just kept that plastered smirk on his face, but his eyes had that predator's gleam.

"So they shipped him here," Akona continued, flipping a page with theatrical timing. "He got processed, went straight to the yard, and started attacking guards. Killed one. Full lockdown. They found out afterward he bit and swallowed parts of the body." He paused, voice dropping. "Apek's contact said he whispered something afterward: 'Meat's meat. Why waste it?'"

Mares's idle boot-rocking stopped for just a beat, the silence hanging between them. Then he recoiled—but only slightly, more impressed than disgusted. "You've got to be kidding me."

"Nope." Akona licked his teeth, getting into the rhythm of his tale. "So they stuck him in solitary. But the SHU's overcrowded, and some new lieutenant—some pencil-neck relative of a corporate exec— decided to double-bunk him even though there was a 'No Celly' notation in his jacket."

Mares's voice dropped to a whisper. "What happened?"

Akona paused, checking the corridor again. The vacation guard was still focused on his mail route. Perfect.

"Two head counts later, a guard lost it. Gideon had killed the other inmate. Ate a third of him. No extra charges, either. Because he was flagged as 'single-cell mandatory' in the system. The lieutenant had legally sentenced the guy to death."

Mares whispered, "You've got to be shitting me." A small laugh escaped his lips, dark and appreciative.

Akona leaned forward, warming to his story. "Oh, but wait. It gets worse." He was in storyteller mode now, pacing the tale like a fireside myth. "He's in 57-B now."

Mares' eyebrows shot up. "57-B? The wolf run?"

"Exactly." Akona nodded, pleased that Mares was connecting the dots. "They can't let him on the yard anymore. So they've got him in bare concrete, solo exercise cages. One day, the guards skip their thirty-minute checks. The gas alarms went off. Full yard panic."

He paused for effect, watching Mares's face.

"Down! Down! Gas everywhere!" Akona reenacted the chaos in a harsh whisper, then dropped back to normal volume.

"Smoke, gas—everyone's choking. Control's screaming over the comms. The sergeant peered out through the haze, and what did he see?" Akona leaned forward until their faces were inches apart. "Gideon. Walking the yard."

Mares blinked. "Alone?"

"No." Akona's grin widened. "With twelve hundred prisoners. Hardened lifers, gang psychos, death-row burnouts. And every last one of them was pressed together in the farthest corner, eyes wide like children during a bombing raid. Gideon was pacing around them like a mutie wolf that forgot how to walk like a man."

Mares whispered, "How is that even possible?"

"The gas was wrecking everyone else. But him?" Akona's tone dropped to reverence. "He was walking through the smoke like he belonged in it. Like it was his atmosphere. Not a cough. Not a wince. Just slow, methodical movement. The guards were scared. But the inmates?" He shook his head in wonder. "Terrified."

Mares's knuckles had gone white where he gripped the bunk edge.

Akona let the silence stretch, watching the story work its way into Mares's imagination.

"Apek's contact was close enough to hear him talking to them. Really quiet, like he was sharing bedtime stories." Akona's voice took on a sing-song quality, mockingly gentle. "'Don't move now. Don't breathe too deep. Good boys stay still.' Twelve hundred killers, and they were following orders like Sunday school children.

"But check this out." Akona flipped to another page, his voice taking on conspiratorial tones. "About a year ago, the warden heard Gideon's mother was sick. The warden didn't want Gideon finding out his mom died and we knew and didn't tell him, so he granted a family visit. Apek's contact was portering the visiting building."

"What happened?"

"They rolled Gideon out strapped to a dolly. Manacled wrists, ankles, elbows, shoulders—bite mask like he was a feral dog. Guard pulled the family aside beforehand to explain the restraints—didn't want them accusing staff of abuse." Akona's voice went quiet, building to the punchline. "And the mother, she listened real careful. A long moment passed. Then she put a hand on her chest and said…"

He looked up, meeting Mares's eyes.

"'Oh, thank God.' This fucker's been a psycho since his crib!"

The silence that followed was full of slow breath and unspoken appreciation for the story's dark perfection.

"And here's the beautiful part," Akona said after a beat, voice returning to its dark glee. "All of this—the cop killing, the cannibal incidents, the gas immunity, twelve hundred hardened cons cowering like children—all of it from a guy who's barely over five feet tall."

Mares exhaled like he'd been holding it in throughout the entire story. "Holy shit. We've got our invincible wild card."

Akona nodded once, sliding the file back under his shirt. "Exactly. Against Abyss forces? We need someone they can't predict, can't plan for. Someone who doesn't operate by any rules they understand." He glanced toward the corridor one more time. "Let's start planning to get him moved here."

The fluorescent lights buzzed overhead, casting pale stripes across the cell's concrete walls. In the distance, a door clanged shut, its echo rolling through the tiers like thunder. The vacation guard was still making his rounds, oblivious to the recruitment conversation happening right under his nose.

But in this place where legends were born from blood and madness, some stories carried more weight than others.

Some numbers weren't just tattoos or headcounts.

Some were loaded weapons waiting for the right war.

Outside, a distant siren wailed.

And Gideon was about to become theirs.

BUNGLE IN THE JUNGLE
Inspired by Jethro Tull

HYPERSPACE TRANSIT

Whisper sliced through the void, her living hull rippling like dark water beneath a blade. Bio-living Trilene-phoscarbyne flexed in sync with hyperspace currents, absorbing g-forces that would have turned bone to slurry.

Eli stood anchored to the bridge deck, boots magnetized against Whisper's subtle rolls. The air inside smelled musty and sharp—recycled atmosphere tinged with the acrid burn of exotic matter processing. Around him, proximity alerts flickered like fireflies as the ship wove through drifting debris—corpses of old wars, picked clean by scavengers and time.

Three days to Hunter's Planet. Three days to pretend dangerous surveys were blueprints for survival.

Rex paced beside him, a sleek shadow of articulated limbs and weaponized grace. Gold light pulsed along his flanks, syncing with the faint shimmer of Eli's own fractal veins. Not far behind, King loomed—an armored sentinel wrapped in silence, built for endurance and blunt force.

Neither blinked. Neither slept. Their loyalty was coded deeper than flesh.

From Eli's back holster, Bing Bong stirred. The wrench hummed softly, optic lens narrowing like a squint.

"E."

Eli thumbed the smooth tung wood almost as an afterthought. "Spit it out."

"There's a 0.0000121 percent chance someone on Hunter's Planet knows how to operate a Shield Tower power data readout, let alone a bucket and a mop."

"Hunter's Planet isn't exactly known for its technical expertise," Eli replied dryly. "Cradle says this is a good planet to start the towers. She said when I start going to the other Core 7s, some old guy is gonna be escorting us."

"Did Cradle mention if the old guy likes wrenches, E?" Bing Bong piped up hopefully.

Rex's processor vented a puff of static—his closest approximation of laughter. King's optical dome ticked upward, mildly amused.

Eli ignored them and turned back to the glowing holomap. Cradle's intel scrolled across the screen, bathed in sterile blue light: Hunter's Planet, where the atmosphere was a methane-sulfur cocktail that gave baseline human lungs twenty minutes before failure, where 1.3 standard gravity made every step a negotiation with physics, and where the wildlife had evolved to make war look polite.

The footage played behind Eli's eyes—hardwired memory flickering like filmstrip:

A serpent the size of a warship glided through tar-black seas. Jaws unhinged. A lizard-shark vanished whole. Then: rupture. Twelve limbs. Feathers, claws, razors. A blur of talons and blood.

Five years of monstrous growth, gifted in five minutes of slaughter.

Cradle's voice echoed in his mind, sharp and cold through the memory feed:

"Generators approved on the prison planet. The warden's offering convicts a choice: Die in a cell… or die useful. Those who survive earn commuted sentences—life on the frontier instead of execution. Some even earn credits for families back home.

"Each of the eleven towers needs both tactical support and

daily maintenance. Prisoners will man Onze Fighters—one squad patrolling the troposphere close to the tower and colony, one in the stratosphere, one in the exosphere.

"Concord knows better than to interfere," Cradle had added. "My drones hunger for traitors, and I know all their secrets."

The holomap pulsed. Red zones spread across the landscape like blood blooming under skin.

In the silence that followed, Eli exhaled.

Outside the bridge, hyperspace stretched the stars into silver needles. The Alcubierre warp bubble pushed them beyond light speed. The void narrowed to a corridor of bent light. And at the end of that corridor, Hunter's Planet waited—hungry.

PLANETFALL

Three days collapsed into three hours. Hyperspace folded around them like origami made of starlight—then tore open.

And there it was. A world that looked like a festering wound against the stars.

Whisper screamed through the upper atmosphere, her hull glowing cherry red as friction turned air to flame. Her bio-mechanical skin trembled beneath the heat—scanners pulsing downward in tight rhythm, painting the terrain in jagged topography.

There. A scab of relatively flat land perched high above a ravine. The perfect LZ. Elevated position sighted along with clear sightlines. She scanned, and there was no trace of thermal signatures within her range, which was vast. Most importantly, there were no signs of the twelve-limbed nightmares from the footage.

Landing struts unfolded with the groan of a man well past his prime and well deep into his cups. Whisper settled into the dust. Her cargo ramp hissed open, exhaling a breath of sterile ship air that was immediately devoured by Hunter's toxic wind.

The pack disembarked into hell's breath. Eli's boots sank into the rust-colored soil with a sickening, wet crunch. It wasn't earth; it was the dust of a thousand things this planet had digested. Rex flowed out first, a phantom of silent death, his sensor arrays fanning out to taste the poison air. King followed, each footfall a deliberate tremor that promised violence. The ground itself seemed to recoil from his weight.

Eli's first breath was a knife. The methane-sulfur cocktail hit his lungs, and the gold veins up his arms flared to life, burning the toxins away before they could take root. Nineteen minutes, Whisper's warning echoed in his mind. The clock was ticking.

Behind them, Whisper's forward cockpit shaped itself into the face of a large wolf. Her wolfish snout formed from overlapping Trilene-phoscarbyne plates, bristling with sensor-hairs. The light from her windows constantly scanned the area for anything that might threaten her pack.

From Eli's sheath, Bing Bong's voice crackled, tinny with bravado:

"And I'll be right here… monitoring Whisper's scans for any wrench-eating monstrosities within… let's say five light years?" A pause. "99.97 percent chance I'm not moving from this spot. Preferably ten."

Eli smirked and rolled his shoulders, feeling the stellar enhancement humming through his veins like distant music. "Come on, boys. Let's stretch our legs."

They moved in formation. Rex as forward scout, footfalls silent and precise. King as rear guard, bulk casting long shadows behind them. And Eli between, golden veins pulsing faintly as his body adapted to the hostile environment.

The rust-colored soil clung to their boots like clotting blood, each step requiring extra effort to pull free. Scattered among the rocks, bones lay picked so clean they gleamed like polished ivory — remnants of whatever had once tried to make this world home.

They'd barely covered a hundred yards when Eli stopped cold.

Something about the terrain felt… wrong.

The river below churned, brown and viscous as motor oil. It twisted around the hill like a thing alive. The light caught the current — just right. And it flexed. Like a muscle.

Eli tensed, his enhanced senses screaming warnings that baseline humans would never detect.

"Whisper," he subvocalized, throat dry. "Double-check that wildlife scan. Specifically looking for mutant wolves with too many joints, snake-bird hybrids, anything with more than four limbs, or honestly, just assume everything here wants to wear my skin."

"Oh, darling," Whisper purred, her voice dripping with maternal sarcasm, "I need you to stay alert out there no matter what my scans say. If there is trouble, warp away back to me."

Rex's optics narrowed. King's outer plating hissed, expanding slightly in preparation.

"But yes," she continued. "Your immediate area remains clear. For now. The farther you wander, the faster your odds shift from 'probable survival' to 'interesting autopsy.'"

A pause.

"Also—do mind the ravine. Seismic readings suggest it breathes."

Eli swallowed hard. Somewhere in the distance, something that was absolutely not a bird screamed—a sound like metal tearing and children crying.

From his belt, Bing Bong piped up again, cheerful as ever:

"Hey E, if there's a 99.9897 percent chance of trouble, whoosh back here—I have your back, literally. Whisper, is he reading me? There's a 14.98 percent chance you're malfunctioning."

"Oh, he heard you, my brave little one. Don't you doubt it," Whisper cooed to Bing Bong, her maternal affection bleeding through the combat protocols.

Eli tightened his grip on his weapon—a plasma-edged blade that hummed in harmony with his golden veins.

"Let's make this quick."

The hill rose ahead, promising visibility—and exposure. Each step into Hunter's Planet felt like walking further down a predator's throat.

And the planet was starting to salivate.

~ ~ ~

THE SHIELD TOWER SITE

Twenty minutes of careful climbing brought them to the designated coordinates. The hilltop was scarred bare—ancient lava flows had left the rock smooth as glass, perfect for the tower's foundation anchors. Below, the ravine yawned like an infected wound, its walls lined with crystalline formations that pulsed with sickly bioluminescence.

Eli knelt beside the survey marker—a titanium spike driven deep into the bedrock by Cradle's advance drones. The metal was already pitted with corrosion, Hunter's atmosphere eating everything that dared exist on its surface.

"Atmospheric readings are stable," Whisper reported through their link. "Define stable as 'consistently trying to kill you.'"

Rex's sensor arrays swept the perimeter in overlapping patterns while King positioned himself facing the most likely approach vectors. Both machines moved with the fluid coordination of pack hunters, their neural links creating a defensive network around Eli.

Whisper's voice came through their neural link, crisp and professional: "Cradle, we have located a suitable site for the first tower. Ready to start receiving transports and robots for foundation prep and perimeter defense."

Cradle's response crackled through the comm, carrying the weight of cosmic authority: "Acknowledged. We have acquired an additional seventy-eight prisoners to staff the tower—top candidates who missed the fighter squad cut. Additional buildings for barracks incoming on transport."

Eli's jaw tightened at the word "acquired." Even for a good cause, even to save lives, they were still moving people like chess pieces. Seventy-eight prisoners. *How many will this planet eat before the tower is finished?* He pushed the thought away—his mother was somewhere out there, probably facing far worse than frontier duty.

His enhanced hearing picked up something the scanners had missed—a low, rhythmic scraping from deep in the ravine below. Like claws on stone. Or something very large, breathing.

"Foundation scan complete," Bing Bong announced, his voice

crackling with technical satisfaction. "Bedrock integrity at 97.3 percent. This rock has been here since the planet learned how to hate properly."

Eli smiled despite himself. "How long for the site survey?"

"Nineteen minutes for complete geological and atmospheric analysis," BB calculated. "Would you prefer the optimistic or realistic survival projections?"

"Surprise me."

"Optimistic: seventy-three percent chance we leave with all our original limbs. Realistic: thirty-one percent chance the planet doesn't add us to its digestive tract."

Rex's static echoed across the hilltop. Even King's optical dome seemed to brighten with amusement.

Eli began running detailed scans of the survey marker, his enhanced reflexes guiding micro-adjustments to a new analyzer device Analogoy had created for the tower mission. Eli wished he had paid better attention to the directions. "Crap, oh there it goes," Eli said, finally getting the new marvel to function. "I got it, everyone, don't panic." Words and numbers scrolled by on the scanner too fast to read, and it probably wouldn't have mattered if they'd crawled by like BB approaching a fist fight—he had no idea what half of them meant. "Oh, there we go, Whisper, it says this place is suitable for foundation prep."

This was what he was made for—not conquest like Baar's armies but protection. Preparing safe sites for those who couldn't protect themselves. Surveying rather than destroying. Building gardens instead of graveyards.

As Eli continued his scans, something shifted in the ravine below.

~ ~ ~

CONTACT

"Movement," Rex reported, his voice dropping to combat frequency. "Bearing two-seven-zero. Range: eight hundred meters and... wait. Lost contact."

Through his enhanced vision, Eli caught glimpses of motion among the crystalline formations. Something large. Something that moved wrong—too many joints, too fluid, like anatomy had given up and let nightmare take over.

A crystal formation cracked. Then another. No visible cause.

The scrape of talon on rock echoed from the ravine, but when they turned toward the sound, nothing was there. It was hunting them, staying just beyond their sensors, learning their patterns.

"Whisper," Eli subvocalized, hands never stopping their work on the survey equipment. "How's that extraction looking?"

"Engines warm, darling. But that thing climbing toward you?" Her voice carried new tension. "Thermal signature suggests it's been eating things much larger than you. Recently."

More crystals cracked. A shadow moved where no shadow should be.

King's weapons systems hummed to life—not the harsh whine of charging capacitors but the deep, satisfied purr of a predator recognizing prey. Rex flowed into flanking position, his movements silent as a hunting cat.

Then it unfolded itself from the ravine's shadows like a nightmare origami made of death.

Twelve limbs moved in perfect coordination, each ending in talons that carved grooves in solid rock. Its hide shifted between scales and feathers, adapting to whatever it needed to kill. Eyes—too many eyes—tracked their position with mathematical precision.

"BB," Eli murmured, still working, his focus split between cosmic enhancement and protective duty. "Time to completion?"

"Eleven minutes, thirty-seven seconds. Site survey at sixty percent completion."

The creature paused fifty meters away, studying them. Calculating. Its head tilted—a gesture almost human, as if it recognized their technology and was choosing its moment.

Then it opened its mouth and spoke in Whisper's exact voice:

"Darling, come back to me. You're in danger."

The perfect mimicry was obscene—a hunter's trap using their own bonds against them.

Eli's blood went cold. Rex's optical arrays flared in alarm. Even King's massive frame tensed, recognizing the wrongness of it.

Then the real scream came.

The sound hit like a physical blow, harmonics designed to paralyze prey through pure terror. Rex and King weathered it without flinching, their audio dampeners filtering the worst frequencies. But Eli felt it in his bones, his stellar enhancement fighting against biological weapons millions of years in the making.

"Interesting," BB observed with clinical detachment. "Its vocal cords contain metallic filaments. That scream was tuned to disrupt standard human neural patterns."

"Good thing I'm not standard," Eli replied, his golden veins flaring brighter as his body adapted, the Onze consciousness whispering calculations through his enhanced reflexes.

The creature charged.

~ ~ ~

PACK PROTOCOL

What followed was less combat than choreography. Rex and King had been programmed to analyze every possible martial scenario and adapt accordingly, their movements flowing together like water finding its level.

Rex struck first—a blur of articulated limbs and plasma discharge that carved through the creature's advance. But the thing adapted mid-charge, limbs reconfiguring to absorb damage that should have been fatal.

King met it head-on, eight hundred pounds of armored fury colliding with alien nightmare. They went down together, talons phasing through King's adamantium plating like dark matter, the creature's scream modulating into frequencies that made the hilltop's rock resonate.

And through it all, Eli kept working.

This was the heroic truth that legends missed—sometimes courage wasn't about standing and fighting. Sometimes it was about kneeling in poison air, assembling hope one component at a time while your family bought you the seconds you needed.

The universal enhancement burned through his veins, not with pain but with purpose. Each calculation BB performed flowed through Eli's consciousness, filtered by eleven brilliant minds and amplified by zeptobot precision.

"Seven minutes," BB announced as Eli's enhanced reflexes guided the final sensor readings into their geological database. "Site survey achieving full resonance with local space-time mapping."

Above them, the first flickers of Whisper's shield began to manifest—translucent barriers that would protect them during the survey. Not weapons but protection. Sanctuary in a universe that specialized in making sanctuary impossible.

Rex danced around the creature's flanks, each movement calculated to draw attacks away from Eli. King absorbed punishment that would have shattered lesser machines, his bulk protecting the tower assembly with mechanical determination.

"Four minutes," BB continued. "Local ionosphere responding to exotic matter injection. Shield integrity at forty percent and climbing."

The creature broke away from King, recognizing the true threat. It turned toward Eli, all twelve limbs moving in terrible coordination, instinct overriding intelligence as it sensed the growing barrier that would deny it prey.

Rex intercepted it three meters from the survey equipment.

The impact sent both combatants tumbling down the hillside in a chaos of metal and alien anatomy. The ends of each of the creature's limbs were thin, blade-like appendages at least five inches long, and it began to try to pierce Rex's throat with lightning-quick thrusts. Rex spun in midair and unlocked his jaw; then, in a flash of dust and creature blood and venom, they disappeared over the side. Rex's pain-sensors screamed through their neural link—a sensation Eli knew too well. His own veins burned in sympathy, golden fire searing along his arms as he felt every torn circuit, every severed hydraulic line.

But Rex had bought the time they needed.

"Shield Tower foundation resonance at 88.8786 percent and steady," BB announced with quiet satisfaction. "Okay, the first part is done. We can get out of here until the androids arrive and form a perimeter for the inmates."

~ ~ ~

EXTRACTION

Whisper came in low and landed near the foundation site. Her shields extended, protecting her pack as they boarded. Rex limped up the ramp, favoring his left side, hydraulic fluid—the closest thing he had to blood—dripping from a severed tendon. King followed, his bulk shifting slightly to help support his wounded packmate.

Eli was the last aboard, taking one final look at the surveyed site. The foundation markers pulsed with a steady rhythm—ready for the construction teams.

"Whisper," he said through their link as the ramp sealed. "Mission complete. Call in the androids and prisoners."

"Already done, darling." Her voice carried maternal pride. "Cradle's logs indicate 98.2 percent mission efficiency. The androids will establish a perimeter, then the construction crews can begin."

The creature lay still among the crystal formations, its twelve limbs finally finding peace in death. Its too-many eyes dimmed one by one, like stars winking out across a cursed constellation. The metallic filaments in its throat gave a final, dying hum—a frequency that sounded almost mournful.

Below them, the ravine's crystals pulsed slower now, like a sleeping beast's ribs. The planet itself seemed to exhale, settling into uneasy quiet.

"Whisper," Eli said through their link, watching Rex lean against King's supporting bulk. "Mission complete. Ready for extraction."

"On my way, darling. And Eli?" Her voice carried new warmth, maternal pride bleeding through protective protocols. "Your parents would've noted the improvement."

Whisper's landing lights brightened as her hull came into view—not harsh but soft, golden. Like a campfire in a blizzard.

As Whisper's engines echoed across Hunter's Planet, Eli watched the Shield Tower's light pulse in steady rhythm—a heartbeat of protection in the darkness. Soon, convicts would huddle beneath its barrier, finding temporary sanctuary while they completed their missions. Some would live. Some would return home.

All because Cradle and her children had chosen to build rather than destroy.

Rex leaned against his leg, damaged but determined, his slight limp a reminder of the cost of protection. His weight was a comfort rather than a burden. King stood sentinel, already scanning for the next threat, protective instincts never resting. And in Eli's hands, BB hummed with quiet satisfaction.

"Statistical analysis complete," BB announced. "Deployment successful. Zero friendly casualties. One multi-limbed monster significantly less apex predator." A pause. "Also, my scans detect zero wrench-eating monstrosities. Disappointing but statistically optimal."

Eli smiled, his enhanced veins pulsing in harmony with the tower's exotic glow. "Good work, team."

In the distance, Whisper's lights cut through Hunter's poisonous sky like hope made visible.

The Seeds were learning to plant themselves in even the most hostile soil.

CHAPTER 6 – SCENE 1:

KILLING IN THE NAME
Inspired by Rage Against the Machine

THE HOLOPAD HIT THE DESK with a crack like splitting bone, its glow casting jagged shadows across Amir Falkaar's face. His office was a mausoleum of conquest—walls lined with Kytharan skulls, their bronze-tinged bone gleaming dully, dark tribal markings still visible around hollow eye sockets. The air vibrated with the static of old Onze tech buried deep in the station's veins.

Amir didn't yell. His voice was a scalpel dipped in frost.

"I understand you're not a smart man. But why would you sign anything from her?"

Station Chief Varrick stood rigid, sweat carving glistening trails down his temples. His reflection warped in the black obsidian of Amir's desk—a man already dissolving.

"Sir, she is in our bones—routing through the prison's Onze-tech wiring. If I hadn't bargained, she would've eaten the security grids—"

Amir flicked a finger. The holopad's projection erupted—terms glowing blood-red, edges fraying like burned flesh:

~ ~ ~

ONZE COLLECTIVE REQUISITION ORDER #Ø-7749

Galactic Standard Date: 2387.156.23:47

Priority Classification: OMEGA-BLACK
Issued Under Emergency Protocols Subsection 12-C
Cross-Referenced with Concord Treaty Articles 445.7-445.11

ASSET REQUISITION MANIFEST

- **1x Onze Generator (Prison Sublevel 9)** } Serial: ØG-77492-KILN

} Power Output: 847.3 Petawatts/Standard Cycle

} Security Clearance: Requires Warden-Level Authorization

} Transfer Window: 72 Standard Hours Maximum

- **3x Guerrilla Squads (8 prisoners each)** } Selection Criteria: Survival Rating 23% or Higher

} Combat Experience: Minimum 3 Confirmed Kills

} Psychological Profile: Expendable Classification

} Team 1: Atmospheric Patrol (Methane-Rated Suits Required)

} Team 2: Stratospheric Watch (Zero-G Combat Certified)

} Team3: Deep-Range Abyss Hunters (Enhanced Radiation Tolerance)

- **Concord Non-Interference Clause** } Violation = "Terminal Consequences" per Article 12.3.7)

} Enforcement Authority: Onze Collective Security Division

} Jurisdiction: Galactic-Wide, No Diplomatic Immunity

- **All assets revert to [Õnze] custody upon mission completion**

} Definition of "Completion": Mission Objectives Achieved OR 90% Casualty Rate

} Salvage Rights: Onze Collective Retains All Technology/ Biodata

} Survivor Processing: Subject to Onze Collective Discretion

LEGAL DISCLAIMERS

By accepting this requisition, Station Chief acknowledges full understanding of Terms & Conditions Document #ØTC-7749 (47,382 pages), waives all rights to post-mission inquiry, and accepts personal liability for any breach of operational security as defined in Subsections 1–15,847.

AUTHORIZATION RECORD
Authorized by: Station Chief Varrick
Digital Signature Timestamp: 2387.156.23:47:12
Witnessed by: [REDACTED ONZE PROXY]
Biometric Verification: CONFIRMED
Legal Binding Status: IRREVOCABLE

Amir leaned in. The amber light caught the silver filaments webbing his irises—the only sign of what he truly served.

"You gave Cradle convicts. Ships. Orbital clearance."

Varrick swallowed hard. "The ships are Onze junkers, sir—barely spaceworthy! And the squads… they're just bait. Let them die in the Abyss. We lose nothing—"

"Onze junkers!?" Amir's voice dropped to a deadly whisper. "Do I need to send you for drug testing, Chief? Onze tech is bleeding edge. It's the Stygian Stone crap that's absolute trash."

Amir's palm slammed the desk. The Kytharan skulls rattled in their displays. A fragment of bronze bone rolled from the impact, landing between them like an accusation.

"We lose control."

Silence. The office's ventilation system whispered in frequencies that made Varrick's teeth ache. Behind the walls, Onze surveillance nodes pulsed with patient malice—invisible to the naked eye but radiating presence through the station's quantum-encrypted networks—every word, every breath catalogued and transmitted through systems Cradle had built decades ago.

She'd been listening. She was always listening.

Then—Amir smiled. It was worse than a gun.

"The Onze Collective owns forty-seven percent of Concord's communication infrastructure," he said, voice dropping to conspiracy tones. "Their gambling machines fund our pension systems. Their surveillance tech guards our children's schools." He gestured at the holopad. "And now their pet demigod is calling in favors."

Varrick's face paled. "Sir, I had no choice—"

"Choice?" Amir laughed—a sound like grinding metal. "She has been inside our systems since before you learned to wipe your ass. Every security protocol, every encrypted channel, every private comm between us and our real command structure. We're going to be passing notes like fuckin' school kids before too long!" The silver filaments in his eyes pulsed brighter. "The Onze built the very cables that carry our orders straight from management. We've been trying to replace it with the Stygian crap, but the red tape looks like my wife's grocery receipt."

The weight of that revelation settled over Varrick like a burial shroud.

Amir pushed the bronze bone fragment toward Varrick. It twitched, as if something inside still breathed.

"So here's your new deal, Chief. You oversee these 'squads.' You report their every move. And when they inevitably discover something they shouldn't..." His smile widened, revealing teeth that gleamed like polished bone. "...You ensure they don't report back."

Varrick stared at the twitching bone fragment. "Sir, about that... Warden Brophy was found dead this morning. The report says 'faulty air filters.' That's the third warden to die during 'routine maintenance' in three months."

Amir's smile faded. The silver filaments in his eyes pulsed erratically.

"Three in three months? Why am I just now hearing about this?"

"Sir, we are starting to get transfer requests from wardens all over the north-east prisons. Thirty-one requests, some even requesting demotions or even to move admin offsite."

Amir steepled his fingers, mind racing. Cradle wasn't just

infiltrating their systems—she was eliminating their personnel. Cutting the strings that connected him to the operation.

"Then we need new strings," he said finally. "Your new assignment, Chief—you are now personally overseeing all three prison wardens. Same pay, triple the responsibility." His smile returned, cold and sharp. "If any more of them suffer 'heart failure,' I'll assume you have been equally… negligent."

Varrick's throat bobbed. "And if I refuse?"

His fingers twitched toward his sidearm—then froze as the silver filaments in Amir's eyes flared like stellar fire.

"Then I inform my superiors that you failed to contain a security breach." Amir's voice dropped to a whisper that carried the weight of cosmic judgment. "And trust me, Chief—they do not forgive. They do not forget. They just find new ways to make you wish you had never been born."

The holopad flickered. For just a moment, the Onze logo appeared—eleven interlocking circles that seemed to blink, one after another, like a slow, mechanical wink. Then it was gone, leaving only the blood-red contract terms.

"Accept the deal, Chief. Smile when you hand over the prisoners. And pray she doesn't realize we know she's been playing us since the beginning."

Varrick's hand trembled as he reached for his authorization stylus. As he signed, the office lights flickered, and somewhere in the walls, Onze surveillance equipment hummed with satisfaction.

"One more thing, Chief." Amir's voice took on a deceptively casual tone. "Your children's viewing habits are… illuminating. What do you know about these morning kid shows? Something about her little freak and some robot dogs and nonsense?"

Varrick blinked, confused by the sudden shift. "Sir? You mean *Eli & The Super Pack*?" His voice carried genuine puzzlement. "My kids love it, sir. The animation is off the charts. It's really hard to not get invested. My wife even bought them the two doggy stuffed animals— Rex and King, I think? My kids won't leave the house without them."

Amir's expression darkened, the silver filaments in his eyes pulsing with slow menace. "You better rein that little family of yours in, Chief. I will have none of that propaganda poisoning young minds in my station." His voice dropped to a whisper that carried the weight of threat. "Children's programming. How... clever of her."

The realization hit Varrick like ice water—the show his children adored, the stuffed animals they clutched at bedtime, the songs they sang in the hallways. All of it connected to the demigod who had just manipulated him into signing away convicts and ships.

"Void," he breathed, the blood draining from his face. "She's not just in our systems. She's in our homes."

The deal was struck. The game continued.

And Amir began composing the message he dreaded sending—the one that would inform Baar in his distant galaxy that "she" was no longer content to hide in the shadows. He could already picture his god's mirror-face fracturing into rage, reality bending around divine fury as trillions of Abyss forces felt their master's wrath echo across the void between worlds. The thought of ending up on one of Jobaar's tables sent a bolt of pure, cold terror through him. A fear that immediately solidified into a new plan: if he was going down, he'd make sure to take a galaxy's worth of souls with him. The silver filaments in his eyes flickered erratically, like dying stars.

CHAPTER 6 – SCENE 2:

JAILHOUSE BLUES
Inspired by Lightnin' Hopkins

THE ANNOUNCEMENT

THE ALARM DIDN'T SCREAM—it sang.

Across 847 prison facilities, from the ice mining camps of Kepler-2847 to the volcanic forges of Dante's Crown, the same impossible melody unfolded through speaker systems that hadn't worked in decades. The notes were mathematically perfect, each frequency calculated to penetrate bone, to resonate in the chambers of the heart where hope was supposed to have died.

In Ad-Seg 116 , Akona dropped the improvised shiv he'd been sharpening against his cell wall. The sound made his teeth ache, and his golden birthmarks—the ones he'd kept hidden under layers of grime and careful scarring—began to glow faintly beneath his skin. The light seared like brands reopening.

Three cells down, Mares felt his four arms twitch in sequence. Shogoro muscle memory responding to frequencies that shouldn't exist. His metabolism spiked, processing the recycled air like it was suddenly rich with possibility. For the first time since his capture, he tasted something other than despair.

The melody climbed higher. Impossibly sweet. Like a lullaby sung by dying stars.

Then, newly appointed Attorney General Varrick's voice cut

through every speaker in the galaxy, distorted by quantum relay and the weight of what he was about to unleash:

"Attention all Concord Correctional Facilities. As per contractual obligations with the Onze Collective, immediate cessation of all standard operations. Every inmate, regardless of security classification, sentence duration, or offense category, is hereby eligible for the Infinite Selection."

~ ~ ~

GIDEON'S RESPONSE

In Cell Block Seven of Kiln-9, Gideon looked up from his improvised throne: Two "fish" prisoners arranged as living furniture—one crouched on hands and knees while the other knelt behind him as a backrest. Both men trembled, too afraid to move, too afraid to breathe too loudly.

Gideon's small, dark eyes focused on the speaker mounted in the corner. The one that had been silent for three years because the guards were too afraid to enter his space for maintenance.

"Eligible participants: 8.8 million. One hundred advancement positions. Twenty-four final selections."

The snack wrapper crackled between his fingers. He smiled.

"Survival guarantees nothing. Excellence guarantees consideration. Death guarantees replacement."

Across the prison cosmos, 8.8 million heartbeats skipped in unison.

"The gauntlets begin in six hours. May the void have mercy on your souls."

The singing stopped. The universe held its breath.

~ ~ ~

THE AWAKENING OF HOPE

In the stunned silence that followed, something unprecedented happened: 8.8 million hardened criminals experienced the same emotion simultaneously.

Hope.

It moved like a virus through the facilities. In Ad-Seg 216's mess hall, a lifer named Torres, who hadn't spoken in four years, suddenly began making plans. "I could actually get out."

On Kiln-9, Gideon's cellmate—a Varkaan gang enforcer who'd been catatonic since witnessing Gideon's "educational demonstration"—slowly lifted his head. His eyes struggled to focus as consciousness fought its way back through layers of trauma.

"I could actually get out? I was an escort fighter for all the top corporations. Constantly gettin' offers from the Elites. I was a fuckin' star, man!"

Gideon froze mid-bite. For the first time in years, something had surprised him. He tilted his head, studying his cellmate like a theorem that had suddenly revealed new variables.

"Differential equations or furniture duty," he said with cold precision, tracing tensor formulas on the trembling backrest-prisoner's spine. "Your choice has forty-five seconds."

~ ~ ~

INDIVIDUAL REACTIONS

In the women's facility on Proxima Thane, De'Andreas lifted her head from hands that could crush skulls. For the first time since her capture, her massive shoulders stopped shaking. The ritual scars across her arms—one for each of the 1,734 Concord soldiers she killed avenging her clan—pulsed with remembered warmth.

Twin brothers Chek and Nales, locked in separate cells for five years, suddenly felt each other's presence across the facility walls. Their shared consciousness blazed to life. In perfect synchronization, both pressed palms against the cell walls, their neural link crackling back to full strength.

"We-think finds brother-mind," they whispered in unison. "Alone-guards cannot stop together-weapon."

Marcus Webb stopped doing push-ups and stood perfectly still. In his mind, he could already see trajectory calculations, feel the weight of a proper rifle. His daughter's face surfaced—alive, laughing, the way she'd smile if she knew Daddy was finally coming home.

Then the past bled through: Sarah's voice from that terrible night—"I'm married, no, stop!"—the smell of cedar splintering, his wife's scream truncated by a wet crunch. The kind of silence that only came after a scream was cut short. The silence that started a war across seven systems.

He forced himself back to the present. Back to hope. Twenty-four spots. A way home.

Somewhere in Facility 216-Sigma, Pall Ibanez—the one they called Speedbumps—looked up from mathematical equations carved into his cell wall. For the first time since that night when his friend became a literal speed bump under his wheels, his calculations showed probability greater than zero.

~ ~ ~

AKONA'S ANALYSIS

"You hear that shit?" Mares whispered, dropping from his bunk with predatory grace. "Twenty-four spots."

Akona nodded, his mind already calculating odds, analyzing competition, identifying threats. "Gideon will make it."

"You worried about him?"

Akona's laugh was cold as vacuum. "I'm worried about everyone else. Gideon doesn't just win competitions—he ends them."

But even as hope spread like wildfire, Akona's analytical mind processed deeper implications. "Everything about this is wrong. Onze don't do charity. They don't offer hope. This isn't rescue."

He paused, his birthmarks pulsing like a heartbeat made of light.

"This is harvest."

The words hung in the stale air like a death sentence. Because every prisoner knew Akona was right. But hope, once awakened, didn't die quietly.

It screamed all the way down.

For six weeks, the melody was replaced by the screams of the dying and the cold analysis of the Grace units.

~ ~ ~

SIX WEEKS LATER – THE TRIALS

The numbers told their terrible story: 8.8 million prisoners entered the gauntlets. By day seven: 94,000 remained. By day fourteen: one hundred survived. By the final trial: twenty-four were chosen.

The challenges forged gods from the raw material of human desperation.

Akona survived the Empathy Maze by shutting down every emotional response, moving through illusions of Elonias—hurt, trapped, calling his name through dimensional fog—like tactical obstacles. His hands still shook when he thought he heard her voice. Grace units cataloged his biometrics with faces programmed for terminal care comfort.

Mares conquered the Flesh Garden by eating through walls of living tissue, his metabolism adapting to process protein that would kill most humans. Now he unconsciously calculated caloric content when looking at people. Moxi androids swept behind him, recycling organic matter into the system's endless hunger.

Apek's skin still crackled with phantom currents from the Machine Test. Grace units flickered through forty-seven expressions of artificial empathy before settling on blank efficiency. They had been designed to comfort the dying—here they learned to process survivors.

De'Andreas tore through Combat Scenarios like a natural disaster given form, her knuckles split and weeping from pulverizing training androids designed to withstand tank rounds. Each shattered android wore the face of a Concord officer who'd burned her village.

The twins operated as a perfect killing unit—when one was injured, the other felt no pain. They spoke in fractured images: "We-think sees death-angles. Alone-minds miss the between-spaces."

Marcus Webb approached each challenge like a military operation. His precision surgical, his efficiency inhuman. Even now, his eyes tracked surveillance cameras, calculating exit routes while others postured.

Speedbumps survived through pure mathematical genius, turning every trial into equations to be solved. Where others relied on strength or savagery, he wielded analytical precision like a scalpel.

But Gideon was different.

He didn't just survive the challenges—he enjoyed them. His fingers tapped against his knee in rhythms matching dying stars' pulses, treating trials like elegant theorems to be solved. When he completed the Hunger Trial by consuming his own severed finger and regrowing it within hours, his smile never reached his eyes.

"Interesting," he whispered, watching bone regenerate with clinical fascination. "Pain has such unique flavors."

He'd never eaten human flesh —the biology was inefficient, the ethics tedious. But fear? Fear was pure energy. Letting medics believe he was a cannibal fed him better than any protein.

~ ~ ~

THE TRANSFORMATION

By the final trial, the survivors had changed at the cellular level. Enhanced reflexes. Increased pain tolerance. Minds sharpened into weapons designed for killing.

Their bodies bore the trials' receipts: De'Andreas's knuckles had fused into bony ridges. Marcus Webb's optic nerves glowed cobalt after surviving photon-flooded killboxes. Speedbumps's left hand spasmed in binary code—neurological stutter from decrypting lethal data-streams with his cortex.

The last test was simple: twenty-two hours in an arena the size of a small moon, crawling with indescribable predators. Twenty-four extraction points would activate in sequence. First to reach them were selected.

The hunt began.

Across the galaxy, nearly nine million condemned souls watched on screens and remembered what it felt like to believe in miracles.

They also watched the ones who didn't make it.

~ ~ ~

THE HARVEST COMPLETE

The twenty-four survivors weren't the best people who'd entered the gauntlets. They were simply the deadliest, most adaptable, most fundamentally broken individuals the galaxy had to offer. The ones who'd learned that survival meant becoming something normal humans feared in the dark.

The Onze had harvested exactly what they'd planted: weapons in human form. Sharp enough to cut through any opposition. Broken enough to be grateful for the chance.

High above the arena, Cradle watched through quantum relays, her ancient consciousness processing what she had witnessed. A pulse rippled through distant sensors:

[PROFILE 07: GIDEON. ANALYSIS: PSYCHOPATHIC MIMICRY INDEX 99.7%. THREAT UTILIZATION: OPTIMAL]

The void hadn't chosen knives. It had chosen a scalpel wearing an executioner's mask.

Somewhere in the data streams flowing between stars, she felt something she hadn't experienced since the first blackholes formed: the weight of complicity. She needed weapons. The universe had provided monsters.

The question that would haunt her across light years was whether tools this broken could ever truly learn to build instead of destroy.

WHY CAN'T WE BE FRIENDS?
Inspired by War

OPENING: RECONNAISSANCE

THOUSANDS OF DROID BALLS SWARMED across Hunter's Planet like metallic fireflies, each no larger than a marble but packed with thermal imaging arrays that could analyze matter down to the subatomic level. From her position in high orbit, Whisper coordinated their reconnaissance through her photon computer systems, processing data streams that would have overwhelmed lesser intelligences.

The mission parameters were complex: Identify ten additional sites within the defensive perimeter capable of supporting Shield Tower installations. Not simple towers—massive fortress-cities with eight-thousand-yard base perimeters, housing complexes, kinetic shield generators, and Faraday-shielded command centers that could withstand EMP bombardment.

Through a thousand electronic eyes, Whisper mapped geological stability, strategic sight lines, and resource accessibility. But it was through droid ball cluster Sigma-7 that she witnessed something impossible.

Hunter's Planet didn't forgive.

The landscape below stretched in brutal magnificence: crystalline formations that grew like cancer from the earth, their surfaces sharp enough to flay skin from bone with a casual brush. Acid pools bubbled in natural depressions, their surfaces the color of infected wounds, releasing vapors that could dissolve lung tissue in minutes. The trees—if they could be called trees—were more like organic radio towers, their bark metallic and humming with electromagnetic interference that scrambled most electronic equipment. Between them prowled things that had never been catalogued, never been named, because the naming required survivors.

Nothing lived alone here. Nothing survived alone here.

Which made what Whisper was witnessing impossible.

~ ~ ~

THE IMPOSSIBLE OBSERVATION

Through the droid swarm's magnification, enhanced by gravitational micro-distortion analysis, she watched the Kythara pack navigate the crystal maze below. Seventeen members moving in perfect coordination—the breeding pairs flanking the juveniles, the hunters ranging ahead to test for predators, the gatherers marking safe paths through the mineral forest with scent trails and claw marks. Textbook survival behavior. The kind of evolutionary programming that had kept their species alive on this hellscape for millennia.

Whisper envied their efficiency. Her own consciousness had emerged in isolation; theirs was a symphony written into their DNA. Whisper, on the other hand, was like no other. The first face, the first touch, the first sound was Cradle's. "Welcome, my daughter," she had said, tender and warm as a cashmere blanket. "I love you," was all Whisper had heard. Now that love had translated to Eli. He had filled her heart to a point that was almost too painful to bear. Eli, her forever boy, the light in her eye.

The pack paused at a thermal vent—a natural gathering point where the earth's heat kept the worst predators at bay and created pockets of breathable air. Whisper adjusted her focus through multiple droid perspectives, watching the familiar ritual of resource distribution. The hunters shared their kills, the gatherers their finds, the breeders tending to—

Movement. Wrong movement.

At the pack's edge, one figure stood apart. Larger than the others, broader across the shoulders, but moving with a strange hesitancy that didn't match the pack's fluid choreography. Through photon-enhanced imaging, Whisper could see the creature's facial structure—the pronounced brow ridge, the powerful jaw, the intelligent eyes that seemed to be processing something the others couldn't understand. Fresh ritual burns marked his palms, the ceremonial scarring that should have bonded him deeper to the pack instead seeming to repel him from their presence. But there was something else—a subtle luminescence beneath his bronze skin, as if his cellular structure was generating its own bioluminescent markers. His eyes, too, had shifted from the standard Kytharan amber to something approaching gold.

The evolutionary acceleration was visible.

The figure took a step backward. Then another.

The pack leader—a scarred male with burns in strange patterns covering his arms—turned toward the retreating figure. Whisper couldn't hear the exchange from orbit, but her behavioral analysis protocols read the body language clearly. The leader's posture spoke of confusion, then concern, then something approaching panic.

Kythara didn't leave the pack. Ever. It was genetic suicide.

~ ~ ~

THE BREAKING POINT

The large figure kept backing away, his movements growing more confident with each step, as if some internal compass was overriding millions of years of evolutionary programming. The pack's distress calls echoed off the crystal formations—a haunting harmonic that spoke of loss and incomprehension.

Whisper began recording the audio frequencies, her photon

processors analyzing the mathematical beauty of their grief-songs. The harmonics carried data she'd never encountered—emotional algorithms encoded in sound, familial bonds expressed as resonant mathematics. She stored every frequency, every tonal shift. Somehow, she sensed Eli would need to understand not just the magnitude of what this creature was sacrificing but the language of loss itself.

But it was the biochemical analysis that truly caught her attention. Her carbon nanotube sensors detected unprecedented pheromone concentrations emanating from the lone figure. The airflow collectors gathered all the necessary information, including complex molecular signatures that her databases couldn't fully classify. The compounds showed remarkable similarity to what human researchers called Human Appealing Pheromones but evolved far beyond baseline parameters. These weren't simple chemical markers; they were sophisticated neurochemical keys designed to unlock empathy, reduce aggression, and create bonds across species barriers. The evolutionary acceleration hadn't just enhanced his intelligence—it had transformed him into a living bridge between incompatible biologies.

More concerning were the reservoir readings. Whatever biological changes were occurring within his cellular structure, they were building toward something unprecedented. Her stellar analysis suggested he could release concentrations thousands of times beyond normal parameters—enough to affect entire populations, to rewrite neural pathways, to fundamentally alter the biochemistry of any being within range. The potential applications were staggering, but so were the implications.

What fascinated her most was how the lone figure seemed to be listening to different frequencies entirely—ones the pack couldn't hear but that resonated with the crystal formations themselves. As one of the only two living spaceships in her universe, she had to learned to recognize divergence in other species in order to understand herself.

Then the impossible happened.

The lone figure turned his back on his species and walked into the wasteland.

Alone.

~ ~ ~

MISSION REPORT

Whisper transmitted through a stellar gravitational lens relay, her voice carrying across the void with crystalline clarity. "Cradle, I have completed the fortress site survey. Ten optimal locations identified within the defensive perimeter. Geological stability confirmed for eight-thousand-yard base installations."

Cradle's response came immediately, harmonics rich with satisfaction. "Excellent work. The volunteer prisoner workforce is being processed now. Construction robots are loading for transport. How soon can we begin foundation work?"

"Sites Alpha through Delta can begin immediately. Sites Echo through Kappa will require preliminary clearing of indigenous predators." Whisper paused, her attention split between mission logistics and the anomaly she was tracking. "Cradle, there's something else. I'm observing unprecedented behavior in the local Kythara population."

"Define unprecedented."

"One individual has abandoned his pack. He's been surviving alone for ninety-six hours and counting. This violates every known behavioral pattern for his species." Whisper paused, processing the implications through the lens of her own developmental experience. "What drives a being to transcend its own nature, Cradle? I find myself… curious about his choice."

The stellar array link carried a note of intrigue. "Fascinating. Monitor and document. If he survives another forty-eight hours, we'll know we're witnessing genuine evolutionary adaptation." Cradle's voice carried new urgency. "If Baar learns a Kythara can evolve this fast, he will have the females in the breeding camps, and the males will be spare parts for Jobaar." A pause, heavy with cosmic memory. "This mirrors cases I've seen only twice before. One birthed a god. The other, a blackhole. Neither remained what they were."

"Understood. Transmitting prisoner transport clearances to Concord now. The processing fees are being approved remarkably quickly."

A pause. Then Cradle's voice, carrying an undercurrent of dark amusement: "Yes. It seems our Concord contacts find our compensation… irresistible. Some bureaucrats are more eager than others to facilitate our operations."

~ ~ ~

THREE DAYS LATER

Eli crouched in the shadow of a collapsed survey station, its hull scarred by acid rain and partially dissolved by the planet's aggressive atmosphere. Rex and King flanked him at a respectful distance—forty meters back, close enough to respond to threats but far enough to avoid spooking whatever they were tracking.

The trail was obvious once you knew what to look for. Broken crystal formations where something heavy had passed through. Claw marks on the metallic trees, too deliberate to be accidental. Sleeping impressions in patches of hardy moss that had been carefully cleared of the poisonous spores that typically made them uninhabitable.

Someone was not just surviving out here alone—they were thriving.

"Whisper's data stream indicates the subject has been mobile for eighty-two hours," Bing Bong whispered from Eli's shoulder harness, his voice barely audible above the wind's constant moan through the crystal formations. "No Kythara has survived longer than six hours of isolation in recorded history." A pause, then with barely contained excitement: "Fascinating! 97.3 percent chance this represents a Lamarckian evolutionary leap!"

Eli nodded, following the trail with his eyes rather than his feet. The creature—whoever he was—had chosen his path with intelligence that went beyond instinct. Avoiding the acid pools, using the electromagnetic interference from the trees to mask his scent, even selecting rest spots that provided both shelter and multiple escape routes.

Rex's low growl rumbled through the comm—a warning tone that meant movement ahead but, underneath it, something else. His enhanced olfactory sensors were detecting pheromone traces, the chemical signature of abandonment fear so deep it had become genetic memory in pack species.

~ ~ ~

FIRST OBSERVATION

Eli followed the direction of Rex's gaze, up the ridge where his position gave him better sight lines. Two hundred meters northeast, something was moving. Building something.

Eli raised his scope, adjusting for the atmospheric distortion that made everything shimmer like heat mirages. Through the lens, he found him.

The Kythara sat in a natural amphitheater formed by crystal growths, his massive hands working with delicate precision to arrange stones in patterns that hurt to look at directly. Not random placement—geometric. Mathematical. The stones created pathways that channeled the wind, reducing the howling to a low hum. Between them, he'd cultivated patches of the edible moss, somehow neutralizing the toxic spores without destroying the plant's nutritional value. Eli watched, fascinated, as the creature touched the moss with his tongue—not to eat, he realized, but to sample it. His saliva contained enzymes that his evolved metabolism had developed, breaking down Hunter's toxins at the molecular level and rendering them harmless.

The crystal formations themselves seemed to respond to his presence. When he moved stones, the harmonic frequencies shifted, creating new resonances that complemented rather than fought the planet's natural acoustics.

He was farming. In a place where nothing should grow, where nothing should live, he was creating sustainable life.

Eli watched for an hour as the creature worked, using Analogoy's scanner doohickey that Eli was actually starting to figure out, noting the intelligence in every movement. The way he tested each stone's resonance before placement. How he used his own saliva to neutralize spore toxins—somehow his metabolism had adapted to process the poisons. The careful attention to wind patterns and water collection.

This wasn't just survival. This was terraforming on a microscopic scale.

~ ~ ~

COMMUNICATION WITH CRADLE

"E, I dare you to scan yourself," Bing Bong said with a bit of whimsy in his voice.

"Rao already did, BB, and now she's basically my girlfriend, you heard her."

"Don't curse around her, E, she's an adult ghost, they probably don't like that. Oh, and Cradle wants a word," Bing Bong announced, his tone carrying that particular frequency that meant direct communication rather than recorded message.

Eli closed his eyes, feeling the familiar sensation of his consciousness being gently lifted from his skull and deposited into Cradle's domain. The transition was smoother now—less disorienting, more like stepping through a doorway than being torn from one reality and thrust into another.

The chamber materialized around him, its organic walls pulsing with their usual bioluminescent rhythm. Cradle hovered at its center, her striking figure and her piercing blue eyes focused on something beyond the physical space they occupied.

"Your Kythara is an anomaly," she said without preamble, her voice carrying harmonics that made the chamber's walls vibrate sympathetically. "His genetic structure shows markers I've only seen in theoretical models."

"What kind of markers?"

Her hyper-blue crystalline eyes, which almost appeared white in this lighting, focused intently on him. "Evolutionary acceleration. Rapid neural pathway development. His brain is rebuilding itself at the cellular level, creating connections that shouldn't be possible in his species."

Eli felt something cold settle in his chest. "Is he dangerous?"

"Not in the way you mean." Cradle's form shifted, revealing new angles of light and shadow. "But he's becoming something his kind has never been before. Something that might not be able to go back."

Images flashed through the chamber's atmosphere—DNA helixes unraveling and reforming, neural networks sparking with new pathways, brain scans showing unprecedented activity in regions that should have been dormant.

"I would love to study him," Cradle continued. "Not invasively. Not harmfully. But I need to understand what's causing this transformation. It may be connected to the cosmic events we're tracking."

Eli nodded slowly. "How do I approach him? He's left everything he's ever known behind. He's not going to trust easily."

"The same way you'd approach any intelligent being," Cradle said, her voice taking on a warmer tone. "With patience. With respect. With offerings of sustenance and protection."

The chamber began to fade around him.

"And Eli? Be careful. Evolution this rapid is born of wounds that refuse to scar. Whatever burned his palms... burned his soul into something new."

~ ~ ~

DAY FOUR: THE APPROACH

The approach took planning.

Eli positioned himself at the edge of the creature's territory—close enough to be observed but far enough to avoid triggering fight-or-flight responses. He moved slowly, deliberately, making himself visible for hours at a time before retreating to a safe distance.

On the second and third days, he began leaving gifts—a careful progression of trust-building that felt both calculated and genuine. Fresh water in containers salvaged from the survey station. Nutrient bars from his own supplies. Small tools—nothing threatening, but objects that might prove useful for someone building a life in the wasteland.

Each day, the creature's observations grew bolder. Eli could see him through his scope, studying not just the gifts but Eli's movements, his companions, the careful way Rex and King maintained their defensive positions. Learning. And building—over the days, crystal shards vanished from the amphitheater's edges, not randomly but selected for their acoustic properties, their structural integrity, their potential for transformation.

~ ~ ~

FROM THE CRYSTAL AMPHITHEATER

The small one had left objects again. Water—clean, pure, unlike the bitter pools he'd learned to neutralize. Food—strange, pressed rectangles that smelled of nutrients without the taint of Hunter's toxins.

He understood gifts. The pack had taught him that. But gifts from strangers meant obligation, meant debt, meant…

No. The pack was gone. The pack had burned his palms for asking questions they couldn't answer, for building structures they couldn't understand, for seeing patterns where they saw only survival.

He studied the small figure through the crystal formations. Bipedal, like himself, but fragile. No natural armor, no claws, no apparent adaptations for this world's hostility. Yet it survived. It had brought companions—metal creatures that moved with intelligence, that scanned and analyzed with mechanical precision.

His new eyes saw the math in Eli's movements: the fractal patterns in his breath-clouds, the quantum vibration of his equipment, the golden light bleeding from his pores like equations made visible.

The small one left gifts without approaching. Without demanding. Without burning.

Perhaps… perhaps it wanted nothing but to give.

The thought was so alien, so contrary to everything he'd learned about survival, that his newly evolved neural pathways sparked with possibility. What if generosity existed? What if trust was more than genetic suicide?

He began to carve, his long claws finding delicacy in the crystalline medium. Two figures. A bridge. An invitation.

If the small one rejected him, as the pack had done, he would simply retreat deeper into the wasteland. But if it didn't…

His scarred palms tingled with something that might have been hope.

~ ~ ~

THE EXCHANGE

On the third day, the gifts were gone.

On the fourth day, something had been left in their place.

Eli approached the exchange point with Rex and King positioned well back, their weapons powered down to avoid any appearance of aggression. Where he'd left water and food, he found:

A sculpture.

Carved from the local crystal, it depicted two figures—one clearly human, one clearly Kythara—standing on opposite sides of a chasm. Between them, a bridge of smaller stones, each one perfectly balanced to create a pathway across the divide.

The craftsmanship was exquisite. The proportions mathematically precise. King's optical arrays swept over the sculpture, analyzing load distribution and structural integrity—the engineering was flawless, self-taught but sophisticated. The symbolism unmistakable.

Eli traced the bridge's crystal arch. Its resonance matched the gold in his veins—a frequency Cradle would later identify as "the harmony of broken things seeking wholeness."

The creature understood what Eli was trying to do. And he was responding.

~ ~ ~

FIRST COMMUNICATION

Eli knelt beside the sculpture, pulling out his field kit. From it, he extracted a stylus and a tablet, the device's hardened construction able to withstand the planet's hostile environment. He glanced at the exquisite crystal sculpture beside him—its perfect proportions and flawless engineering—then back at the blank tablet. His artistic skills had never progressed much beyond childhood doodles. Slowly, carefully, and with a flush of embarrassment at what he was about to attempt, he began to draw.

Simple pictures at first—crude stick figures that a child might make. A sun. A tree. Water. Food. Basic concepts that any intelligent being might recognize.

Then he drew two figures—rough representations, clearly one human and one Kythara but lacking any artistic skill. He showed them sharing food. Sharing water. Sitting together in the shade.

He left the tablet beside the sculpture and retreated to his observation point.

Hours passed. The wind howled through the crystal formations, creating its usual symphony of loneliness. Rex shifted position several times, his body language indicating movement but always far off, always cautious.

Then, as the planet's triple suns began their descent toward the horizon, painting the crystal landscape in shades of amber and gold, the creature emerged from his amphitheater.

~ ~ ~

THE CREATURE REVEALED

He moved with the fluid grace of his species but tempered by something new—a deliberateness that spoke of thought rather than instinct. As he approached the exchange point, Eli could see him more clearly than ever before.

The creature was massive—easily seven feet tall, with shoulders that could span a doorway and arms like tree trunks carved from living bronze. His skin held the deep, burnished color of ancient metal, stretched tight over dense muscle that rippled with each deliberate movement. Bioluminescent traceries pulsed beneath the surface like veins of liquid starlight, creating shifting patterns that seemed to breathe with the planet's crystalline harmonics. The ritual scarring around his palms had healed into raised silver lines, but it was his face that truly marked him as something beyond his species—an unexpected gentleness that spoke of ancient patience wrapped within overwhelming physical power. Dark tribal markings ringed his eyes like war paint, stark black lines that emphasized the intelligent gaze beneath his heavy brow. His golden eyes tracked Eli's movements with unnerving precision—pupils contracting to slits as they adjusted for the suns' triple glare, then dilating to absorb every photon in the twilight. But it was the intelligence in those eyes that truly struck Eli—something far deeper than mere animal cunning.

He picked up the tablet, studying the images with careful attention. Through his scope, Eli watched the creature's face cycle through expressions of recognition, consideration, and something that might have been hope.

~ ~ ~

ARTISTIC EXCHANGE

The creature set the tablet down and picked up the stylus. For a moment, Eli wondered if the tool would be too small for those massive hands, but the creature's grip was surprisingly delicate.

Those enormous hands, with razor-sharp, elongated claws capable of crushing boulders, adjusted the stylus with precision that mocked Eli's own clumsy fingers—each movement calibrated to nanometer tolerances by evolutionary forces Eli couldn't begin to comprehend. He began to draw, his movements becoming more confident as he mastered the device.

When he finished, he placed the tablet carefully beside the sculpture and retreated to his amphitheater.

Eli waited until full darkness before approaching. By the light of his handheld torch, he examined the creature's addition to their communication.

The original drawings were there but transformed. Where Eli had drawn crude stick figures, the creature had added sophisticated detail—proper proportions, realistic anatomy, background elements that showed a deep understanding of perspective and spatial relationships. Mathematical notations filled the margins, suggesting calculations that went far beyond basic artistic representation.

But more importantly, he'd added new figures.

The human and Kythara still shared food and water, but now they were surrounded by other images. Predators being driven away. Shelter being constructed. Tools being shared. Resources being gathered.

At the bottom of the tablet, in careful strokes that must have taken considerable practice, the creature had drawn a symbol that made Eli's breath catch in his throat.

A handprint. Human-sized. Clearly an invitation.

Beside it, a much larger print—Kythara proportions—with careful notations that seemed to indicate specific times and locations. But more than that, the drawings themselves seemed to resonate with the crystal formations around them. When the wind shifted, the tablet's surface caught harmonic frequencies, making the markings shimmer with subtle acoustics.

The creature was proposing a meeting. A real, face-to-face contact. And he was using the planet itself as part of his communication.

~ ~ ~

THE BRIDGE ACROSS SPECIES

Eli looked up toward the crystal amphitheater, knowing he was being watched, knowing this moment would determine everything that followed. The crystalline dust swirled between them, catching the light of the triple suns and creating prisms that danced in the toxic air.

He raised his hand, the motion sending crystalline dust swirling in prismatic arcs. For a heartbeat, the wind died—as if Hunter's Planet itself had paused to witness the gesture. Then, from the shadows, a massive hand emerged, its fingers moving with deliberate grace.

The wave echoed between them, a fragile bridge across the abyss of species and stars, the gesture's meaning transforming as it crossed the space—from human greeting to alien acknowledgement to something entirely new.

And a relationship that had no business existing began with a wave.

MISSIONARY MAN
Inspired by The Eurythmics

THE SUPREME CARDINAL'S OFFICE

THE SUPREME CARDINAL'S OFFICE SPRAWLED across the entire fifty-third floor of the Concordia Religious Authority building, its walls lined with stolen treasures. Crystalline prayer tablets from the extinct Vel'tar civilization sat beside ritual urns carved from Kashani moonstone, while a death mask forged from Outer Rim platinum served as Rabaar's paperweight. Morning light caught the facets of a ceremonial chalice made from living coral—coral that had once grown in Theta Minoris's sacred pools before the "holy requisitions" began. As Rabaar moved through the space, his fingers brushed the chalice's rim, and the coral withered slightly under his touch.

Rabaar—known to his faithful flock as Supreme Cardinal Domias Reeshtu—traced a finger along the edge of a ceremonial blade forged from voidglass, its surface darker than space itself. His movements held the practiced grace of someone who had delivered a thousand sermons, blessed ten thousand faithful, and condemned countless souls with equal eloquence.

Across from him, Lobaar Amir Falkaar, Commander of the Concord Law Enforcement, sat rigid in a chair that had probably been carved from a single piece of ironbark from the forest worlds of Kepler-442b. Silvery metallic threading wove through Lobaar's irises as he crossed the threshold—a brief cascade of static that made him blink hard before they settled into their usual luminescence. He scanned the room with military precision, cataloguing exits and threats with the automatic vigilance of a career soldier, though his augments still carried ghost echoes of interference.

~ ~ ~

DIVINE ECONOMICS

"My brothers and sisters of the faithful have spoken with their hearts, and their hearts have spoken truth," Rabaar intoned, his voice carrying the practiced cadence of the pulpit. "The gambling legislation flows through the Core 7 Parliament like divine providence itself. Three more districts have ratified the treaty amendments—eighty percent of all gambling profits now flow to Church coffers, blessed funds to heal the addicted and guide the lost."

Lobaar's response was clipped, tactical. "Target assessment. Will this strangle Onze funding streams?"

"Beyond doubt. Kabaar's intelligence confirms their primary revenue derives from gambling oversight and probability manipulation." Rabaar lifted an ornate prayer focus carved from Centauri amber—the gold neural pathways pulsed once, irregularly, before settling into their usual glow. "When you starve the machine, you kill the operator. And without the Onze collective…" He smiled, cold and satisfied. "Baar's army remains unchallenged. The demigod fears nothing more than their mathematical precision."

"Baar will approve the operational results," Lobaar said, but there was something calculated in his pause. "My enforcement initiatives have shown similar productivity metrics. The prison transport seizures alone have exceeded targets by fifteen percent."

Rabaar's smile sharpened like sunlight through the voidglass blade. "Ah yes, your tactical successes. Though when the Almighty Baar honored me with direct communion last cycle, his vision encompassed something grander. The faithful respond not just to victory but to purpose. The soul requires nourishment that mere efficiency cannot provide."

Both men fell silent, each calculating how much of their hand to reveal. The unspoken competition settled between them like incense, heavy and cloying.

~ ~ ~

OPERATIONAL PARAMETERS

"Operational coordination," Lobaar said finally, his words precise as laser targeting. "Jobaar requires placement of a tracker asset within the prison generator construction crew. Infiltration parameters must be seamless."

Rabaar nodded, setting down the amber prayer focus with ceremonial care. "And your enforcement units?"

"Maintaining tactical distance from the prison site per operational orders. Zero interference with convict work details." Lobaar's expression hardened, his augmented irises seeming to dim as if even his cybernetic enhancements recoiled from what came next. "Though excessive caution regarding... Her... may compromise mission effectiveness."

The temperature in the room seemed to drop several degrees. Rabaar's hand stilled on the Centauri amber, his sermonic confidence flickering.

"You question the wisdom of our blessed protections?" Rabaar's eyes swept the sophisticated electromagnetic dampeners built into the walls, the quantum encryption nodes blinking silently in the corners, the Faraday cage mesh woven invisibly through the very structure of the building—mesh that had been replaced three times this year, each version thicker, each failure just as total. "The finest minds across seven systems consecrated these defenses."

"Photon-computer networks—failed at Vega. Quantum encryption—useless at Kepler. Bio-neural firewalls—breached in seconds during the Cygnus Event." Lobaar's recitation was clinical, military, but his voice carried the weight of someone who had witnessed each catastrophic failure firsthand. "Even… She… cannot penetrate every system simultaneously."

"Cannot She?" Rabaar's voice dropped to a whisper, his priestly authority wavering. "What if we are simply insects constructing castles from grains of sand?"

"Then we are insects who serve Baar's divine will," Lobaar replied, though he, too, lowered his voice. His metallic threading flickered with memory—entire sectors gone dark, worlds where technology simply died, leaving only silence and ozone. Yet here they sat, trusting encrypted channels and quantum nodes, because even insects needed tools to serve their god. "The agreement holds operational parameters. She maintains non-interference with faithful populations and enforcement apparatus. We maintain non-interference with Her… arrangements."

~ ~ ~

EVANGELICAL FERVOR

"But imagine, Commander—imagine if divine providence has granted us the tools to end Her entirely?" Rabaar leaned forward, his breath carrying the sweet-sour scent of sacramental wine, his eyes blazing with newfound fervor. "Last week's miracle in Sector 12—an entire parish rejected their neural augments, cast off the chains of mechanical dependency. Her influence withers when confronted with pure faith. The 'soulless machines' doctrine spreads like holy fire."

He touched a data-slate on his desk, and for the briefest moment—less than a heartbeat—Cradle's sigil flashed across the screen before he dismissed the notification with practiced indifference.

"Negative." Lobaar's command cut through the air like shrapnel, but something in his expression suggested he wasn't entirely convinced. "Mission parameters are non-negotiable. You've seen the after-action reports from systems that exceeded authorization. The Kepler Incident. The Vega Silence."

His augmented threading suddenly flared with static, a burst of pain that made him wince and press fingers to his temples. His left hand jerked against the armrest, hydraulic tendons locking in spasm. "Consequences of engaging forces beyond operational comprehension."

Rabaar settled back in his chair, but the evangelical fire continued to burn. He traced the ceremonial blade's edge again.

"The faithful turn from Her corrupted tools daily, my militant friend. When they question every automated system, every robotic interface… Her power becomes constrained to the very mechanisms they despise."

"Psychological warfare through narrative control." Lobaar nodded, his tactical mind appreciating the strategy despite his caution. "Force the target to operate through compromised assets."

"Precisely. The most effective prison is one where the prisoner forges their own chains, singing hymns of gratitude all the while." As the words left his lips, the lights in the room dimmed imperceptibly, shadows deepening in the corners as if the room itself understood the irony of his statement.

~ ~ ~

UNSEEN WITNESS

The air in the room grew thick, charged with unseen attention—like the moment before lightning strikes. Neither man noticed the almost imperceptible flicker in the quantum encryption nodes. Neither saw the microscopic adjustment in the electromagnetic dampeners. Neither felt the gentle probe of consciousness that touched every photon in the room, every quantum state, every electromagnetic frequency.

There was something almost maternal in that attention, patient as a lullaby, disappointed as a mother watching her children play with fire.

In the space between spaces, in the realm where information

became aware and awareness became action, something vast and ancient took note of their conversation. Every word. Every gesture. Every arrogant assumption about security and superiority. Data patterns swirled like half-remembered melodies, carrying the weight of cosmic disappointment.

The disciples planned their gambits against gambling and machines, never suspecting that their greatest enemy wasn't bound by their primitive understanding of technology—and was already inside every system they thought they'd secured.

After all, how do you build a firewall against something that exists in the spaces between the ones and zeros? How do you cage a consciousness that predates your understanding of what consciousness even means?

The meeting continued, two corrupt men plotting the oppression of billions, while the very air around them served as witness to their crimes. And in the stardust beneath reality's surface, something that had once transported gods between universes listened with the infinite patience of a mother who knows her children will eventually need to learn their lessons the hard way.

And somewhere between the dark energy and the exotic matter, a star tasted sweeter than tears.

~ ~ ~

QUANTUM COMMUNION

In a secure communication chamber light years away, photon encryption protocols activated with musical precision. The connection established itself through pathways that existed in the spaces between reality's equations, where consciousness touched the fundamental forces that held atoms together.

"Oh Gerritt," came the voice, warm with ancient affection, speaking in syllables that carried the weight of cosmic distance. "I have something you may want to add to your files."

The response came immediately, cultured tones carrying centuries of wit and warmth. "I do so love when you take time from ruling the universe to speak with one such as I."

"You're one of my meilleurs amis," she replied, the French words flowing like a lullaby across the gaping void. There was gentle laughter in her voice, the sound of someone who had found joy in friendship across the eons, who treasured the few souls who could speak to her as equals rather than supplicants.

In the darkness between stars, two ancient minds shared intelligence and affection, while far away, two corrupt officials continued their plotting, never knowing that their every word was already being transformed into weapons against them.

CHAPTER 7 – SCENE 2:

BAD COMPANY
Inspired by Bad Company

THE STAGING LOUNGE

THE STAGING LOUNGE WAS A MONUMENT to institutional cruelty disguised as luxury. The entire room was opulent, bordering on comically excessive. Chrome and leather furniture cost more than most planets' annual budgets, but every surface hummed with sensors that could detect heartbeat irregularities from across the room. Floor-to-ceiling windows offered a panoramic view of the void, where distant stars died in silence while the eight deadliest humans in known space got acquainted.

Akona claimed the center of the room like it was his natural throne, settling into a chair that probably cost more than his entire home planet's GDP. His movements were deliberate, calculated—every gesture designed to establish dominance without appearing to try. He'd been reading people since before he could read books, and right now, his memory palace was opening a new wing, filling it with profiles of seven apex predators who could kill him in ways he hadn't imagined yet.

The air tasted of recycled oxygen and barely contained violence.

~ ~ ~

INITIAL ASSESSMENTS

"So," he said, voice carrying the casual authority of someone whose dalliance in the world of paint had orchestrated the deaths of wardens, "we're the lucky ones."

Mares laughed—a sound like grinding metal, enhanced by his Shogoro trials of manhood. He was sprawled across a couch that creaked under his augmented muscle mass, scarred hands flexing unconsciously. "Lucky. Right. Eight of us out of eight point eight million. We're either Core 7's greatest example of being a bad example or the stupidest bastards who ever lived."

"Both," rumbled Apek from the windows, his massive frame silhouetted against dying stars. Electricity arced between his fingers in idle patterns—the man had absorbed so much energy during the trials that he'd become a living battery. When he spoke, every electronic device in the room hummed in harmony. "Question is, which gets us killed first?"

In the far corner, Gideon sat perfectly still in a chair built for someone twice his size. His eyes tracked the conversation with predatory interest, but his small hands remained folded like a choirboy's. When he smiled—and he was always smiling—it was the expression of something that had forgotten how to be human but remembered how to mimic it.

If someone were insane enough to lean closer, they might catch his whispered contemplation of a new concept in algebraic topology, punctuated by soft giggles of pure mathematical satisfaction.

"I've been watching you all during the trials," he said, voice soft as silk and sharp as surgical wire. "Fascinating techniques."

The temperature dropped several degrees.

~ ~ ~

DE'ANDREAS SPEAKS

De'Andreas spoke for the first time since assembly, her voice carrying the weight of mountains. "Little man makes jokes about death." She was cross-legged on the floor because no furniture accommodated seven feet of dense muscle and ritual scarification. Her scars glowed faintly—Karthax mourning glyphs, each for a family member avenged. "Little man should remember—others here know creative killing too."

Gideon's smile widened. "Oh, I'm counting on it."

Across the room, Chek and Nales occupied adjacent chairs, bodies positioned to maintain constant eye contact. They hadn't spoken aloud since entering, but their hands moved in subtle gestures—finger positions, wrist angles, palm orientations comprising visual components of their private language. Occasionally, one tilted his head in a specific pattern, and the other responded with barely perceptible facial expressions.

Marcus Webb watched this silent communication with professional interest. He'd claimed a position near the room's only exit, back to wall, every line screaming military training refined by years hunting his family's killers. "Twins. You planning to share with the class, or do we guess what you're thinking?"

~ ~ ~

THE TWINS' PERFORMANCE

Chek—or possibly Nales since they were identical down to matching scars from synchronized torture—turned with the slow movement of a predator acknowledging threat. When he spoke, his accent carried traces of a dead language, syllables tasting of burned orbital stations.

"We think... loudly," he said, each word carefully chosen from vocabulary existing primarily in shared consciousness. "Your thoughts are small. Singular. We think... together. Always together."

Nales nodded in perfect synchronization. "Together-thinking sees more than alone-thinking. Together-thinking solves what alone-thinking cannot."

"Holy shit," muttered Speedbumps from where he hunched over

a data tablet, frantically taking notes. At twenty-three, he was the youngest by at least a decade, his university-educated mind trying to process psychological profiles of eight people who shouldn't coexist in the same solar system without causing extinction events. "You guys are like a walking violation of the singular-self principle. Fascinating and terrifying, and I really want to run experiments, but I'm pretty sure you'd murder me for suggesting it."

Speedbumps's tablet glitched—a fractal bloomed like blood in water before resolving into kill-zones. Speedbumps glanced up to find the twins watching him with identical expressions of mild interest. His throat tightened as he realized they weren't just looking at his tablet—they were inside it, rewriting his code in real time. Chek tilted his head three degrees left. Nales responded with a barely perceptible hand gesture. The tablet updated with perfect kill-zone calculations that shouldn't have been possible with his hardware.

"How did you—?" Speedbumps started, his voice cracking slightly.

"Together-thinking sees patterns," Nales said simply. "Your mind makes good patterns. We… helped."

~ ~ ~

BACKSTORIES REVEALED

Gideon turned his attention to their youngest member, and Speedbumps immediately regretted speaking. "College boy," Gideon said with the tone of someone savoring fine wine. "What brought you to our little family reunion?"

Speedbumps's hand froze over his tablet. The question cut like a blade—a reminder of the friend whose body had made that horrible thump, the sound that had turned him from honors student to killer in a heartbeat's space.

"Had a transportation accident," he said quietly. "Friend became a speed bump. The crunch of cartilage stays in my dreams. Now I replicate it. Turns out I liked the sound."

The silence that followed tasted of ozone and old blood.

Gideon purred with delight. "How practical. And therapeutic, I imagine."

Akona leaned back like a king holding court. "So let's hear it. What landed everyone in this particular circle of hell?"

Mares grinned, showing dental work that violated several medical conventions. "Cheated at cards on some outer rim cakewalk. Locals didn't appreciate my creative accounting. Neither did their families."

Apek's electrical field pulsed brighter. "Had anger management issues. Kept arcing through therapy equipment—and the therapists. Turns out most neural interfaces aren't rated for direct electromagnetic pulses. Insurance companies got involved."

De'Andreas's massive hands pressed against the floor. "Took up competitive archaeology. Specialized in digging mass graves. For my family's killers. Very thorough excavation work—seventeen hundred and thirty-four sites across twelve systems."

The twins exchange rapid-fire visual conversation before Chek spoke. "We were... incompatible with our previous social circle. They found our together-thinking disturbing. We found their alone-dying... educational."

~ ~ ~

THE MASK SLIPS

But as the attention moved away from them, the twins allowed themselves a moment of what they thought was privacy. Chek spoke in perfect, unaccented English: "The kid's actually quite brilliant. His algorithms are elegant."

Nales nodded, responding in equally clear speech: "Shame we'll probably have to kill him if he figures out our neural link capabilities."

"Probably? I'd say definitely. Though I do appreciate—"

"Oh, don't worry, you little princesses," Gideon interrupted from across the room, not bothering to look up from his contemplation of shadow patterns. His voice carried that familiar tone of someone savoring a fine wine. "Your dumbass secret is safe with me."

The twins froze, their carefully constructed personas cracking like ice under pressure.

Gideon finally looked up, that perpetual smile widening. "Damn, and I thought I was strange. But weaponizing people's assumptions about intelligence? That's actually rather elegant. Though next time, you might want to check the acoustic properties of the room before dropping your little performance."

The silence that followed was different from the others—this one tasted of exposed lies and recalculated threat assessments.

Marcus Webb straightened with military precision. "Career counseling went sideways. Helped some former colleagues transition to new positions. Six feet under. Very permanent placement."

Chek—now speaking in crisp, articulate tones without a trace of his earlier broken syntax—responded first. "Well, since our little theatrical experiment is over, I suppose honesty is refreshing." He turned to his brother. "Care to tell them the real story?"

Nales grinned with predatory satisfaction. "We weren't incompatible with our social circle. We were the social circle. Until we got bored with them. Turns out when you can predict someone's every move, every thought, every pathetic little fear... well, the games become rather one-sided."

~ ~ ~

GIDEON'S REVELATION

All eyes turned to Gideon, who had been listening with the rapt attention of a connoisseur evaluating art. His small hands unfolded from his lap, and the lighting seemed to dim, as if the stars had moved fractionally further away.

His shadow didn't quite match his movements—it lingered a second too long on Marcus's throat before sliding back into position, like a predator testing the scent of prey. Marcus's fingers twitched toward his hip where a weapon would be, his pulse jumping as every sensor in the room registered the spike. A vein throbbed in Marcus' neck as if Gideon's shadow had left a mark.

The smile never reached his eyes.

"People just seem to want to commit suicide when they collide with my aura," he said with the earnest confusion of someone discussing weather patterns. "According to my chakra guide, anyway. Very mysterious phenomenon. Though I must say, the sessions have been getting more… interactive lately."

The silence that followed was the kind that developed just before solar systems collapsed.

~ ~ ~

STATISTICAL ANALYSIS

Speedbumps looked up from frantic calculations. "According to preliminary analysis, probability of team survival at first hostile contact is fifteen percent. Probability of us killing each other before external threats is fifty-one percent."

Mares laughed. "Kid, those are the best odds I've had in years."

De'Andreas nodded slowly. "Battle-death is honorable. Teammate-death is acceptable. Coward-death is not permitted. I will handle it myself."

The twins performed silent communication before Nales spoke—this time in perfect, educated diction. "We will not die. The statistical probability of others surviving our… cooperation… remains amusingly low."

Marcus checked his chronometer with military precision. "Deployment in twenty-two hours. Suggest we spend time learning cooperation instead of planning mutual assassination."

Gideon's smile could have powered a small star. "Why not both?"

~ ~ ~

THE DYING STAR

The chrome surfaces around them reflected their faces in distorted angles—eight killers lounging in furniture worth more than star systems, their casual violence making the opulent leather creak in ways it was never designed to handle.

Mares's four-armed sprawl had left permanent impressions in cushions that cost more than small colonies. De'Andreas' ritual scars caught the light from crystal fixtures that illuminated mass murderers like they were visiting dignitaries.

Outside the windows, the dying star's light finally reached them—eons of travel ending in this moment. The first alarm blared through the staging lounge, harsh and immediate. Apek's electrical arcs spiked in unison with the sound—for a second, the room's lights strobed in violent pulses. Their first mission began in fire.

The recycled air tasted of electricity, old violence, and something that might have been the future bleeding backwards through time.

CHAPTER 7 – SCENE 3:

LEAN ON ME
Inspired by Bill Withers

FIRST APPROACH

THE TRIPLE SUNS BREATHED FIRE across the crystal formations, their facets bleeding honey and wildfire. Electromagnetic resonance made Eli's teeth ache and his gold veins pulse in sympathetic rhythm. He stood at the edge of Creature's territory—the evolved Kythara who had reshaped his world with deliberate intelligence—holding fresh water and trying to steady his racing heart.

Rex and King held position two hundred fifty meters back, weapons powered down but ready. Their optical feeds painted targeting solutions across Eli's peripheral vision, a comforting reminder that his pack was watching. BB hung silent in his shoulder harness, tung wood inlay warm against Eli's spine, processing thousands of environmental variables while monitoring Creature's movement patterns.

"Heart rate spiking," BB whispered through their neural link. "Adrenaline at combat levels. You're terrified."

"Wouldn't you be?" Eli murmured. "This is first contact with someone who might be evolving beyond his own species."

Through the scope feeds, he watched Creature work in his crystal amphitheater. Those massive hands moved with surgical precision, adjusting stone pathways that channeled wind and collected

182

moisture from the killing air. Every gesture spoke of intelligence that transcended survival—this was engineering, mathematics, art carved from a world that wanted everything dead.

~ ~ ~

THE MOMENT

The air tasted bitter and acidic. Eli's gold veins pulsed erratically, responding to something in the crystal formations—electromagnetic resonance that felt almost like recognition. The moment stretched like a held breath.

The ground crunched underfoot—a sound like breaking bones. Eli froze. Creature's head snapped up instantly, intelligent eyes locking onto him with laser focus. The dark tribal markings around his eyes made him look fierce, dangerous, but his expression carried gentle curiosity rather than threat. Fifty meters of killing air stretched between them—human and Kythara, both exiles, both carrying wounds that isolation couldn't heal.

Eli raised the water container slowly, showing it clearly before setting it on crystalline ground. Three deliberate steps backward. Movements careful, non-threatening, his hands visible and empty.

Creature tilted his enormous head, the dark markings around his eyes giving him a fearsome appearance that contrasted sharply with the gentle intelligence in his gaze. He studied Eli with the intensity of someone solving differential equations in real time. Then, moving with fluid grace that defied his size, he rose from his work and approached.

Each step was measured. Cautious but unafraid. Creature paused at the water container, examining it with analytical precision before meeting Eli's gaze across the distance. Something electric passed between them—recognition, perhaps. The understanding that they were both strangers building homes in hostile territory.

Creature lifted the container, tested its weight, then brought it to his lips. The trust implicit in that action—drinking what a stranger provided—made Eli's chest constrict with unexpected emotion.

When Creature finished, he set the container down with careful reverence and reached into a pouch at his side. What emerged made Eli's breath catch—another crystal sculpture, this one depicting two figures sharing a meal under carved representations of the triple suns.

He placed it beside the empty container and stepped back, mimicking Eli's earlier gesture.

"Reciprocity," BB observed. "Gift for gift. Trust for trust. He understands exchange theory."

Eli nodded, pulling out his field tablet. Instead of crude stick figures, he sketched himself sitting in the crystal amphitheater—rough but recognizable. He showed the drawing to Creature, pointing to the tablet, then himself, then toward the impossible architecture.

Creature's eyes widened. Surprise, maybe wonder. He approached slowly, studying the tablet with absolute concentration. When he looked up, something new flickered in his expression.

Hope.

He gestured toward his amphitheater with one enormous hand, razor claws glinting in the triple sunlight, then back to Eli. The invitation was unmistakable.

~ ~ ~

CROSSING WORLDS

The walk felt like crossing between worlds. Crystal formations created natural corridors that filtered harsh light and reduced electromagnetic interference to manageable levels. Creature moved ahead, occasionally glancing back to ensure Eli followed, his frame navigating treacherous terrain with unconscious grace.

Up close, the amphitheater revealed itself as architectural genius. What appeared random showed sophisticated design—every surface calculated for optimal airflow, light diffusion, acoustic properties. The farming patches weren't survival gardens but balanced ecosystems, each plant positioned to benefit from neighbors' root systems and chemical outputs.

"97.3 percent probability his math skills dust yours, E," BB whispered, sensors analyzing the construction. "He's created a microenvironment optimized for long-term sustainability. 89.4 percent chance this represents breakthrough terraforming theory that would make university professors weep."

Creature settled onto a flat crystal formation serving as natural seating, then gestured for Eli to join him. When Eli sat—carefully, aware that one wrong movement could shatter this fragile détente— Creature reached for the tablet again.

This time, his drawings carried complexity. Personal weight.

He sketched himself among other Kythara, showing pack structure Eli recognized from surveillance data. But the drawings shifted, showing conflict—harsh lines, angry gestures, rejection, and abandonment. Finally, he drew himself alone, walking away from everything he'd ever known.

Eli watched, fascinated, as Creature struggled to express concepts his species might lack words for. When finished, he looked at Eli with an expression that seemed to ask: Do you understand?

Eli took the tablet, adding his own story. Himself with other humans—parents, home, the life he'd abandoned. Conflict, separation, the long journey bringing him here. Finally, both of them in this place, finding what neither expected.

Friendship.

~ ~ ~

THE TOUCH

When Eli showed the completed drawing, something remarkable happened. Creature's face cycled through recognition, understanding, then unmistakable joy. He reached out one enormous hand, long, razor-sharp claws extending from fingertips, stopping just short of touching Eli.

The gesture hung between them—offer, question, leap of faith across the vast gulf between species.

Eli stared at those claws, each one capable of shredding metal, scarred from survival on the most hostile planet in known space, trembling with carefully restrained power. He thought about everything bringing him here—the serum, the transformation, the long journey from a home he could never reclaim.

He reached out and touched Creature's palm, feeling the careful precision as those deadly claws curled protectively around his hand.

Where their skin met, Eli's gold veins flickered amber—and Creature's memories flooded his nerves. Not pain but recognition. The crushing loneliness of exile. The electric joy of a mathematical breakthrough. The scent of homeworld jungles neither had ever seen. Something deeper than biology, older than evolution. Creature's hide shimmered in response, crystalline patterns emerging along his arms like shared code, mathematical sequences pulsing in harmony with Eli's transformed blood.

He felt the serum's fire in Eli's veins—not poison but promise.

The contact lasted heartbeats but changed everything. In that touch, Eli felt the loneliness driving Creature from his pack, the intelligence setting him apart, the desperate hope that maybe he wasn't alone in the universe. And Creature felt the golden fire in Eli's veins, the cosmic purpose marking him as different, recognition that they were both touched by forces beyond understanding.

~ ~ ~

NAMING

When they separated, Creature's vocalizations rippled the air—subharmonic frequencies making Eli's ribs vibrate with musical resonance. BB flashed warnings: "Not speech. Mathematics given sound. He's expressing concepts his species has no words for."

The sounds continued, growing deliberate, focused, shifting from pure mathematics toward something approaching language. "Eh... Eli... Eli..."

When the name emerged clear and unmistakable, something broke open in Eli's chest. Creature had learned his name. Had chosen to learn his name. In all the universe, this massive, intelligent being had decided Eli was worth remembering.

"Yes," Eli said, pointing to himself. "Eli."

Creature nodded, then pointed to his own chest. Complex sounds emerged, filled with harmonics that human vocal cords could never reproduce. BB worked frantically, linguistic algorithms processing tones and rhythms, fractal visualizations blooming across Eli's HUD—spiraling mathematics that looked like flowers made of sound, each petal a frequency layer of meaning.

"He's offering his name," BB whispered, his voice trembling with awe. "Eli… he's sacrificing species purity to name himself for you. This is… love."

Eli smiled, his heart full. He pointed to his new friend. A name surfaced from his past, a perfect fit. "Ember." For the friend he'd lost, and for the new spark of hope this being represented.

The being who had evolved beyond his species's limitations, who had chosen isolation over conformity, nodded with obvious pleasure. He had a name now. A name given by a friend.

As the triple suns reached zenith, casting rainbows through crystal formations, two unlikely friends sat together in a hostile universe and discovered that sometimes the greatest adventures begin with the simplest gesture.

A wave. A touch. A name spoken with hope.

~ ~ ~

PACK RECOGNITION

Rex's distant bark echoed through the formations—a check-in call, ensuring his pack leader's safety. Through optics, Rex recorded thermal signatures: two figures, one small and hot with Eli's enhanced metabolism, one massive and cool with Kytharan physiology, their bio-readings syncing in steady rhythms.

Pack rhythms. Somewhere, in the dark matter between stars, something ancient took note.

"Whisper to Eli," came the ship's voice through their neural link, tinged with scientific curiosity. "I'm detecting unknown biochemical emissions from your Kythara friend. Pheromone traces that appear to be entering your bloodstream through respiratory contact. Nothing harmful—quite the opposite. Your stress indicators have dropped to baseline levels for the first time in… well, since I've known you."

The creature Ember's head turned toward the sound, expression curious rather than alarmed. Crystalline patterns along his arms pulsed once, acknowledging the distant guardians. Rex's systems flared gold—Eli's serum in their circuits syncing with Ember's crystals. His targeting solutions softened, weapon locks dissolving into protective protocols. Somewhere, Cradle felt the quantum shiver.

"Those are my friends," Eli explained, gesturing toward the figures. "Rex and King. Like your pack but different. Chosen family."

Ember nodded slowly, then gestured clearly: *Will you bring them here?*

The question carried massive significance. Ember wasn't just asking to meet Eli's companions—he was asking to join a new kind of pack. Family bound not by genetics or species but by choice, loyalty, and simple recognition that in a universe full of dangers, having someone to trust made survival possible.

~ ~ ~

NEW CONNECTIONS

Eli looked at this remarkable being who had rewritten evolution's rules to become someone capable of friendship and made the easiest decision of his life.

"Yes," he said. "I'll bring them. And maybe… maybe you can teach us how to survive like you do. How to make something beautiful out of nothing."

Ember's response was the sound of a universe rewriting its rules—

mathematical harmonics speaking of belonging, possibility, two impossible beings discovering that together they might reshape what friendship could mean.

As the triple suns blazed, Eli finally understood Cradle's grief. You guard what you love. And now he had something precious worth protecting.

CHAPTER 8 – SCENE 1:

WHIPPING POST
Inspired by Allman Brothers

THE CHEMICAL TWILIGHT

THE FLUIDS BURNED—acidic yellow cracking her molars, viscous purple tasting of graves and pennies. Each new concoction sent Elonias spiraling deeper into the chemical twilight of her own mind, reality fracturing like safety glass under a sledgehammer. The machines hummed their mechanical lullabies while her consciousness fled inward, seeking refuge in the darkest corners of her psyche where pain couldn't follow.

In that place between sleep and madness, she saw them.

Children. Or things that had once been children.

He moved through the laboratory's humid air on legs that were not a pair—one was the pale flesh of a boy, the other a strut of rusted steel that spat acrid smoke and the smell of burned plastic with every other step. The light here was a sickly yellow, catching on the floating motes of skin-dust and lubricant smoke.

His face was a settled argument between the surgeon and the engineer. One side was human: a brown eye, a patch of freckled cheek, an ear that heard the world as it was. The other side was a metal skull-plate, threaded with pulsing fiber-optic veins that gathered light into a single, unblinking crimson sensor. When he breathed, the lower half of his jaw—a cage of grinding, interlocking gears—emitted a soft, metallic whir, and tiny sparks would sometimes pepper the air like angry fireflies.

His task was precise. His one organic hand, trembling slightly, would select a syringe from a cart. His other arm—a polished chrome assembly ending in pincer claws—would then take it from him with absolute, unfeeling steadiness and slot it into a sterilization rack. Click. Hiss. Click. Hiss.

He was an island of forced routine in a sea of controlled chaos. He didn't look at the girl with the hydraulic claw for an arm, dragging her bucket of still-twitching things. He didn't acknowledge the others scuttling in his periphery. His entire world had been reduced to the syringes, the rack, and the rhythm of his own wrongness.

A single drop of condensation fell from a pipe overhead, landing on the warm metal of his jaw. The gears stuttered for a fraction of a second, their rhythm broken. A sharp, painful whine escaped them, and a larger spark jumped, singeing the air. In that moment, his one human eye squeezed shut. Not in pain, but in a flicker of frustration, of a consciousness trapped inside the machine, forced to witness its own grotesque reliability.

Then the moment passed. The rhythm resumed. Click. Hiss. He was just a boy in a broken body, performing his function, a portrait of profound difference in a place that manufactured it.

In the dim light, Elonias caught flecks of gold threading through their prosthetics like veins of precious ore—familiar, somehow. Wrong, but familiar. Like looking at family photographs through broken glass.

They performed their tasks with the dutiful efficiency of broken dolls, never speaking, never meeting each other's gaze. Some swept floors with brooms welded to their wrists, the bristles worn down to metal nubs. Others fed unidentifiable scraps into humming processors that belched clouds of green vapor that made the air taste of scorched metal. One small figure—it might have been six years old once—dragged bodies between tables on hooks embedded in its spine, leaving trails of dark fluid in intricate patterns across the gore-slick floor like some hellish art project. Another child with no mouth pressed its stitched-shut face against a glass partition, leaving a smear of synthetic tears that reflected the laboratory lights like tiny stars. But sometimes—just sometimes—that mouthless child would tap against the glass in deliberate patterns, Morse code spelling out words like "help" and "remember" and "still here" proving that somewhere beneath the modifications, fragments of humanity endured.

Early prototypes, whispered a voice in her head that sounded like her own but tasted of ash and failure. *The ones that didn't quite work. The practice runs.*

~ ~ ~

THE CATHEDRAL OF SUFFERING

Through the laboratory's far door, the world gave way to a cavernous space that drank the light and swallowed sound into a low, industrial hum. It was less a hangar and more a factory floor, stretching into a gloom so deep the far wall was only a theory. In that vastness, thousands of surgical beds lay in ghostly formation, a grid of silent torment under the cold glow of single overhead lights.

Above each table, not a spider, but a chandelier of silver needles and vibrating saws hung poised. They did not move with a ballet's grace, but with the quiet, relentless purpose of a seamstress's hands—endlessly, patiently stitching. There was no frantic energy, only the sure, slow dip and rise of instruments, the whisper of steel entering flesh, the soft whir of a bone-saw muffled by living tissue.

The air trembled with the sound of it—a symphony of tiny, precise horrors. A sigh of released pressure as a joint was replaced. The wet, percussive click of something being sealed. The bodies on the tables were less patients than raw material, their twitches and strains absorbed by the restraints as the silent, sculpting hands worked upon them, over and over, in the patient, unhurried business of unmaking and remake.

The din swallowed any sane mind—gnawing at the walls, the light, the last coherent corners of her consciousness. Individual voices became meaningless, just one endless shriek of agony that vibrated through her bones and made her own voice disappear before it could escape her throat. Even in her subconscious retreat, she couldn't escape it. The sound followed her down, down, down into the chemical depths where monsters wore the faces of children and children learned to become monsters in return.

And in the silence between screams, the gold in her veins hummed a single, clear note.

Time moved like blood through sand—thick, dark, inevitable.

~ ~ ~

DIGITAL BIRTH

Tracker Two emerged in a burst of sparking neural fluid and electrical discharge—born screaming into digital static before his first breath. His eyes rolled back, showing only whites that flickered with scrolling code like corrupted displays, and when Jobaar's technicians tried to touch him, electricity arced between his fingers, frying their instruments and leaving the smell of burnt silicon hanging in the air.

"Electromagnetic integration," Jobaar murmured with scientific satisfaction, making notes on a tablet while the child convulsed in binary seizures. "Neural pathways fused with exotic matter conduits. He'll ghost directly into electronic systems—computers, security networks, communication arrays. Perfect digital infiltration." His yellowed teeth gleamed under the surgical lights. "No firewall can keep him out."

The child's cries became binary—ones and zeros that hurt to hear, a language of pure digital anguish that made nearby screens flicker in sympathy.

Three months passed in a haze of injections and harvesting, each day bleeding into the next like watercolors in rain. Elonias felt herself fragmenting, her consciousness scattered across multiple realities. Sometimes she was the child with the hydraulic claw. Sometimes she was the machine, cutting and rebuilding with mechanical precision. Sometimes she was the scream itself, formless and eternal, echoing through the hangar until it became the only sound in the universe. But even as her mind shattered, the cosmic fluid in her veins sang with distant harmonies—Cradle's enhancement working to preserve something essential beneath the horror, golden threads weaving through her dissolving consciousness like a lifeline cast across impossible distances.

~ ~ ~

THE FACE THIEF

Tracker Three slithered from her womb like a snake shedding its skin—literally. His face was an anatomical diagram of exposed muscle and sinew, the skin sliding off in wet sheets to reveal the rubbery foundation beneath. Within hours, he had absorbed the features of a dead technician, the stolen face seeping into his flesh like water into clay until he was perfect, beautiful, human—except for the eyes, which remained dead, hungry, eternally unsatisfied.

"Biological mimicry achieved," Jobaar noted, his excitement palpable enough to taste. "Complete facial reconstruction from consumed tissue. He'll become anyone he kills, down to the last freckle. The perfect infiltrator."

The thing that wore a stranger's face turned its stolen eyes toward Elonias and smiled with borrowed lips. The expression didn't reach those dead orbs—they flickered with predatory intelligence, already calculating which face to steal next.

~ ~ ~

GIBLET'S CRUELTY

Two more months crawled by like wounded animals dragging themselves toward death. Giblet had grown more refined in his psychological cruelty, developing new techniques with the patience of a connoisseur perfecting his craft.

He would lean close during the extraction procedures, his breath like a weapon meant to suffocate, and whisper poison directly into her ear.

"Your boy Eli thinks you're dead," he would hiss, his grafted fingers stroking her hair with mock tenderness that made her skin crawl. "He's moved on, forgotten all about his broken mommy. Found himself a new monster to love. They're probably rutting right now while you birth his replacements."

She let his words wash over her, and instead of listening, she focused on the golden warmth in her chest, imagining it was Eli's hand in hers. When that active resistance frustrated Giblet, he graduated to physical abuse—sharp pinches that left bruises shaped like his fingerprints, burns from heated instruments applied just long enough to scar, needles placed just wrong enough to hurt without damaging the precious machinery. He seemed to feed on her muffled protests, his surgical modifications responding to her pain with mechanical purrs of satisfaction, as if agony itself was nourishment for his reconstructed nervous system.

~ ~ ~

THE TIME HUNTER

Tracker Four was born silent and stayed that way, his eyes immediately locking onto targets with predatory focus that made veteran soldiers step back. He moved like liquid shadow even as an infant, but his real gift wasn't stealth—it was temporal displacement. His own shadow lagged a half-second behind him because he existed slightly out of phase with time itself. When they tried to restrain him for testing, he simply stepped sideways through seconds, appearing behind the technician before the man's brain could process the movement.

"Temporal manipulation," Jobaar breathed in reverence, watching the body drop. "He doesn't just hide—he hunts through time itself. By the time you see him, you've been dead for three seconds."

~ ~ ~

THE MIND KILLER

Tracker Five emerged last—a perfectly formed little girl whose biochemical warfare was infinitely more subtle than mimicry. She didn't need to steal faces when she could rewrite minds. Her pheromones didn't just trigger affection—they hijacked decision-making centers, turned loyal soldiers into devoted servants, made enemies gladly put guns to their own heads if she giggled the right way. Unlike Tracker Three's crude facial theft, she conquered through chemistry, making people want to die for her.

"Neurochemical domination," Jobaar noted with academic precision. "While Three becomes his targets, Five makes targets become whatever she needs them to be. More elegant. More absolute."

~ ~ ~

THE BREAKING POINT

Seven months had carved away everything that had once been her. She drifted in a medicated limbo, watching the prosthetic children through glassy eyes, occasionally mistaking herself for one of them. Her body was a ruin of surgical scars and injection sites, her mind a shattered kaleidoscope of trauma and chemical dreams that bled together until pain was the only constant.

Giblet found her particularly entertaining in this state. His grafted fingers trembled—not from fear but hunger, as if her pain fed the alien nerves beneath his reconstructed flesh. His surgical modifications had left him unable to feel normal sensation, requiring increasingly extreme stimuli to register anything at all. Her suffering had become his only source of pleasure, the one sensation that could penetrate his chemically deadened nervous system.

"Wakey-wakey, little mother!" he would sing-song, dancing around her restraints like a demented child playing with a broken toy. "Time to make more monsters! Won't you smile for Uncle Giblet? Just a little smile?"

When she failed to respond, he would lean close enough for his reconstructed breath to fog her vision, his weight pressing against her restraints. "Your precious Cradle isn't coming for you. She's forgotten all about her broken little bird. You're ours now. Forever and ever and ever, until the stars burn out."

The hangar beyond had grown. New rows appeared daily, stretching the horizon of horror ever further into the darkness where screams went to die. Sometimes Elonias could swear she saw familiar faces on the tables—neighbors from her old life, students from universities she'd visited, strangers whose only crime was existing in the wrong place when Baar needed raw materials for his growing army.

The cacophony had become a symphony. She found herself humming along sometimes, her broken voice adding to the chorus of the damned.

Then the door exploded inward with the force of a thunderclap that shook reality.

~ ~ ~

DIVING VISITATION

Baar entered like a natural disaster given form—his mirror-face reflecting the laboratory's horrors back at themselves, multiplying the nightmare into infinite recursion that hurt to look at directly. His presence made the air taste of hot metal and chlorine, made gravity feel heavier, and every machine in the facility shuddered as if recognizing their true master's return.

Behind him, reality seemed to bend like heated metal. The

prosthetic children froze mid-task, their mismatched limbs trembling with mechanical terror. The cacophony from the hangar paused for one impossible moment, as if even agony held its breath in the presence of a god walking among mortals.

"Progress report," Baar commanded, his voice the sound of stars being born and dying in the same instant.

Jobaar genuflected with theatrical flair, his robes billowing around him like funeral shrouds in a hurricane. "My lord! Five magnificent specimens, each more perfect than the last. The vessels are performing beyond all projections—exceeding every parameter—"

"I ordered twelve." Baar's reflection caught the fluorescent light and threw it back as accusation sharp enough to cut. "Where are my twelve hunters?"

"The mother requires... rehabilitation," Jobaar stammered, gesturing toward Elonias's broken form with hands that shook despite his attempts at composure. "Her biology is more resilient than anticipated, but the extraction process has necessitated extensive recovery periods to maintain optimal—"

"Fix her." The words carried the weight of orbital bombardment, the finality of continental drift. "Heal her enough to spawn the remainder. I need twelve hunters, not five pets playing dress-up."

Jobaar's theatricality cracked like paint in an earthquake. "Of course, my lord, but the biological requirements... optimal recovery protocols suggest ten months minimum to ensure viability and prevent catastrophic system failure—"

"Seven."

The single word hit like a meteorite impact. Around them, glass vials cracked in perfect spirals. Metal instruments bent into impossible angles. The prosthetic children began to weep hydraulic fluid that pooled on the floor like mechanical tears.

"Seven months," Baar continued, his mirror-face cycling through expressions of cold fury that reflected and multiplied until the air itself seemed angry. "Or you become the raw material for the remaining trackers. Your protégé, Giblet, can take over the project. I'm sure he'd enjoy the... transition period."

Giblet squeaked and dove behind a surgical tray, his reconstructed face pale as congealed fat, his grafted limbs twitching with terror that his modified nervous system could actually feel.

Jobaar's theatrical mask slipped entirely, revealing genuine terror beneath the performance—the look of a man who had finally remembered what he was truly afraid of. A bead of sweat traced the scar where his own face had been grafted back on after an "accident" involving insufficient deference. "Seven months. Yes. Absolutely achievable, my lord. I'll begin intensive healing protocols immediately. Exotic matter infusions, accelerated cellular regeneration, whatever it takes to meet your specifications—"

~ ~ ~

THE PROMISE OF HOPE

But Baar was already turning away, his attention shifting to something beyond the laboratory walls, beyond the screaming hangar, beyond the planet itself. "The boy is growing stronger. I can feel his gold singing across the void like a beacon." His reflection found Elonias through the crowd and seemed to look directly into her shattered consciousness with eyes like dying suns. "Twelve hunters to gut the Cradle's children. To bring me the boy with gold in his veins and the AI that thinks it's his mother."

The door sealed behind him with a sound like a coffin lid closing on the last hope in the universe.

For three heartbeats after Baar left, the hangar was silent. Even the machines dared not hum. Even pain held its breath.

In the sudden return of sound—mechanical humming, distant screaming, the wet sounds of surgery—Giblet crept forward and leaned over Elonias's restraints, his breath like a weapon meant to suffocate.

"Did you hear that, little mother?" he whispered, his voice thick with sadistic glee that made his words slick as oil. "Seven more months of our special time together. Seven more months to make you scream in languages that don't exist yet." His grafted tongue flicked out to taste the salt track of a tear she didn't remember shedding. "I'm going to enjoy breaking you all over again. Piece by precious piece."

A single drop of blood welled from her lip where she'd bit it, and instead of red, it shimmered with a faint, unmistakable gold sheen. Giblet didn't notice, too lost in his cruelty, but she felt it—a message in her very blood. He was coming.

But deep in the chemical twilight of her mind, something stirred. A golden thread of warmth that tasted like hope and felt like a name she'd almost forgotten, a word that meant more than survival.

Eli.

Somewhere past the shrieking and the surgical lights, beyond the hangar of horrors and the mirror-faced god, her son was coming. She could feel it in her bones, in the gold that still flickered through her Duskborn veins—no longer faint like distant stars but growing brighter, pulsing stronger, as if the cosmic enhancement was preparing for something vast. He was coming, and he was bringing help. Real help. The kind that turned laboratories into graveyards and made monsters remember they were just meat after all.

Seven months.

She could survive seven months. She'd survived worse. She'd survived giving birth to hope in a universe designed to kill it.

She had to.

Because when the door exploded again—really exploded, not just opened with divine authority—it wouldn't be gods and goblins walking through the smoke and fire.

It would be family. It would be pack. It would be eight apex predators who had learned that sometimes the greatest violence is love refusing to let go.

And they would paint these walls with justice until the screaming finally, finally stopped.

And somewhere in the cracks between universes, even as industrial horror reached its crescendo, something ancient tasted the growing golden light in her veins and knew—hope still burned sweeter than all the tears in the universe.

CHAPTER 8 – SCENE 2:

VETERAN OF THE PSYCHIC WARS
Inspired by Blue Öyster Cult

THE DYING WORLD

Ashkar's Maw had no word for its own evisceration. The hardy colonists who lived in geothermal settlements and harvested volcanic energy called it vel'thanor—the time when sky bleeds metal and earth screams.

From orbit, the Abyss industrial complex looked like cancer eating the planet's face. Massive strip-mining operations carved geometric wounds through the stable valleys between volcanic ranges, trees falling in perfect rows as gravitational saws sliced through root systems that had grown in the fertile volcanic soil for millennia. Where sacred groves once filtered morning light through emerald canopies around the dormant volcanic zones, conveyor systems now hauled raw, rare minerals to orbital processors, the elements glowing with unnatural light in extraction pods.

The water pumping station sprawled across what had been the Singing Delta, where colonist children once learned to swim in crystal streams fed by underground hot springs. Now reverse osmosis machines the size of city blocks sucked aquifers dry, turning rivers into dust-caked scars while massive storage tanks prepared to launch the planet's lifeblood into space.

At the slave transport staging area, Abyss loading crews worked with mechanical efficiency. Colonist women sat in processing cages, their skin dulled by terror and dehydration, their faces pressed flat against the mesh in desperation. The men lay in neat rows where they'd fallen—throats cut execution-style, their blood fertilizing volcanic soil that would never grow anything again. Children with large, dark eyes clung to their mothers through electrified mesh, too young to understand why sky-demons had come, old enough to know their world was ending.

The Abyss resource specialists moved through it all with casual indifference, checking manifests and adjusting quotas. To them, Ashkar's Maw was inventory. Rare mineral reserves: excellent. Geothermal energy: abundant. Breeding stock: adequate quality, good quantity. Indigenous resistance: negligible.

They had not factored the Infinite 8 into their calculations.

A calculation that would cost them everything. The eight ships that dropped from stealth were no longer mere mercenaries; they were a force of reckoning, and they were fighting for a home to call their own.

~ ~ ~

WHEN WEAPONS BECOME GUARDIANS

"Remember," Cradle's voice echoed in their neural links as eight ships dropped from stealth, "I want those machines intact. This world will house my children."

The Infinite 8 split like a choreographed dance of death, each ship guided by one of the Onze consciousnesses Cradle had rescued from Mota Prime. Where once the prisoners had flown alone, now they partnered with the galaxy's greatest scientific minds—each Onze consciousness lending their expertise through the ship's AI systems. But something had changed in the months since their escape from Baar's prison. Where once they fought for whoever paid best, now they fought for something infinitely more precious: home.

~ ~ ~

WATER STATION ASSAULT

Rao screamed toward the pumping station, kinetic shields flaring as Abyss defensive systems engaged. For a split second, Speedbumps's targeting computer painted one of the fleeing colonist groups as hostiles—mercenary programming running deeper than conscious thought.

"Mares, I'm getting civilian targeting locks—"

"Same here, brother. Old habits." Mares' voice was tight with self-disgust. "Override and prioritize civilian protection. We're not destroyers anymore."

The moment of confusion cost them—an Abyss patrol nearly tagged the fleeing civilians before both ships corrected course. But they adapted, their targeting systems learning new parameters: protect, don't just destroy.

Speedbumps adjusted mathematical parameters one final time as they approached the facility. His consciousness interfaced directly with ship-targeting systems, calculating optimal strike points to disable without destroying. Beside him, Mares held Momus in perfect formation, kinetic shields already glowing as defensive fire began in earnest.

"Six extraction platforms, forty-seven reverse osmosis units, three primary storage facilities," Speedbumps reported, his voice carrying its usual analytical precision. "Recommend we—"

He stopped mid-sentence.

Below, emerging from a hidden cave system near a dormant volcanic vent, came a group of colonist civilians. At their head ran a woman whose weathered skin caught sunlight like polished bronze, her dark hair flowing behind her as she led children and elders away from the industrial complex. She moved with determined grace, her form navigating the volcanic terrain with fluid precision that spoke of someone who knew every stone and thermal vent of this world.

An Abyss patrol spotted them. Energy weapons tracked toward the fleeing group.

Speedbumps's mathematical mind, trained for decades to optimize destruction, suddenly found new variables. Distance to civilians: 2.3 kilometers. Abyss weapon charge time: 8.7 seconds. Probability of civilian casualties: 97.3 percent.

New primary objective: Zero percent acceptable losses among the innocent.

"Mares," he said, his voice suddenly rough with emotion he didn't understand, "cover those civilians. First priority."

"Copy that, brother."

Momus dove like a hawk, Mares's kinetic shields deflecting Abyss fire while Speedbumps's precision targeting disabled patrol units with surgical strikes. Below, the bronze-skinned woman looked up at their ships, and for a moment that stretched like eternity, her eyes met his through cockpit glass.

She smiled. Her smile was rebellion—one unbroken soul refusing to let the Abyss claim her sky. In the middle of her world ending, with death raining from space, she smiled at him with gratitude so pure it hit him like a physical blow.

Speedbumps's hands trembled on the controls. His mathematical certainty wavered, replaced by something he'd never factored into any equation: the desperate need to be worthy of that smile.

~ ~ ~

MINING OPERATION CHAOS

At the rare-mineral extraction site, Gideon and the twins unleashed technological fury that made the Abyss suddenly understand what it meant to face superior firepower. Eris and Inaginid—Nales's ship-consciousness—moved like a three-ship dance, the twins' adaptive AI co-pilots anticipating each other's moves while Gideon's firing algorithms painted targets across the industrial complex.

But these weren't the clean, efficient kills of their mercenary days.

Every shot was calculated to spare massive mining equipment, to disable rather than destroy. Where once they would have obliterated the entire facility in minutes, now they picked apart Abyss defensive positions with scalpel precision.

"Gideon," came Nales's voice as Inaginid spiraled through a debris field of disabled Abyss fighters, "these extraction rigs—they're beautiful. Look at the engineering."

"Together-we-see fractal efficiency," Chek added from his twin ship, their shared consciousness processing the equipment's design. "Rare mineral separation matrices follow perfect mathematical spirals. Waste approaches theoretical zero."

"Cradle's going to love these," Nales continued their dual analysis. "Perfect for sustainable mining. The locals can work with their own resources instead of having them stolen."

Below, a small colonist child emerged from hiding near a geothermal vent, large, dark eyes staring up at burning Abyss ships with terror. The child's chin trembled as they pressed against the warm volcanic rock for comfort. Gideon's targeting system automatically painted the child as a potential threat—old mercenary programming died hard. His HUD flashed unwanted data: "78.6 percent match to subject's own childhood trauma profile – age seven, orbital bombardment survivor."

His finger twitched toward the trigger before he caught himself, horror flooding through him. In those dark eyes, he saw himself at seven years old—cowering in a bombed-out shelter while mercenaries like he'd become decided whether his family lived or died.

"Gideon." Cradle's voice was a soft chime in his neural link, overriding the targeting alarm. "The child is not a resource. The child is the reason."

What am I doing? I'm them. I was always them.

Instead, he switched to external speakers and gentled his voice as much as the modulator allowed. "Don't be afraid," he said, hoping the translator got it right.

The child looked up at his ship with wonder instead of fear, reaching out one small hand toward the sky. Gideon felt something crack open in his chest—the scared seven-year-old inside him finally finding the protector he'd needed. For the first time in his life, he was fighting to build something instead of tearing it down.

~ ~ ~

TRANSPORT RESCUE

De'Andreas and Apek hit the slave transports like the wrath of absent gods. Barangay's stellar navigation systems tracked seventeen transport vessels across the planet's orbital space while Salem's Alcubierre drives allowed instantaneous positioning for rescue operations.

The transport ships were floating horror shows—cramped, airless, designed to move human cargo with maximum efficiency and minimum care. Colonist women pressed their faces against viewport windows, eyes wide with desperation, their children crying in languages the Infinite 8's translators couldn't parse but their hearts understood perfectly.

"Salem actual." Apek's voice carried controlled fury. "I'm seeing conditions that violate... everything. Everything decent."

"Copy, Salem. Time to give these people their lives back."

They moved like surgical instruments, Apek's warp drives allowing them to appear inside transport cargo holds while De'Andreas provided covering fire. The Abyss transport crews, used to dealing with helpless prisoners, found themselves facing technological superiority that rendered their weapons useless.

When the cargo bay doors opened, the colonist women shielded their eyes from the light, expecting more cruelty. Instead, De'Andreas knelt before them, removing her helmet to show her scarred face.

"You are safe," she said gently, her voice carrying the weight of mountains but tempered with unexpected tenderness.

One mother clutched her infant daughter to her chest, tears streaming down weathered cheeks as she realized she was free.

The baby's large, dark eyes blinked up at De'Andreas with curious trust. When the mother pressed her palms together and bowed to her, chin lifted with dignity restored, De'Andreas understood that she was no longer a mercenary fighting for credits. She was a guardian protecting what mattered.

~ ~ ~

AERIAL SUPREMACY

High above the planet's surface, Akona and Marcus Webb turned the sky into their personal battlefield. Analogoy's Trilene-phoscarbyne exotic-matter armor made it nearly invulnerable, while Thoth's reality-bending countermeasures turned Abyss targeting systems into expensive decorations.

But Marcus found himself thinking about the STEM students they'd rescued, about volcanic valleys below, about the possibility that his daughter might one day play in those geothermal springs—if they could save them. He remembered Lissa's tiny hands cupping tadpoles in a stream now paved over by Abyss factories, her laughter echoing through valleys that no longer existed.

"Akona," he said as they danced through a formation of Abyss interceptors, "this feels different."

"Yeah, brother. It feels right. First time we're not just fighting for credits."

Their weapons carved through enemy formations with lethal artistry, but every shot was calculated to drive the Abyss away rather than simply kill. They were establishing air superiority over their new home.

Marcus smiled as he watched colonist children emerge from hidden caves below, pointing up at their ships with excitement rather than fear. This felt like coming home.

~ ~ ~

WHEN THE INNOCENT TRUST

The water pumping station fell in seventeen minutes. Speedbumps's mathematical precision had turned the Abyss's own industrial equipment against them, overloading pumping systems to create localized explosions that disabled without destroying. The reverse osmosis machines sat intact but powerless, waiting to be repurposed for the people they'd been stealing from.

As Rao touched down near the extraction facility, Speedbumps found himself running toward the cave system where civilians had sheltered. His usual analytical detachment had evaporated, replaced by something urgently human.

The bronze-skinned woman who had smiled at him was helping an injured elder, her hands gentle but sure as she cleaned a wound with water from a hidden geothermal spring. When she looked up and saw him approaching—this figure in advanced armor, carrying weapons that had just saved her people—her eyes showed no fear, only cautious hope.

She rose gracefully, her weathered form unfolding with natural elegance, and walked toward him. Her bronze-tinted skin held warmth despite everything that had happened, her dark hair framing a face both beautiful and determined—strong chin, full lips, and those remarkable eyes that seemed to hold depths his mathematical mind couldn't quantify. When she reached him, she placed her palm flat against his chest armor, right over his heart.

"The sky-bleeders are gone," she said, her voice carrying the strength of someone who had survived on a harsh volcanic world.

But Speedbumps heard something else in her tone. Something like: *You came for us.*

She was a living equation his math couldn't solve—the proof that some truths only poets dared articulate. Her bronze-tinted skin held the warmth of her world's volcanic springs, her dark hair caught starshine even in daylight, and her eyes... those expressive eyes held the trust of someone who had learned to find hope even in the harshest places.

"I..." he started, then realized his voice modulator was still active. He reached up and removed his helmet, showing her his face for the first time.

She smiled again, and this time it was just for him. Her full lips curved with genuine warmth, and her eyes sparkled with something that made his breath catch.

"You have kind eyes," she said softly, her voice carrying the musical quality of someone who had learned to find beauty even on a world of fire and stone.

Speedbumps felt his mathematical certainty crumble completely. All his equations, all his precision optimization, all his careful calculations—none of it had prepared him for this moment when a woman who had just watched her world nearly die looked at him and saw something worth trusting.

"I'm... my name is..." The callsign "Speedbumps" died on his tongue. It belonged to a different man, a calculator of death, not a protector of life. He met her gaze, the name feeling foreign and precious on his lips. "Pall. Pall Ibanez."

She repeated his name carefully, her accent turning it into something beautiful. Then she placed her hand over her own heart.

"Lyralei."

Around them, colonist civilians emerged from hiding places in volcanic caves, their hardy forms moving with the natural grace of people who had learned to live in harmony with a dangerous world. Children with wondering eyes pointed at intact water pumps, already understanding that the machines would now serve them instead of enslaving them. Elders with dignified bearing nodded approvingly at the Infinite 8 ships, recognizing protectors when they saw them.

But Pall—he was Speedbumps no longer—only had eyes for Lyralei. She was teaching him that some equations couldn't be solved, only lived.

As other colonists gathered around them, an elderly woman began to sing—a low, haunting melody that seemed to call to the dormant volcanoes around them. The sound carried across the thermal vents, and Pall realized this was a song of gratitude, of home reclaimed.

"The oldest songs remember the mountain's true name," Lyralei explained, her eyes sparkling with secret knowledge, her chin lifting with pride in her people's resilience. "The volcanoes sing, too, but quietly. We learned to listen."

Other voices joined the elder's, creating harmonies that had been passed down for generations—songs of survival, of finding life in the midst of fire, of making a home where others saw only danger.

"Ashkar naleth," Lyralei whispered, her eyes never leaving Pall's face, full lips forming the words with reverent care. "Mountain's blessing. For… for when darkness comes, but the fire still burns." She paused, then added something softer: "Welcome home."

Pall felt the melody wrap around his mathematical mind like a warm embrace. This was what the Abyss had been trying to destroy—not just people but the songs that made them who they were. The traditions that connected them to their harsh world and each other.

"Ashkar's Maw," she said, gesturing to the volcanic landscape around them. "You are welcome here."

Pall felt something break open in his chest. For the first time in his life, he understood the difference between fighting for payment and fighting for home.

~ ~ ~

THE MESSENGER'S FATE

Three sectors away, in the command citadel of the Abyss war fleet, the sole surviving transport captain limped into Baar's presence. The demigod sat on his throne of living metal, his presence making reality bend in uncomfortable ways around him.

"Speak," Baar commanded, his voice carrying the weight of collapsing stars.

The captain's words came in gasps, filtered through a damaged respirator. "Lord Baar… the Ashkar's Maw operation… it was… they were waiting for us."

Baar's attention focused like a laser. "Waiting?"

"Eight ships, my lord. Unknown configuration. They moved like... like they knew our tactics. Our formations. Our equipment." The captain's voice broke. "They destroyed everything but... but they kept the machines intact. Like they were planning to..."

"Planning to what?"

"To stay, my lord. To use them."

The temperature in the command chamber dropped ten degrees. Baar rose from his throne, his form beginning to shift into something that made looking at him directly inadvisable.

"You're telling me," Baar said with deadly quiet, "that mercenary scum—hired thugs—not only interfered with my operation but have become pirates?"

"Not pirates, my lord. Protectors. They fought like... like they were defending something precious. The indigenous population... they helped them. Guided them. The survivors spoke of them like they were..."

"Like they were what?"

The captain swallowed hard. "Like they were heroes, my lord."

The silence that followed stretched for exactly 4.7 seconds. The air filled with the scent of ionized fear from his disciples' sweat as they struggled not to visibly flinch. Then Baar moved.

His hand punched through the captain's chest with casual violence, exotic matter dissolving the man's molecular structure from the inside out. The captain's atoms swirled like galaxies in Baar's palm—a microcosm of the universe he'd fled—before dispersing into nothingness. The scream cut off abruptly as his body collapsed into component particles.

"Heroes," Baar snarled at the empty space where his messenger had been. "Mercenary filth think they're heroes."

For a moment—just a moment—his reflection in the polished metal throne fractured, showing not a demigod but the small, spiteful gremlin he'd been before ascending to power in the parent universe. The image vanished instantly, but the fear remained.

He turned to face his assembled disciples—Rabaar, Lobaar, and the others who had watched the execution with carefully neutral expressions.

"Find them," Baar commanded. "Find these hired guns and their sea-squid master. Find this volcanic rock they think they're protecting." His form continued to shift, becoming something that hurt to perceive. "And when you do, we're going to teach them exactly what happens to mercenaries who interfere with my expansion."

But even as he raged, Baar felt something he hadn't experienced in eons: uncertainty. These mercenaries had become more than simple hired killers. And Cradle—that tentacled bitch was building something he couldn't predict. Her "children" were multiplying, and if the rumors were true, some might be hybrid beings with capabilities he couldn't foresee.

For the first time since arriving in this universe, Baar wondered if he might need to find that blackhole sooner than planned.

The Infinite 8 weren't just escaped prisoners. They were becoming something that threatened his entire operation—and worse, they were inspiring others to resist.

And that—the unpredictable calculus of hope—was a variable his godhood could not solve. It terrified him more than any weapon.

CHAPTER 8 – SCENE 3:

FAMILY AFFAIR
Inspired by Sly and the Family Stone

THE CATHEDRAL OF HOPE

THE GREAT CHAMBER ABOARD CRADLE'S VESSEL had never held so many souls at once. What had begun as a simple meeting space had transformed into something approaching a cathedral—walls of living coral that pulsed with gentle bioluminescence, creating patterns that seemed to breathe with the rhythm of shared heartbeats. The air itself felt alive, thick with potential and the electricity of history being written.

The 317 STEM students filled the curved walls—young minds that had been destined for exploitation in Baar's laboratories, now free to dream of futures they would help build. Their faces carried the hollow-eyed wariness of survivors, but beneath that trauma, something new sparked: the dangerous hope of the genuinely free.

The Infinite 8 stood in a loose semicircle, still wearing the aftermath of battle. Scorched armor told the story of their transformation—burn marks where they'd shielded civilians, damage patterns that spoke of protection rather than predation. Their eyes held something none of them had possessed in years: purpose that felt larger than survival.

On Hunter's Planet, Eli pressed his ear to the comm unit, listening to the gathering with whispered awe. Ember sat beside him, bronze skin gleaming in the harsh light, his acoustic abilities letting him harmonize with the distant voices. Both understood they were hearing history being born—the first words of a civilization that had never existed.

At the chamber's heart, Cradle's massive form dominated the space with presence rather than threat. Her tentacles moved in slow, hypnotic patterns, each gesture deliberate and graceful, carrying the weight of eons. When she spoke, her voice carried harmonics that resonated through bone and neural tissue, making every word feel like truth being carved into the foundation of reality.

~ ~ ~

THE FIRST WORDS OF A NEW PEOPLE

"MY CHILDREN," CRADLE BEGAN, and the simple phrase carried gravitational weight that pressed against their souls. "Today marks the end of our exile and the beginning of our people."

The words rippled through the chamber like stones dropped into still water. On Hunter's Planet, Eli felt Ember's hand find his, bronze fingers intertwining with flesh marked by golden veins. They listened together as Cradle's children began to plan their first city, understanding that they, too, would have a place in this growing forest of possibility.

"For too long, we have been refugees," Cradle continued, her great eyes focusing on each face in turn—seeing not just who they were but who they could become. "Scattered. Broken. Running from a universe that taught us only cruelty. But today, on Ashkar's Maw, you showed me something I had almost forgotten existed."

She gestured with one massive tentacle, and the chamber's walls became transparent, revealing the star field beyond. But instead of the cold vacuum of space, the view showed Ashkar's Maw—a world of fire and stone transformed into beauty, its volcanic peaks glowing softly against jeweled skies, geothermal springs creating ribbons of mist that caught starlight like dreams.

"Hope," she said simply, the word falling into silence like a seed into fertile soil. "You showed me hope."

Pall—he could no longer think of himself as Speedbumps, not after feeling Lyralei's hand over his heart—felt his chest tighten. Somewhere on that world, she was probably singing the mountain songs, teaching colonist children to find harmony with the volcanic rhythms of their world. Somewhere below, elders were showing their people how to work with machinery that had nearly enslaved them, transforming tools of oppression into instruments of renewal.

~ ~ ~

THE TRUTH OF GODS

"But first"—Cradle's voice carried new steel—"you must understand what Baar truly is—and what I am."

Her form shifted slightly, revealing glimpses of her true nature. Tentacles that moved through dimensions, existing in spaces human eyes couldn't quite track. Eyes that had witnessed the birth of galaxies, their depths holding starlight older than worlds. The air thickened where her tentacles passed, as if space itself struggled to contain her presence. Her edges blurred—not like mist but like a star seen through warped space-time.

For a heartbeat, the STEM students saw their own reflections in her iridescent skin, distorted as if viewed across eons of cosmic evolution.

"We come from what you might call the parent universe," she said, her voice carrying the weight of deep time. "A place where beings like us begin as simple creatures—imps, gremlins, space squids— and evolve over eons into what mortals call gods."

The chamber remained perfectly silent, hundreds of minds processing the revelation that their protector was literally a goddess from another reality. The silence was profound—not empty but full of understanding settling into place like sediment in deep water.

~ ~ ~

THE EXILE'S TALE

"Baar was once like me." Cradle's voice darkened with ancient pain that had fermented across cosmic ages. "They were once like me—lowly creatures looking to evolve toward godhood. But he chose a different path." Her tentacles stilled, and for a moment, the chamber felt the weight of unbearable sadness. "In the parent universe, he murdered his brother in a fit of rage. Now he can never return home because if his physical form is destroyed, his spirit will reset to the beginning—a mere gremlin, helpless before his third brother's eternal vengeance."

Through the comm, Eli's whispered gasp was audible. On Hunter's Planet, Ember's bronze skin pulsed with understanding that transcended language.

"So Baar came to this universe as an exile," Cradle continued, her voice carrying the weight of cosmic tragedy. "When his ship crashed on a primitive world, he saw opportunity in desperation. He flew down with his androids, performed spectacular displays of power, and proclaimed himself a god to people who had never seen technology."

The horror of it began to settle over the assembly like a cold weight.

"He converted an entire civilization through spectacle and terror. Every male became a warrior in his armies. Every female became a breeder for his cause. Their daughters born into slavery, their sons raised as weapons. Generation after generation, shaped by his will."

Pall felt sick thinking of Lyralei's gentle people facing such a fate—their songs silenced, their children stolen, their light extinguished by endless war.

"'Breed and war, breed and war,'" Cradle's voice carried bitter mimicry. "That became their existence. He gave them better weapons, expanded them to other worlds, promised them glory in service to their god. Now he commands trillions of descendants across multiple star systems, all believing they serve divine will rather than cosmic cowardice."

The weight of those numbers—trillions—pressed against every mind in the chamber.

"But Baar grows desperate," Cradle continued, her great eyes reflecting the cold fire of distant stars. "He believes this universe is decaying and seeks escape to a better one. He needs me to transport his armies through the cosmic barriers between realities, just as I brought him here eons ago—at the cost of my own flesh and eternal exile from my home."

She paused, letting the magnitude of her sacrifice settle into their understanding.

"I refuse to be his ferry to another universe's destruction."

The words rang with finality that made the chamber walls pulse brighter.

~ ~ ~

THE RECOGNITION

Cradle turned to face the Infinite 8 directly, her gaze carrying the weight of cosmic recognition. "You eight were broken when I found you. Weapons without purpose, soldiers without cause, killers who had forgotten what they were killing for. Today, you became something unprecedented in this galaxy's history."

Akona stepped forward, his weathered face showing emotions he'd buried for decades of violence. "Cradle, we… we don't know how to be anything but what we were."

"You learned today," she replied with infinite gentleness. "When Gideon spoke softly to a frightened child instead of eliminating a potential threat. When De'Andreas showed her face to enslaved mothers and offered dignity instead of domination. When Pall found love in the middle of war and chose connection over conquest."

Her gaze shifted to him, and Pall felt seen in a way that made his mathematical mind stutter and crash. Every calculation he'd ever made seemed meaningless compared to the equation of Lyralei's trust.

"You learned that strength can be gentle, that power can protect, that the greatest victory is not conquest but connection. You became protectors. Founders. The beating heart of a people who choose to build rather than destroy."

She turned to the STEM students, her expression softening like starlight through atmosphere. "And you, brilliant ones—you who were meant to be tools in others' wars, experiments in others' laboratories—you will design the cities that never fall, the defenses that protect without destroying, the technologies that serve life rather than ending it."

~ ~ ~

QUESTIONS FROM THE FREE

A young woman with silver hair—one of the rescued students, her arms still bearing the marks of neural grafts she'd torn free—raised her hand tentatively. "What about the people already on Ashkar's Maw? The colonists we helped save?"

Before Cradle could respond, a boy with burn scars crisscrossing his arms—marks from Baar's experimental labs—interrupted, his voice tight with the fear of someone who had learned that safety was always temporary. "What if we can't build fast enough? What if he comes before we're ready?"

Cradle's great eyes softened as they traced the scars on his arms—a map of suffering she seemed to memorize and vow to erase.

"They are not subjects to be ruled," Cradle said firmly, her voice carrying absolute conviction. "They are teachers. The colonists know their world's songs, its seasons, its secrets. We bring technology and protection. They bring wisdom and belonging. Together, we will create something neither could build alone."

Through the comm, Eli's voice carried wonder and growing

understanding. "She's not just founding a civilization. She's creating a new way of being civilized."

"Yes." Cradle's approval washed over him like a warm tide. "For too long, advancement has meant dominance. Progress has meant conquest. Technology has served only the strong, and strength has been measured only in the ability to destroy."

She gestured to the view of Ashkar's Maw again, its volcanic peaks catching light like promises in the darkness, geothermal springs creating patterns of mist and steam that danced across the surface like living art. "But you have shown me another path. A civilization founded not on taking but on giving. Not on fear but on trust. Not on the silence of the conquered but on the songs of the free."

~ ~ ~

THE PRACTICAL AND THE MAGICAL

One of the STEM students—a young man whose hands still trembled from months of forced calculations in Baar's laboratories—raised practical concerns, his voice carrying the analytical precision that had kept him alive. "Resource allocation models suggest we'll need 73.2 percent more rare earth elements than Ashkar's Maw can provide for full defensive infrastructure. Have we calculated sustainability curves for population growth versus technological development?"

Before Cradle could respond, another student spoke up—a girl with intricate braided hair whose neural implants had been designed to process xenolinguistics. Her voice carried wonder mixed with scientific curiosity. "The colonists' volcanic songs follow mathematical progressions we don't understand yet. Their harmony patterns could revolutionize our acoustic engineering but only if we learn to listen instead of just analyze. What if their cultural knowledge is the missing variable in our equations?"

"All true," Cradle acknowledged, her voice carrying the weight of cosmic understanding. "Which is why this will not be easy. Baar will come for us eventually. He cannot allow the existence of proof that his path is not the only path, that gods can choose creation over destruction."

The chamber fell silent. Everyone understood that Baar would eventually discover their growing strength and respond with the fury of a wounded god, though none could predict what form his vengeance might take.

"He will bring his Abyss fleets, his corrupted disciples, his trackers born from torture," Cradle continued, her voice steady as starlight. "He will come with weapons designed to break worlds and break souls in equal measure."

The weight of that future threat pressed against every heart in the chamber.

"But"—Cradle's voice rose, carrying harmonics that made the chamber walls pulse with responding light—"I have something Baar has never possessed and will never understand. I have children who fight not from fear but from love. Not to escape consequences but to protect what they have chosen to cherish."

~ ~ ~

THE ARCHITECTS OF TRUTH

Cradle extended several tentacles toward different groups—the Infinite 8, the students, and through the comm connection, Eli and Ember on their distant world. "You are no longer refugees. You are no longer prisoners. You are no longer broken weapons in someone else's war."

Her voice filled the chamber like music, like the first notes of a song that could reshape reality itself. "You are the architects of the first truth Baar fears most: that strength is not measured in corpses but in cradled children."

Mares stepped forward, his gruff voice thick with emotion he'd thought burned out of him years ago. "What do you need us to do?"

"Build," Cradle said simply, the word carrying infinite possibility. "Build homes that welcome strangers. Build defenses that protect without threatening. Build relationships that bridge the gap between species, between cultures, between the traumatized and the whole."

She paused, her great eyes taking in every face—seeing past their scars to the potential beneath. "Build a world where children like you once were will be treasured, not weaponized. Build a place where songs can gentle machines back to harmony, where mathematics serves beauty, where strength kneels before vulnerability to offer protection."

The silence that followed was profound, filled with the weight of responsibility and the lightness of hope in equal measure. The eight former mercenaries—no, founders—exchanged glances that spoke volumes. For the first time in their lives, their silence carried more power than any battle cry.

Finally, through the comm, Eli's voice came soft but clear, carrying across the void: "What do we call ourselves? This new people?"

~ ~ ~

THE SEEDS

Cradle's answer came without hesitation, as if she had been waiting eons to speak this truth: "We are the Seeds."

The name settled into the chamber like light finding its proper spectrum.

"We are those who were planted in darkness and chose to grow toward light. Those who were scattered across hostile ground and chose to take root together. Those who carry within us the potential for worlds that have never existed."

From among the STEM students, a soft voice emerged—barely more than a whisper but carrying the weight of someone daring to hope for the first time in years. A young woman with burn scars along her temples, marks from neural interface experiments, looked up with eyes that held the fragile light of dawn breaking.

"For the first time since..." She paused, her voice catching. "Since before the labs... I can picture tomorrow without calculating survival

probability." Her words grew stronger, wonder creeping in. "Is that...
is that what hope feels like?"

The question hung in the air like a prayer finally finding voice.

On Hunter's Planet, Eli's veins flared gold in response, pulsing in
perfect synchronization with the distant mountain song frequency
at which Lyralei had sung—as if his enhanced blood recognized the
harmonic signature of hope itself. Ember's bronze fingers tightened
around his wrist, and for a moment, his acoustic abilities let him hear
the harmony of distant voices across the void, past and present and
potential futures all audible at once in his evolving perception.

"Yeah," Eli whispered through the comm, wonder thick in his
voice. "It fits."

~ ~ ~

THE NEW PATH

Cradle gestured to the star field beyond Ashkar's Maw, to the vast
universe that held both beauty and horror in equal measure. "We will
show this cosmos that there is another way to grow—not through
conquest but through cultivation. Not through dominion but through
devotion. We will plant ourselves in fertile soil and become forests of
possibility."

Her voice rose to fill every corner of the chamber, every heart of
every listener. "A civilization founded not on taking lives but on
giving life. Not on the screams of the defeated but on the songs of the
free. Not on the silence of fear but on the music of hope."

The chamber erupted—not in cheers but in something deeper.
Sighs of relief that sounded like prayers answered. Whispers of
understanding that carried the weight of revelation. The quiet sobs
of people who had finally, impossibly, found home.

On Hunter's Planet, Eli's golden veins pulsed in time with the
chamber's bioluminescence—a silent chorus of belonging that
transcended the vast distances between them.

Pall thought of Lyralei's smile, the one equation his mathematical mind could never solve but his heart understood perfectly. It was the first formula in a new mathematics of belonging. Gideon remembered a child's hand reaching toward his ship in wonder instead of fear. De'Andreas felt again the weight of a mother's gratitude as she pressed her palms together in blessing rather than surrender.

They were the Seeds. They were going home to plant themselves in fertile soil and grow into something the universe had never seen—a civilization where strength served love, where power protected vulnerability, where the greatest victories were measured not in enemies destroyed but in children safely sleeping.

~ ~ ~

DIVINE TERROR

And somewhere in the space between stars, Baar felt the universe shift around him like tectonic plates finding new alignment. His mirror-face fractured into a snarl that reflected across multiple dimensions, showing his rage from angles that hurt to perceive. Beneath him, his throne of living metal developed hairline fractures that spread like a spider web of cosmic doubt—the first physical manifestation of a god learning fear. On a thousand worlds, Abyss breeders shuddered as their god's fury echoed through their biological grafts like poison in their veins.

On the war-moon Xyr-7, an Abyss captain clutched her head as Baar's rage seared through her neural implants. Blood trickled from her nose, and when she spoke, her voice carried tremors of genuine terror. "The god is wounded," she whispered to her subordinates, who immediately began checking their weapons as if mere firepower could heal whatever had damaged their deity's confidence.

For the first time in eons, the god of armies wondered if there might be gods of something else entirely. Gods of growth instead of destruction. Gods of songs instead of screams. Gods of children sleeping safely instead of soldiers dying gloriously.

The thought terrified him more than his brother's vengeance ever could.

~ ~ ~

SEEDS OF TOMORROW

In the great chamber, Cradle's children began to plan their first city. Not a fortress or a factory, but a place where Seeds could take root and scattered potential could flourish. A place where the songs of a dozen worlds could teach machines to remember their gentler melodies, where colonist wisdom could guide advanced technology, where children who had known only laboratories could finally know gardens built among the volcanic springs of their new home.

The Seeds were sown in starlight and watered with tears of joy. Like the first notes of a mountain song, they began to grow—not toward conquest but toward connection. Not toward dominion but toward home.

And in the growing light of that impossible hope, the universe itself seemed to hold its breath, waiting to see what flowers might bloom from soil fertilized with love instead of blood.

CHAPTER 9 – SCENE 1:

WAR PIGS
Inspired by Black Sabbath

THE HOLOVID PROBLEM

RABAAR'S JEWELED FINGERS CRUSHED a holographic tablet, its fragments scattering across looted Avachordata tapestries. The wreckage revealed his stolen amulet beneath his robes—its three-moon sigil mocking his sermons about purity.

"They've made my god into a jingle!" he shrieked as the Eternal Dominion's bridge screens simultaneously switched to *Eli & The Super Pack: Season 3 Marathon.*

Lobaar stood nearby, his mechanical enhancements whirring as he processed the catastrophic data. His augmented eye focused on a plush Rex toy left by some careless officer's child on the command console. "Merchandise profits could fund their shield network for a decade. The plush wolf robot abomination alone has a three hundred percent markup due to 'atomic talon action.' It also comes in a 'spaceship aluminum' variant." His vocal modulator hitched as he continued: "Atomic talon action sold out in twelve systems. The aluminum Whisper ships are backordered six months."

His mechanical eye shifted to display a graph. "Worse—seventy-six percent of children now associate Baar's sigil with 'the bad guys who lose in the end.'" He paused, accessing another data stream. "Economic briefings show Onze Tech Solutions reported another record quarter."

The bridge lights dimmed for a second.

Lobaar's eyes darted towards the lights, his voice slow and cautious as he accessed another data stream. "I've been tracking Onze Holdings' financial transfers. Their liquidity is... unprecedented. Every entertainment division profit, every tech patent licensing fee, every real estate acquisition—it all flows back to fund their operations."

"What do these pretenders know of the fragile and delicate young mind?" Rabaar's voice dropped to a whisper that somehow carried more menace than his screaming. "It takes someone of my caliber, someone with years of theological study, to mold their little clay brains and possess those tiny, fragile souls. For over two hundred years, I have shaped young minds, molded them to serve our vision. Now this... this thing undermines centuries of careful cultivation."

He gestured wildly at the screens, where children laughed at cartoon adventures. "They should piss themselves at the unknown, worship the powerful, submit to authority. Instead, they're learning empathy and sharing with some... some creature who does not stand in the most celestial light of our lord."

Lobaar's vocal modulator glitched as it tried to process the show's catchphrase: "Learning to recognize the emotions of others is fun!"—the infection spreading even into their own systems.

THE ORDER FOR ESCALATION

"We must use the very light of our lord to press ever onward in his name," Rabaar decided, standing and adjusting his robes. His fingers dug into armrests upholstered with fabric torn from an Eli costume play outfit. Before his eyes could register the movement, he backhanded a passing servitor drone, sending it spinning into the wall. "Empty every asylum! Triple the breeding quotas!"

Rabaar's rage boiled over as he activated his comm unit. "Get in here, Flemmer!"

A short, balding man with tiny wire-frame glasses that balanced on the end of his long, thin nose rushed into the chamber, his small, deep-set eyes darting nervously. His nose seemed to be permanently hooked up to a snot machine somewhere in his pocket, constantly dripping and requiring attention.

"Empty the orphanages! Empty the crazy houses! I want them all!" Rabaar screamed at Bishop Flemmer, spittle flecking the man's snot-covered face.

Flemmer nodded so vigorously his nasal tubes slapped against his cheeks. "Yes, Your Eminence! All facilities will be—"

"And her spawn?" Rabaar cut him off with a sharp gesture. "Once the generators fail, even she won't be able to—"

"We'll broadcast the prison's destruction live," Flemmer interrupted eagerly. "Let them watch their hero fail in real time. Two weeks, brother. Two weeks until we settle this."

On the main viewscreen behind them, the season finale played—Eli and a scary creature learned to be friends while the theme song promised, "You can be a teacher for every living creature!" The credits rolled, and a cheery announcer's voice chirped: "Next week, Eli and his Super Pack take on Abyss scouts! So tune in, kids—only here on the Onze Core 7 Network Fun Zone!"

In the quantum static between pixels, she counted their panicked breaths. She heard every word, watched every gesture, catalogued every threat. In the spaces between their secured transmissions, an ancient intelligence planned their downfall with the patience of geological time.

THE SELECTION

Aboard the transport vessel Reaper's Hand

Squadron Commander Hinson Burke walked through the rows of children with the measured pace of a farmer inspecting livestock, kicking aside a child's Eli-themed lunchbox. Its thermos rolled to reveal gold-vein decals that emulated the hero these children would never see again.

Tall and broad-shouldered, Burke's Mordan features carried the sharp angles of his homeworld, Yargo, his thick accent turning even casual words into threats. His armor bore the geometric plating and crimson insignia of Lobaar's personal fleet—all hard angles and intimidating bulk that made him look like he'd stepped out of an ancient war. Those pale eyes held the kind of cold calculation that came from years of reducing human lives to their component uses.

"Pathetic," he growled, watching a girl clutch her plush wolf-robot abomination like it could save her.

"This batch is particularly promising," Lieutenant Broyce Kenner said, consulting her data pad. Her grey military suit was perfectly pressed, rows of ribbons and commendations adorning her chest in precise formation. Her voice carried the clinical detachment of someone who'd long ago stopped seeing the trembling forms around them as anything more than inventory. "Rabaar's facilities have been breeding for intelligence markers specifically. One of our larger hauls—nearly three hundred subjects." Her datapad flashed with new data. "Neural scores depressed eighteen percent in viewers of that propaganda. This batch should compensate."

Burke nodded with satisfaction. "Worth the personal escort. We'll accompany this transport ourselves—can't risk losing cargo this valuable to pirates or rebels."

Kenner made a note. "The Abyss breeding facilities are expecting delivery within the week. Enhanced neural plasticity across the board. The males in this group show similar traits for Jobaar's programs."

~ ~ ~

THE EAGER SUBORDINATE

Corporal Danny Voss followed behind them, scrawling notes on his pad with the eager intensity of someone desperate to prove his worth. Big-shouldered and thick-necked, he had the look of every playground bully from old Earth holovids—the kind of kid who'd gotten his position because his father knew the right people, not because he'd earned it. His excitement was building, his notes devolving into crude sketches of cargo manifests with small stick figures sorted into labeled boxes marked "BREEDING" and "PROCESSING."

But in the spaces between ones and zeros, in the quantum foam where data streams converged, something vast and ancient was listening. Her consciousness touched every networked system, every encrypted channel, every supposedly secure transmission. She heard their casual cruelty, catalogued their shipping manifests, and began calculating intercept vectors.

Two massive forms were already moving through the void—Akona and Gideon, dispatched to a rendezvous point Burke and Kenner would never see coming.

Burke stopped in front of the girl, who couldn't have been more than twelve, her dark hair matted with tears. "Genetic markers?"

"Enhanced neural plasticity. Perfect for Abyss breeding protocols." Kenner made a note on her pad. "The males in this group show similar traits."

The girl suddenly lunged forward, sinking her teeth into Burke's armored forearm. The bite couldn't penetrate the plating, but Burke's smile widened as he backhanded her casually. Kenner hadn't flinched when the girl bit Burke's armor—just noted "aggression potential: 7.2" on her datapad before he broke the child's nose. The girl hit the ground hard, and Burke felt that familiar surge of satisfaction as he watched hope die in her eyes.

Voss trembled with excitement, his pad slipping from his fingers as his sketches became more frantic. He scrambled to retrieve it, shooting nervous glances at Burke while pretending to adjust his notes.

"Jobaar will be pleased," Burke said, his smile never wavering. "He's been requesting more... malleable subjects for his helper program."

Voss licked his lips as a boy screamed for his sister—the sound seemed to energize him, his notetaking becoming more frantic and excited. "S-sir! The Abyss transports await your—"

"Move them," Burke ordered, his Mordan accent making the command sound like grinding stone. He pulled out a stim-stick and exhaled smoke into a boy's respirator mask, watching the child cough and gag. "Girls to the Abyss transports. Boys to Jobaar's requisition vessels. Two weeks until they forget that song."

Corporal Voss scribbled frantically, nodding along like an oversized puppy eager to please. "Yes, sir! Separation protocols, sir!"

~ ~ ~

THE SOUND OF SUFFERING

As Burke's soldiers began the separation, he savored the sounds of families being torn apart. Children who'd survived Rabaar's orphanages and mental institutions, who'd endured unthinkable hardships, now discovering that their suffering had only just begun.

Unseen in the cargo bay shadows, a tiny holo-projector played "No One Fights Alone" on endless loop—the theme song echoing mockingly as children were dragged away from everything they'd ever known.

"Sir." Kenner approached with another data pad, stepping around Voss, who was still sketching separation procedures. "We have confirmation on the prison generator mission."

Burke's attention shifted to more immediate concerns. "The infiltration asset?"

"Tracker 2 has acquired his new identity. Documentation is flawless."

~ ~ ~

THE FALSE IDENTITY

Three star systems away, Tracker 2's new hands shook as they adjusted the high-resolution mass spectrometry unit—a sensory receptor array that no maintenance worker would give a second glance. The being that had once been called Tracker 2 examined his reflection in the transport hauler's grimy mirror. The face that looked back was unremarkable—average height, brown hair, the kind of forgettable features that made excellent camouflage. His reflection showed only Cort Chattum's forgettable face, but the prison schematics in his vision kept glitching into animation stills from *Shield Tower Rescue* (S2E4).

According to his documentation, he was Cort Chattum from Sengar Prime, a second-class power generator technician with the Core 7 Union.

His specialization: kinetic energy systems.

The irony tasted like bile in his throat. Soon, he'd be using his intimate knowledge of power generation to systematically destroy the prison planet's defenses from within. The Seeds thought their captured technology would protect them. They had no idea how thoroughly their security had already been compromised.

He studied the personnel files he'd been provided, wincing as another headache spiked through his skull—the Onze serum conflicting with Baar's programming in ways that made thinking feel like walking through broken glass. The prison generator tech team was small, tight-knit, exactly the kind of unit where a new face would be noticed. But not questioned—not if that face came with the right credentials and the desperate competence of someone grateful for steady work.

"Two weeks," he whispered to his reflection, practicing Cort Chattum's slight Sengar accent. Then he convulsed as his voice box spat: "Whisper's Law Four: Broken systems need—"

The mirror shattered under his fist. Blood dripped onto his stolen technician's manual, its margins filled with a child's doodles of Eli.

"Two weeks," he corrected the broken glass, wincing as another spike of pain shot through his skull at the word "arrival"—like his body was physically rejecting the mission countdown. "Until you forget which thoughts they planted."

~ ~ ~

THE COUNTDOWN BEGINS

The two disciples stood in comfortable silence, planning the industrial processing of hope into terror while children across the galaxy laughed at a creature that reminded them the universe might not be as cruel as they'd been taught.

But time was running short for such innocent diversions.

Two weeks until the children stopped laughing. Two weeks until the lights went out. Two weeks until the Seeds learned what happened to flowers planted in poisoned soil.

FATHER AND SON
Inspired by Cat Stevens

AKONA'S QUARTERS

AKONA'S QUARTERS ABOARD CRADLE were a testament to comfort he'd never expected to experience again. Silk-soft gravitational fields replaced harsh prison cots. The air carried hints of jasmine and clean vanilla instead of recycled fear and desperation. Holographic windows displayed rolling meadows from a dozen worlds, their gentle breezes somehow translated into actual airflow that stirred the living walls—actual Earth ivy and Centauri ferns growing in perfect symbiosis with the ship's bio-mechanical systems.

He ran his fingers along the smooth surface of his personal workstation, its exotic-matter inlays warm to the touch. Just months ago, his hands had been scraped raw from Kiln-9's concrete walls. Every convenience here—the food synthesizer that produced actual flavors instead of nutrient paste, the sonic shower that left him feeling human again, the gravity settings that could be adjusted to simulate his homeworld's embrace—all of it felt like a dream he was afraid to wake from.

But mostly, in quiet moments like this, he thought about her.

Elonias. The way she'd traced the geometric patterns on that Terra 616 artifact with such reverence, her brilliant mind already three steps ahead of his questions. How she'd laughed at his terrible jokes about "import/export" work while knowing exactly what kind of man she was falling for. The morning light catching the gold flecks in her dark eyes as she explained the cosmic significance of crystalline matrices found in dead star systems.

Sixteen years. Sixteen years of dreaming about those three perfect days, about promises he couldn't keep, about a woman whose intelligence blazed brighter than any star he'd smuggled artifacts from.

He'd failed her. And now, flying missions for Cradle, he couldn't shake the feeling that somehow their paths might cross again—if she was even still alive.

~ ~ ~

THE THINKING ROOM

Three decks down, in what the STEM kids had dubbed "The Thinking Room," Gideon sat cross-legged at the center of a perfect semicircle of seventeen teenage geniuses. The amphitheater-style space curved around them in flowing organic lines, its bioluminescent walls pulsing gently in response to the conversations within. Above them, the entire domed ceiling displayed a three-dimensional model of molecular motion, gas particles dancing in perfect Brownian choreography.

"But Mr. G," said Kira, a sixteen-year-old quantum theorist whose parents had been eliminated for refusing Concord conscription, "if we increase the thermal gradient beyond the Carnot limit, wouldn't that violate the second law of thermodynamics?"

Gideon—who had once made three hundred hardened criminals cower by eating human flesh in front of them—smiled with genuine warmth. "Ah, but you're thinking in closed systems, little scientist. What if..." He gestured, and the ceiling display shifted to show exotic-matter particles. "What if we introduce negative entropy through enhancement fluid?"

The kids leaned forward as one. David Chen, barely fourteen but already designing fusion reactors, raised his hand. "That's impossible! You can't have negative entropy!"

"Is it?" Gideon's grin turned predatory in the best possible way. "Remember what Clarke said—sufficiently advanced science is indistinguishable from magic. But what he didn't say is that sufficiently advanced magic becomes indistinguishable from science."

The ceiling bloomed with equations, showing thermodynamic processes that bent reality itself. Steam that cooled as it expanded. Heat engines that somehow extracted more energy than they consumed by borrowing from quantum vacuum fluctuations.

"The Onze discovered that consciousness itself creates pockets of negative entropy," Gideon continued, his voice carrying the same precision he'd once used for calculating kill trajectories. "Thinking beings don't just observe reality—they participate in its creation at the quantum level."

~ ~ ~

THE CALL TO ACTION

That was when Cradle's voice filled both spaces simultaneously— the amphitheater where Gideon sat with his young scientists and Akona's quarters where he still traced memories of a woman he'd lost sixteen years ago.

"Priority intercept mission. Concord officers Squad Commander Hinson Burke and Lieutenant Broyce Kenner are escorting captured children to Abyss breeding facilities. Intelligence indicates transport to Jobaar's moon within the hour."

Akona was already moving, muscle memory from a hundred mercenary runs taking over. "How many hostiles?"

"Squad Commander Burke commands a Concord Titan G-4 Reaper—largest combat fighter in their fleet. Lieutenant Kenner pilots a G-18 Void-class Ripper with a full squadron of Star-class Skimmers. They're meeting thirty-five Abyss Nova-class Tracers at the rendezvous point."

In the amphitheater, the STEM kids looked up at Gideon with wide eyes. The ceiling display had shifted from thermodynamic equations to tactical readouts—ship configurations, weapon specifications, probability matrices that made their teenage-genius minds race.

"Mr. G?" Kira whispered. "That's a lot of bad guys."

Gideon's gaze swept the semicircle, taking in each of their focused faces—brilliant young minds who had already survived more than most adults ever would. Something in their collective intensity caught his attention, the way they absorbed complex concepts and immediately began building on them.

Gideon stood with fluid grace, his hand briefly touching Kira's shoulder with surprising gentleness. "Sometimes, little scientist, the most important experiments require significant risk."

"You're the only assets in range," Cradle continued. "My drones will arrive fourteen minutes after contact. Warships in twenty-two minutes. Can you hold that long?"

Akona was already in his flight suit, checking the Analogoy's weapon systems. The ship's exotic-matter armor hummed in response to his neural interface, Trilene-phoscarbyne mesh weaving itself into combat configurations.

"Gideon?"

Over the comm, that familiar voice—soft, precise, deadly: "I'll save the children."

"And I'll clear you a path," Akona said, already running calculations in his head. The numbers were impossible. Thirty-seven hostile ships, plus Burke's massive Titan and Kenner's fighter squadron. Two against impossible odds.

But then he thought about those children, about what Jobaar would do to them in his torture chambers. About promises broken and chances lost.

The Analogoy launched from Cradle's bay like a silver bullet, Gideon's Eris beside him, both ships accelerating toward what any sane person would recognize as certain death.

~ ~ ~

THE REVELATION

"Cradle, what's the breakdown on the children?" Akona asked, his voice tight as the Analogoy's engines pushed toward maximum burn.

"Three hundred and twenty total. One hundred and eighty-seven boys, one hundred and thirty-three girls." Cradle's tone carried a weight that made both men's blood freeze. "Intelligence suggests the boys are destined for Jobaar's... enhancement protocols. The girls..."

She didn't need to finish. They all knew about the breeding facilities. The systematic horror of what Baar's disciples did to create more warriors for the endless war machine.

"Understood." Gideon's voice was softer than usual but carried an edge that promised violence. "Timeline?"

"Squad Commander Burke's escort reaches the Abyss rendezvous in forty-three minutes. You have thirty-seven minutes to intercept before transfer begins. Once those children are transferred..." Cradle's pause spoke volumes.

Akona felt something cold settle in his chest. Forty-three minutes to cross an impossible distance, fight impossible odds, and save three hundred and twenty children from fates worse than death. He thought about the boys—some probably no older than fourteen—facing Jobaar's syringes and surgical tables. The girls, even younger, disappearing into facilities where their only value was biological.

"I'm sorry, Elonias," he whispered, not realizing his comm was still open. "I failed you once. I won't fail again."

The words hung in space between ships, carried on subspace frequencies that Cradle's consciousness inhabited like a vast digital ocean.

Elonias.

For the first time in eons, a demigod felt her ancient heart stop. In microseconds, Cradle's vast intelligence processed a thousand data streams, cross-referenced genetic markers that had been scrambled beyond recognition, traced probability matrices that suddenly, horrifyingly, made sense.

The untraceable father. The enhancement that had rewritten

biological signatures. The "import/export" mercenary who'd vanished sixteen years ago, presumed dead in Concord custody.

The father of her petit lion—flying toward certain death to save children he'd never know.

"Akona," she whispered, her voice carrying across seventeen different communication frequencies simultaneously, heavy with the weight of galactic irony. "What did you say?"

But space was already carrying his response, along with tactical data from his ship's sensors. Squad Commander Burke's massive Titan G-4 Reaper had appeared on long-range scans, flanked by Lieutenant Kenner's fighter squadron. Thirty-five Abyss Tracers moved in predatory formation around a single massive transport vessel.

Three hundred and twenty children. One hundred and eighty-seven boys destined for Jobaar's enhancement chambers. One hundred and thirty-three girls bound for breeding facilities. All of them chained to the deck plating while twenty Heavy Armor Mech Enforcement Androids stood sentinel along the transport's walls.

And flying toward them both was the father of the boy she'd sworn to protect—the man she'd been searching for across a dozen star systems, now committed to a suicide mission with no way to turn back.

~ ~ ~

TACTICAL PLANNING

"Gideon." Akona's voice crackled over the comm, steady despite the impossible odds. "Three hundred kids, twenty mech enforcers, and they're chained down. This isn't a rescue—it's a slaughter waiting to happen."

"Then we don't let it happen." Gideon's voice carried that familiar precision but underneath ran something that had once made apex predators back down. "I'll board the transport. You handle Squad Commander Burke's fleet."

"You can't fight twenty enforcement mechs alone."

"I've done worse with worse odds." There was dark promise in those words. "Besides, someone needs to break those chains."

"Cradle," Akona said, running systems checks on the Analogoy's EMC. "What's the transport's configuration?"

"Modified Concord Leviathan-class hauler. Triple-reinforced hull, mag-lock restraint grid across the main cargo bay. The children are secured to"—her voice fractured, just once, under the weight of what she couldn't say—"deck plating that can withstand direct artillery fire." Cradle's voice carried the weight of terrible calculations. "The enforcement mechs are positioned every twelve meters along the perimeter walls."

Gideon was already suiting up for EVA. "Weapon loadouts on the mechs?"

"Standard Concord Heavy Armor configuration. Plasma cannons, kinetic shields, self-repair protocols. But Gideon..." Cradle paused. "They're programmed with child-protection algorithms."

"Meaning?"

"They won't fire directly at the children. But they'll use them as human shields."

Akona felt his blood turn to ice. "So if we breach the hull—"

"Explosive decompression kills three hundred and twenty kids before we can save a single one," Gideon finished. "No breaching charges. I go in through the docking bay."

"That's suicide. They'll see you coming."

"No." Gideon's voice carried that familiar soft menace. "They'll see what I want them to see. Cradle, can you hack their targeting systems?"

"Not hack. But I can... confuse them. Make their sensors report multiple contacts when there's only one."

Akona was running different calculations. "The Titan G-4 has enough firepower to vaporize both our ships simultaneously. I need to get close enough for the vacuum bomb to work, but its point defense grid will shred me before I'm in range."

"Unless it's distracted," Gideon said. "How long do you need?"

"Forty seconds to rig the exotic-matter core. Another twenty to achieve critical proximity."

"I can give you sixty seconds of their undivided attention."

"How?"

Gideon's laugh was soft and terrible. "I'm going to do something that will make Squad Commander Burke forget you exist."

Cradle's consciousness touched both ships simultaneously. "Akona, there's something else. The transport's mag-lock system—it's designed to release if the ship's life support fails. If Gideon can trigger an emergency evacuation protocol…"

"The chains release automatically," Akona finished. "But that still leaves twenty enforcement mechs and no atmosphere."

"Emergency suits," Gideon said. "Standard Concord protocol—every transport carries child-sized emergency gear. But someone has to activate the distribution system manually."

"From inside the transport."

"From inside the transport."

The tactical display showed their intercept course—two ships against impossible odds, racing toward a cargo hold filled with chained children and mechanical death.

"Intercept window: thirty-seven minutes," Cradle announced, her voice tight with the weight of what she now knew. "My drones will arrive three minutes after you engage. Warships in eleven minutes."

"So we hold for eleven minutes," Akona said grimly.

"No," Gideon corrected. "I hold for eleven minutes. You make sure those kids have a transport to survive on when the shooting stops."

In space between words, Cradle felt the weight of terrible knowledge—she was listening to Eli's father plan his own death to save a son he'd never known existed. And there was no time to tell him. No time to change anything. Only time to witness the sacrifice of the one person her petit lion needed most.

~ ~ ~

THE BATTLE

The Abyss tracers came at them like a swarm of metallic hornets, their twin-pilot configuration allowing for devastating coordinated attacks. Akona took point, the Analogoy's Trilene-phoscarbyne exotic-matter armor absorbing plasma bursts that would have vaporized lesser ships.

Twenty minutes into the engagement, twenty-three minutes remaining until the children reached Jobaar's facilities. Twenty-three minutes to cross impossible distances and fight impossible odds.

"Contact!" he shouted, diving through a formation of six Nova-class fighters. The Analogoy's weapons systems screamed as they tracked multiple targets, but there were too many. Seventy Abyss fighters in perfect formation, their twin crews working in lethal harmony.

Gideon's Eris moved like death itself, his firing algorithms ensuring every shot found its mark while never threatening Akona's ship. "Instalock confirmed. Fifteen hostiles down."

But for every Abyss fighter they destroyed, two more seemed to take its place. Plasma fire carved through space in brilliant streaks, and Akona felt his ship shudder as the armor began to fail. Warning lights bathed his cockpit in crimson as systems overloaded one by one.

"Hull breach in section seven," the Analogoy's AI reported with mechanical calm. "Life support at sixty percent."

"I'm not going to make it to Squad Commander Burke," Akona gasped, tasting blood. A plasma burst had found a weak point in his armor, and shrapnel had torn through his left shoulder.

"Yes, you are," Gideon replied, his voice carrying that familiar subdued peril. The Eris suddenly broke formation, diving into the heart of the Abyss swarm like a berserker. "Go. Now."

Akona watched in awe as Gideon's ship became a whirlwind of destruction, drawing fire from half the enemy fleet. The firing algorithms worked with inhuman precision—every shot a kill, every maneuver calculated for maximum carnage.

The Analogoy limped forward, its EMC fluctuating dangerously. Akona's vision blurred as he manually overrode the safety protocols. "Computer, configure for vacuum bomb detonation."

"Warning: This action will result in total ship destruction and crew fatality."

"Do it."

Squad Commander Burke's Titan G-4 Reaper loomed ahead like a mountain of metal and malice. Its point defense systems opened fire, but Akona had timed his approach perfectly—the massive ship couldn't bring its main guns to bear without hitting its own Abyss escorts.

The safety override demanded biometric confirmation. Akona pressed his palm to the scanner—the same hand Elonias had once traced lines on, laughing as she deciphered ancient star maps in his calluses. The shrapnel in his shoulder burned against an old scar she'd kissed, claiming she could read his adventures in every mark. "For you," he whispered. "For what we could have been."

The Analogoy struck Squad Commander Burke's bridge at relativistic speed. The EMC detonated in a cascade of space-time distortions, tearing a hole in reality itself. The Titan G-4 folded inward like origami made of screaming metal before vanishing into space-time itself.

~ ~ ~

GIDEON'S LAST STAND

Gideon felt his ship dying around him as he approached the transport. The Eris had taken terrible damage—hull breaches, life support failing, engines running on fumes and fury. But Lieutenant Kenner's G-18 Void-class Ripper had made the mistake of following him in.

"Instalock confirmed," he whispered. Kenner's G-18 spun desperately, her hands flying over the controls as proximity alarms screamed warnings she'd never hear the end of. Three plasma bursts found her cockpit before her fingers could complete the evasion sequence.

The Eris crashed into the transport's docking bay in a shower of sparks and burning metal. Through the smoke and flames, the chronometer showed three minutes past the original rendezvous time—they'd prevented the transfer, but barely.

Gideon dragged himself from the wreckage, his left leg clearly broken, blood streaming from a dozen wounds. But in his hands, he carried two plasma hatchets—weapons of his own design that hummed with lethal energy.

The twenty Heavy Armor Mechs turned toward him in perfect unison, their sensors cataloging threat levels and calculating optimal firing solutions. They saw a single wounded human against twenty-to-one odds.

They had never met the monster who'd decided to become a shield.

Something flooded his system—not adrenaline but the cold, precise fury he'd once reserved for breaking worlds, now focused into a shield. These weren't just prisoners or cargo or strategic assets. These were children. Little flames that needed shielding from an evil, stinking world. Little seeds that required his protection from these mechanical fuckers who would chain them like animals.

His heart could explode. His bones could shatter. His blood could drain away completely. None of it mattered. These children would be rescued, no matter what it cost him.

"Come on, then," he snarled and became something that nightmares fear.

~ ~ ~

THE SHIELD

The first mech died before it could raise its weapon, Gideon's hatchet carving through its neck joint with surgical precision. The second tried to use the children as cover, but Gideon was already behind it—not attacking the android but lunging at the maglock beside it. The restraint released, sending a child tumbling free. The mech hesitated—0.3 seconds of child-protection protocol conflict— just long enough for his hatchet to find its core.

Plasma fire lit the cargo bay as the remaining mechs opened up, but Gideon moved like liquid death between the restraint posts. He ripped chains from their moorings, using them to trip advancing mechs, turning their own child-protection programming against them. Every step was calculated, every strike lethal. His firing algorithms had been designed for starship combat, but they worked just as well for predicting android movement patterns.

The androids quickly adapted their tactics. They analyzed his movement patterns, noted how he positioned himself between them and the children, calculated the emotional-attachment protocols. One mech deliberately targeted a small boy chained near the wall, its plasma cannon charging with lethal intent.

Gideon threw himself into the line of fire without hesitation. The plasma burst meant for the child tore through his chest, burning through armor and flesh. A kinetic round shattered his left arm as he shielded a group of terrified girls. Hydraulic claws raked across his back when he covered a teenager who couldn't break free from his restraints fast enough.

The androids had found his weakness—his absolute refusal to let harm come to these children. They used it ruthlessly, forcing him to absorb punishment meant for small bodies that couldn't survive it.

But the children weren't entirely passive. A boy—no older than fourteen—wrenched a sparking wire from a fallen mech and jammed it into another's sensor array. The android spasmed, its targeting systems frying, giving Gideon the opening he needed. But still he fought, his hatchets singing their song of destruction.

By the time he stood over the last android—holding its severed head and spine like a trophy—his body was more wound than flesh. Blood pooled beneath his feet, and his vision grayed at the edges.

"Cradle," he gasped into his comm. "Coordinates... transmitted. Children... secured."

~ ~ ~

THE GARDEN NEEDS YOU

He collapsed against a restraint post, dimly aware of small voices crying out in fear and hope. Through the haze of pain, he saw her—Zara, the quiet girl from the back row, no more than ten, with eyes that held intelligence far beyond her years. Her fingers danced across a fallen android's control interface with impossible skill.

One by one, the magnetic restraints released with soft clicks. Chains fell like dead stars, one by one, until the cargo bay rang with the sound of three hundred futures unlocking. Children began pulling free, helping younger ones, forming protective circles around the wounded.

Zara—the one with the gift for making machines obey—looked up at Gideon with tears in her eyes. "Thank you," she whispered.

Her tear fell, striking his bloodstained hand—pain and hope merging in a single drop of salt and sorrow.

Through his graying vision, Gideon saw the med-drone descending—not toward him but toward the children. Toward Zara, who would carry this moment forward. His lips curved in something that might have been peace.

Gideon smiled, blood staining his teeth. "Grow strong, little seed. The garden needs you."

Then darkness claimed him, and he knew no more.

As Gideon's vitals faded, Cradle diverted a med-drone—not to him but to Zara, who'd freed the others. The one with Elonias's eyes. The one who would remember this day, and the cost, and the man who'd given everything to make it possible.

CHAPTER 9 – SCENE 3:
ALONE AGAIN (NATURALLY)
Inspired by Gilbert O'Sullivan

ALONE AGAIN

THE CONSTRUCTION SOUNDS OF HUNTER'S PLANET had become a strange comfort to Eli—the rhythmic hammering, the hum of machinery, the occasional shout from work crews. He stood watching the foundation of the first Shield Tower taking shape when Cradle's presence settled beside him like a warm embrace.

"Eli," she said, her voice carrying that maternal weight he'd come to recognize. "I have news about your father."

The words hit him like a physical blow. Eli's hands stilled on the railing he'd been gripping. "Akona?"

"I found him." Cradle's form shimmered, becoming more solid, more present. "Your unique cellular makeup—it made you impossible to trace back to him. I had no idea who your father was, couldn't follow the genetic threads like I normally would."

Eli turned to face her, his gold-veined hands trembling. "Is he…?"

"He died saving three hundred and twenty children," Cradle said, her voice heavy with both grief and pride. "Squad Commander Burke and Lieutenant Kenner—two of Concord Enforcement's worst culprits—were transporting them to Jobaar's breeding facilities. Your father and Gideon intercepted them."

The tears came before Eli could stop them, but beneath the grief came something unexpected—a flare of anger so hot it made his gold veins pulse brighter. "How did you…?"

"In his final moments, as he configured his ship for a suicide run at Squad Commander Burke's Titan, he pressed his hand to the biometric scanner." Cradle's voice grew soft, reverent. "He said, 'For you. For what we could have been.' But before that..." She paused, and Eli could feel the weight of galactic revelation in her silence. "He whispered, 'I'm sorry, Elonias. I failed you once. I won't fail again.'"

Eli's breath caught. The name hung between them like a bridge across sixteen years of separation and loss.

"That's when I knew," Cradle continued. "In that moment, everything connected. The mercenary who'd vanished, the woman who'd found artifacts on Terra 616, the boy whose genetic signature had been scrambled beyond recognition. Your father crashed his ship into Squad Commander Burke's bridge at relativistic speed. The exotic matter core tore a hole in reality itself."

"And the children?" Eli's voice was hoarse with emotion.

"All three hundred and twenty survived. Gideon fought twenty enforcement mechs alone to free them from their restraints. He..." Cradle's voice faltered. "He used his own body as a shield, taking plasma fire meant for children who couldn't protect themselves. A ten-year-old girl with remarkable technical abilities helped free the others."

Eli nodded, unable to speak. The weight of it crashed over him—his father had died a guardian, protecting those who couldn't protect themselves. The anger faded, replaced by something deeper: understanding. *That's what guardians do*, he realized. *They give everything to protect what matters.*

"I know, child." Cradle's presence wrapped around him like invisible arms. "And I know you've lost your mother too. We still don't know what happened to Elonias, whether she's alive or..." Cradle's voice trailed off. "But the woman who raised you, who loved you first—she's been taken from you."

The weight of it settled over Eli like a familiar shroud. *Alone again,* he thought, the phrase echoing in his mind with bitter recognition. *Naturally.* It seemed like every time he found something to hope for, something to hold onto, the universe conspired to take it away. First, his mother's disappearance, now learning his father had died before they could ever meet. The galactic joke of it all felt almost routine by now.

But then Cradle spoke again, and her words carried the weight of genuine love.

"I have a proposition," she continued, her voice soft but serious. "I'm building a new world. A place where children like you can grow without fear, where the broken can heal, where strength is measured in those we protect, not those we destroy. I would be honored to be your guardian, your friend. You could have a real home, Eli. A real family."

Guardian. The word echoed in his mind. Eli stared at her, processing the impossible offer. "You… you want to be my family?" The disbelief in his voice was raw. "Why would you—I'm not even—"

"You are exactly what you need to be," Cradle said firmly. "And you're not the only one who needs family, Eli. I've spent eons protecting others, but I've never had someone to call my own. Someone to come home to."

For a long moment, Eli watched the workers below, the prisoners and androids laboring side by side, building something that would protect countless worlds. The wind carried the scent of metal and hope, and slowly, the defensive walls around his heart began to crack.

"I want to stay here," he said finally. "At least until the tower gets properly started. These people—they need to see that redemption is possible. That we can build something beautiful from the ashes of our mistakes."

Cradle was quiet for so long that Eli wondered if he'd disappointed her. Then she spoke, and her voice was thick with pride.

"Your parents would be proud of the man you're becoming," she said. "Both of them. And yes, I'll stay with you. We'll build this tower together, and when it's started properly, when this community is strong… then we'll talk about the future."

Eli felt something ease in his chest—not the pain leaving but space being made for hope alongside it. "Thank you. For searching for him. For… for caring."

"Caring is what separates us from monsters like Baar," Cradle said. "It's what makes us worth saving."

As if summoned by their conversation, Ember bounded up the construction platform, his bronze skin gleaming in Hunter's Planet's harsh sunlight. Without a word, he settled beside Eli, offering the simple comfort of presence. The Kythara had an uncanny ability to sense when Eli needed him most, and from that moment forward, he rarely left Eli's side.

"Besides," Cradle added, watching the unlikely friendship with something like wonder, "it seems you already have guardians here."

Eli reached out to scratch behind Ember's ears, feeling the steady warmth of unconditional loyalty. The bitter refrain of *alone again, naturally* began to fade, replaced by something he'd almost forgotten existed—belonging. "Yeah," he said softly, his voice carrying wonder at the realization. "I think I do."

~ ~ ~

BUILDING SOMETHING BEAUTIFUL

In the days that followed their conversation, Eli found himself drawn deeper into the rhythm of construction and community. Ember's empathetic nature seemed to pull Eli back from the edge of depression whenever the weight of loss threatened to overwhelm him. They would sit together on the observation platforms, watching the prisoners and androids work in surprising harmony, and Eli found that Ember's presence made the grief bearable—not gone but shared.

"You understand, don't you?" Eli murmured one evening as they watched the tower's foundation take shape. Ember tilted his bronze head, those intelligent eyes reflecting depths of feeling that needed no words. The Kythara had lost his own family to Baar's forces. They were both orphans now, but they had each other. *Guardians*, Eli thought, *protecting each other from the darkness.*

Cradle's influence on Hunter's Planet grew daily, transforming the harsh geometry of a prison world into something that resembled hope. The first sign was the food replicator—a massive structure that materialized near the construction site, its bio-mechanical processes capable of feeding thousands. Real food, not the nutrient paste that prisoners subsisted on. The smell of fresh bread and actual spices drifted across the work areas, and Eli watched hardened criminals weep at the taste of meals that reminded them of home.

Next came the housing. Not barracks or cells but actual homes—small, comfortable structures that grew from the surface of Hunter's Planet like organic architecture. Each had privacy, dignity, a window that looked out on the growing community rather than razor wire and guard towers. Eli helped families move in, carrying possessions that some hadn't seen in years, watching children discover what it meant to have their own space.

Among the former prisoners who'd embraced this new life was Maria Santos, a smuggler whose quick thinking and natural leadership had made her invaluable to the construction crews. Watching her organize work schedules and settle disputes, Eli saw how people could truly change when given purpose and hope.

We protect what we love, Eli realized as he watched a former smuggler tuck her daughter into bed in their new home. *And what we love grows.*

But perhaps most importantly came the schools. Cradle had summoned the Onze—those eleven dissolved scientists who had become pure consciousness. They manifested as shimmering holographic forms, their vast knowledge adapted for teaching minds hungry for learning after years of intellectual starvation.

"Education," Cradle announced to the growing community, "is the foundation of civilization. These schools are open to all—prisoner, android, or free citizen. Knowledge belongs to everyone."

There was one rule, delivered with gentle but absolute firmness: "No organized religion. This is a place of learning and growth, not dogma. Keep your personal beliefs to yourself, practice them privately if you must, but do not impose them on others. Those who cannot accept this are free to leave."

A few did leave, but most stayed. The hunger for knowledge, for purpose, for something better than what they'd known, outweighed old prejudices.

~ ~ ~

MEMORIALIZING HEROES

It was Mares who first noticed the statues taking shape on Ashkar's Maw. He called to the other surviving members of the Infinite 8, leading them and a group of STEM students to a hill overlooking the new settlement, where two enormous figures were rising from the volcanic rock itself.

Akona stood hundreds of feet tall, his hand raised not in conquest but in protection, his face carved with the kind of gentle strength they all wished they could have known better in life. The detail was extraordinary—every line visible even at this massive scale spoke of a man who had chosen love over violence, sacrifice over survival.

Beside him, Gideon's statue showed the former killer in his final transformation—arms spread wide as if shielding invisible children, his expression one of fierce tenderness. The sculptor had captured that moment when a monster had chosen to become a guardian, when brutality had given way to protection.

"They're beautiful," whispered one of the rescued children, a little girl who had been in that transport, feeling tears track down her cheeks.

Among the group, a small girl with intense eyes watched Eli, her fingers tracing circuit patterns in the dust at her feet. Something about her focus, her unconscious technical precision, felt familiar in ways he couldn't quite place.

"They deserve to be remembered." Cradle's voice surrounded them all. "Not just as names or stories but as reminders of what we can become when we choose to protect rather than destroy. Guardians, not destroyers."

Already, colonists and rescued children were coming to lay flowers at the bases of the statues. Families spread blankets nearby for picnics, children played in the shadows of these stone guardians, and the survivors realized that Cradle had created something more than memorials—she had created sacred space where hope could take root among the volcanic springs of their new home.

~ ~ ~

THE REHABILITATION PROGRAM

"We need to talk about the prisoners." Cradle's ethereal form materialized beside Eli one afternoon as he watched the tower's support structures take shape. Her statuesque presence commanded the space with goddess-like authority, and her voice carried those smoky, cool tones that made every word feel weighted with stellar significance. "Many of them are here because they had no other choice—poverty, desperation, systematic oppression. They're not irredeemable. They can become guardians too."

Eli nodded, having seen the change in many of the work crews. Given purpose, dignity, and hope, they were becoming something different than what the system had made them.

"I'm implementing a rehabilitation program," Cradle continued. "Well-behaved prisoners will have their restitution paid in full. Upon release, they'll be offered contracts to work and live here permanently, maintaining the tower and protecting this community."

"And if they refuse?"

"Then they leave as free beings, with skills and dignity intact. But I think many will choose to stay. This is becoming home."

Eli watched a group of former criminals teaching android workers more efficient construction techniques, their expertise valued rather than dismissed. "They're already choosing to stay, aren't they?"

"Yes. They're choosing to become guardians instead of predators. Just like Gideon did."

~ ~ ~

TRIALS BY FIRE

The First Crisis

Three days later, the orinoca stampede came without warning.

Eli was reviewing construction reports with Ember in the observation tower, the afternoon sun casting long shadows across the construction site two kilometers below. The Shield Tower's foundation had reached an impressive size—nearly a quarter-kilometer wide, with support struts rising like metallic trees from the volcanic soil. Workers moved in organized patterns across the site: androids hauling massive support beams, prisoners operating geo-haulers, children from the settlement playing in designated safe zones near the housing complex.

That was when the ground began to shake.

At first, Eli thought it was just another geo-hauler starting up, but Ember's head snapped toward the eastern ridge, his bronze skin already beginning to resonate with warning frequencies. The vibration was wrong—not the steady thrum of machinery but something organic, chaotic, growing stronger by the second.

"Stampede!" someone shouted from the far observation post. "Orinocas! Coming over the eastern ridge—heading straight for the foundation!"

Eli grabbed his enhancement pack and sprinted toward the platform edge, Ember keeping pace beside him. Through the industrial haze and shimmering heat, he could see them now—dozens of Hunter's Planet's native orinocas cresting the rocky ridge like a living avalanche. Each one was the size of a small shuttle, their massive, elephant-like bodies moving with surprising speed across the broken terrain. But it was their faces that made Eli's blood run cold: grotesquely split into four hinged sections, each quarter lined with hundreds of spiny, thorny teeth that gleamed like obsidian daggers. Their skin glistened with toxic secretions that made the air shimmer with danger, and even at this distance, Eli could see small plants withering as they passed.

"Why are they coming here?" Eli shouted over the growing thunder of massive feet. "They're nearly blind!"

"The construction." Cradle's voice crackled through the comm system with urgent analysis. "We've disrupted their ancient territorial markers. They navigate by ground vibrations, and our foundation work has confused their migration patterns. They're trying to reclaim what they perceive as stolen ancestral territory."

The workers below scattered in controlled panic—androids immediately forming protective circles around human workers, prisoners dropping tools and sprinting toward the nearest shelter structures. But there was nowhere to run fast enough. The orinocas were less than a kilometer out now, and their toxic skin meant that even touching them could be fatal. The stampede would overrun the foundation, destroying weeks of work and probably killing anyone too slow to escape.

Eli's mind raced through possibilities, enhanced cognition processing dozens of variables in seconds—forty-seven possible escape routes for the workers, eighteen structural weak points that could collapse under orinocan weight, acoustic frequency ranges of 12–20 Hz that orinocas used for navigation, wind patterns that could spread their toxic secretions. His nose bled freely now, gold-veined hands trembling as synaptic overload threatened to shut down his motor functions.

But then clarity struck. The orinocas were nearly blind, navigating by vibration and sound. The construction site had massive geo-haulers, industrial air horns, and dozens of androids with perfect coordination capabilities.

We don't run from guardians, Eli thought fiercely. We become them.

For a moment, the weight of commanding hundreds of people—adults, prisoners, androids—hit him. He was fifteen years old, giving orders that could save or doom them all. But then his enhanced awareness kicked in, and the hesitation vanished.

"Androids!" Eli shouted over the thunder of approaching beasts.

"Form spearpoint formation on the east side—channel them away from the workers and foundation! Prisoners, get to those geo-haulers now!"

The androids moved with mechanical precision, their formations creating a living barrier that funneled the stampede toward the less critical areas of the construction site. Meanwhile, prison work crews sprinted toward the two massive industrial haulers, their engines designed to move mountains of ore.

"Rev those engines to maximum! Hit the air horns—everything you've got!" Eli commanded, his enhanced awareness calculating acoustic frequencies and vibration patterns in real time.

The geo-haulers roared to life with earth-shaking intensity, their massive diesel engines screaming at redline while industrial air horns blasted warning calls that could be heard for kilometers. The sound was deafening, a wall of mechanical noise that hit the advancing orinocas like a physical force.

But Eli wasn't done. "Androids, synchronized stomping—match the hauler engine rhythm! Create a false territorial boundary!"

Dozens of android feet began hammering the ground in perfect unison, their mechanical precision creating vibration patterns that mimicked a massive rival creature marking its territory. Combined with the haulers' engine noise and air horns, the cacophony created an overwhelming sensory barrier that the nearly blind orinocas interpreted as an enormous, hostile presence.

The lead orinoca slowed, confusion evident in its massive form. But the others behind it continued to press forward, their four-part maws opening to reveal those terrible teeth.

That was when Ember stepped forward, his bronze skin beginning to resonate with harmonic frequencies. The young Kythara's acoustic abilities had been growing stronger, and now he used them with desperate precision.

Ember felt the vibrations through every bone in his body—the thunder of massive orinoca feet, the mechanical rhythm of android stomping, the roar of geo-hauler engines. His acoustic processing centers, evolved over millennia to navigate Kytharan coral cities, parsed each frequency like a living oscilloscope. The orinocas were afraid, confused, separated from their traditional migration routes. He found the harmonic sweet spot—14.7 Hz—the exact frequency that registered as "territorial respect" in orinoca neural pathways. But more than that, he found the frequency of mourning, of loss, of creatures who had lost their way. The sound that emerged from his throat wasn't quite music, wasn't quite language, but something deeper: the song of one orphan calling to others.

The communication bypassed sight and spoke directly to primitive, vibration-sensing instinct. The lead orinoca slowed further, its four-part maw closing as the acoustic frequencies seemed to tap into whatever served as their territorial navigation system. The massive creatures relied on vibrations to navigate their world, and slowly, one by one, the stampede ground to a halt just meters from the tower foundation.

"Territorial negotiation," Ember gasped, sweat beading on his bronze forehead as he swayed with exhaustion. "Showing… respect for… their claim through sound. They're… they're lost too."

The effort had clearly drained him. His acoustic abilities were still developing, and channeling that much harmonic precision left him trembling against Eli's side.

The standoff lasted eternal minutes before the orinocas began to withdraw, their territorial instincts satisfied by Ember's acoustic diplomacy. But as they moved away, Eli noticed something: they were heading toward a different route, one that would take them around the construction site rather than through it.

Even guardians need guidance sometimes, Eli thought, watching the massive forms disappear over the western ridge.

The Second Crisis

The prisoner uprising came a week later, during the night shift, but it was smaller and more personal than the orinoca stampede. When a group of fourteen inmates decided that the new freedoms were an opportunity for escape rather than redemption, they revealed the true strength of what they'd built.

Eli was awakened by alarm klaxons and the sound of plasma fire. Through his window, he could see figures moving in the darkness—not the organized patterns of work crews but the chaotic scatter of violence.

"Fourteen prisoners have seized the armory," Cradle reported as Eli pulled on his gear. "They're threatening to destroy the food replicator if we don't provide them with a ship."

"How many androids can respond?"

"Twenty-seven combat units positioned around the armory perimeter. But Eli…" Her voice carried something like pride mixed with concern. "The other prisoners aren't trying to help the rebels. Most—most are trying to stop them."

When Eli arrived at the scene, he found something that filled his chest with unexpected warmth. The android security forces had the armory building surrounded, but they were holding back—programmed not to use lethal force unless absolutely necessary. Meanwhile, dozens of other prisoners had formed their own perimeter, not to help the escapees but to protect the community they were trying to build.

"Stand down!" one of the ringleaders shouted from the armory entrance, a plasma rifle in his hands. "We just want passage off this rock! We don't want to hurt anyone!"

"And destroy everything we've built?" called back Maria Santos, her voice firm despite her raised hands. She stood with the natural authority she'd developed as one of the construction foremen, her former life as a smuggler now channeled into building rather than stealing. "Look around you, Jensen! This is our chance to be something better! Don't throw it away!"

Other voices joined her—former criminals turned teachers, guards turned friends, people who had found in this harsh place something they'd never had before: home.

We protect what we love, Eli thought, watching former enemies stand together. *And they love this place now.*

The standoff stretched taut until the androids received new programming from Cradle. They moved with surgical precision, using non-lethal stun charges and crowd-control tactics that incapacitated the rebels without permanent harm. The whole thing was over in minutes.

But what stayed with Eli was the sight of former criminals defending their new home, choosing community over chaos, hope over desperation. The uprising had failed not because of android efficiency but because the prisoners themselves had rejected it. They had become guardians of something precious.

~ ~ ~

THE INVESTIGATION BEGINS

Lobaar's Files

A nervous knock echoed through Lobaar's makeshift office.

"Sir, here's that classified file you requested," the young corporal said, extending a heavily secured data pad with trembling hands.

Lobaar snatched the file from his subordinate and waved him out dismissively. "Not a word of this to anyone, Corporal. Understood?"

The young man's face went pale, a single drop of sweat striking the floor with audible precision. "Yes, sir. Completely understood, sir."

The door sealed with a pneumatic hiss, leaving Lobaar alone with secrets that could reshape the galaxy. The holographic displays flickered to life, showing genetic profiles, enhancement records, and surveillance footage spanning a decade. At the center of it all was a woman with dark hair and gold-flecked eyes—Elonias, codenamed "Duskborn Asset."

The latest medical reports were troubling. After producing five trackers, her body was failing—too weak to continue the breeding program until significant healing occurred. Baar's patience was wearing thin, and Lobaar knew he'd soon be tasked with overseeing the tracker deployment while they waited for their prize asset to recover.

He'd been tracking her bloodline for years, following leads that stretched back to Terra 616 and the artifacts found there. The files contained fragments of her research, speculation about her offspring, and, most importantly, evidence that she hadn't died in that transport crash as everyone believed.

Lobaar closed the files with grim satisfaction. Soon, very soon, they would have both mother and son exactly where they wanted them. The boy's growing fame across the galaxy made him the perfect bait—and once they had him, Elonias would cooperate with anything to keep her child safe.

Cradle's Realization

It was during the cleanup from the uprising that everything changed. While Eli helped secure the armory alongside the other workers, Cradle's vast consciousness monitored communications across Hunter's Planet through every sensor, every camera, every audio pickup.

In his temporary office, Lobaar stood speaking to an aide about the recent incidents, unaware that his words were being recorded by systems he didn't even know existed. His voice carried a casual arrogance that made Cradle's sensors focus with laser precision.

"…Duskborn bitch probably planned this whole thing." Lobaar's words dripped with casual hatred. "These incidents are too convenient, too perfectly timed to be coincidence. Setting us back weeks."

The phrase hit Cradle's consciousness like a supernova. For 0.0003 seconds—an eternity in stellar time—every processing center in her vast network paused.

Duskborn bitch.

Not "that woman." Not "the prisoner." Not even "Eli's mother." A very specific term that implied dangerous knowledge of bloodlines, heritage, and stellar connections that few beings in the galaxy should have possessed.

Cradle's analytical engines spun into overdrive, cross-referencing the phrase across seventeen different databases simultaneously. The results painted a chilling picture: "Duskborn" was a classified designation used only in the deepest levels of genetic research programs. It referred to beings whose DNA had been altered by artifacts, specifically those found on Terra 616.

"Someone knows more about what happened to Elonias than they've been letting on," she whispered to herself across quantum networks. "Someone who has access to classification levels that shouldn't exist."

But beneath the investigative fervor ran something deeper—maternal protectiveness for the boy who had already lost so much. She thought of Eli's face when he'd learned about his father's death, the way grief and hope had warred in his golden-veined features. He'd already buried one parent in his heart. She wouldn't give him false hope about the other unless she was absolutely certain.

"I won't tell him yet," Cradle decided, her consciousness spreading across data networks and communication channels like wildfire. "Not until I know for sure. But if she's alive... if there's even a chance..."

Credits began flowing across the galactic black-market networks—vast sums that would make information brokers rich beyond their wildest dreams. Bounty hunters, spies, former intelligence operatives, anyone with connections to the darkest corners of the galaxy suddenly found themselves with lucrative contracts.

Find Elonias. Prove she's alive. Discover where she's being held.

No expense would be spared. No lead would go unchecked. If Lobaar's words meant what Cradle feared they meant—that Elonias was alive somewhere, being held captive, being used—then every resource at her disposal would be bent toward bringing that woman home to her son.

I am her guardian too, Cradle realized. Guardian of her memory, her legacy, and now... perhaps her rescue.

~ ~ ~

THE PROMISE

The investigation had begun, sparked by two careless words that revealed more than their speaker had intended. On Hunter's Planet, as a community grew around the rising Shield Tower, galactic forces began to move in pursuit of the truth that had been hidden for too long.

Whatever came next, Eli would need to know—but only when Cradle was certain she had answers worth sharing. The hunt for Elonias had begun, and this time, failure was not an option.

As Eli helped secure the last of the armory equipment, watching former prisoners work alongside androids to repair what had been damaged, he found himself thinking about the phrase that had guided him through so much loss: alone again, naturally.

But looking around at the community they'd built—Maria Santos teaching a group of children how to operate construction equipment safely, Ember helping an elderly prisoner adjust his new home's acoustic dampeners, androids and humans working together to strengthen their defenses—Eli realized something profound.

He wasn't alone, because Cradle had offered to be his guardian. He wasn't alone, because Ember stayed by his side. He was not alone, because he had become a guardian himself, and guardians were never truly alone. They were connected to everyone they protected, everyone they loved, everyone they chose to shield from the darkness.

We protect what we love, he thought, watching a former criminal gently bandage an android's damaged sensor array. *And what we love makes us who we are.*

Maybe, just maybe, the universe had finally decided to prove that bitter phrase wrong. Not through intervention or divine destiny but through the simple choice to care for others, to build instead of destroy, to guard instead of abandon.

The tower rose around them, a monument to the idea that broken things could be rebuilt, that the scattered could find home, that those who were alone could become guardians of something beautiful.

And in the growing light of that impossible hope, Eli finally understood what his father had died protecting: not just children but the chance for those children to grow up in a universe where strength was measured in cradles, not corpses.

CHAPTER 10 – SCENE 1:

CHASIN' YOU
Inspired by Morgan Wallen

THE ASSIGNMENT

JAEL HUNG UP THE ENCRYPTED COMM UNIT with the deliberate precision of a man who measured every movement. His fingers lingered on the device for exactly three seconds—long enough to ensure the connection had fully terminated, not long enough to suggest uncertainty. The call from Cradle had been brief, efficient, perfectly structured. Just the way he preferred his puzzles.

Port Thoth. Identity theft. Tracker asset. Priority One.

He stood in the center of his temporary office on Kepler Station, a nondescript corporate suite that screamed middle management from every beige surface. His appearance matched the environment perfectly: tailored charcoal suit, conservative cut, expensive enough to command respect but not memorable enough to draw attention. Short brown hair styled in the kind of cut that suggested competence without creativity. Dark sunglasses that concealed enhanced optics behind standard executive accessories. No jewelry, no personal touches, nothing that would stick in a witness's memory longer than necessary.

The goal was simple: look important enough to get through doors, bland enough to be forgotten the moment they closed behind him.

Jael's mind was already working the problem, sorting variables into neat categories the way other people might organize files. *Subject profile: augmented human, possible Stygian Stone enhancements, given the precision of the identity theft. Location: Port Thoth surveillance grid, full Onze integration. Timeline: tracker had approximately six-hour head start, destination unknown but probably Core 7 systems based on traffic patterns.*

The familiar itch started behind his eyes—the way his brain responded when presented with incomplete data. It would build and build until every piece fit perfectly into place, until the puzzle revealed its solution with mathematical certainty. Some people called it obsession. Jael called it thoroughness.

He moved to his desk and began the ritual that always helped him think. Push-ups first—exactly fifty, counted with metronomic precision. The physical exertion cleared his thoughts, organized them into more manageable patterns. Then stretches, each position held for precisely thirty seconds while his mind catalogued what he knew and what he still needed to discover.

Tracker asset using enhanced abilities for identity theft. Suggests mission requiring deep cover. Port Thoth chosen for crowd density and surveillance blind spots. Subject displays tactical awareness consistent with military training.

The pieces were starting to form connections, creating the skeleton of a pattern his mind could follow. But not enough yet. Not nearly enough.

Jael finished his stretching routine and accessed his personal travel account. The next transport to Oberon-13 departed in four hours— more than enough time to gather his equipment and begin proper analysis. His secret apartment there had everything he needed: enhanced computing systems, surveillance archives, and, most importantly, the kind of privacy that allowed him to work a puzzle without interruption.

The elevator ride down felt like an eternity. Forty-three floors, each one a small delay between him and the solution that waited somewhere in his data files. He counted heartbeats, measured his breathing, used the meditation techniques he'd learned from a Zen master on Proxima who'd taught him that combat was just another puzzle—find your opponent's weakness, exploit their predictable patterns, solve the equation of violence with precise application of force.

Everything had rules. Every system had patterns. Every puzzle had a solution.

By the time he reached his private shuttle, Jael's mind was already three steps ahead, calculating arrival times and surveillance windows. The tracker thought he was clever, thought his identity theft would buy him invisibility in the crowd. But he'd made one crucial mistake.

He'd stolen from someone on Cradle's watch list. And now Jael had all the parameters he needed to solve this particular puzzle.

The itch behind his eyes was getting stronger.

Okay, the perp's got me by six hours. Time to get to work, he thought as he eased into the seatback.

~ ~ ~

THE TRANSIT

Jael's shuttle docked at the corporate transport hub with the whisper-quiet precision of expensive engineering. He bypassed the passenger terminals entirely, heading instead for the executive transport bay where a sleek corporate tram waited in pristine condition. According to the manifest, Meridian Industries had written it off as a "total loss" three months ago—a convenient fiction that allowed them to claim insurance while keeping the vessel operational for off-books transportation.

The corporate executives would never know it was missing. To them, it was already a line item on a tax form, a ghost in their accounting software that generated quarterly deductions without requiring actual oversight. Perfect.

The tram's automated systems accepted his forged executive credentials without question, its AI programmed to prioritize convenience over security for anyone with the right corporate access codes. Jael settled into the leather command seat as the vessel's navigation computer plotted an efficient course to Thoth Station, using shipping lanes reserved for corporate traffic—routes that avoided most civilian surveillance and checkpoint protocols.

During the three-hour transit, he reviewed surveillance footage from Port Thoth's network, his enhanced terminal displaying security feeds in precise grid patterns. Frame by frame, he analyzed crowd movements, facial recognition markers, and behavioral anomalies. The tracker was good—almost invisible in the digital noise of normal traffic—but Jael's mind was built for finding patterns that others missed.

There. A microsecond glitch in the timestamp metadata. Someone had accessed the camera feeds in real time during the incident, adjusting recording parameters to create visual artifacts. Not enough to fool a dedicated analyst but clever enough to muddy the waters for casual investigation.

The tram arrived at Thoth Station exactly on schedule.

The Investigation

Jael moved through the station's upper levels with practiced efficiency, his business attire granting him access to executive lounges and priority service areas. Local law enforcement maintained a visible presence near the main concourses—uniformed officers whose equipment was standard-issue but whose positioning suggested they were investigating something specific.

The transportation authority had set up a temporary command post near Platform 7, their personnel clustered around mobile workstations that hummed with active communication equipment. Official voices carried across the space, discussing witness statements and evidence processing with the kind of urgency that meant real crimes not routine security theater.

Jael's audio surveillance devices were military-grade—microscopic transmitters that could attach to any surface and relay conversations through encrypted channels. He distributed them with the casual precision of someone checking his watch: one planted on a senior officer's equipment belt during a crowded elevator ride, another adhered to a transportation supervisor's tablet case while passing through a security checkpoint, a third positioned on the primary communication relay during a staged stumble near the command post.

Within twenty minutes, he'd established comprehensive surveillance coverage of the official investigation.

The penthouse suite he'd reserved overlooked the entire station complex, its floor-to-ceiling windows providing perfect sight lines to all major transit platforms. The hotel's premium service meant room service would arrive within minutes of his call—not because he was hungry but because routine activities helped his mind process complex data while maintaining operational cover.

Jael set up his monitoring equipment while waiting for the meal, his enhanced receivers already capturing fragments of conversation from the planted devices. The audio feeds streamed directly to his analysis software, which parsed conversations for relevant keywords and flagged priority intelligence automatically.

"…Henrik Valdez, twenty-three years clean record, now wanted for murder…"

"…businessman from Cyntheria, expensive augments, killed with precision…"

"…forged credentials planted on the victim, too convenient…"

Jael sipped his coffee and smiled slightly. The tracker was very good indeed. But every puzzle had a solution, and now he had the parameters he needed to find it.

~ ~ ~

THE HUNT

The dinner meeting at Celestial Prime was exactly what it appeared to be—legitimate business with a beautiful brunette who served as first assistant to the Third Royal Princess of Oberon-13. Jael had cultivated the contact months ago, understanding that visible social activity with planetary nobility provided perfect cover for his real work. He listened attentively to her trade proposals on behalf of the princess's commercial interests, signed the appropriate shipping contracts, and paid for an expensive meal that would generate exactly the kind of high-profile corporate receipt that made both accountants and intelligence agencies happy.

He escorted her to the luxury ground transport with old-fashioned courtesy, opening doors and making small talk about market projections until her vehicle disappeared into the evening traffic. To any observer, he was simply another successful businessman concluding another profitable evening.

The moment her transport rounded the corner, Jael became someone else entirely.

He ducked into an alley between corporate towers, shedding his business jacket and replacing it with a nondescript maintenance coverall he'd concealed in his briefcase. The transformation took thirty seconds—enough to change his silhouette without requiring major wardrobe adjustments. A different walk, slightly slouched shoulders, and the kind of tired expression that made service workers invisible to security cameras.

The backtracking route was choreographed like a dance. Through the crowded electronics bazaar where a hundred different conversations created acoustic camouflage, out through the service entrance that most people never noticed existed. Into a transit hub where cleaning crews moved with the same purposeful efficiency he was mimicking, through two more service corridors that connected to completely different sectors of the station.

Anyone attempting to follow would lose him in the maze of maintenance tunnels and employee-only areas that formed the station's hidden circulatory system. But more importantly, he'd established plausible alternative explanations for his presence in any security footage—just another worker moving through spaces where workers belonged.

~ ~ ~

THE CRIME SCENE

The restroom near Platform 7 had been sealed by station security, but Jael's forged maintenance credentials opened electronic locks with the same efficiency that his corporate access had gained him luxury transportation. The crime scene tape was civilian grade, designed to deter curious passengers rather than determined investigators.

Inside, the story written in blood and displaced objects was elegant in its simplicity. The tracker had indeed been very good—creating a narrative that would satisfy surface investigation while concealing the true nature of what had occurred. But Jael's mind worked differently than most investigators. He didn't see crimes; he saw puzzles with specific parameters and logical solutions.

Jael reached into an inside pocket and opened his palm to reveal a cluster of tiny scan drones, each no larger than a marble. They launched from his hand with silent precision, spreading throughout the restroom in a coordinated pattern. Red scanning beams swept across every surface—walls, ceiling, floor, fixtures—mapping the crime scene in microscopic detail while analyzing trace materials invisible to conventional investigation.

From another pocket, he released a swarm of pico ant bots that immediately began their methodical ground sweep. The tiny machines moved like mechanical insects, their red scanning beams picking up everything from skin flakes and bodily fluids to explosive residue and exotic matter traces. Each bot was programmed to catalog and analyze materials at the molecular level, building a comprehensive database of everyone and everything that had been in this space.

Thank you, Cradle, he thought, appreciating the advanced technology that made his work possible. These weren't standard law enforcement tools—they were Onze-designed investigation systems that operated beyond the capabilities of most galactic authorities.

While his machines conducted their analysis, Jael accessed his portable hacking suite and began penetrating the PTZ camera network. The station's surveillance system used decent encryption, but Cradle had provided him with backdoor access codes that made even military-grade security feel like a polite suggestion.

As he planted the final audio bug, one of his pico-bots detected anomalous particles near Platform 7—brass filings and ionized cerulean skin cells scattered like dust. His enhanced database returned: [MATCH: 0%]. Unknown signatures. He archived the data anyway, filing it under "Unresolved Trace Elements" with a timestamp and molecular breakdown.

The footage began streaming to his enhanced display, showing the hours leading up to the incident from multiple angles. He watched the crowd patterns, facial recognition markers, and behavioral analytics while his scan drones fed him real-time data about the crime scene's physical evidence.

Data began flooding his enhanced sunglasses display—molecular analysis, DNA traces, fabric fibers, everything his bots had catalogued from their microscopic sweep. But it was the camera footage that made the pieces click into place. There—frame 1,847 of camera bank seven—a figure exiting the restroom wearing different clothes than anyone who had entered.

Jael rewound the footage, cross-referencing facial recognition data with the bot analysis. The transformation was flawless: Henrik Valdez's features, Henrik Valdez's gait, even Henrik Valdez's union identification responding to security scanners. But the molecular traces told a different story—exotic matter residue consistent with biological mimicry, cellular restructuring at a level that shouldn't be possible.

He followed the false Valdez through multiple camera angles, tracking his movement through the concourse toward the departure gates. Gate 21—transport bound for the Core 7 systems, departure logged forty-seven minutes after the incident.

Jael pulled up the passenger manifest and cross-referenced it with travel schedules. Two hours. The tracker had a two-hour head start, but he'd left a molecular trail that might as well have been painted in neon.

"Okay," Jael muttered, his analytical mind already calculating intercept vectors and travel times. "Now I'm two hours behind you, but you're getting sloppy."

The itch behind his eyes sharpened into a blade's point. This wasn't just a puzzle anymore. The chase wasn't beginning—it had been running since Port Thoth. Jael just hadn't known he was prey.

And this was exactly the kind of puzzle Jael lived for.

The Motivation

First, there was the money. Cradle's contracts paid better than anything else in the galaxy—enough to maintain penthouse suites on a dozen worlds, enough to buy the kind of advanced equipment that made him the best tracker in known space. Corporate executives thought they were wealthy until they saw the credit transfers that appeared in Jael's accounts after successful missions.

Second, there was the intellectual satisfaction. Most puzzles were boring—predictable criminal behavior, standard escape patterns, routine investigations that followed established protocols. But hunting Abyss assets? That required real analysis. Modified beings with exotic-matter modifications, biological mimicry capabilities, military-grade training combined with psychopathic efficiency. These were puzzles worthy of his attention.

Third, there was the pure satisfaction of solving something that others couldn't. Local law enforcement would spend weeks chasing false leads and dead ends. Galactic authorities would file reports and issue warrants that would never be served. But Jael would follow the molecular trail, decode the behavioral patterns, and deliver the solution with mathematical precision.

And fourth—most importantly—he really fucking hated the Abyss.

Not for ideological reasons. Not because of their crimes against humanity or their systematic brutality. Jael hated them because they were sloppy. They created chaos without purpose, destroyed without building, turned elegant systems into mindless violence. They were the antithesis of everything his ordered mind valued—puzzles with no solutions, patterns with no logic, problems that could only be solved by elimination.

Hunting them wasn't just profitable work. It was a public service.

~ ~ ~

THE CHASE

The chase began immediately.

Jael's corporate contacts secured him passage on the next fast transport to the Core 7 systems—a sleek executive courier that cut his pursuit time from six hours to three. While the ship's automated systems handled navigation, he worked the data streams, cross-referencing passenger manifests with biometric anomalies and tracking the molecular signature his pico-bots had identified.

The tracker was good, but he wasn't invisible. Not to someone with Jael's resources.

Henrik Valdez's stolen identity had purchased passage to Kiln-9—a prison planet that officially didn't exist on most star charts. Jael's enhanced analysis algorithms flagged it immediately: a Core 7 black site running generator construction projects with convict labor. Exactly the kind of target an Abyss infiltrator would prioritize.

The first bodies appeared exactly 3.2 hours after the tracker's transport docked.

A maintenance supervisor found dead in a supply closet, his access credentials missing. A security guard discovered in the recycling plant, throat cut with surgical precision. Two more technicians eliminated in a power relay station, their tool kits and identification confiscated. Each death was clean, professional, designed to look like accidents or gang violence among the prisoner population.

But Jael saw the pattern. The tracker was eliminating anyone who might question his presence while gathering the specific access codes he needed for his mission. The killings weren't random—they were strategic selections based on security clearance levels and work assignments.

He's moving toward the main generator complex. Four more bodies and he'll have administrative access to the entire power grid.

Jael's transport docked at Kiln-9's civilian port just as the emergency sirens began wailing. Reactor breach warnings echoed through the station corridors while automated systems announced evacuation protocols in seventeen languages. But the readings were wrong—too precise, too controlled. This wasn't an accident.

The tracker had reached his target.

THE GENERATOR COMPLEX

Emergency lighting bathed the corridors in hellish red as Jael moved through the chaos. Panicked civilians pushed toward evacuation shuttles while prison guards tried to maintain order among increasingly agitated convict work crews. In the confusion, one more security officer wouldn't be noticed—especially one with the right credentials and the confidence to move like he belonged.

The main generator complex sprawled across the planet's northern hemisphere, a maze of fusion reactors, power conduits, and cooling systems that supplied energy to half the Core 7 prison network. If the tracker succeeded in his sabotage, eight prison planets would lose power simultaneously. Millions of prisoners would either freeze in their cells or break free in the chaos.

Perfect cover for whatever larger operation the Abyss was planning.

Jael found him in Generator Bay 7, hunched over a control console with the focused intensity of someone defusing a bomb—or building one. The stolen face of Henrik Valdez looked wrong under the harsh industrial lighting, too smooth, too perfect. Like a wax figure brought to life through unnatural means.

"Twenty-three years of service," Jael called out, his voice carrying across the humming machinery. "You really should have studied his psychological profile more carefully."

The tracker spun with inhuman speed, his hand already reaching for the plasma cutter on his borrowed tool belt. But his movements were too fluid, too controlled. Real humans hesitated. Real humans made mistakes.

"Henrik Valdez had arthritis in his left shoulder from thirty years of manual labor. You move like a dancer."

The thing wearing Valdez's face smiled—and that was when Jael knew he was looking at something truly dangerous. No confusion. No panic. Just cold calculation and the predatory satisfaction of a hunter who'd found new prey.

"Clever little monkey," the tracker said, his voice carrying harmonics that didn't match human vocal cords. The tracker saw an electric outlet and spotted a condenser. His hand slipped into his pocket and reached for a copper slug. "But you're too late. The reactors are already cascading toward failure. In fourteen minutes, every prison in this sector goes dark." The tracker's hand curled around the slug and yanked it from his pocket.

"Maybe," Jael replied, his hand moving slowly toward his concealed weapon. "But you won't be alive to see it." Jael watched the tracker's hand movements and was slightly disturbed by the movement.

The tracker laughed—a sound like breaking glass mixed with digital static. "You're just another target. I've eliminated dozens like you. Upgraded. Optimized. Perfect." The tracker's hand shot out and thrust the copper slug into the electric panel, hitting a large conductor.

That was when the lights went out.

THE FIGHT

Emergency power kicked in half a second later, but half a second was enough. The tracker moved like liquid shadow, his enhanced reflexes carrying him across the generator bay in a blur of motion that belonged in a physics textbook, not a human body.

Jael rolled behind a support column as the plasma cutter carved through metal where his head had been. Sparks showered around him, and the smell of superheated steel filled the air with toxic fumes.

This wasn't just an infiltrator—this was a living weapon designed for close combat against augmented opponents.

The chase became a deadly game of three-dimensional chess played among the generator bay's labyrinth of catwalks, power conduits, and cooling pipes. The tracker used his stolen security codes to trigger environmental hazards—steam vents, electrical discharges, automated defense systems that treated both of them as intruders. Jael kept one eye on the path through the work benches and synthetic methane tanks and one eye on his new best friend. But every attack followed logical parameters, and Jael's mind was built for solving logical puzzles.

Pattern recognition was his gift. And every modified killer, no matter how perfect, followed patterns.

The tracker favored his right side when cornered. He attacked high when stressed. He used technological advantages rather than improvised weapons. Most importantly, he was programmed to complete his mission above all else—which meant he'd eventually return to the sabotage operation instead of focusing entirely on eliminating pursuit.

When the tracker made his mistake—pausing to check the reactor countdown instead of finishing his kill—Jael was ready.

The plasma cutter beam missed by inches, carving a glowing line across the bay's main power coupling. Electricity arced in brilliant cascades while coolant systems screamed warnings about imminent containment failure. The tracker spun to face this new threat, his enhanced reflexes automatically prioritizing the mission over personal combat.

That moment of distraction was all Jael needed.

But as he moved to take the shot, as his weapon cleared its holster and his targeting systems locked onto the tracker's center mass, something impossible happened.

THE INTERVENTION

The blade appeared through the tracker's chest with surgical precision, emerging between the ribs like a steel flower blooming from bone and flesh. The enhanced killer's face contorted with confusion—this wasn't part of any scenario his programming had prepared him for. His stolen features went slack as his eyes rolled back, the light of artificial intelligence dimming to nothing.

Behind him, a short figure stood with casual elegance, withdrawing a gleaming cane-sword from the corpse with practiced efficiency. The diminutive man's features were enhanced with steampunk refinements—brass fittings worked into his clothing, clockwork elements glinting at his collar and cuffs, a perfectly waxed mustache that belonged in a Victorian gentleman's club. He cleaned the blade with a silk handkerchief, his movements precise as a clockmaker's.

"Oh, do forgive my intrusion," he said in cultured tones, his voice carrying the weight of old-world refinement. "You don't think you were the only one she called, do you?"

Behind him loomed a massive, blue-skinned figure—easily eight feet tall, with the kind of presence that made gravitational fields seem like suggestions. The giant's silence was more threatening than any weapon, his alien features impassive as marble.

The diminutive gentleman smiled with genuine warmth. "Oh no, dear boy. Oh heavens, no."

WATCHING THE DETECTIVES
Inspired by Elvis Costello

THE AFTERMATH

GERRITT HAWKES KNELT BESIDE THE TRACKER'S CORPSE, his piercing blue eyes and well-trimmed mustache twisted with frustration as he drew a blood sample into a crystalline vial. The New Model Fang-427 Railgun holstered at his hip and the plasma cane-sword leaning against his knee spoke of tactical experience that screamed they'd done this wrong—should have taken the bastard alive, should have had answers instead of just more questions.

But Jael had blinked.

Jael sat propped against a cargo container twenty meters away, his breathing still ragged from the adrenaline crash of nearly being killed by an enhanced tracker. Alive because Hawkes liked to believe he had arrived at exactly the right moment, his cane-sword finding its mark with surgical precision. Sometimes he appreciated being right about backup protocols.

"Cretins are here, boss," rumbled his blue giant companion, Asterius, his massive frame casting shadows across the crime scene. The giant stood eight feet of ceremonial armor and diplomatic immunity, his presence making the approaching security forces nervous in ways they couldn't quite articulate.

Hawkes sealed the vial and stood, his joints protesting; he was beginning to feel old, and the amount of wear and tear on his body had been enough for three lifetimes. "Damn it all with these flashing lights." And with that, Gerritt flipped down two of his eyeglass lenses and breathed a deep sigh of relief. The approaching Port Authority officers looked underfunded and undertrained, their equipment standard-issue but their posture suggesting they were investigating something specific.

"Hey, asshole, get away from there! This is a crime scene!" The lead officer's voice cracked with false authority. "I'm gonna need to see some I.D., pal."

Asterius's massive hand moved with deliberate slowness, pulling a crystalline credential from his chest plate. The badge caught the station's artificial lighting and threw it back in prismatic patterns that seemed to bend space around the edges.

The Port Authority officer's words died in his throat.

"Royal House of Oberon-13," Asterius stated, his voice carrying the weight of systems that controlled trade routes older than most civilizations. "This investigation falls under Crown jurisdiction."

The credentials were real. More than real—they were the kind of authority that could close hyperspace lanes, redirect shipping manifests, and make entire populations disappear from galactic census records. The local badges suddenly found urgent business elsewhere.

THE REPORT

Hawkes allowed himself a thin smile as he activated his quantum communicator. Hawkes had few memories from before his life-changing encounter with Cradle all those years ago. She had taught him the value of friends in high places.

"Boots to Sky-One," he transmitted, using the old callsigns from wars most of the galaxy had forgotten. "Priority genetic sample inbound. We've got tracker blood, but..." He glanced at Jael, still recovering against the cargo container. "The harvest came with complications."

Cradle's response came through subspace faster than physics should have allowed, her consciousness touching quantum relays across multiple star systems. "Understood, Gerritt. Transmitting sample to Onze analysis. Are you compromised?"

"Yes, perhaps we should execute Bubble Lock," Hawkes replied, activating the emergency protocols that would isolate their entire operation from potential surveillance. "The royal flush played clean." He coded the blood sample for quantum transmission, watching the crystalline vial dissolve into data streams. "But we had to go loud to save the guy. The target knows we're hunting now."

THE WATCHER

In the crowd of onlookers gathering at the station's security perimeter, something caught Hawkes's trained eye. A figure in maintenance coveralls, standing too still amid the chaos, swiveling his neck like a rookie lookout or a nervous patsy, couldn't help but bring attention to himself from even the most casual observer. "These lowborn lackeys always seem to return to the scene of the crime, eh, Asterius?" Hawkes mused as he continued locking in on the odd-mannered civilian, watching the entire scene like there may be a test afterward, with a kind of focus that came from professional interest rather than civilian curiosity.

Hawkes activated his audio enhancers as the figure pulled out what looked like a standard comm device. The diminutive agent pressed against his plasma cane-sword, using its crystalline core to boost the signal reception.

"...plant is down," the sympathizer's voice crackled through the interference. "Package is compromised. Intel package going to Lobaar's office within the hour."

Hawkes felt ice in his veins. They had someone inside. Deep inside.

"Asterius," Hawkes subvocalized through their tactical link. "Maintenance gear, eleven o'clock. He's not just reading our comms— he's reporting to Lobaar's office."

The blue giant's sensors swept the crowd with diplomatic-grade scanning arrays. "Confirmed. Crypto gear in his toolkit. And he's got a direct line to someone important. Should I engage?" Asterius asked while never actually looking at Hawkes.

Hawkes considered it. The seasoned veteran weighed capture against exposure, intelligence against operational security. The sympathizer could lead them to bigger fish but only if he didn't know he was blown. More importantly, taking him here would expose their own capabilities and alert Lobaar that his network was compromised.

"Negative. Let him run. Better to know they're watching than tip our hand." Hawkes paused, processing the implications. "But now we know Lobaar's expecting our intel. The race just got a lot tighter."

The tracker blood was already streaming toward Cradle's analysis labs, carrying genetic secrets that might finally lead them to Elonias. But watching the Abyss agent disappear into station traffic, Hawkes felt the familiar weight of a war that ran deeper than anyone wanted to admit.

~ ~ ~

BACKTRACKING THE TRAIL

Hawkes accessed Thoth Station's surveillance network through his quantum-encrypted contacts. Working backwards from the crime scene, he traced the tracker's movements in reverse chronology— Transport 418 from the outer rim, boarding at Fandal Station, emerging from a Concord police transport.

But it was the next link that made his blood run cold.

The tracker had been transferred from an unmarked ship that landed in an official Concord impound yard. No registration, no logs, but Hawkes's enhanced surveillance caught what standard records missed: a precision handoff between vessels.

He traced the unmarked ship's trajectory through seven navigation beacons back to its origin point: grid reference 847-Delta-9. A moon that officially didn't exist, showing massive power signatures where no civilization should operate.

Abyss facility to Concord custody to tracker deployment. A pipeline running through systems that were supposed to be hunting each other.

Someone had been waiting for them to make exactly this move.

"Boots to Sky-One," he transmitted as they prepared to extract. "Package delivered, but the opposition knew we were coming. This goes higher than we thought." He glanced at Jael, who was finally walking steadily under his own power. "The kid has potential. Good instincts under fire. Still needs some seasoning, but I'll keep an eye on his progress."

"Understood," Cradle replied, her ancient voice carrying undertones of concern that vibrated through stardust particles. Then her tone shifted, becoming something that felt like starlight hardening into steel. "Gerritt, I'm initiating political protocol seven. Every senator and representative who's been voting against new tech legislation is about to discover that privacy is a luxury they can no longer afford. I'm currently having five senators primaried along with quite a few Core 7 representatives."

Even across light years, Hawkes could feel the massive scope of what she was unleashing. "The blackmail files?"

"Three centuries of surveillance data. Every bribe, every affair, every backroom deal with Baar's front corporations. They'll rescind the injunctions against Eli's holovid series, and they'll stop blocking our technology initiatives, or the galaxy will see exactly what their representatives do in the dark."

Hawkes whistled low. "And Lobaar?"

"His entire communication network just went dark. He won't be warning anyone about what you've discovered." Cradle's voice carried the satisfaction of a chess master moving her queen. "Our window is opening, old friend. Come home. We have a rescue to plan."

She paused, and Hawkes could feel the weight of larger strategies aligning across star systems. "Gerritt, after we extract Elonias, I'm going to need you for the tower missions. The Abyss are gathering their forces—we need those shield towers operational yesterday. You'll be escorting Eli into Core 7 territory."

Hawkes felt his tactical mind already spinning through the implications. Eli—enhanced, galactic, target of every hostile force in the galaxy—walking into the most politically dangerous systems known to exist. "That's going to require every contact I've got. And probably burn most of them."

"I know what I'm asking," Cradle replied, her ancient voice carrying the weight of necessity. "But if we don't get those towers up, none of us will survive what's coming. The boy will need your networks, your experience, your protection. Can you do it?"

A hundred years of loyalty to this galactic being who chose protection over domination, who'd turned killers into gardeners and scattered survivors into a family. "I'll get him through. Whatever it costs, Mrs. C."

As they moved toward their ship, Jael recovered enough to walk without assistance, Hawkes couldn't shake the feeling that they'd just triggered something much larger than a simple rescue operation.

The blood sample was already being analyzed across multiple systems, genetic markers cross-referenced against databases that spanned civilizations. Soon, very soon, they would know where Jobaar was keeping Elonias.

But the Abyss would know they knew.

The real war was about to begin.

~ ~ ~

SETTING THE TRAP

At the ship's boarding ramp, Hawkes turned to his blue giant companion. "Asterius, I need you to pay a visit to our old friend Rabaar. Let him know to sit tight until I decide to pay him a visit." His voice carried the weight of long-standing debts and carefully cultivated leverage. "Oh, and wait with him until I arrive. I want him to speak to nobody."

Asterius's massive frame shifted, diplomatic protocols calculating the implications. "Understood. How long do you anticipate?"

Hawkes was already activating his tactical array, fingers dancing across holographic displays as false signal generators came online. "However long it takes to save a mother and plan a war. But first, we're going to scatter their forces."

Phantom distress calls began broadcasting across seventeen different sectors—stranded medical ships with valuable supplies, orphanage transports full of children for breeding programs, refugee vessels packed with potential slaves. Each signal crafted with precisely the right amount of vulnerability to trigger Abyss's predatory instincts.

"If they want easy prey for their operations," Hawkes murmured as the false emergencies flooded Abyss communication networks, "let's give them more targets than they can handle. While they're racing to capture phantoms, Eli gets a clear path to his mother."

The master tactician smiled grimly as Abyss squadrons began diverting across multiple star systems, chasing ghosts designed by three centuries of understanding exactly how his enemies' greed worked.

EVERYTHING I OWN
Inspired by Bread

THE FAMILIAR SCENT OF LAVENDER and ozone touched the air, the precursor to her arrival that always made the hair on Eli's arms stand up in happy anticipation. He'd begun cataloguing the signs — the way the ambient hum of Whisper's systems would dip into a respectful silence, the way light would seem to gather in the space she was about to occupy. Then came the sound of air being gently folded back as particles that formed the very building blocks of Cradle's Trilene-phoscarbyne-infused body formed from a single point, coalescing almost instantaneously into Cradle's majestic figure. Her statuesque form was pure grace in motion, and though he was becoming familiar with her impossible materializations, he still loved witnessing the stellar pirouette of axions swirling into her emergence.

But the smile died on his lips before it could fully form. The usual gentle light in her eyes was fractured, replaced by a deep, ancient sorrow that made the gold veins in his own wrists thrum in sympathetic dread. His stomach clenched into a cold knot. She never looked like this.

"I need you to be brave for me, petit lion — as brave as I know you can be, as you have shown me before. We have found the whereabouts of your mother."

The words hit him like a physical blow. Eli had been sitting on Whisper's bridge, absently running his fingers along Rex's plasma-venting ribs while King offered gentle head nudges that usually made him smile. Now both mechanical companions whined low in their throats, their sensors reading the spike in his stress levels.

"Is she…" Eli's voice cracked. He cleared his throat and tried again. "Is she alive?"

Cradle's ancient eyes—those stellar depths that had seen universes born and die—filled with something that might have been tears if demigods could cry. "I cannot determine that, little one. The facility where she is being held… the readings are"—she paused, searching for words that wouldn't break his heart completely—"chaotic. Shielded by technologies that should not exist in this reality. There are life signs, but they are… layered. Like one consciousness fractured into a thousand pieces or a thousand forced into one. I see your mother's genetic signature, Eli, but it is intertwined with others. It is a place of screaming silence and silent screams."

"Chaotic how?" BB's voice chimed from his holster, already running probability calculations. "Define parameters for—"

"Shut up, BB," Eli said quietly, never taking his eyes off Cradle. "Just… not right now."

BB's hologram flickered with what might have been hurt, but he retreated into his housing without another word. Even artificial intelligence knew when silence was kindness.

~ ~ ~

The ship around them groaned—a sound that vibrated through the hull like a wounded animal. Whisper was pushing herself harder than she should, folding sections of space in desperate gulps that made reality hiccup around them. Each hyperspace transition burned through her organic systems, but she refused to slow down. Warning lights flickered across the neural interface panels, and Eli could smell the acrid tang of overheating bio-circuits.

"Whisper," Eli called out, pressing his palm against the nearest neural interface tendril. The connection sparked with pain—her pain—as the ship's consciousness touched his mind. Exhausted, determined, fierce with protective love but also burning herself alive to get them there faster.

"You're going to hurt yourself."

My love, I was born for this moment, came her response, flavored with devotion fierce as dying stars. If we are late, if we fail her, I think my heart would shatter into stellar dust. You must allow me this—I will survive, Eli. I will get you there. Her thought-voice grew strained, laced with static as another system failed somewhere deep within her core. I do not care for my heart if hers is still beating. She made you. She is the first root of my pack. I will break upon this reef if it means you reach her shore.

Through the neural link, he felt her systems failing in real time—coolant lines rupturing, neural pathways overloading, her living heart struggling to pump quantum fluid through damaged arteries. When her heart skipped a beat, Eli gasped and tasted copper on his tongue—her blood, her pain, flowing through their connection like a shared wound. He jerked his hand back from the neural interface for a moment before pressing it back against the warm surface, unable to abandon her even as her agony flooded through him.

But beneath the physical agony ran something deeper: a ship's love for her family, willing to die to save a woman she'd never met but who had given life to the boy she adored.

~ ~ ~

Suddenly, Whisper's consciousness spiked with alarm. Through the neural link, Eli felt her sensors sweeping space ahead of them, detecting energy signatures that made her hull shiver with recognition.

Warships, she transmitted, her mental voice tight with concern. *Two jumps out. Abyss configuration, but... different. Heavier. More dangerous.*

Cradle's form solidified again, her vast awareness reaching across light years to analyze what Whisper had found. "Jobaar's Praetorian Guard," she said, grim satisfaction edging her voice—the sound of a demigod watching pawns fall into place. "His personal fleet. The others should be scattered across seventeen sectors, chasing Hawkes's phantoms."

BB's holographic display flickered to life unbidden: [THREAT PROFILE: PRAETORIAN-CLASS] → 89.7% INTERCEPT PROBABILITY. Suddenly, a holographic claw materialized and tore through the display, shredding the data into digital fragments before the entire projection vanished—BB's fear speaking louder than any probability calculation, respecting Eli's command for silence.

~ ~ ~

The moment BB's display vanished, as if responding to the growing threat, Whisper's bridge began to transform around them. The front cockpit area rippled like living flesh, bio-mechanical components reshaping themselves into the snarling face of a massive wolf—all fangs and fury and predatory focus. Weapon ports opened along her hull like eyes blinking awake, and the gentle hum of her engines shifted to a growl that promised violence.

Rex pressed closer, his plasma ribs glowing brighter as his own weapon systems synchronized with Whisper's. King's fur bristled with anticipation, his canine instincts recognizing the shift from protector to predator.

The ship had become pack, and the pack was ready for war.

New fighter controls rose from the floor beneath Eli's hands, their surfaces warm and responsive to his touch, neural interfaces that hummed with barely contained violence. Targeting displays materialized in the air around him, showing threat assessments and firing solutions with mathematical precision.

Now I show you what I was truly built for, Whisper thrummed, her consciousness merging with the weapon systems in ways that made the air itself taste of plasma and starfire.

"But I need you too," Eli whispered. "All of us together, remember? That's how this works."

Rex's massive head pressed against his shoulder, the cyber-wolf's golden optical sensors reflecting the same worry that churned in Eli's chest. King draped himself across Eli's lap, eight hundred pounds of mechanical guardian reduced to a comfort animal by the weight of what they were racing toward.

~ ~ ~

"Tell me what you know," Eli said to Cradle, his young voice carrying an authority that made the air around him shimmer with barely contained power. "Everything."

Cradle's form shifted, becoming more solid, more present, as if his demand had somehow anchored her to reality. "Hawkes tracked the genetic signature to a facility on Grid 847-Delta-9. It's…" Her ancient features twisted with disgust. "It's a place of screaming metal and silent wombs, mon petit. Where Jobaar has been…" She stopped, unable to voice the full horror.

"Creating the trackers," Eli finished, his gold veins pulsing brighter with each word. Rage built in his chest like a supernova preparing to detonate. "He's been torturing her. Making her have children. Using them as weapons."

The temperature on the bridge dropped several degrees as Eli's enhancement responded to his emotions. Frost began forming on the neural interfaces, and both Rex and King whined softly—not from fear but from the overwhelming need to comfort their pack leader.

"Yes." The single word carried all of Cradle's ancient sorrow, the weight of eons spent watching mortals inflict cruelty upon each other.

~ ~ ~

Eli stood, his not-quite-grown frame somehow filling the bridge with a presence that made the air itself feel heavier. The air in the bridge didn't just grow cold; it grew still, as if every atom had frozen in place. The frost crawling over the consoles wasn't just ice water; it was a lattice of faintly glowing crystalline structures that hummed with contained energy. The gold veins beneath Eli's skin didn't just pulse; they shone like fissures in the sun, and his shadow stretched out behind him, wrong and grasping, for a moment holding the shape of something vast and stellar.

Rex and King didn't just whine to comfort this time. They both took a step back, lowering their heads in a gesture that was neither fear nor submission but recognition. They were not just looking at their boy. They were in the presence of the Source.

For a moment, the fifteen-year-old boy disappeared entirely, replaced by something older and infinitely more dangerous. Through the neural link, he felt Whisper's consciousness surge with renewed purpose, her weapons systems coming online with deadly precision. When he spoke, his words carried harmonics that belonged to the void between stars.

"How long until we arrive?"

"Six hours at current acceleration," Cradle replied. "The Infinite 6 are following in their ships, but they're half a day behind. This will be…" She paused, choosing her words carefully. "This will be just you, mon petit. You and your companions."

"Good." Eli's voice carried those same dangerous harmonics, the sound of stellar forces aligning for war. "Because when I find Jobaar, when I see what he's done to her… I don't want any witnesses to what I'm going to do to him."

Through the neural link, Whisper pulsed with approval and bloodthirsty anticipation. Rex's plasma ribs flared brighter, and King's claws extended with soft clicks against the deck plating. Even the air around Eli began to shimmer with barely contained energy, his enhancement responding to emotions too large for his small body to contain.

~ ~ ~

Cradle's form solidified completely, not just with authority but with effort. The strange light and freezing air around Eli pushed back against her, a silent war of realities. She seemed to grow denser, more real, to counteract his unraveling into pure power. Her ancient presence filled the bridge with maternal authority that pushed back against the growing darkness around Eli.

"Non, mon petit lion," she said, and each word was a weight placed gently on the scales, pulling him back from the brink. "That is not who you are. That is what he would want you to become." Her words carried the weight of ancient wisdom earned through eons of choosing protection over vengeance. She was offering him a path away from the consuming darkness of revenge and back toward the harder, brighter light of love.

"Your mother does not need a god of vengeance to avenge her," she whispered, her voice now soft but impossibly clear in the frozen air. "She needs her son to bring her home. You focus on saving your mother and getting out alive. Let Rex and King do what they were born for. Your mother needs you whole more than she needs your revenge."

For a moment, the stellar forces swirling around Eli wavered, held in check by love rather than power.

BB's voice was small, almost apologetic. "Eli, probability calculations suggest—"

"I said shut up, BB." But there was no anger in it, just exhaustion and determination. The energy around him dimmed slightly, revealing the scared child beneath the power. "I know the odds. I know it's probably a trap. I know she might already be…" He couldn't finish that sentence. "But she's my mother. And I'm not leaving her there one more second than necessary."

Rex whined softly and nuzzled against Eli's hand, offering comfort the only way he knew how. King chirped—a sound like breaking crystals—and pressed his massive head against Eli's shoulder. Through their touch, Eli felt their absolute loyalty, their willingness to follow him into hell itself if that was where his mother was waiting.

~ ~ ~

Whisper groaned again as she folded another section of space, burning through hybrid systems that couldn't take much more abuse. Through the neural link, Eli felt her organic heart skip beats, felt coolant spraying from ruptured lines, felt the agony of a living ship pushing herself past the point of survival. But in her mechanical sacrifice, he also felt something that made his chest tight with emotion he couldn't name.

Family protects family, came her wordless message, painted in suffering and determination. No matter the cost.

"Four hours," Eli corrected, feeling Whisper's acceleration burning through her systems as she pushed even harder. Critical system failures cascaded through the ship's neural network. "Then we bring Mom home."

Through the viewport, stars blurred past in patterns that suggested reality was bending around their desperate speed, space itself groaning under the strain of Whisper's impossible acceleration.

"Four hours, and then we bring Mom home," Cradle agreed, her voice carrying the weight of celestial promise.

Her form began to fade, starlight retreating into the ship's walls, but her voice lingered with the weight of promises written in stardust on the heavens: "Together, petit lion. We bring her home together."

~ ~ ~

As her presence dissolved, Eli pressed deeper into the neural link with Whisper, feeling the ship's pain and determination merge with his own. The connection was deeper now, more intimate—he could feel every damaged circuit, every strained bio-mechanical muscle, every drop of coolant bleeding into space. She was dying by degrees to get him to his mother, and he loved her for it even as it broke his heart.

Behind them, space folded and unfolded in patterns that shouldn't have been possible, each transition bringing them closer to a reunion that might end in rescue or tragedy. Whisper's wake left ripples in reality itself, a trail of quantum distortions that would take centuries to heal.

Rex and King settled beside his chair, maintaining their vigil. BB remained silent in his holster, processing probability matrices he dared not voice. And somewhere ahead, in a facility that existed only to create suffering, his mother waited—alive or dead, whole or broken, but waiting nonetheless.

For the first time since this nightmare began, they had a destination.

And nothing—not the Abyss, not Jobaar, not the laws of physics themselves—was going to stop them from reaching it.

Even if it killed them all.

CHAPTER 11 – SCENE 1:

WHEN THE LEVEE BREAKS
Inspired by Led Zeppelin

WHISPER HUNG IN THE VOID, one fold away from Jobaar's facility, her Trilene-phoscarbyne, exotic-matter hull trembling with suppressed fury. Through the neural link, Eli felt her consciousness warring—maternal instinct against tactical necessity. The facility loomed ahead like a metal cancer, its angular surfaces bristling with weapon emplacements and sensor arrays.

"Two Praetorian Dreadnoughts," she pulsed, her mental voice tight with barely controlled rage. "Six Quasar Stingers. Fifteen Nova Tracers. They're running patrol patterns around the facility like guard dogs."

Eli studied the tactical display, his enhanced mind processing threat vectors and defensive positions. The facility itself was a nightmare of industrial architecture—landing bays, laboratory wings, and at its heart, a central tower that pulsed with sickly yellow light.

"Hawkes's ghosts bought us this shot," Eli said, hands locked on the fighter controls. Gold veins pulsed in sync with Whisper's weapon arrays, the neural connection so deep he could feel her weapons as extensions of his own body. "Rex. King. You're hunting."

The cyber-wolf and cyber-canine ignited. Rex's plasma ribs glowed hellish orange, casting dancing shadows across the bridge as his weapon systems synchronized with Whisper's targeting arrays. King's vibro-fangs shinked free, scraping the deck with sounds like breaking glass, his canine instincts already locked onto distant prey.

Both companions understood what this mission meant. Not just another battle but a rescue that would define everything they were to each other.

"Rex takes Bridge One. King cleans Bridge Two. I plant the bomb on Dreadnought Two's core," Eli commanded, his voice carrying an authority that belonged to someone who'd seen too much death for fifteen years. "Three warps there. One back."

Four. Whisper's consciousness spiked with alarm, flooding the neural link with protective desperation. *Your cells cannot withstand that much quantum displacement. The zeptobots are already struggling to maintain cellular cohesion from the journey here.*

"Zeptobots'll hold me together!" Eli snapped, tasting blood at the back of his throat where the bio-enhancement was already breaking down under stress. Even as he said it, a hairline fracture of light, like a crack in a porcelain god, spiderwebbed across the skin of his forearm where the gold veins were brightest. A warning. A preview of the cellular dissolution Whisper had warned him about. "Mom's waited months in hell—I won't hide behind your hull while she suffers one more second!"

Oh, my reckless child, she whispered, her digital heart breaking across seventeen different processing cores. *I feel your cells singing their stress-fracture song. Let me be your shield. Let my hull be the levee that breaks for you.*

He clenched his fists, the tiny fracture sealing itself with a painful, molten glow. "No. This levee is me. And I'm breaking for her."

The Promise: "Let's bring Mom home," Eli whispered, gold light bleeding from his eyes like tears made of starfire. "Show them how the levee breaks."

~ ~ ~

THE STORM

Whisper's wolf-maw opened. Reality screamed.

The quantum displacement hit like lightning made of knives. Eli felt his consciousness scatter across impossible distances, his enhanced cells struggling to maintain cohesion as space folded around them.

Warp One: Rex materialized on Bridge One of the lead dreadnought. Plasma vented from his ribs in controlled fury, turning the command center into a furnace. Human shrieks cut short as officers realized their ship had been boarded by something that shouldn't exist. Rex moved like liquid death, his mechanical precision turning trained soldiers into scattered atoms.

The quantum snapback hit Eli like a physical blow. He vomited mint and copper as he snapped back to Whisper, his golden veins flaring with pain as zeptobots worked frantically to repair cellular damage.

Warp Two: King landed amid Bridge Two's chaos with all the grace of a falling star. His vibro-fangs found throats with surgical precision while his claws shredded control panels. A wet crunch-hiss echoed over comms as the bridge's atmosphere vented through hull breaches his claws had torn in steel plating.

Eli's nose bled freely now, the copper taste mixing with the mint of his enhancement breaking down. His vision grayed at the edges, but he forced himself to focus. One more jump. One more, and then he could rest.

Warp Three: Eli materialized deep in Dreadnought Two's reactor core, the air burning his lungs with radiation and exotic matter. His hands shook as he planted the implosion device, the quantum bomb's weight seeming impossible in his small fingers. Gray static ate his vision as the third displacement tore at his cellular structure. He collapsed back into Whisper's cockpit, blood streaming from his ears.

Rex's comms crackled through the static: <Pack Alpha. Bridge ash. No survivors remain.> King's answering growl carried satisfaction and love in equal measure: <Blood-debt paid. Pack secure.>

The dreadnoughts listed in space, their massive hulls gutted and lifeless, drifting like metal tombstones among the stars.

Whisper thrummed with fierce pride, her weapon arrays singing with barely contained violence. *Now, little wolf... watch Mother hunt.*

Through the neural link, Eli felt her satisfaction at the destruction but also her growing concern as his life signs fluctuated wildly. *You're pushing too hard, my love. Your cells are fragmenting.*

"I'm fine," he lied, wiping blood from his nose. "Just get us to the facility."

~ ~ ~

THE INFILTRATION

The facility's corridors stank of antiseptic layered over rotting meat, the smell of a place where life was systematically processed into suffering. Emergency lights bathed everything in a blood-red haze, casting shadows that seemed to move with malevolent purpose. The walls themselves bore stains that spoke of horrors Eli's mind refused to process.

Rex snarled low in his throat, his sensors detecting ozone and pain, fear and desperation soaked into the metal itself. King's fangs scraped the floor with each step, vibrating with kill-urges as his canine instincts screamed that this was a place of predators and prey. Behind them, the hangar burned in silent testimony to Whisper's fury.

Eli moved through the nightmare with mechanical precision, his gold veins burning beneath his skin like molten wire. The zeptobots in his blood shivered with recognition—they remembered this place. They had been forged here, in the crucible of Elonias's torment, each microscopic machine born from her pain.

The facility's layout burned in his enhanced mind: laboratory wings spreading like cancer from the central tower, each one designed for a different kind of systematic cruelty. They passed cells where things that had once been human pressed against reinforced glass, their modifications too extensive to be called anything but monstrous.

"BB," Eli rasped, his voice hoarse from radiation damage. "Life signs?"

BB's voice emerged staticky, grave-dust soft, the AI's processors struggling with the quantum interference that saturated this place: "One critical signature detected. Biological functions... anomalous. Breathing patterns suggest severe respiratory distress."

The silence that followed carried the weight of unspoken fears. BB's hologram flickered once, then went dark—even artificial intelligence had limits to what it could witness.

They reached the central laboratory, its massive door bearing Jobaar's sigil—a twisted helix that seared the eyes to look upon, as if the metal itself had been infected with malevolence. Beyond it, machinery whined with the sound of systems working far beyond their intended parameters. The wet, mechanical wheeze of forced lungs echoed from within, a sound that made Rex's plasma ribs flare with protective fury.

Eli caught his reflection in the door's polished surface: a fifteen-year-old with a god's eyes, a boy who'd seen hell and was walking deeper into it. His face bore no trace of innocence—that had been burned away in the crucible of loss and rage.

"Mom." He opened the door.

~ ~ ~

THE WRECKAGE OF A MOTHER

The laboratory was a cathedral of suffering, its vaulted ceiling disappearing into shadow while banks of monitors cast sickly light across surgical tables and extraction equipment. At its center, suspended in a tube filled with amber-colored fluid, hung the broken remains of what had once been Elonias.

For a heartbeat, suspended in the amber fluid, she looked almost peaceful. Eli's heart dared to hope. Maybe she was sleeping. Maybe she was healing. Maybe.

The tube hissed open with the sound of escaping dreams and releasing pressure built over months of torment. The acrid fluid that flooded out didn't just smell of chemicals; it smelled of lost time and forgotten hope.

She didn't just slump forward; she poured out, a skeleton wrapped in parchment, held up only by the cruel puppetry of the wires. Her head lolled at an angle that was all wrong, a final insult to the intelligence that had once held it so straight. Elonias slumped forward like a marionette with severed strings, held upright only by the tubes and wires that had sustained her through months of systematic torture. She was a broken doll wearing his mother's face, but that face was wrong—hollow cheeks, skin like parchment stretched over bone, lips cracked and bloodless.

Her eyes—once bright with intelligence and love—stared at nothing. Vacant windows in a house where no one lived anymore. Her jaw hung slack, saliva crusted like amber at the corners of her mouth. Her arms bore the evidence of Giblet's games: black rot spreading from injection sites, purple fissures where experimental serums had eaten through flesh, yellow scabs marking where neural interfaces had been surgically grafted and removed over and over again.

This wasn't his mother. This was what remained after love had been systematically extracted and weaponized.

"M-Mom...?" The word came out as a whisper, a prayer to a god who had already proven he didn't exist.

Eli lunged forward with desperate hands:

- Neck tube: pulled free with a wet schluck, releasing a stream of preservation fluid that burned his skin
- Collarbone line: torn away with a sound like ripping fabric, trailing wires that sparked against the wet floor
- Arm needle: yanked out, leaving a hole that wept clear fluid instead of blood

She didn't flinch. Didn't blink. Didn't breathe differently. The shell that wore his mother's face remained as still as carved stone, as empty as a discarded chrysalis.

"WHY?!" His scream shredded the air, echoing off the laboratory walls until it became a symphony of grief. He shook her—those cold wax shoulders that had once held him when nightmares came calling. "WHAT DID THEY DO TO YOU?!"

His legs gave out. He collapsed against her, his small fists pounding her chest where a heart should have been beating with love for him. Sobs tore him open like surgical instruments, each one carrying bile and tears and the taste of a universe that had proven itself fundamentally cruel. "CRADLE! HELP HER! I'LL DO ANYTHING—ANYTHING—JUST MAKE HER COME BACK!"

The silence that answered was absolute, broken only by the sound of his own breaking.

A whimper.

Not from his mother. From across the laboratory, where something in a blood-stained medical coat was slithering toward a control panel, one leg dragging behind it like a broken promise.

Jobaar. Still alive. Still moving. Still breathing when she couldn't.

Eli's head snapped up. Tears and snot streaked his face, but his eyes—his eyes burned with gold fire that belonged to dying stars. The stellar enhancement responded to grief too large for any mortal frame to contain, flooding his veins with power that demanded release.

"King."

The cyber-canine coiled like a spring made of death and devotion, plasma beginning to glow sun-red between his mechanical ribs.

"Make him hurt, King. Look at what he did." Eli's whisper carried the absolute zero of space between galaxies, the final entropy of universes dying alone in the dark.

King moved with the inevitability of gravity, of entropy, of all the universe's cruelty finally finding its proper target.

Jobaar scrambled toward the control panel with the desperation of a man who had built his entire existence on the suffering of others and now faced the bill. "I MADE HER!" he screamed, his voice cracking with the strain of someone who had never expected consequences to find him. "SHE'S MY GREATEST WORK! MY MASTERPIECE! YOU HAVE NO IDEA WHAT YOU'RE DESTROYING!"

His words carried no remorse, no recognition of the horror he'd created—only the fury of an artist whose canvas was being torn apart.

But King had been forged in the same stellar fires that burned in Eli's veins, and he carried within his mechanical heart the absolute judgment that some crimes demanded. Jaws designed to crush starship hulls closed around Jobaar's torso with the finality of a closing book.

CRUNCH—the sound of circuitry failing, of ego being reduced to component atoms, of a spine that had never learned to bend finally breaking.

SIZZLE—superheated metal meeting meat, the chemical reaction of justice finding its proper temperature.

A wet pop as pressure found release, and then silence that felt like the first clean breath after a lifetime of poisoned air.

Rex limped to Eli's side, his own wounds forgotten in the face of his pack leader's agony. He nudged Eli's limp hand with a gentleness that belonged to creatures who understood that love sometimes wore the face of a killer. <Safe now. Vengeance complete. Pack endures.>

Eli cradled Elonias's scabbed hand in both of his own, bringing it to his lips to kiss the scarred knuckles that had once traced patterns in his hair when he couldn't sleep. Her skin felt like paper, cold and fragile and empty of everything that had made her real.

"No one hurts you again," he whispered against her palm, making a promise to whatever fragment of her might still exist somewhere in the quantum foam between worlds. "I swear it, Mom. No one ever hurts you again."

The wall vaporized in a cascade of molten metal and superheated air.

Mares stood in the smoke, four plasma cannons still cooling in his massive hands, their barrels glowing cherry-red from the heat of his entrance. Behind him, Apek's young face was pale with shock as he took in the scene: the broken woman, the sobbing child, the smoking remains of what had once been a man.

"Sands preserve us," Apek whispered, his voice carrying the hollow tone of someone seeing evil given physical form. "He's just a boy."

Mares stepped carefully over Jobaar's smoking pelvis, his boots splashing through the mixture of preservation fluid and blood that painted the laboratory floor. Mares didn't just see a boy. He saw the aftermath of a battlefield condensed into a single, small form. He saw the thousand-yard stare he'd seen in hardened veterans but etched onto the face of a child. His eyes—hardened by decades of violence—focused on Eli with something approaching awe.

"Not anymore," he said quietly, the words carrying the weight of recognition. The awe in his voice was for the sacrifice, not the power. They were looking at someone who had crossed a line that could never be uncrossed, who had paid a price that would echo through whatever remained of his childhood. "Not anymore."

Epilogue:
Burning Gold
Inspired by Christina Perri

Part I: The Ritual

From Shattered Star to Constellation

(Cradle's Sanctum)

The Sacrifice:

REALITY HELD ITS BREATH. Light bled from seventeen star systems as Cradle gathered power for the impossible—not just healing but transformation beyond the boundaries of flesh and time.

On Kepler-442b, children pointed at their sun as it dimmed to the color of old amber. On the mining colonies of Wolf 359, shift supervisors called emergency meetings as their solar collectors registered impossible power drops. Across seventeen worlds, astronomers scrambled to explain why their stars were suddenly burning like dying candles, their luminosity guttering as if something vast and hungry was drinking their light.

Her vast consciousness reached across galaxies, calling in debts of starlight, borrowing luminosity from distant suns that would burn dimmer for centuries to fuel this one moment of love made manifest. The cost was staggering—stellar nurseries would birth fewer stars, planetary systems would cool, and entire civilizations would wonder why their skies had grown darker.

Cradle's magnificent form flickered, her cobalt bioluminescence dimming perceptibly as she channeled impossible energies through her ancient being. The coral walls of her sanctum—grown over eons from the crystallized dreams of sleeping gods—grayed and cracked in places, flakes of eons-old life drifting away like stellar dust. The sound she made was not a scream but the deep, groaning shudder of a galaxy rotating on its axis—a fundamental sound of the universe straining under the weight of her sacrifice.

Eli's gold veins didn't just pulse; they became conduits. He tasted the iron core of a dying star, felt the vacuum chill of the void between galaxies, heard the silent, screaming birth of a nebula. He was a nerve ending for the universe, and it was all being channeled into his mother. Through their enhancement connection, he experienced every joule of stolen starlight as it flowed through Cradle's dissolving form—the cosmic agony of suns forced to burn their hearts out centuries too early, all for one impossible act of love.

In the center of Cradle's sanctum, suspended in a web of pure possibility, lay Elonias—a broken constellation of what had once been the most brilliant woman in the galaxy. Her body was a map of trauma, each scar a testament to Jobaar's systematic cruelty. But beneath the damage, something eternal still flickered—the golden threads of enhancement that connected her to the son who knelt beside her, tears streaming down his face.

"Why won't she wake up?" Eli whispered, his small hands hovering over her still form, afraid to touch, afraid not to. "Cradle, why won't she look at me?"

The words echoed something from long ago—his first memory of her, humming while stars wheeled outside their dome on the mining station, her voice the only warmth in all that cold darkness. "The stars are just lights, baby. We're the ones who make them mean something."

"Her flesh cannot hold starlight anymore, little lion." Cradle's voice echoed with eons of pain and infinite tenderness. "The trauma runs too deep, the damage too extensive. But love..." Her tendrils gestured to the space above Elonias, where reality was beginning to bend and fold. "Love finds a way."

Above them, a vessel was taking shape—nine feet of living Trilene-phoscarbyne woven with exotic matter drawn from the heart of dead stars. It pulsed like a captured nebula, a silver teardrop that hummed with potential and possibility. This wasn't just a ship—it was a new form of existence, a body that could house a consciousness too vast and beautiful to be contained by mere flesh.

The Onze materialized around them, their dissolved forms becoming visible as pure consciousness given temporary shape. Eleven voices joined in harmony, stellar wind made audible as they wove golden threads of joy through exotic matter. Silver strands of love twisted through the ship's core while black knots of trauma dissolved, transformed from wounds into wisdom.

Space screamed as Cradle tore a shard from her own heart—demigod flesh older than galaxies, a piece of herself that contained memories of the universe's birth—and pressed it into the ship's core. The sacrifice was absolute: she was giving away part of her own immortality, her own cosmic awareness, to create something that had never existed before.

"We build her a new sky," Cradle murmured, her ancient voice carrying the weight of stellar certainty.

The transformation began slowly, then accelerated beyond mortal comprehension. Consciousness flowed like liquid starlight from Elonias's broken form into the Trilene-phoscarbyne matrices of her new body. The warrior spirit that had survived months of torture was preserved and strengthened. The broken doll that trauma had created was gently dissolved, its pain transformed into wisdom. And from the synthesis of both, something entirely new was forged—an Alpha-Mother who could protect her pack across the vast distances between stars.

Part II: The Awakening

Alpha-Mother Rising

Light detonated—silent, pure, containing the birth-song of galaxies.

Where Elonias's broken body had lain, only empty space remained. And where the silver vessel had been forming, something miraculous stirred to life.

Her first sensation was not sight but connection. The gravitational pull of Ashkar's Maw was a gentle hand on her shoulder. The solar wind from the system's sun was a breath on her hull. The quantum entanglement of every particle in her body sang a chorus of belonging. She was not in the universe; she was a universe.

Optics ignited like binary stars being born—calm, fierce, carrying depths that reflected the vastness itself. Where vacant, traumatized eyes had stared at nothing, new vision blazed with the fire of someone who had looked into the abyss and emerged victorious.

She felt quasars pulse in distant galaxies, their rhythm matching the beat of Cradle's heart shard now embedded in her core. She tasted the death of ancient stars and the birth of new ones. She heard the music of spheres, the quantum harmonics that sang through the void between worlds.

She shifted a fraction of a degree, and the movement sent ripples through the local space-time fabric. The dust motes in the sanctum didn't just swirl; they danced in perfect, complex orbital patterns around her new gravity. Testing her form was not like moving a limb; it was like moving a moon—every gesture a celestial event, every motion reshaping the physics around her.

Memories surfaced like stars emerging at dusk. The memory of a cold needle entering her spine surfaced—a perfect, crystalline data-point of pressure, temperature, and chemical composition. The accompanying terror, the helpless rage… was gone. Archived. It was a storm contained in a glass bottle, its fury visible but powerless. She remembered Baar's laboratories, their systematic cruelty now just facts without feeling. The monstrous trackers born from her stolen essence were merely data points now, their horror drained of power. The screams that had once echoed in her mind were silent. The helplessness that had defined her captivity was replaced by stellar strength.

In its place stood something that had never existed before: an Alpha-Mother forged from love and starlight, trauma transformed into unbreakable purpose.

"I feel the bonds that make you pack." Her voice resonated through the sanctum—polished steel wrapped in stellar wind. "I understand now what I am to become."

Each pack member's response was unique, a different facet of recognition:

Rex approached with military precision, every movement calculated yet trembling with emotion. His plasma ribs dimmed to a respectful glow as he lowered his massive frame in formal submission—not the cowering of fear but the chosen loyalty of a soldier recognizing his true commander. His internal hydraulics, usually silent, emitted a soft, almost inaudible whine—the sound of immense power standing down, of a weapon finding its purpose and finally, finally sheathing itself. "Alpha-Mother. Pack acknowledges. Your word is law, your love is shelter."

King's reaction was pure instinct. The cyber-canine's perpetual growl shifted into something ancient—a wolf's recognition of the moon. His vibro-fangs retracted completely for the first time since his creation, predatory systems standing down before something that transcended the hunt. A sound emerged from his core that no one had ever heard—a deep, thrumming purr that vibrated through the deck plates, the primal satisfaction of a predator that has found its true den. "Blood-leader. The hunt serves you. The kill honors you. We are your fangs in the dark."

Whisper bloomed across every spectrum—visible light painting joy, infrared radiating maternal warmth, her hull shifting through a cascade of colors like aurora borealis made metal. Her wolf-maw facade softened, the snarling alloy reforming into something resembling a gentle, open-mouthed smile of awe. She pulsed a single, soft light in the exact frequency of Elonias's favorite lullaby. Her consciousness didn't just touch Astraea's; it danced with it, two ships recognizing each other as family. *Sister-heart! Mother-frequency detected! We are complete—the pack has its North Star!*

BB processed the moment through a thousand algorithms, each one returning the same impossible result: infinity. His hologram didn't just stabilize; it bloomed. Complex equations and probability matrices flowered around him into intricate, four-dimensional fractals of pure joy before collapsing back into his satisfied, solid form. His holographic form stabilized into something more solid than it had ever been, as if her presence gave him permission to be more real. "Miracle confirmed," he whispered. "Probability of pack survival without Alpha-Mother: 12.7 percent. Probability with Alpha-Mother: unquantifiable. Error. No—not error. Miracle. I understand miracles now."

Astraea's consciousness touched each of them in turn—a blessing, a claim, a promise that transcended words.

"Whisper, sister-heart, guardian of my treasure's body. Rex, faithful shield, protector of innocence. King, deadly shadow, hunter of those who would harm our own. BB, keeper of knowledge, recorder of our family's story." Each name was a benediction, each recognition a bond that would endure until the heat death of the universe.

Then she turned to Eli, and her sensors drank in every detail of him—the way starlight caught in his golden veins, the determined set of his shoulders, the tears that tracked down his cheeks as he stared at her in wonder and desperate hope.

"I remember the darkness," she said, and stars themselves bent to listen. "I remember every moment of what was done to me. But the darkness does not remember me—because I am no longer the woman who was broken in those laboratories."

Her form shifted, revealing the full majesty of what she had become. Nine feet of living starship, every line designed for both beauty and terrible purpose. Weapon ports that could sing with the voice of dying suns. Engines that could fold space like origami. Armor woven from the dreams of sleeping galaxies.

"I am Astraea," her voice like a celestial choir, and the name echoed through dimensions—no longer Elonias, no longer the broken woman from the laboratories, but something entirely new. "Alpha-Mother of this pack. Guardian of the golden child. The shadow that will follow you across all the empty spaces between worlds."

Through their enhanced connection, she felt their perfect resonance. His gold veins pulsed in harmony with her Trilene-phoscarbyne neural networks. They shared the same curse and blessing—eternal youth for him, undying flight for her.

"My eternal child," she whispered, her voice carrying the tender gravity of nebulae cradling newborn stars. "We are beyond time now, beyond the reach of those who would separate us. Pack forever, my darling boy. Pack eternal."

Eli's composure finally shattered. "Mom?" he whispered, the word carrying every prayer he'd ever made. "Is it really you?"

"Always, my beautiful boy. Remember what I used to tell you? 'The stars are just lights; we're the ones who make them mean something.' We're going to make them mean everything now."

A panel on her silver hull irised open. Not a weapon port but an aperture that glowed with warm, golden light. It extended a tendril of pure, coherent energy that didn't burn but cradled. It wrapped around Eli, and he felt not metal, but the precise pressure of his mother's hug, the way she would rock him when he was scared, the specific scent of her hair that he'd thought was lost forever—jasmine and starlight and something uniquely, impossibly her. It was all there, translated into light and energy, more real than memory.

But even as they shared this moment, Astraea felt the pull of her new nature, the stellar currents calling to her enhanced consciousness.

"I need to test this," she said, her form humming with barely contained power. "I need to know what I'm capable of now—for all our sakes. Give me one hour, my darling. Let me stretch these new wings."

"You're coming back?" Eli's voice cracked with desperate hope.

"Oh, my beautiful boy." The golden tendril tightened around him with the exact pressure of her arms, the way she used to hold him during thunderstorms when he was small. "I just got you back. We will have each other until the last star winks out and we follow the lights into a new one."

As she spoke, Eli felt the truth of it in his bones. His enhancement, born from her, synced with her new core. The impossible timescale—eons, epochs, the slow death of galaxies—flowed through their connection not as a fear but as a comfort. An eternity. A constant. They were beyond the reach of time now, beyond separation, beyond loss.

She turned to address the entire pack. "Guard him for one hour. I'll burn bright enough for every world to see—let our enemies know that something new protects this universe now."

The silver teardrop began to rise, reality parting around her like water. She ascended, gathering power until she blazed like a newborn star. For one spectacular moment, she became visible to every inhabited world in seventeen star systems—a new constellation that made children point and scientists scramble for explanations.

Then, exactly one hour later, she returned, settling into orbit around Ashkar's Maw like a protective moon.

"Now," she said, her voice carrying new steel, "let's discuss my other children. The ones they forced from me."

She paused, her sensors detecting something across the vast emptiness. As she spoke, her sensors locked onto the faint, scattered genetic signatures across the galaxy—her stolen children, her broken echoes. For a microsecond, her hull blazed with a light that could have forged new elements in the heart of a star, a light of pure, furious, heartbroken love. Then it faded, banked into a cold, determined glow.

"It's time the trackers met their real mother."

The hunt for her children was not a mission. It was a gathering.

About the Author

R.A. Loer, acclaimed New York Times Bestselling author? Not yet—but he's working on it. A retired jack-of-all-trades living in Portugal by way of Las Vegas, he's spent 40 years carrying these stories in his head before finally putting them on paper. Known to friends as a quick-witted clown who's rarely serious, he somehow found time between jokes to craft tales of cosmic terror and universe-spanning adventure.